SATAN RIDES YOUR DAUGHTER

One Hellish Anthology

A HellBound Books Publishing LLC Book

Austin TX

**A HellBound Books LLC
Publication**

Copyright © 2021 by HellBound Books Publishing LLC
All Rights Reserved

Cover and art design by Luke Spooner for
HellBound Books Publishing LLC

www.hellboundbookspublishing.com

Printed in the United States of America

Contents:

SATAN RIDES YOUR DAUGHTER

The Pit and the Basket
L. G. Merrick

1.

When Warren Ledlow was four, his father returned from Afghanistan. It became one of Warren's earliest memories, vivid forever. Dad showed up at the front door in uniform. Smiled. Said nothing. Walked straight through the house to the back yard. Stripped off his uniform, doused it in lighter fluid on the kettle grill, and set it ablaze. The crowd in the yard went silent, uneasy. So much for his welcome-home party. Warren's dad, in skivvies, laughed grimly.

His father also brought home souvenirs that he seemed to regret. A colorful kite went straight to the basement. A hand-carved tobacco pipe on a display stand went to a prominent shelf—where a row of true-crime paperbacks soon got placed in front of it. An embroidered vest, Warren recalled, his father donned once, during an afternoon of merry drinking. At dinnertime it was ruined forever in a prolonged, helpless roll on the floor in overturned spaghetti and vomit. But the souvenir that most stood out to Warren was a wicker basket.

It was big enough for him to sit inside, but he never did.

It was barrel-shaped, with a wicker cap. It was woven from sticks once varnished a dark glossy red, now worn mostly to a dull, dried blood color, and furthermore, the weave was tired, no longer tight, so here and there thin crevices opened onto the interior. Exactly how old the basket was, who could say. What about it had spoken to his father—went unexplained. The basket sat empty in a corner of the living room.

Occasionally, while playing with Fisher-Price trucks on the scratchy green rug in that room, Warren felt unsettled. As if being watched. He would not look at the basket then. If the feeling persisted, he left the room. He would not go back to those toys the rest of the day.

When he was six, his father disappeared.

It happened slowly. Some nights Warren awoke to incoherent yelling from the living room, to the crash of hurled furniture. Some mornings his mother moved as if with sore ribs. His father became unemployed, then sold the car, then the police stopped by a few times, then he sold the TV—and then he was gone. It felt sudden.

Warren's mother said, "Your father went to get fresh air in the mountains, to get better."

Weeks later, on a trip to the supermarket with his mother, he spotted his father in the parking lot. Passed out beside the dumpster.

Shortly after that, Warren was playing with trucks on the rug when again the feeling of being watched crept over him. This time, angered by it, to his surprise—he turned to face the basket. And through the weave, he saw the silhouette of a boy about his own size.

His anger melted. Maybe here was a potential friend. Warren wanted a friend. So he edged closer. He waved. He inched closer still, and reached for the lid. But before his hand touched it, he halted. Through a crevice, he saw the boy's eyes staring out at him.

Their intensity did not portend friendship.

The eyes were strange, too, with irises as black as the pupils, and whites not white but the gray of dishwater. And spotted, as if mildewed. The colors seemed so unlike eye colors that Warren suddenly relaxed, deciding they were not eyes, and not ominous, but some innocent, ordinary thing. His mother had put a pillow in the basket. With two buttons on it.

When the eyes blinked, Warren ran.

2.

Warren was alone in the house eating a peach that his mother had sliced up. He was watching cartoons. She had run down the street to Ms. Turnbull's house for an emergency meeting. Ms. Turnbull was his babysitter sometimes. "Emergency meeting" was what they called it with a laugh when they opened a bottle of cheap white wine. His mom said she'd be back real soon and he should stay on the couch.

Okay.

Except he was eating the peach. And its pit was on the plate. And he popped that in his mouth too.

He knew you couldn't eat pits. A peach tree would grow in your stomach. But he devised a game. He lay flat on the couch and spit the pit—*pwoof!*—straight up, then caught it in his mouth when it came down. That was the game, anyway, but it turned out to be hard. Every time, the pit flew up at a slight angle, so it didn't fall straight back into his mouth. He had to jerk left or arch his back to try for it—and he missed every time.

Until he didn't. That time, the pit went right in, didn't even graze lip or tooth—but he didn't have time to feel proud of himself. The pit fell straight to the back of his throat and bounced downward, and stuck.

Startled, he sat up. He could feel it, it felt like a knuckle inside his throat.

He could not breathe. He got up and jumped in place, hoping to make it fall all the way down, but no, it stuck, and his lungs burned.

He lay down and writhed. He crawled, he beat his chest. He couldn't make noise. Tears streamed across his face from the strain, but even they were silent.

He staggered for the front door. Ms. Turnbull lived five houses down and suddenly that seemed to be miles. He felt as if someone big, an adult, was standing on his chest with a foot on each lung. Gray sparkles clouded his vision.

Then it occurred to him that he was not alone.

The boy in the basket could help.

The boy would know what to do. It was a burst of luck to have this basket in the house. He felt as if he had been choking for months. He fell against it and shoved the lid off.

It was not a boy, crouched in the basket.

I'll help you, it croaked.

Its toadish lips moved to form the words, but they did not carry through the air. They resonated in the center of Warren's brain as if originating there.

It added, *On one condition.*

Anything!

I will save your life so you can live a number of years and then, when that number is up exactly to the day, I will take you to Hell. Do we have a deal?

The world looked no wider than a keyhole now. All Warren could see was the long tendrilled warts that sprouted instead of hair from the creature's scalp. He was terrified of it, but he said *Deal!*

It drew closer. *How many more years would you like to live?*

In his head Warren screamed a number that seemed enormous.

Twenty!

3.

For the next nineteen years, Warren Ledlow lived a normal life. He played sports poorly and video games all right, he could have gotten better grades in high school, he learned to drive a car, he worked part-time at a knife factory, he managed to get serious with two different girls, one for three months and one for ten, he got high sometimes, he thought about becoming a dog trainer, or a bounty hunter or a millionaire, sporadically he took classes at the county college, he couldn't quite get money together for continued studies, or for a great car or better apartment—but he got through. He was okay.

And I'm alive, he thought. *Which was not in the cards.*

He told the first girlfriend that he would be dead if not for a helpful monster.

"It had long, skinny arms. It reached one into my mouth, right down my throat. It pulled out the pit—and said I'd live twenty more years. So here I am, on borrowed time."

He had hoped that finally telling the story would make it feel fun, like a joke. In truth, death weighed on him. It felt close, and had for nineteen years. Its finality. Its unknowns. No one else seemed to think about it all the time like he did. He always felt like a stranger because of it, alone. He supposed everyone else had an easier life, not knowing when death would come. He supposed death was okay if it happened after a very big number, like eighty. And if there was a Heaven. But nothing was certain—except his death, which was on its way, on a schedule.

The girlfriend didn't laugh at his monster story. She said, "You sound disturbed," and it changed how she looked at him. So he didn't tell the second girlfriend.

As for the thing in the basket, after the day he choked, he never saw another sign of it. So some days he was able to convince himself he had hallucinated. Not enough oxygen to the brain. The pit simply popped out. He wasn't going to die when he was twenty-six.

He had night sweats, though, that twentieth year. He wished he knew the date he'd choked. If he'd choked on January 15 and was still alive on January 16—well, then it *was* a hallucination. A weight would lift.

How heavy a weight? Immeasurable. Carrying this burden was the way he lived, had lived ever since. Like a man asked to shoulder his own corpse and never allowed to set it down. He couldn't wait to turn twenty-seven. Then he would be out from under death, for the first time since eating a peach watching cartoons. On that day, he would wake up as a completely different person. It was impossible even to imagine who. A person who could stand up straight. Run. Laugh easily. He would be—finally—for once—*happy*. He had never successfully imagined what it might be like to be a happy person.

It was a sticky night in July, the year he was twenty-six, when he was visiting his mother and she left him alone for a minute. With the basket.

"I need a beer!" she called. "You want one?"

"Sure!" he said.

Then he heard the dusty croak. It was unmistakable, even after decades, right in the center of his head.

It said, *Two days left*.

He spun to face the corner. Gray eyes stared from a gap in the weave, and he fled the room like a child.

4.

At the end of the visit, at the door, he asked his mother, in a voice pitched embarrassingly high, "Hey, I'd like a souvenir of Dad. Maybe I could take that old basket with me?"

She chewed on her thumb.

"Let me think it over."

"Sure. I'll come back tomorrow for it."

He wanted to burn the basket.

"It's a fifty-mile drive," she said. "You're not doing that two days in a row."

"I don't mind seeing my own mother twice."

"I have lunch plans. And book club. Listen, forget the basket. It's all I have to remember him by."

"There's a pipe. A kite."

"I, uh, went through a thing where I sort of curated my memories of him. I only kept the basket. He belongs in the corner."

Warren needed to destroy the basket. He said, "I'll just borrow it."

She frowned. "You're sweating. Are you on someth—are you sick?"

"Just give me the goddamn basket."

"I think you should lie down."

"Okay, no. Sorry. I'll go. Sorry, I love you, I'm sorry."

5.

At home he got into bed telling himself he hadn't heard any voice, he'd had a stress attack. Demons were not real, obviously. As a kid, a very stupid kid, he'd let this dumb idea into his head and it had taken over his whole life—and it wasn't real. He wanted to go back in time and smack that kid.

As he fell asleep, he even convinced himself today's panic attack was good news. The voice said two days, so all he needed to do was survive three days, and he'd become that new happy person.

In the morning, though, he woke with a fully restored terror of mortality. So he drove to his mother's house and hid in a bush.

When her car pulled out, he moved fast. He broke a window to get in, he turned over furniture, he poured her Jack Daniels and beer down the sink. He wanted to make it look like kids got in (he did swig from the Jack; he needed that) and he grabbed the wicker basket. After all these years, she still kept it empty—and he walked around the house dumping items into it. A thermos, a framed photo of his grandmother, a handful of pieces from a jigsaw puzzle, volume N-O of an old encyclopedia. He used to steal like this when he was fourteen, break into houses around town and grab random items—nothing worth anything—to entertain himself by wondering how long before someone noticed each was missing. A lipstick? A fork? A clock? A harmless prank.

At home he put a sheet on the living room floor and cut the basket into pieces with a hacksaw. Whenever the pile of pieces got big enough, he fed them into the fireplace. It was a gas fireplace trimmed in cheap pink tile. The red wicker turned the blue flame purple, crackled, sent up white sparks. The apartment filled with the smell of wood burning—and occasionally surprising odors, as if he were cooking with exotic spices. The scent of spell ingredients, he decided with a laugh, that had been used to trap a demon in the basket.

I'm setting you free, buddy. Now you can go home. So we're even.

Occasionally the odor was horrendous. A garbage reek. Sour milk. An outhouse. When the putrid stench of a rotting corpse rolled out of the fireplace, Warren ran to the kitchen gagging, and stuck his face under cold water.

When the last of the basket turned into purple flame, he felt safe.

His mother phoned. Upset. The police had just left.

"You were robbed?"

Probably kids, she said. "They drank up my liquor, but you know what? The only missing things? One book from the old encyclopedia and a photo of my mom." She started to cry. "My favorite photo."

"Maybe—maybe it'll turn up," he said. "What are kids going to do with that?"

"She's gone forever. She's just—gone."

Warren's grandmother had died years ago. He was surprised to hear emotion come so quickly to his mother. He had not taken her for... sentimental.

6.

A sulfuric smell woke him. The malodor of rotten eggs, thick as smoke.

He jumped from bed, but the fire alarms were silent. He turned on the lights. No smoke visible. He turned them back off. It was 3 a.m.

He stood puzzled in the living room. The smell, strong enough to wake him, already was fading. He crossed to open a window to let out the last—

He froze.

Something had moved in the fireplace.

He wanted to believe it was an animal that had come down the chimney, but he knew better. Even before he saw the gray eyes.

They peered out of a face blackened to charcoal.

The creature blinked and flakes of burnt flesh drifted off its eyelids, into the room.

It said, *One day left.*

He fought his instinct to cower.

He asked, *Tomorrow? What time?*

Today, at 4:34 p.m.

Warren said, *I want to change our deal.*

He felt an unexpected thrill, saying that, because—suddenly—he realized this was not only the moment he'd been dreading all these years. It was also the moment he'd been prepping for. He had imagined hundreds of times, maybe a thousand, exactly how he would negotiate if he ever "really did" meet a demon. All he had to do was get the thing to talk, and this time—this time, he would prove a formidable opponent.

The stiff metal curtain clanked as the demon unfolded from a crouch to step onto the pink hearth. Soot wafted off it. Skinny and charred and three feet tall, it regarded Warren neutrally.

A deal is a deal.

I was six. It isn't fair.

Nothing's fair. Oh well.

It looked back to the fireplace, as if done talking, ready to get back in there.

Wait! I don't even know who you are. Or what you are.

What's your guess?

You're a demon.

I see. And you know what a demon is?

You work for the devil.

The thing sighed drily and looked away, as if weary of the misconception—then, as if deciding to help him understand, back at Warren. As if Warren might be worth helping.

I work for chaos and ruin. I like decay, it said. *In the grand scheme, I'm a little guy, just like you, Warren. We do what we can, don't we? We stay busy, we feed ourselves. But "work for" the devil? Do you "work for" the president?*

Well. I don't report directly to him. But I believe in America.

Ah, then you understand me. The demon seemed genuinely impressed. *It's the same way. To be honest, the devil doesn't even know I exist. Just like the president doesn't know you do.*

Warren bristled at the suggestion that the president didn't know about him, though of course it had to be true. *He's just very busy*, Warren said.

Mm, it's a big country. Same problem in Hell. And the

truth is, Hell is not very organized.

Chaos, Warren said, suddenly seeing his chance. *So you could just—lose our deal. No one would notice.*

The thing's lips flattened in disapproval. *That kind of chaos doesn't interest me. Although...* The lips stayed flat but stretched wide, a smile; wider, until the burnt flesh cracked. *Let's see what you do with your last day.*

7.

Warren spent the next two hours driving aimlessly, anxious. What could he do to make the demon spare him? Eventually he decided he needed to be around people. People would distract him from reality.

He drove to the only thing open at 5 a.m., *Adult Playtown* on Route 41. It was a double-wide with a gravel parking lot, always a couple of cars. He'd been twice before, poked around the magazines and left, feeling weird.

This time he ended up in back, in a booth, watching a girl through Plexiglas. But not even this distracted him completely. Fear and despair mixed into his lust. It hit him that being in love had been his favorite thing and he hadn't got nearly enough of it.

"Any way we can get closer?" he asked, sliding a twenty into a slot.

A few minutes later he was on a couch in a room still farther back and she was pressing her boobs to his face. She looked bored but he had an anguished urge to throw her down and take her and pretend she wasn't. *Go out with a bang*, he thought.

He supposed he didn't need to save his money, if he was going to die in eleven hours. He said, "I saw an ATM in front. How far can we go if I get a hundred dollars?"

She said, "Two hundred."

Back in his car an hour later, he called in sick to work.

Raleigh's Grill would open at 6:30. He got there early

and through a window watched waitresses tie on aprons, the cook fire up the griddle. He tried to savor his rapidly fading post-girl calm. Maybe those minutes with her—it was the power of love, right? Love would count in his favor. Maybe.

At 6:32 he was sitting at the counter ordering black coffee, waffles, bacon, sausage, a cheeseburger, and chocolate pie.

As he ate, he used his phone to post on Facebook that he realized he had a lot to be thankful for, and was glad about his time on Earth. He did this because he wanted everyone to remember him as a man who lived life to the fullest.

Except then he realized he did not know how he was going to be killed. If the demon made it look like a suicide, then this would read like a suicide note. He didn't want to be thought of as a suicide. He wanted people to say there was no way Warren Ledlow killed himself, no matter how it looked. So he deleted the message and posted some funny memes instead.

He went to Murphy's Bar and pointed to the top row of whiskeys, the ones he could never afford.

"Pour me the most expensive one."

"Special occasion, War?"

The tiny shot cost twenty-five dollars, but at least he found out what he'd been missing. It tasted like someone had stabbed out a cigarette in it. He chased it with a couple of Buds.

When he stepped back outside, the sky looked like rain. Maybe he'd be struck by lightning.

Around the side of Murphy's, a man in rags accosted him, stinking of piss, with a suppurating cyst on his neck.

"Excuse me, sir," the man said, "anything you could—"

"What's your name?" Warren said immediately, taking out his wallet. "I'm Warren."

"Bob," the man said. It sounded like a lie.

"Hi, Bob. You got someplace to go if it storms?"

"I do."

That might also have been a lie, but Warren decided to respect the man's privacy and handed him two twenties. "Bob" did a double-take.

"These are the wrong—you meant two singles—

"Bob, those're yours."

He felt good about it, driving away.

Suddenly he thought, *Oh!—the demon is going to hand me a peach. That's how. I take a bite, I choke.*

But if we can talk first... As he drove, he played through a whole imagined dialog, in which he was ruthless, clever, sardonic, and this boy-sized godlike bastard came to respect him.

It occurred to him that he should go to church, if Hell was coming up at 4:34. Except for weddings, he hadn't been inside a church in—nine years? But it was Monday. Churches were closed.

Buzzed from Murphy's, he went to the movies. As a kid, he loved going to movies buzzed. Well—he'd done it only a couple of times, but those had come to represent to him all that was decent in eighth grade (against all that was shit, which was the rest of it). So he watched a movie, and alone in the theater he felt half good, half sorry for himself.

When the movie let out it was 4:14. Twenty minutes left. It was raining, but not dramatically. No thunder, no lightning. The universe seemed to be gearing up to barely mark his exit. He thought he might go sit in a park to await—whatever.

Then, with a start, he remembered that the photo of his grandmother was in his apartment.

He had to get there. Had to. If he died, his mother would come over to go through his belongings. She'd find that photo, she'd know he was the one who broke in—he was the one who stole it. He thought of her crying and he couldn't bear it.

He raced home and burst in the door panting, glanced at the clock—4:31. Three minutes! He had to get the photo out of here. The proof that he was a bad son. He should have died back then, that's what she'd think, should have choked on the peach pit. *And yeah,* he thought, *if I did, she would have been better off, lived a better life, not stuck with a stupid kid.*

He dashed down the hall, down the stairs to the garage where the dumpsters were, he didn't think he was going to make it, didn't want to die with the evidence right in his hands, so he tossed the photo—it twirled through the air—and it landed atop the piled plastic bags and broken desk lamps and cracked flowerpots and loose banana peels. He saw it land in the dumpster, and only then did he stop running and double over, hands on his knees. He thought *Oh, god, it's going to be a heart attack.* He wanted to get back upstairs and die on his carpet.

Don't go anywhere, said the voice. *We'll do this right here.*

Slender fingers wrapped over the top of the dumpster and the creature pulled itself up from the trash. Its flesh was gray again, not charcoaled, but horrifically scarred by the burns.

I watched you all day, and I have a new deal to offer.

Relief washed through Warren like a flash flood.

Yes! Let's talk!

Allow me to ask you some questions. First, how much more life would you like?

Warren grinned as he fought to catch his breath. This was it. His moment.

Two thousand years—and I don't grow old.

Ah! Two thousand, and you stay young. And healthy?

Yes!

And then you go to Hell.

No. Heaven has to be an option.

Sorry. I won't renegotiate that part.

Okay, if I have to go to Hell—he had gamed out this angle too—*make it a million years.* He could not imagine anything still existing in a million years. Even Hell. *And I don't age!*

You have to age. It's a law. But I can slow it. You will age one day per year. Would that suit you?

It sounded good. He said, *Yes!*

So what's our deal, Warren Ledlow? Tell me, so I know there are no mistakes.

I live one million more years—human Earth years. It was important to stipulate, lest the demon try switching to dog years or years on Mercury. *During that time, I only age one human Earth day per year. And no cheating by putting me in a coma, or framing me for a crime so I get a life sentence. I'm healthy as can be, free in the world, making my own choices. Then I go to Hell—if Hell still exists.*

The thing sank into the dumpster until only its hands showed, gripping the edge. Warren got the impression it felt cornered.

I'll have to ask for one condition in return. But you have to agree to it before you hear it.

No way.

So I take you to Hell right now.

Okay—okay. Will your secret condition interfere with my conditions?

Not at all. The demon pulled itself up enough to peer over the lip. *It actually gives you more choice in your fate. And it will be easy for you to do. As easy as taking out the trash. Do we have a deal?*

He thought a long time about what detail he might have missed. At last he said, *Deal.*

The thing chuckled.

It said, *The condition is this. Starting now, to add each year to your life, you must murder someone. If you want to live your full million years, then murder a million people, one a year. If you get tired of life before the million is up, simply live a year without a murder, and I'll come and take you.*

I don't want to be a killer.

Then don't be one. You've got a year from today to decide if you really don't want to be a killer. Oh, and Warren? One last favor I'll do for you.

Angry, he said, *I don't want your favor.*

You do. I'm going to let you take a peek at Hell. What you see will help you make your decision each year.

Warren backed away and turned to run but he fell. The creature had tripped him, somehow—and now he was looking at a crack in the cement of the garage floor an inch from his face and suddenly the crack was an orifice like an anus gaping wider to show him a nearly lightless landscape sprouting hair like dense tall grass that whipped and lashed to and fro in biting wind, that tangled and knotted, while struggling deep down in it were forsaken souls and over the plain crawled enormous spiders searching for them, and now Warren was tangled in the hair and here came a spider, chittering, chittering, its body bigger than a car, Warren could not be still because he was terrified, the way a child is terrified, he thrashed to get free but failed, and the hair whipping above parted and exposed him and when the spider loomed into view over him, it had his father's face and it shrieked laughter and it vomited into his face, a boiling green sludge of poison some of which he couldn't help but swallow.

A second later Warren was ralphing painfully on the garage floor, splashing his hands, but otherwise safe.

Safe, he thought, *thank God that wasn't real.*

Oh, that was real, said the voice from the dumpster.

8.

Warren Ledlow lucked out with his first victim. He was ten months into the year, stress mounting every day about what he had to accomplish. Then he witnessed a man collapse in a parking lot, and ran to help. Right away he could see the man was having a stroke, the cataclysmic kind no one recovers from, probably. Seized by a sense of wild luck, Warren covered the man's mouth and pinched his nose.

For weeks he expected to feel sorry, but it never happened. He *had* helped that guy.

He decided he could use the next year's murder to improve the world. In the news there was a dirty cop named Popov, recently acquitted. Guy planted evidence, got kids put away. Kids with disadvantages. Warren cased his home. The man lived alone, divorced, and Warren got into his fridge and poisoned the orange juice.

It surprised him how good that murder felt. Righteous. He'd had run-ins with cops as a kid. He hated to think what Popov would have planted on him. He started to think he could do this forever, if he picked the right people. People who deserved to go down.

His third victim was nearly eighty, so already what did it matter, and he knew she was a bad person not from the news, but from his own life. She'd been his third-grade teacher. All the kids were supposed to write a report on a historic figure. He chose George Washington. At the time, his mother was seeing a guy who liked to yell and—well, a real louse. The day all the other children handed in their reports, Mrs. Genitoro demanded Warren explain why he didn't. No, Warren, I can't hear you, *Warren*, you better stand up and explain, that's right, *stand up* and explain to me and *all* the other *children*, Warren, who all did *their* reports, what makes you *so* special that *you* didn't have to *bother*.

He meant to smother her with a pillow, but when he saw her sleeping peacefully, every syllable of that speech crowded into his head as if he'd heard it yesterday and so instead, he put his hands around her skinny, corded neck and shook her awake, and choked her dead while looking her in the eye and saying "Remember me?" over and over.

For his fourth year, he murdered a boss who had fired him from a part-time job when he was trying to pay for college. He had not been stealing, or not as much as he stood accused of. The guy had yelled in front of about fifty customers and all his coworkers, "I gave you a shot and you *robbed* me, you worthless turd," and the only comeback Warren had mustered was, "Zero evidence, old man." That memory had stung him with shame every time it surfaced. He stabbed that boss through the lungs, five, six, maybe nine perforations, and while the man's eyes still had light, Warren stole the wallet from his back pocket and waved it in front of his face. He said, "I know you remember me."

Warren was not as clean a killer as he thought. But he never was caught because the thing from the basket secretly performed many favors for him. Erasing fingerprints, picking up fibers, smudging the lens of a security cam. It was fun keeping Warren in business. The demon began to like Warren, and spoke with him more often.

Warren, of course, did not forget his vision of Hell. It spurred him to attend church, to volunteer at a soup kitchen, to apply himself at his job. He bought a gigantic pickup truck and used it to drive around looking for homeless people, to hand them care packages, which he assembled himself.

However, the demon was not bothered by his good deeds, as a deal is a deal, and frustration at their uselessness may even have contributed to the increasing cruelty of Warren's kills. One day the demon emerged from the truck's glove compartment to discuss the situation pleasantly.

I see you have become friends with Father Babbo at your church.

Yes. He's a wise man.

And you told him about me.

That's right. He's going to help me break the deal.

No. He doesn't believe you. Also, you didn't tell him you're a murderer.

Warren's hands tightened on the steering wheel. *I will.*

I see. And then he'll forgive you, because you bought this truck to pass out blankets?

He'll tell me how to break the deal. He's a holy man.

Warren, holy men are often a disappointment. Let me ask you a question.

Frustration cinched in Warren's chest. *Your questions always go badly for me.*

This question will not obligate you.

So ask. You're going to anyway.

If Babbo could send you to Heaven, but you had to go right this instant... knowing you could live a million years instead... would you go?

Warren paused before answering. The demon laughed.

There's my answer!

Warren frowned. *You're a moron*, he said angrily. *If Father Babbo could get me out of the deal right now, then in a thousand years there'll be some other priest who can get me out, or in half a million years! Why should I throw away all that life?*

You're right, said the demon, *I am chastened.*

He withdrew into the glove compartment.

Warren cursed and jammed down the gas and plowed through a mailbox and a rosebush and a dog and wanted to jump something. Fury overwhelmed him. He had never been so crazed with rage, up to that point in his life.

It was about forty years later that he killed Father Babbo.

The homicide detective assigned to the case had seen a lot of awful shit in his time on the force, but when he walked into the home for retired priests and beheld *that* atrocity, he lost his lunch and the last dangling shred of his faith.

Meanwhile Warren, as always after a murder, was in a great mood. All burdens had lifted, stress melted, the deal felt fair. In a few weeks, he knew, tension would return, and begin to ratchet steadily back upward. He would again feel every betrayal he suffered, every failure of the world, and true, every year he felt these more acutely. But for now, he was the person he'd always hoped to be. He was happy.

The Works of His Hands
Henry Myllylä

Rain pierced the dim of eve. Abrupt drumming and cymbalic splashes halted the silence as the wind began to scourge the forest in thunderous fashion. John damned and lowered the chisel and the hammer from his hands. The storage door slammed outside as the storm swept across the yard of his small rural workshop. He made haste through the yard, picking up tools lying on the ground and tied the storage door shut. By the time he got back to the safety of his workshop, his linen tunic was already cold and soaked throughout. He went to the brick fireplace opposite to his workstead and placed two logs upon the still glowing embers and blew gently underneath. Soon orange, smouldering coals began to burst into a full-fledged fire, crackling. The warmth shone from the fire as he pulled a wooden chair beneath him and sat down, his eyes fixed on the flames.

Following morning, the rain had stopped. Cold, white mist lingered upon the puddles, reflecting the thick grey haste above. As he walked towards the storage in order to continue his daily work, his eyes caught something on the ground. A line of clear, crooked footprints came from the forest and circled the storage, continuing until they stopped not far from his door. They were easy to distinguish from dirt; two tear-like shapes with slightly curved tips.

A goat, he thought. *A big one.* He bent down and tried one with his fingers. Standing up, he followed the line with his eyes. As he inspected the trail further down to the treeline, he grew troubled. Not because of their size; a male feral goat could easily grow into proportions such as these. It was their formation. Instead of the usual pattern, in which four hoofs form a cohesive waving line, these ran rather straight; way too straight. One hoof after another. *This walked on two.*

The day passed unfocused. The chisel and the hammer were left untouched, just as the ornamental door he had carved. Instead, his hours passed on the porch, eyes transfixed down to the treeline, his mind bewildered. His focus made constant, repeating circular patterns, moving back and forth between the humming branches and the ground, in which those water filled hoofprints mirrored the inevitably darkening sky above. From there his gaze turned right back onto the trees wavering in the wind, as if not wishing to leave this barrier in unguard for a second.

By evening, the wind had stopped and the crisp, cold moisture was gone. The darkness descended quietly. Still having his eyes vigilant towards the forest, he placed an axe by the doorway and tucked a knife behind his back onto his brown leather belt. If it be that the trespasser comes, it won't go unnoticed this night. He knew all too well that allowing unusual things go undealt through one's land could cost dearly. He came to this remote place for solitude and peace, nevertheless he was no fool. No one would stand up for him. He had carved his own niche here with austere toil and he'd be the only one to defend it, if needed.

It was in the depth of darkest night hours that the silence ended. A screeching, sombre sound cried out from the darkness, heralded by a rattle of dead branches and leaves. His pulse rushed as he stood by the doorway, incessantly gazing at the treeline. He reached his right arm to the side and gripped the axe. Then, other voices cried aloud. Dry rattling of branches cracking under swift steps and a low, discoherent humming like wind coalescing with a strange, high-pitched—*humane*—resonance. An eerie discomfort choked his heart as the sounds grew closer, so that they were coming right from between the two of the closest trees encircled in shadows. He gasped in terror, unable to turn his eyes away, though every cell in his being wanted to.

Then, as if being a sinister play of fortune, the dark clouds that had dominated the skies for days opened and the white hues of the moon in her prime bled down. Either, because of an instinct or because of sheer terror, he squeezed his eyes tightly shut and held his breath. Praying he'd wake up, his last chance to avoid what was to come had arrived. But way too soon, the forceful exhale broke free through his lips and his eyes opened a little. It was there. His hands shook.

He gazed feverish at a humane figure standing in the treeline. The pale skin bathed in moonlight, it's silhouette masking into it as if being part translucent. As it approached, a bare female with a filthy, cadaverous complexion and thick black fur from waist down disgraced his eyes. Beneath, two black hoofs made sharp, almost clapping noises and underneath it's black, disheveled hair, grew horns that circled around its temples, towering wide over its ears. Ghast, malformed eye sockets grew partially into the horns, so that the upper face was merely a sick parody of a humane facade, as the red, serpentine tongue lolled sickly back and forth from a mouth frozen into a delirious, gnawing misposition. Above it, a pair of skeletal nostrils pointed gaunt ahead; resembling those of a pig, as no nose hid them beneath, and similarly to its red, inhumane eyes at the roots of the horns and other furrows, they were filled with black, moist dirt. He smelled a strangely sweet, rancid odor, as if a decomposed body was anointed with garlic and honey. The axe fell to the floor crumbling, as he could not but turn around. Eight numb steps lead him to his bed, and he laid down, his mortified face pressed against the wall. Graceless, rugged knacks followed not far behind. Petrified, he stared at the blurring wood. "God forgive," he plead as a sour, pungent stench reached his bedside and the floor planks crackled. Sinisterly, it laid down on him.

II

John loved wood. Always had. His sturdy grip and hardened palms had tamed it since he was a child, learning to read it and find ways to shape it to his will in the most delicate manners. In exchange, it gave him freedom and expression. He cherished this bond with such passion, that it eventually led him to become an apprentice of the old James Gallaway—the famed carver. With the guidance of his mentor, he commerced himself into the precise art of carving, even to the degree of receiving orders from clients of his soon-late teacher. This was by no means a surprise, since John had an intuition that allowed him to cherish the natural shapes and qualities of the wood so that one could not distinguish between the natural and man-made. It was this inner receptivity, *the eye* as they called it, that also his teacher first recognized. Already in his teens, he could make the natural reflect his visions with such tenderness, that it was nothing short of marvelous. Every piece he made was a unique, exhilarating mixture of nature, a highly skilled craftmanship and tireless search for beauty and perfection flowing seamlessly together. He sought them in such precision, that ornamental works of his hand became known for their graceful, lively elegance that was almost beyond compare.

However, it was 5 years later, at the demise of his wife in

labour with their first-born, that his quest for beauty reached its tragic zenith. Birch became his sole friend, as he submitted to a penitential meditation of loss by carving statues of women and children in a draining fervor. Doomed to finish none of them according to a zealous perfection he sought, the works were but shadows of a fundamentally flawed destiny; a wound that could not be undone. For two years he lived alone amidst those carved, humane elegies—which, finally numbering in dozens for his unwillingness to sell them—flooded his workshop that he had begun calling them his *Valley of the shadow of death.*

Then, one night, just before the break of dawn, this miserable retreat came to an end, as an abrupt fire engulfed the neighboring house and spread to the thatched roof of his home. The dark Valley had finally found its apocalyptic redeemer. By dawn, the whole settlement was but a charred desolation and save but one, a statue of a hooded young lady carrying a swaddled child in her arms, the silent, carven dreams of John were gone. Sunken back to that same darkness, from which he first desperately summoned them forth to make right what he could not contain.

Some time later he said that he had found a spot from the woods. A small cove, where birches grew around a little pond. Situated deep down into the valley, the warmth of the sun stayed there during the days and the wind was tranquil. The whole cove had seemed to be as if peacefully asleep, when he first arrived there by accident. There, near by the pond, in the center of a green, lush meadow, he found a place for the statue. The carven remnant of his tattered dreams had finally found a resting place equally beautiful as it, under a serene song of a nightingale. Something seemed to come into conclusion, yet also to begin, as not many miles from there, he managed to get himself a property from the edge of the woods and began to build himself a new workshop.

III

I had not heard of him since the last fall. It was odd, considering the fact that even at his worst he would pay a visit every now and then. Also, the letter I sent this January passed unanswered. Last time we talked must have been in early August, when I kindly commissioned new doors for my drawers. Not that there was any actual need for them. I knew that he was in dire need of provision, since his hardship had driven many of his trusted customers elsewhere and somewhat shaken his reputation. Besides, furniture that he made was always of highest quality and those ornamental details worth praising. Therefore, a friendly commission had felt more than reasonable, making it also an investment into the continuity of his career that I most heartedly wished to see.

It took two days journey to reach the forest passage that he had first walked when arriving here. If I'm correct and remember his account right, it was near this steep hill where he turned off-trail and eventually ended at his small, miraculous pond. I, however, had no inclination for turning away from the trail that passed winding through cliffs and enormous treelines, allowing sun to shine on the ground only on brief occasions. I had no other knowledge of the area, except that following this trail would inevitably lead me to him. In his letter last summer, he'd said that by spring his workshop should be fully operating, and I would be warmly welcomed to visit him anytime I could. Beside those greetings, the letter included exact instructions on how to find him.

First, I should take a trail north from the old mercantile road just before the village, then walk until the trail splits. There I should take the path going uphill, straight towards the top before turning to circle it. A half day from there, I should reach the destination. In retrospect, the instructions seemed precise. I had just chosen the trail uphill and circled around a thick wooded top, arriving on a cliff on the other side and paused to admire a beautiful view over the valley underneath. It was easy to see the appeal in this solitude. The sun shone gently over the birchwood below and had begun to bloom in its brightest. Further away I could see sunlight reflecting and sparkling amidst the green coat, marking the pond at the far end of the valley. A deep sense of apotheosis filled me in regards of him, as I looked over this place that had become his shrine of remembrance. Imagining, I could see the peaceful image of a mother and a child standing together in a meadow, encircled by those lush, green leaves and white trunks that held them up high, with the blue pond glittering behind. With a spontaneous smile for the assurance that a lifelong friend of mine had passed through the darkness of his former days, I continued along the trail, so that the night would not reach me before the shelter of his house.

From thereon, the trail crooked tortuously by steeps and slopes. Rocks and thick roots swept across the way, making the ascent slow and draining. To make it even worse, walking downhill had to be made with especial care for similar reasons. A misstep or a slip was not an option I wanted to think of either way. The thick foliage of trees was nearly impenetrable, allowing the sunlight to touch the ground only sparingly. It was easy to feel that the summer was only coming, since the shades grew cool in thickest parts of the woods and the vibrant moisture was still lingering in the air. However, in case of having to travel by rain or storm, the place would certainly keep its underneaths dry.

The forest ended by a small stream after couple of hours, when the sun had already begun to align with its western exit in the horizon, nearing the tips of the highest trees. Knowing I was already close, I kneeled down and cupped my hands, sprinkling the running water upon my face. After a short pause I pushed myself up, despite the tire I would have likened to appease a little longer by this charming little stream, and took a long, almost leaping step across to continue what was left of the journey.

But as soon as I entered a small brownish meadow right beside the stream, my journey was halted by an eerie occurrence. Walking past the meadow's murky ground and scattering hays, I arrived at a small mound. Rocks were assembled to encircle this otherwise barely recognizable spot of tilled earth, marking it apart from the surroundings. As I kneeled down to examine it closer, a bizarre revelation dawned on me. Hidden behind a brush of yellowish hay stood a small, wretched cross of decayed wood, shambly assembled to face the mound between us, with a corroded nail crudely protruding from its heart. This spot was a grave, yet way too small for a man, as it neared only about one cubit in height and a half in width. Ghast premonitions ran tortuously through my mind as I stood up, only to see another such spot crudely displaying itself some three yards away. All of a sudden, this spring-like meadow, preparing to shed its pale, brownish winter coat to finally awake blooming, had turned itself into a sidereal portray of some nether realm. When I examined the area further, the sense of this place being enclosed in some forbidden atrocity came even clearer as I, to my horror, spotted an empty pit dug in the ground. Similar in size and shape as the two others, with rocks encasing its borders, it was yet to be fed with whatever it was meant to enseal. Unlike the others, this cross was not decayed, neither the nail rusty. Though similarly crude in design, its condition was good. I shuddered for acknowledging that whatever purpose this strangeness was serving, it was unfinished; something that was yet to be. An iron shovel laying abandoned on the ground nearby made no mistake about that as I started to move hastily away from there and the sun began to leap upon its crimson wings beyond the blackening treeline.

In the last red wreaths of a waning sun, the ridge of a

darkly brown roof and a chimney came out from the distance. Panic I had felt eased a little, as I was finally able to catch my breath and depart from a race against the death of a day. After a little ascent by a hillside I was nearing, a tar coated log wall began to stand out and grow in size. It seemed that I was approaching the house from behind, since no door or windows were visible this way. Soon another, a rather shafty house of similar design began to show from behind it, its door visible this way. The two seemed to exist on a blackening, lively canvas as thick, dark woods waving slightly in the wind, circled them on the opposing side.

As I got closer, approaching the houses from their far right, a strange feeling began to stir within myself. No light was visible from the windows, nor smoke rose from the chimney. As if being caught from a motionless, picturesque sleep, the place stood dark and quiet against the descending twilight.

"Hello!" I called out, my voice dampening and drowning into the thick woods. "H-hello?"

As neither sight nor sound of a living soul answered, I began to feel almost an intruder. Strangely ashamed for disrupting something I should have not. Only the wind droning in the trees and a black spider creeping in its web against a dusty, dark windowpane distorted this painting-like stillness, as I saw nothing but jet-black reflecting from a gap in between the closed window shutters. Upon entering the front of the house, my wonder was seized by an acute alertness. The door hung wide open. Almost painfully dislocated and upheld only by a crooked lower hinge. The black doorway stood stoically gaping at me. Mere instinct turned my steps cautious as I came closer and the threshold snarled deep as I pressed my foot on it, leaning slightly over to have a look.

"John?" I immersed my face into the darkness.

Then I had an answer. The dark innards of the house impregnated my lungs with a sickening, bitter stench that itched and clawed through my spine, as an audible choir of flies swirled and buzzed, churning madly in unison with the putridity. Drowning to this sickening swell, my eyes caught a glimpse of what appeared to be a white cloth bundled upon a bed in the far end corner. Disoriented, gagging, I stepped further in, forcing myself through this revulsive thickness, onwards to what appeared to be its axis. The revel of flies grew denser at each step, as I saw that the cloth had been tied to form a small, contorted sack. It was stained in deep, almost blackening crimson, whereas its bottom was so soaked throughout, that a pool of dark, putrid secretion had appeared on the floor underneath. The denser the stain upon it, the more flies rallied at it, gratifying and spawning at the height of its excessiveness. Protecting my lower face with a sleeve of my jacket, I took a lengthy piece of scrap wood from the floor. Trying to open the sack carefully with it, every inch that I managed to peel open this rancid cloth, reminding merely of a putrid, oozing womb, unveiled a new wave of even denser miasma heralding from inside with flies flying scared away from their deathly dwellings. The smell was unbearable, but nothing in comparison to what I was about to unveil, as I turned open the last leaf of this sinister banquet. At first, the narrow opening gave but a glance at the unrecognizable gory heap encloistered tightly into the fabric. But as I poked it slightly in order to remove some of the cloth attached to it, my heart wrenched in repulsion as a soft form of a pallid infantile hand and five wringled fingers bent in a ghastly malformed position came to my sight. Gasping in hammering nausea, I peeled this uteral shrine further to uncover a pale armpit, shoulder line and neck sheltered in a rotten membrane. Then a lower back and an inch-thick thigh were revealed, bent in a gaunt misposition underneath a swollen, purple patched stomach, swelling in a thick pool of dark secretions. I grinned in a woeful obnoxion as tears flooded from my eyes. Through their wet, salty veil, I saw that the bent leg partly underneath this miserable being perverted unnaturally into an embryonic shape of bestial origin in resemblance of a hoof. Kneeling in exhaustion, I could do nothing but cry, shivering for this madness. Spasming, as my stomach purged its content along the floor, I began to crawl towards the door on all fours. Outside I spat my woe unto the darkness of the woods, rubbing my hands to my face like a fool.

At dawn I found him. In the wreaths of first light a splattered trail of blood was easily visible outside. Beginning from his bedside, crooking towards the woods through the yard. Following it, I noticed scattered crimson stains upon trunks of the two closest pines that had textures of skin imprinted on them. Tufts of brown hair had tarnished into the blood and into the scratches that bored into the wood itself. It took but a few steps past these moribund, marked pillars to have a glimpse of his bloody, pale feet gleam behind a morass of dry bushes. Coming closer, a sinister, shaming scene opened in the woods not far behind the toolshed.

Bent down on his knees, he laid against an old, thick pine. His upper body pressed against the tree so tight, it kept him up in this obscene position where his head stood upright against the trunk while his loose arms stretched grievously around as if still trying to embrace it. His blood drenched face contorted against the bark in a fierce, ecstatic expression as a foggy, dislocated stare in his dim, grey-glazed eyes surged upwards reflecting the wind-swept foliage on their barren surface. His pallid nakedness was covered in dark filth and filled with cuts and bruises, whereas his bottom stood high towards the woods behind his deeply arched back. At first, most of the blood seemed to be upon his thighs and lower back. But a wretched shame filled me as I saw his loins soaked in a filthy crimson mixture with dark, membraic tatters and, what appeared to be some visceral cord hanging from in between his buttocks where flesh had bulgingly torn into an open orifice. I stared at him breathless, enchanted, choked in terrifying awe. My vision blurred as my heart pound feverish, unable to unsee the nightmares this altar had dreamed.

Hours passed dazed until I became numb enough to act. My reflection echoed from the nether of his eyes as I tried to push him away from the tree, kneeling on his front. As he moved barely an inch, I circled around him, placing my linen coat over his loins and took a steady grip of his ankles. A haunting gurgling whistled from his mouth and nauseating stench flood out of him, as the air in his cavities was released by a single, surging pull that straightened his crooked posture. Unreleased blood bled still out of his mouth, nostrils and that gaping lower wound, as I dragged him past the trees to the yard and from there into his house. Wooden planks rumbled underneath us, as I placed him next to the bed, lying on his back. I took my coat off from his loins and placed it over his face that was frozen in repeat of the abominations it had seen. Then, I gathered some wood and began to prepare a fire in his fireplace. Soon crackling, lively warmth began to shine outwards, dispelling my numbness a little. I felt dirty. Disgraced. The dry lifelessness of his ankles lingered still on my palms, as my eyes were upon abominable darknesses that were not here, but in his gaze; in his inhumane crookedness; in deviations that had begotten this sick being on his bed. Soon, as the fire had grown strong and steady, eagerly expecting further feeding, I scattered its burning heaps around the house. Then I went outside and waited.

I felt stories of old being retold, as I watched the churning pyre unfold. I found myself wandering in the darkness of Babylon, inside its temples and houses abandoned. I studied its remnants of godless glories and temples that sanctified whoredom over its holies. Gazed in awe at things that danced in their shades, those beasts of darkness a day shuns out in shame. I prayed, "Fire is a decent grave, my old friend. With peace your name shall I never attend. John, forgotten, abandoned now hush—in time I'll take you with me down unto dust."

Afterwards I carried his bones to the statue down in that valley and granted them rest. His skull was as pure as the work of his hands and until the end of my days, I shall remember the beauty under which he now lays.

The Goat
Alan Derosby

I sat alone in my office, staring at the envelope. Just the return address sent shivers up my spine. It had been two decades since I had gone there; the last time to grab some paperwork so I could apply to college. I had attempted to get them mailed, but my adopted parents—an aunt, and uncle on my father's side—convinced me it was for the best to visit. At the time, I was eighteen and old enough to get myself a hotel room, far away from my grandfather's farm. As a child, I returned every summer, an order that was placed in my mother's will. She wanted me to keep close to her side of the family, which I did until that one evening, when I was sixteen. I refused to return and, until this moment, believed that I would never see that farm again. Now, the contents in the envelope dictated that there would need to be one final trip, a deed in my name for full ownership of the farm at the death of my grandfather.

The drive was long, just me and my thoughts, from Pennsylvania to Maine, to gather the belongings I might want and to prepare the farm for sale. I hadn't wanted it; not the house, not the land and not the responsibility. In the back of my mind, I believed my grandfather knew this; one final "fuck you" to the girl who ran.

"Marisa, please stay on the farm. Just a few days." Grandfather begged me when I came for the paperwork. By that time, he was already reaching eighty-five years of age, still looking in decent shape for a man who worked the fields for many decades. I made up some excuse as to why I couldn't; perhaps an early flight or a date night with some old friends. Both were utter bullshit. I just couldn't sleep in that same bedroom, the one that looked out into the garden and that damned statue that rested directly in the center.

Now, as I pulled into the driveway, after making every stop I could to avoid arriving here, I sensed it, waiting for me out behind the farmhouse; the goat. It wasn't a real goat, those were not allowed on the farm, especially once my grandmother passed away so tragically. I wasted no time, immediately walking around back. The house could fuck with my head later. Right now, I needed to see if the source of my nightmares still existed. And just like I remembered, though no longer in a well-manicured garden with the brightest and wildest flowers, sat the goat. The white marble, once so clean and bright, was faded and smooth. Time and the elements had taken its toll.

The goat stood on all fours, its eyes slightly off to the side, a slight grin across its lips, and a braided beard that hung below its chin. Under its belly was a large utter, swollen, and un-milked. A pair of horns adorned its head, long and curled. Though it was nothing but a simple statue of a goat, it was a concern of fear as a child. To always look down from my window to see it, staring up towards me. I ran my fingers over it, touching what for many summers I was told not to approach. There was no spark, feelings of sadness or anger.

"You're not so bad," I said, smirking. Behind that shitty grin was a tint of fear, for a tale told to me that one evening when grandfather drank too much Allen's Coffee Brandy.

Inside the farmhouse was much like I remembered. The smells of cigarette smoke and stale coffee, once so familiar to me, lingered in the air, sticking to cupboards and closed curtains. The squeaky screen door slammed, a notice to the ghosts that someone familiar had returned. I had no desire to spend any more time than I had to in the farmhouse, a place filled with sadness. I had not planned on staying the evening, already renting a room at a local bed and breakfast just down the road. As if the universe knew my plan, the sky grew dark and opened up, heavy rain pouring down. I waited for close to an hour, hoping the torrents would let up, and when they refused, I made the uncomfortable decision to stay the night. I ran to my car, grabbing a suitcase and bottle of wine I picked up at a convenience store, to make it through the evening. Soon, I was back inside, a fire roaring to warm my chilled body.

My mind raced back to the statue, and I rushed upstairs, into my old bedroom, to a lookout. There stood the goat, fighting against nature, standing stoic in the garden while being pelted with raindrops. Just the thought of what it represented scared me, and without another wasted minute, I closed the door and returned to the living area, to bunk on the couch. I spent the next hour, drowning my sorrows in cheap red wine, thinking of the loss, this place, and that damned statue. My grandmother had died before I was born; my mother, much like myself, growing up without a strong female role model. My own mother died on this farm as well, a death that devastated my grandfather. He survived many years after her passing but was never the same, closing himself up like a hermit. However, all that changed that one evening, while I was flipping through family photo albums that had been stored in the attic. I was still a child, in need of nurturing from the only real family I had left. My grandfather could not provide that.

"Grampa, where are the pictures of Mom or Grammy?" I asked when he came outside to join me on the porch. For a moment, I thought he'd turn on his heels and walked back inside, a common reaction for him when dealing with uncomfortable situations. This was not one of those. Instead, he sat down in a rocking chair, closed his eyes briefly, and began.

"It's too hard to look at them, Marisa." Grandfather wiped tears from his eyes.

"My teacher says time heals all wounds." As a teenager, I was easily influenced by adults that showed an interest in me. My grandfather wasn't one of those.

"I wish that were true. But that damned goat is here to remind me, staring and waiting for me." Grandfather sighed. I could smell the alcohol on his breath and knew he was inebriated. Against my better judgment, I pushed forward.

"It's just a statue. Take it down if it bothers you." I reached over, grabbing his shaking hand. For a brief moment, I felt close to him, bonding with a man who refused to connect with me. I wish I hadn't.

"I can't take it down. That was the deal. It must stay up to remind me of the pact I made." Grandfather was no longer speaking to me, but beyond me, as if he were unburdening himself of significant hardship.

"What deal? With whom?" I asked.

My grandfather's face transformed from sadness to pure terror. For a moment, he said nothing at all, staring out with his widened eyes into the vast lush farmland. He let out a deep breath, closed his eyes, and told me his story.

"There's never been a time in your life where this farm hasn't produced crops, meat, and milk, all in such ample supply. You've never wanted for anything because of that. But that wasn't always the case. Many years ago, the land suffered a drought, unlike anything I'd seen. Crops dried up, the ground lost its nutrients and became sour, and animals became sick and died. For a young farmer, living off the land handed to him by his father and his father before him, it was a struggle not to be able to provide for the family and community. I tried everything for an entire season, including prayer, though even that fell on deaf ears. Your grandmother never said a word about it, only offering words of encouragement. But, she was pregnant, and I needed to provide. No banks would loan me money, and no neighboring farm would let me work on their land. So, one night, after drinking, I wandered outside and cursed everything. I cursed the farm. I cursed the banks. And I cursed God for doing this to me. I collapsed to my knees, weeping; out of answers.

It was then that I heard a voice. I should have ignored it and went inside. I could have let the bank foreclose on the farm and find happiness with my family somewhere else. But, unfortunately, that's not how the tale ends. I answered the voice; my head still buried in my hands, only looking up upon receiving an answer.

"Perhaps, I could be of assistance." I saw the voice attached to what is best described as a goat-man. The creature was standing on two legs, the entire body covered in thick, black fur. Though it had hooves on its feet, the goat had human hands. A long thin tail wrapped around its body; the tip speared at the end. On the top of its head sat two giant white horns, the only color on it, besides yellow eyes.

"Not unless you can make the farm successful, Goat." I didn't question talking to this animal, though now I look back, I know exactly who it was. This was destined to happen.

"I can do just that if that's what you desire." The creature walked around me, its hooves gliding over the dirt.

"Of course, you can." I laughed in its face. I should have gotten up, excused myself, and walked into the house.

The goat smirked, waved its hands in the air, and before I knew it, the ground beneath me shook. Rows of fully-grown vegetables of all kinds grew up from the dry soil. I leaped out of the way just in time as several rows of corn exploded from underneath my feet.

"How did you do that?" I said, clearly recognizing that I had gone insane. I, in no way, believed that what was in front of me was real. It was the stress and alcohol that provided the hallucinations.

"I can do many things, young man. I can open up the skies and let blood rain down upon you." The goat waved his hands again, and indeed, blood fell from the clouds.

"Why do this for me? Why help?" I asked the goat.

"Hmmm, good question. I am, what you call, an interested party. I offer my services in exchange for a nominal fee." The goat closed both hands, opening his fists to reveal a pen and what looked to be a contract.

"A catch. I knew it. What would I owe you?"

"Your soul, of course. I assumed that was apparent from the start. When you die, and I can promise it will not be for many, many years, I get your soul. Until that time, this farm will be the most profitable in the state. You will never suffer a day without the most delicious crops, the healthiest animals, and the creamiest milk." The goat looked around, each time its eyes fell upon some land, crops shot out of the ground.

"That's it? My soul in exchange for providing for my family." I had not cared about my own damnation and what would happen beyond this night, much less all eternity.

"Well, there are a few small requirements. First, while you become wealthy beyond your wildest dreams, your neighbors' fields will suffer. You may provide them food and support, but in no way, are you ever to tell them of our deal. You will be questioned and blamed for their failures, and, in a way, it will be true. This deal may help you but will destroy those around you. Are you fine with that?" The goat focused on me now, having raised my fields from the dead.

I should have thought of the consequences of my actions. To hurt those around me for my benefit was selfish, but my desires outweighed it. I was very agreeable, only thinking of my family and myself.

"And one other thing; a small token of respect for what I am to do for you. On this location, where I've transformed your life, you are to place a statue of a goat in my honor. All those that see it will wonder of its significance. You cannot tell them the true nature of the agreement. This cannot be moved or tampered with. It must stand on these grounds, even when humanity destroys itself."

"What happens if someone tries?" I was thinking through the logistics. What if a work hand shifted it out of the way to till the soil? Would there be retribution?

"If that is the case, they will die. It is your job to protect this statue at all costs. That is merely the fine print of the deal." The goat held out the contract.

The request of the statue was an odd one but made some sense. For thousands of years, societies and cultures sculpted statues of deities, as a place of worship. Any church in the area had marble statues of Mary or crosses with a crucified Jesus Christ adorned throughout. I agreed to that demand immediately. As far as protecting the figure, a fence, and some scare tactics could solve that. Under no circumstance could anyone lay hands on the goat.

I willingly signed the contract, not thinking through the long-term ramifications of doing so and the pain I would cause all those around me. Pen hit the paper, and as soon as my signature was completed, a statue, the one you see there, rose from the ground, taking its place in the center of the garden. And before the goat-man left, he issued the same warnings as before, to remind me of the deal. I don't remember how I got home, but I was woken up by your grandmother, screaming excitedly about what she saw from the window.

For many years, I convinced myself it was all a dream, but it couldn't have been. The goat stood in the garden as a reminder. And like the Devil said—and yes, I now believe that was who I was dealing with—my farm was extremely successful while others around us struggled and then failed. It wasn't merely the failure that bothered me, as awful as that sounds. It was what was happening after. Several of my neighbors came to me, demanding to know what I did to their fields. I told them nothing, as instructed, per my agreement. It was hard at first to see grown men grovel, but I soon became accustomed to it. But that wasn't the worst part. Over the course of a few years, five local farmers wandered onto my land at night. The following morning, they were found, lying dead in my garden, the goat standing over them. Autopsies always came back looking like a heart attack, but I knew what caused their deaths.

Your grandmother struggled with this, the death of those friends and neighbors we were once close with. She refused to go to the garden and grew to hate the goat that guarded it. Often, at dinner, she would fall into fits of rage, demanding me to destroy the statue and raze the fields, a place that had brought so much death. I couldn't tell her why that was impossible, always trying to refocus her on your mother, who was now a young child. And most evenings, I was successful. However, the Devil enjoys his games.

It happened one night after an extremely explosive argument about the goat. She'd been hanging clothes on the line when she claimed it looked at her. I tried to explain that a statue couldn't move, but I was not being truthful. I do believe it did, to bait her into a reaction. I had thought I'd convinced her that perhaps a therapist would be an excellent avenue to take and went to sleep. That night I was awoken to a blood-curdling scream. I leaped out of bed, rushing outside to see the statue lying on its side in the grass. But that wasn't the part that sent a chill up my spine and forced me to realize how bad the deal I made was. In the place where the statue once stood, was your grandmother, standing in the center of the garden, cursing the goat. In seconds, two black arms shot out of the ground, grabbed your grandmother by the legs, and pulled her down, deep into the soil. She screamed for me to help her until her face disappeared into the ground.

I waited in shock for an hour, thinking back to what I had caused. Greed forced me to make a deal that resulted in my wife's death. I wanted to run inside, grab my shotgun, and end my life. I loved that woman greatly, but your mother needed me. So, after gathering my bearings, I picked up the goat and placed him where he belonged. The next morning, I called the police to file a missing persons' report. It wasn't uncommon for a wife to leave their husband, especially one who was sick of all the neighbors' attacks. A new life, with a new husband, in a new place, was the story, but I knew better. My actions killed my wife.

Life continued, though I was no longer happy. I loved your grandmother, and to let the town speak ill of her because of the actions I caused was a cross I struggled to carry. But the farm was still extremely profitable. I hired many hands to do the work while I fought to get through every day. Before I knew it, your mother was grown, finishing the top five in her class with discussions of a four-year bachelor's degree at the University of Maine at Orono. She'd wanted to get away from here, a place that only brought about sadness and resentment.

The goat knew; could sense it. I believe that. And it was unwilling to let go of anyone that had profited off it. A week after the acceptance at UMO, your mother came to me with another, less favorable information. She was pregnant. Not that your birth is not one of the happiest times of my life. I'd suffered so much that any tiny hint of good tidings was welcome. It was that her plans to leave and build a life somewhere else were dashed. College was put on hold, never to be realized. At that moment, I understood she'd never leave here. None of us would. I tried to keep things upbeat, building a nursery, and providing support with local women to help with the raising of a baby. But nothing helped. Your mother fell into a great depression, frequently sitting in her bedroom window with you in her arms, looking out into the garden. The goat called to her, and one night she listened.

I did not see her disappear into the earth like I did your

grandmother. Instead, I only saw the goat, on its side, pushed to the ground. I again pondered suicide, as losing a child was more painful than anything I'd gone through. But it was the baby inside and the protection I needed to provide you that kept me alive. I put the statue back in its place and moved on. I no longer care about my farm, though it is still the most profitable and successful farm in the state. I do no work, only drinking my day away. I've hired others to do the books, tend the fields, and slaughter the animals. I want to die, but know, when I do, my soul will be damned to hell, the same eternal place I willingly had a hand in sending my wife and daughter." Grandfather stood, wiped his tears away, and went inside without uttering another word on the subject.

I sat, shocked, listening to this story, this crazy tale by the ravings of a man who'd lost everything. To say I didn't believe it was an understatement. But I could tell one thing; he believed it all. The look on his face, one of torture and relief for sharing, let me know that my grandfather, after suffering so much loss around him, had a mental breakdown. What pained me was the way he described the loss of my mother. Was she dead? Still alive living another life? Was that his way of convincing himself that she and his wife hadn't left him? Did he kill them? I didn't know or care. I stayed the remainder of the summer, though neither one of us revisited that night. When the fall came, I left. I was able to contact some of my father's relatives, and soon I was off to Pennsylvania.

I said I'd never return to this place. I don't believe the stories, not one bit. To think that the Devil controls these fields is insanity. But the thoughts that the dead litter the grounds scare me. Perhaps it would be best if I destroyed the stigma of this farm, burning it to the ground instead of selling it. But I won't do that. There's too much money tied up in this place. I do know one thing, however. In the morning, when the sun rises, I will be outside, in the garden, to push that damned goat to the ground.

Route 666, or, the Art of Driving Muscle Cars in Hell

A.K. McCarthy

The car's backfire was his alarm clock, and the cloud of dust was his breakfast.

Farmington Turner grumbled awake, still in the driver's seat of his purple Plymouth Barracuda. The pain in his head was sharp, his memories hazy.

Farm growled, the bits of dust still settling on his broad hood. Through the haze, he saw the black Dodge Coronet racing off across the flat desert road.

Farm reached for his keys, finding them still in the ignition, and turned them. The engine roared like a beast emerging from beneath the earth.

Farm snarled, reaching for the skull-topped gear shift.

Today, I kill you, he thought.

***

The fading center line of the highway wavered back and forth in front of the purple hood like a doomsday grandfather clock. Farm's heavy foot pushed the Barracuda until it got to a hundred and thirty miles an hour. The engine obliged, howling the whole way.

The Dodge Coronet still wasn't in sight, but Farm knew he moved faster than The Duke. The Duke wasn't stupid, but he was prideful. He'd be happy to trade paint with Farm.

It was impossible to tell one spot from another on The Road. It was hard to tell one day from another on The Road.

Was it a day ago or a year ago that he caught up with The Duke the last time? When they'd crashed their cars and fought in the flaming wreckage? They'd traded blows until their hands were bruised and their muscles gave out. Then they'd kept fighting, wrestling each other to the hard, hot ground. Farm leaned on The Duke's throat and put his whole weight into it. The Duke's eyes had bulged, as if they were about to burst. Farm wondered what would have come out of the eyeballs if they had exploded.

Just when he was about to find out, another engine roared nearby. Farm remembered looking up and seeing the grill of a Mustang Mach 1 staring him in the face. What had happened next? Farm forgot. The days ran together out here. The sun dried them up and the wind carried them away.

He looked down and saw he was nearing a hundred and fifty miles an hour. The thick fingers of his scarred left hand closed tighter on the top of the wheel as his gnarled right hand still rested on the gear shift. His hands had no need to open anymore. They closed around the wheel. They closed around the gear shift. They tightened into fists. He no longer needed them to caress a woman's face or shake a friend's hand.

His life was simple these days. He woke up. He drove. He fought. Like an animal evolving to its surroundings over the generations, his body changed the way it worked. Fury pumped through his veins. Anger filled his lungs. Pain slowly digested in his stomach. His head remained bald, though he hadn't shaved in months. Or was it years?

He didn't eat. The car didn't take gas. They were the same. They both ran on hate. Their tanks were both empty and only revenge could fill them.

None of it existed anymore—time, day, night, seasons, weather. Every day was just like the last. Out here there was only the growling of the engines, the squealing of the tires, the crushing of metal on metal. Pain was the new pleasure. Brutality the new beauty. Desolation the new decadence.

The heat coming off The Road and the ground turned the horizon from a straight line to a wavy one, but Farm still thought he saw a black speck coming into view. He growled again as a flame began to grow inside his ribcage.

A hundred and fifty. It wouldn't be long now.

Farm reached over to the passenger seat and ran his hand over his arsenal. There was the axe. The whips—one for close combat and one for long-range lashings. There were the flame grenades and the spider bombs. Spider bombs. The kind of weapon that could only exist on The Road. Not even the war pigs of Europe and America could create something so barbaric.

And of course there was the chainsaw. Never drive on The Road without it.

Farm looked down at the chainsaw for a few moments, running his hand over the smooth steel of the engine. He admired the modifications he'd made.

When he looked up, he found that a white Mustang had appeared in the rearview mirror. A deep breath. A crack of his neck. The game was afoot.

Farm steered the 'Cuda, which was still tearing forward at more than a hundred thirty, to the right side of the road. The Mustang pulled up next to Farm.

Even before Farm and the Mustang's driver were even with each other, Farm heard something land on the soft roof above him. He didn't need to look up to know what it was. Fire grenade.

Quickly, he flipped the clips holding the roof in place. He flung the roof open just as the grenade went off. He felt his scalp singe as the roof burst into flames. For a moment, Farm was blinded and had to crouch down in his seat to get away from the heat.

The misery was only momentary, though, as the wind took the roof and blew it off the back of the car. Farm didn't look back to see the fireball fly away.

He looked over at the Mustang's driver, who was cackling. The driver, clothed in white leather, had brown stumps where teeth used to be. His frosted tips were straight from a boy band music video, as were his sunglasses.

Farm grumbled and reached over to the passenger seat. His gnarled right hand closed around the handle of the long whip.

Farm peered again at the Mustang's driver, whose laugh had morphed into a sneer.

Farm gritted his teeth, and his wrist sprang into action. The whip's long, black tail unfurled, arcing through the air high above the two cars. The Mustang's driver didn't have time to put his hand up before Farm brought the whip down.

Farm's aim was true. The end of the whip's tail struck perfectly between the driver's eyes, snapping his sunglasses in two. The plastic of the shades flew off the driver's hideous face, revealing albino eyes.

His sneering visage stretched into a scream of horror, as he took his hands off the wheel to cover his eyes, which were boiling in their sockets. Steam escaped through the man's fingers as he writhed in agony, and the car wavered for a few moments on The Road. The car decelerated, and a few moments later it plunged off the road and flipped over.

Farm calmly watched the Mustang become wreckage in his rearview mirror. He placed the whip back in its spot on the passenger seat.

One down.

It wasn't long before two more Mustangs approached. Red and black, and closing fast. Farm cracked his neck and braced for their arrival.

They pulled up alongside him in unison, each throwing a large metal hook over the sides of Farm's doors, hooking their cars together. Farm expected this. He grabbed his axe and wedged it so it was down on the gas pedal. Then he grabbed the short-range whip and leapt to his feet. One foot on the driver's seat and one on the passenger seat.

The red Mustang's driver sprung up first, coming at Farm from the left. The driver's short-cropped hair matched the blazing red of his paint job. His eyes also seemed to blaze with an orange tint, and he wore faded red jeans below his black tee-shirt.

The driver raised a baseball bat full of nails—such a cliché, Farm thought—and stepped onto his passenger seat toward Farm. Farm gripped the handle of his whip—one that had nine barbed tassels.

The driver clumsily swung his club at Farm, who crouched and snapped his whip forward. The tassels tore through the driver's red jeans, the steel barbs tearing out chunks of thighs beneath. Farm's wrist snapped again as he brought the whip across again. More rips in the jeans, more flesh flung to the wind.

The driver brought the club down again, and Farm leaned back as the club slammed down on the seat below him. Farm drew his arm back to strike again, but the driver moved faster. He pulled the bat back up, and as Farm whipped, the driver moved the bat in front of him.

The tassels of the whip wrapped around the bat, getting tangled on the rusty nails. The driver yanked, pulling Farm forward and down to a kneeling position. The whip slipped from his hand, and the driver flung his bat away, taking the whip with it.

As he did that, the driver kicked Farm in the chin, sending Farm sprawling across the two front seats. The cloudless sky spun in front of Farm's eyes for a moment.

Then he heard it. From the black Mustang on his passenger side, a beast rattled to life.

Farm instinctively reached below him for his chainsaw. A moment later, the beast from the black Mustang was above him. The long, black chainsaw growled its mechanical battle cry. The driver of the black Mustang smiled, his long, greasy black hair flapping in the wind.

The driver brought the chainsaw above his head and then plunged it down. As he did, Farm brought up his own chainsaw and cranked it to life. He did this with the speed and muscle-memory of a Marine assembling his weapon.

Farm got his chainsaw in front of his face just in time. The black driver's chainsaw crashed into it, causing an eruption of sparks. Farm held strong, pushing up with all his force to keep the driver from shoving his own chainsaw down into him.

As Farm was pushing back, he saw the driver of the red Mustang had pulled out his chainsaw as well. Of course.

Farm pulled his legs up just before the red driver swung his chainsaw through the driver's seat right where Farm's legs had been. Farm kicked the red driver's wrist and could feel the pop as the joint dislocated.

Farm took a deep breath, sparks flying into his mouth, and gave a powerful push that threw the black driver's chainsaw upward and made the driver stumble backward. Farm leapt to his feet and jumped into his backseat.

The two drivers, each standing in their own cars, didn't look as confident as they had a few moments before. The red driver's right arm hung uselessly at his side, the hand dangling at an unnatural angle. The black driver brushed the tangled hair out of his face, glowering at Farm. The black driver wore all black, from his jeans to his shirt to his leather jacket. Dozens of silver zippers crisscrossed the jacket.

The black driver brought his chainsaw up and lunged at Farm. Farm swung his chainsaw defensively, repulsing the attack in a flurry of sparks. The red driver also swung his forward, listlessly. Farm easily defended it.

So it went for what seemed like an eternity. Their cars hurtling down The Road at over a hundred miles an hour, the three grizzled warriors swung at each other. It was a world populated with the gnashing of teeth and the smell of burnt metal.

Farm could tell the red driver was tiring, as he was using just one arm. Farm lunged at him and ferociously swung his chainsaw. The driver got his chainsaw up, but Farm was able to knock him backward. In that instant, Farm reached down and grabbed a spider bomb.

He armed the bomb and flung it straight at the driver's face. The driver's eyes widened in horror and he dropped his chainsaw. Eight metal legs shot out the sides of the orb and latched onto the driver's head. The legs pulled the orb close, right up to the driver's face. The driver thrashed and screamed and clawed at the spider bomb, but it was futile.

The small bomb detonated, sending bits of the red driver's head in all directions. His body crumpled into the front seat of the red Mustang.

Farm swung his chainsaw between the cars, cutting the hook that connected it to the red Mustang. With nothing tying the two cars together, the Mustang slowly angled off the road and crashed into the unforgiving desert.

He turned back to the black driver, whose chest heaved with renewed fury. He lifted his huge black chainsaw above his head and screamed.

Farm quickly reached down and pulled the large hook out of

the side of his car. As the black driver took a step forward and prepared to bring his chainsaw down on Farm, Farm knelt and swung the hook into the driver's midsection.

It stuck through the leather jacket with a pop and crashed through the man's ribs. The man brought the chainsaw down at Farm, but it was a weakened, slow movement. Farm easily got his chainsaw up in time, fending off the attack.

Farm shot up, swinging his chainsaw with blinding speed through the driver's torso. The driver's eyes boggled in his head before his top half slid off into Farm's backseat. The legs remained standing—one leg in the passenger seat and one in the driver's seat—for a moment before toppling.

Farm took a breath, then squatted down and picked up the remains of the black Mustang driver. Farm tossed the halved carcass onto The Road. A death on The Road meant your remains were to be scattered on the asphalt like ashes into the sea. Heavy, dripping, stinking ashes.

Farm slowly moved over to the passenger side, where he ripped the hook out of the door and watched as the black Mustang veered off into the desert.

Farm removed the axe and returned to his spot behind the wheel. He was distantly aware that he was sitting in something wet and chunky, but discomfort was just part of life on The Road.

Life and death coexisted closely, like a parasite and its host. Life fed off death out here, not the other way around.

The 'Cuda's engine bellowed as Farm's pedal foot hit the mat. The leftovers of the third Mustang driver disappeared in his rearview mirror, but Farm wasn't looking back.

After a few minutes of fury-fueled acceleration, Farm saw it. Where the Road met the sky, a dark speck appeared. Farm knew it was a jet-black Dodge Coronet. *The Duke's* jet-black Dodge Coronet.

The roar under the hood intensified. Maybe the 'Cuda had spotted the Coronet too.

It didn't take long to close the gap. The Duke wanted a fight. He always did.

Farm growled as the 'Cuda caught up to the Coronet. The Dodge was so dark that nothing was reflected in its paint. It was a black hole in the shape of a turbo-charged muscle car. Black lettering on a dark red license plate proclaimed *666*.

The Coronet's top was down, allowing Farm to get a clear look at The Duke as he pulled up alongside. The Duke's knotted black hair whipped like frenzied octopus tentacles in the wind. His grin stretched from side to side of his pale face. His mouth was lined with gold teeth. He wore a spotless black tuxedo with a black bow tie. He was a physical contradiction traveling a hundred twenty miles an hour.

The Duke was in a constant state of grotesque euphoria. He gnashed his gold teeth in the wind, as if trying to taste the acrid air. While some spoke in tongues, The Duke screamed in tongues. He was Bulgakov's Master on meth.

And now he was locking eyes with Farm as the two sped next to each other. The Duke howled with laughter. Farm snarled with rage.

They both ripped their steering wheel to the side, slamming the cars into each other. Sparks sprayed, but neither of them broke eye contact. They smashed their cars into each other again. And again. And again.

The Duke hooked the two cars together, just as the Mustang drivers had done before. Farm propped the axe against the gas pedal and sprung to his feet. Neither man picked up a weapon.

As the two cars tore forward at a hundred twenty miles an hour, Farm and The Duke engaged in a fistfight. Farm's muscles showed no signs of fatigue after the clashes with the Mustang drivers. He trained for this every day. Every action was done with The Duke in mind. He slammed his huge fists into The Duke's ribs, but the tuxedo felt like chainmail armor. Farm could tell he wasn't causing much pain to The Duke at all. The fiend's smile never faded.

The Duke struck with similar futility, as his blows were lost in Farm's vast network of muscle spread across his body. There was no cushion of fat. No crack of bone. Farm was a slab of lean beef that fought back.

Then they started swinging at each other's faces. Farm landed the first blow, splashing red across The Duke's line of gold teeth. The Duke, his grin still intact, struck Farm across the face with the back of his hand. Then he kicked at Farm's knee, sending the large man tumbling.

Farm was on his back before he knew it, his head on the driver's seat, and The Duke pounced on top. He had Farm pinned down. He slammed his face down into Farm's. Then he did it again. Both men's noses bled freely, and The Duke screeched with laughter. He screamed in his foe's face, spitting thick blood.

"FAAAAAARM!"

Then he threw his head back in laughter, black hair thrashing in the wind.

In a daze, Farm turned to his left and saw his axe wedged against the gas pedal. He twisted his body slightly, stretching his neck to its limit and closing his teeth around the axe's handle. He pulled, jarring the axe loose.

The 'Cuda began to slow down, dragging the Coronet to the left.

The Duke stopped laughing and looked down. He was still smiling, despite his surprise.

Farm pounced, ripping his arms free of The Duke's clutch and grabbing the axe. The Duke fell forward, off balance from Farm's move and the car's lurching. Farm pulled the axe out from under the steering wheel and held it in front of his face.

The Duke couldn't stop himself and fell face-first onto the axe's blade. The Duke's gold teeth sprayed in all directions, some of them flying out of his mouth and some of them lodging themselves in his cheeks.

Farm could feel The Duke's screams reverberate through the blade and the axe handle. It was time to deal the death blow, and he couldn't hesitate.

But before he could do anything, the linked cars spun out of control. Both cars flipped, sending the two drivers spinning in midair. Everything went black for Farm as he was thrown against the asphalt of The Road at more than a hundred miles an hour.

The blackness didn't last long.

Farm came to, his body pulsating with pain. His clothes were ripped to shreds and his skin hung in tatters in some places. He was confident he'd sustained severe burns on most of his body below the neck.

He groaned his way to his feet and looked around. The air was hazy and carried the smell of melted metal. Miraculously, the 'Cuda had landed back on its tires. The Coronet was totaled, now reduced to an obsidian heap of gnarled metal.

And there the bastard was. His face nearly torn in two, The Duke stood in his tuxedo next to the corpse of his car. His face glinted with gold, as the shards of his teeth poked through his cheeks.

He unleashed a howl, and Farm could tell The Duke was screaming his name. If his jaws had been anywhere near each other, The Duke would be smiling still.

Farm lurched forward through the smoky air. His legs were heavy, and his skin burned. The Duke bent his knees and put his hands forward, preparing for another clash.

Then Farm had a moment of clarity. He suddenly remembered how his last encounter with The Duke had ended. And he remembered why he'd made modifications to his chainsaw and the 'Cuda.

Farm turned back and moved as quickly as he could toward the 'Cuda. He heard the roar of an approaching engine.

A Mustang. The fourth one.

Another screech erupted from The Duke's ruined face as he saw Farm turning away. Farm would finish The Duke, but he needed to finish the Mustang driver first.

Farm saw the chainsaw on the side of The Road near the 'Cuda. He limped over to it, found it to be in working order, and dragged himself over to the 'Cuda. He looked back down The Road and could see the pale Mustang approaching. He'd have to move swiftly. He lifted the hood and got to work.

Moments later, Farm was in the 'Cuda's driver's seat. The Mustang was in clear view now, and Farm could even see the driver's sallow face. His deep red lips were wide open as he howled in rapturous fury. The front of the 'Cuda faced away from the approaching Mustang. Farm didn't want the Mustang driver to see the front.

The Duke, who had seen Farm working on the 'Cuda, tried to signal to the Mustang driver to stop. The driver was focused on Farm, though. He steered the Mustang straight at the 'Cuda. Farm waited to put the car into gear, looking to catch the driver by surprise.

When he could clearly see the driver's face, Farm threw the car into reverse and spun the car. Like a matador tricking a bull,

Farm had the Mustang right where he wanted it.

The driver saw the chainsaw too late. The chainsaw, attached to the 'Cuda's engine, stuck out from the front of the car and churned madly as Farm hit the gas. The Mustang drove straight into the turbo-charged chainsaw, which sliced its way through the car toward the driver.

The driver dived into the passenger seat as the chainsaw tore through the steering wheel and driver's seat. With nobody at the wheel, the Mustang spun out of control. It flipped once and then landed back on its tires.

Smoke surrounded the Mustang as the driver sat up again. He tried to look around but couldn't see. He heard the 'Cuda before he saw it. It was getting louder.

The purple car tore through the smoke, chainsaw leading the way. The chainsaw sliced through the Mustang once again, this time driving straight into the pale driver.

The driver screeched as the chainsaw tore through his midsection. From his seat, Farm saw the driver's blood bubbling and spraying up. It was like he'd struck crimson oil. Farm didn't take his foot off the gas until the blood stopped spraying. Even then, he waited a couple moments more.

Satisfied that the Mustang driver was dead, Farm leaned back in his seat and instinctively put his foot on the brake pedal. He looked in the rearview mirror. The cloud of smoke behind him, created from the squealing of his tires and the burning of metal, was painted red by the brake lights.

Farm saw the figure approaching through the smoke as if it were in slow motion. He felt strapped to his seat as the figure grew closer.

The Duke's ravaged face, red in the brake lights' glow, peeked out from the smoke. Farm saw there was something in The Duke's hand. Farm spun to face The Duke, but it was too late.

Farm turned around just in time to see the spider bomb soaring toward him. Its legs were fully extended. The legs latched on to Farm's head as Farm clawed at them furiously.

The legs dug themselves into his skull, and a deep cracking sound filled his head. The last thing Farm heard was the ghastly howling that spewed from The Duke's decimated jaws. It almost sounded like laughter.

***

The car's backfire was his alarm clock, and the cloud of dust was his breakfast.

Farmington Turner grumbled awake, still in the driver's seat of his purple Plymouth Barracuda. The pain in his head was sharp, his memories hazy.

Farm growled, the bits of dust still settling on his broad hood. Through the haze, he saw the black Dodge Coronet racing off across the flat desert road.

Farm reached for his keys, finding them still in the ignition, and turned them. The engine roared like a beast emerging from beneath the earth.

Farm snarled, reaching for the skull-topped gear shift.

Today, I kill you, he thought.

When the Devil Laughs
Brian James Lewis

Hendricks School of Psychological   Study
575 Granite Quarry Lane
Carbon City, NJ 19760-4055

Graduate Student Project Class of 2015

Date: September 15, 2018

Purpose of Study: To create a written record of the incidents on September 18, 2007 that resulted in former Carbon City Police Sergeant Frank Slade's voluntary commitment to the Angel of Mercy Health Center. AMHC is a long-term care facility for those who've demonstrated a disturbing level of detachment from reality and are hazardous to themselves or others. In the interest of producing a cohesive document, some minor edits have been made. All the words recorded were spoken by Mr. Slade, regardless of how strange they may seem.

*In light of recent events, there is also a short addendum to Slade's file after the record of events. While Hendrick's

University offers our deepest condolences, we do not accept any responsibility for Slade's actions.

It was hotter than hell on the night that Charlie sent me out on the worst call ever. The whole summer had been a scorcher and we'd hoped that the usually rainy Fall season would cool things down. But instead, the heat just kept ratcheting up higher until the simple act of crossing the street felt like the labors of Hercules. The same could be said about all the news people who were constantly around jamming microphones in our faces and asking for comments. I was pretty sure that, "It's fucking hot out here, jack!" wasn't exactly what they were looking for. So I just did the smile and nod thing, but the old folks who sat around the fountain by city hall weren't feeling as restrained.

"Don't you know that Carbon City is the Devil's Cauldron?" Emmaline Schuster hollered at the kid from Channel 5 doing a human-interest bit. She stuck her wrinkled old pan right into the guy's camera and grabbed his pant leg so he couldn't walk away from her. "The Devil is coming! Can't you feel that heat, son? The closer he comes, the hotter it gets! Last time was Afghanistan, but the worst time was Vietnam! We're going to war! WAR!"

That guy just froze and kept saying, "Yes, ma'am!" Until she unclenched her arthritic hand. I'd heard a few whispers about that event and how the Leslie Shoe Factory suddenly burst into flame during the sweltering September of 1972. They'd been churning out a hundred pair of jungle boots a day to outfit soldiers. But when the whole place burned to the ground, all the jobs went with it. While the official cause for the disaster was claimed to be electrical, surviving employees insisted that Satan came right up through the floor and set the place ablaze. I always thought it was kind of a cool local legend, but nothing more.

When the kid got his chance at freedom, he made a run

for it, giving me the old stink eye for not stepping in to rescue him. But that's what you get for riling up some oldsters whose brains are frying like Spam in a pan. Nobody hurt him and we were all getting pretty tired of too much media attention by then. Sure, it was nifty to be featured on *The Weather Channel* and *CNN* every day. Especially when Wanda Weatherly and "Hurricane" Howie Henderson began using Dillon's Diner as the backdrop for their broadcasts! But as the heat and humidity ground on with no relief in sight, the fun value took a hike and never came back. I mean, just doing my job of being a calm, rational police officer was twice the work it normally was. At lunch I had to change into a fresh uniform and replenish the two gallons of Gatorade I carried in my car. Still, in light of how things went, it was nothing to complain about.

After oozing through an awful August, we ended up in sick September. The temperatures continued to soar, and Carbon City got hit by the "super bug." It was like a mean flu on steroids that nothing could touch. Some folks even died from it. The only thing you could do was sit on the crapper all day and stay hydrated. Unfortunately, that became an additional problem when it turned out that our water was full of it. Some people said the virus was incubating in the water tower, while others claimed that it was carried downriver from some Podunk town that didn't believe in sanitation. The water treatment plant responded by raising the chlorine level until a cup of coffee tasted like the city pool heated up. Yum.

After that glamorous development, the TV people hit the road for some California wildfires and left us to roast in our own vomit. They weren't the only ones disappearing either. The super bug cut the Carbon City Police Department off at the knees, bringing us down to 33 percent operating capacity. Big problem! It wasn't as if the criminals were going on sick leave until we could get back on our feet. Those of us who were immune or somewhat healthy, were stuck working doubles until further notice. While the overtime pay was great, the bone crushing exhaustion wasn't. I felt like a cheaply made robot going through the motions. Punch the clock, load a case of bottled water into the cruiser, eat a sandwich, change your clothes and do it again. None of us were ready for the unexpected.

Ironically, my night of hell began with me feeling happy. My shift was almost over, and I had big plans! Nothing romantic, flashy, or expensive. But it was going to be great! On my way home, I was going to pop into Garcia's and grab myself a sixer of Rolling Rock and two bags of ice. Once home, I'd fill a bucket with ice, pop the beers into it, and watch baseball in my boxers until I fell asleep. Man! I smiled just thinking about it. All that remained was my final cruise down Watson to make sure things looked secure. Halfway down, the radio crackled:

"Dispatch to 47…Over."

"Yeah, Charlie…" I replied against my better judgment, "What's the scoop?"

"We got a complaint from a lady over on Rose Street. Something about fireworks…"

"Fireworks?" I shot back as my phone rang.

"Yeah…pick up." I did and he continued. "Carol Feeney at 101 Rose is complaining that her neighbors at 99 Rose keep setting off fireworks. Says they're scaring her kids." Well fan-fucking-tastic! A bullshit neighbor problem. They always took forever to sort out and everybody had to have their say. Then I was supposed to ignore everything else, like the fifteen people in a one-bedroom apartment with the black and blue kids. Shit, there went the ballgame and my ice-cold longnecks! Garcia's would be closed by the time I mopped this up.   "Did you tell her to call back in ten minutes if they keep it up?" I asked hopefully.

"No I did not. C'mon, Frank! You're what, a couple blocks away?"

"Yeah…"

"So drive over there and lay down the law!"

"Rose Street isn't a great place for a lone cop to be sticking his face in the door…You know that as well as I do."

"Yeah, but it's a mom and her kids. So we should check it out."

Nothing like a damsel in distress to get the old man all fired up! I mumbled something under my breath, but Charlie heard me anyway.

"Who the hell are you callin' old? Don't make me come over there and do the job myself!" He shouted. Me and my big mouth.

"No, I got it." I sighed and got my ass in gear.

It was easy for him to be big and brassy on the horn, but there were problems with Charlie's plan. Number one being that we were not checking anything out. It was just me with no partner to watch my back in case anything went south. Number two was that my nearest backup was fifteen minutes away, thanks to the skeleton crew deal. Number three, the East Side wasn't known for its high quality of living, or classy citizens. I might be walking right into a meth lab, drug house, or a gang hideout. Not exactly places to arrive all by your lonely.

After passing the battered "Dead End" sign, I did my best to steer around the worst potholes and mounds of stinking garbage. Rose Street was a nice place, if you were shooting a horror flick, maybe! Otherwise not so much. Streetlights seemed to be optional, as were house numbers. So I clicked on my trusty spotlight and peered into the gloom in search of 99, which surprisingly, had numbers. It just took me a minute because some joker had flipped them upside down and scrawled in an extra digit with a sharpie. 666 Rose was an ugly place that looked as if it might collapse at any moment. I shut the car down and sat for a few minutes, listening for trouble.

Five minutes ticked by in silence.

If somebody was shooting off fireworks, they must have exhausted their supply. That worked for me! Maybe I'd get that six-pack after all…No bullshit required. But just as I grabbed the mic to tell Charlie I was heading in, "BLAMMO!" A huge boom shook the ground, and everything lit up. Damn! What the hell were these people shooting off, a cannon? Without further ado, I heaved myself out of my sweaty seat and strode right up to the front door. Charlie wanted me to lay down the law? You're damn right I would, and screw the warning! It was ticket time for these bozos! Maybe I'd put a couple dents in their door, too…

But it opened before I even knocked, revealing a hot little number in a skin-tight tank top and daisy dukes. She gave me a smile that took the wind right out of my sails. Officer hard ass became office hard on. Oops.

"Well, hello there…Officer." She purred as her body rubbed against my left arm. A wave of perfume that reminded me of high school filled my nostrils with sweet memories. "I'm sooo…Hot…" She smiled. "Wouldn't you like to come…inside?" I smiled, nodded, and stepped right on into the house. It was fun following her short shorts down a long hallway and into the living room. Whoo-Hoo, buckaroo! The night could only get better from here, right? My brain was so busy running off to happy land that it never occurred to me that the whole thing might be a trap.

She smiled. I talked. What a pleasure it was to speak with this beautiful and cheerful woman! It sure was a nice change from the usual drunk guy with puke on his shirt or his angry mastodon of a wife shouting into my face. My stupefied brain was puzzled. How could anyone think that such a hot babe could be a bad person? Probably the woman next door had called us out of jealousy. I gave her my card and told her that she could call me for anything at all. No emergency required. Wink-wink! But as my eyes ran up and down her shapely legs, I saw something I hadn't seen before. There was a gun on the coffee table.

Seeing that I was checking out the coffee table, the babe shifted herself around a bit to bring my attention back to her charms. Instead, it revealed an arsenal of weapons and a huge statue of Satan holding out hands of flame with his head thrown back in laughter. Even in my current blissful state, I knew that couldn't be good! The best course of action for me was to stride briskly out the door before anything else revealed itself. As I looked around for nearby exits, I realized that we were standing in the center of a large pentagram. Great. That wasn't a place I wanted to be any longer, so I tried to wrap things up quick. "Well, thanks for your help." I smiled. "Time to get back out there and chase the bad guys. Ha-ha!"

"Don't move, pig." Said a raspy voice behind me.

Shit! I was screwed, and not in a good way. The speaker had cut off my exit and knew everything I didn't. There could be one guy or a small army behind me. From the look of those guns, I was guessing a crowd. Either way there wasn't much I could do about it. Alarm bells were blaring inside my head and my face flushed with embarrassment. How the hell could I have been so stupid? I was a twelve-year veteran police officer who'd just let a sexy babe turn him back into a rookie again. Damn it!

Figuring that my best chance for escape would be to catch the raspy voiced joker off guard, I braced myself for a quick spin and takedown. All I needed was 30 seconds to fly out the door and into my cruiser, then I'd be gone like the wind. But I stopped with the action hero jazz when I felt cold steel touching my temple and heard that rusty chuckle again.

"Face forward, dickhead." Rasped the guy behind me, pushing what felt like the nose of another pistol into my lower back. "You make any more sudden moves, and I'll blow your balls off. Keep your hands up, too." A cool chunk of ice dropped into my stomach and for a minute, I thought I was going to shit my pants. The girl kept on smiling, but her charm was gone. It was obvious that the sudden change of events did not surprise her as she wiggled over, took my gun, and pointed it at me.

"The Master is going to be so pleased with him, Lucifera."

She blushed and rubbed at her crotch excitedly. "Death makes me wet! Rawwwr!"

"Easy there, tiger…We don't want to kill him until the master gets here"

"Hey! What's going on?" I asked, trying to sound tough like John Wayne and failing miserably.

"It's time for the annual sacrifice to the master and tonight, you're the lucky winner!" Yelled the gravel-voiced dude with a lot more joy in his voice than I was feeling right then. But he didn't have a gun jammed into his back, either. As we stood there, with my captors enjoying their success, I racked my brain for anything I could use to get myself out of this jam. Obviously, my tough guy approach hadn't worked too well. If anything, it just made them enjoy things more. Maybe I could trade places with the person who'd caused all this drama? Yeah, it was kind of lame to throw a citizen under the bus, but what the hell else was I supposed to do? Besides, if that woman lived in this neck of the woods, I was pretty sure that she wasn't a regular churchgoer. You know what I mean?

"Look, the only reason I'm here is because your next-door neighbor called us about the fireworks and my dispatcher made it into a big deal. Me? I could care less! Anything else I saw here is none of my business." Nobody told me to shut up, so I kept talking. "Truth is, your neighbor is the one who got her panties in a bunch, not us. Does the name Carol Feeney ring a bell? She's the one with a problem! You let me loose and you're free to do whatever you want to bitchy old Carol. Sound good?"

Their reaction was not quite what I expected. Instead of

howling in righteous indignation, the babe in front of me cheesed like she was doing a toothpaste commercial and the creep behind me let loose another rusty chuckle. He kept chuckling as he lit a cigar so close to my ear that I could feel the heat from the flame. Plumes of smoke whooshed by my face as the guy laughed like I was a stand-up comic instead of a stupid, overconfident cop.

"Hey, Carroll! Come on in and join the party. I got this dick stain under control!"

A door behind the chick flew open with a crash, letting in demented laughter and a big hairy dude that must've weighed at least 400 pounds. He had a mop of greasy hair and beard to match. Who knew that Sasquatch lived in New Jersey? I sure as hell didn't. Even the guy's hands were covered in hair! But his physique didn't bother me as much as the evil grin on his face did. Between that and the t-shirt he wore, identifying him as a member of the "Devil's Posse," I wasn't sure whether to laugh or cry. But as the saying goes, actions speak louder than words. So when I saw him ignore a nearly naked woman in favor of fondling his shotgun, I knew I'd landed myself in some serious trouble.

"Wait a minute! You…You're…" I stammered. "You're Carrol?" This was just getting too damn weird.

"You betcha!" He bellowed back while stroking off his shotgun.

"But we got a call from a woman in distress!"

Everyone in the room laughed, except me. The guy behind me said "Go ahead and show him, Carrol! He ain't never leaving here anyways!" Carrol stood up straight and as he did, his face softened into waxy mask. Slowly his features morphed into a delicate female face. Whoa! That was creepy! The voice that came out chilled me to the bone. "Please, Mister Officer! My children are frightened! Please send somebody to help us! Please?"

"Fuckin' cool, ain't it?" Hooted my captor, as Carrol's face slowly returned to its hairy self. I was speechless. If that was fun, me and these folks didn't have much in common.

"So, what are we gonna do with him, Chainsaw?" Asked Carrol with his scary chompers glistening. Seriously? The brains of the operation called himself, "Chainsaw?" In better circumstances, I probably would have laughed out loud to hear that. It sounded like somebody spent a little too much time watching professional wrestling and taking bad drugs. But since Chainsaw was still holding a gun against the side of my head, I kept silent.

"We're gonna have us some fun, Carrol!" Chainsaw crowed. "This shitbird is our sacrifice for the master, but we're going to soften him up first!" Carrol cheered loudly in appreciation of this fine news, but I didn't feel nearly as enthusiastic.

"Who's the master? Why are you doing this for him?" Truth was, I was getting a pretty good idea from the scenery and watching Creepy Carrol loving up his shotgun. That, and Lucifera was wiggling around in her tiny shorts as if she was about to blow a gasket. They both looked at me as if I were the main course at an all-you-can-eat buffet and they just couldn't wait to get started.

"Because then we'll get our eternal reward!" They cheered. Sweat was pouring down my face freely and a metallic, coppery taste soured my mouth. I felt myself moving quickly towards hysteria. These folks weren't kidding around.

"What? You can't be serious!" I babbled to them. "If you get caught for this…It's the death penalty for shooting an officer." But all that did was add to their kicks.

"Move it, pig!" Chainsaw rasped, jamming his guns into my back and pushing me towards the door Carrol had just come through. "Don't try anything stupid, either! I've got your ass covered and Carrol here will blast a new hole through your ass if I say so!" In confirmation of this, Carrol jammed his shotgun against my stomach and smiled.

As our little procession shuffled out into the weed choked

backyard, I saw that they were more than ready. There was a creepy looking sacrificial altar of sorts set up between the back porch and the warped wooden fence. It was a mock crucifix made of plywood, rusty car parts, chain restraints and a lot of old tires. As they secured me to it, I got to see what Chainsaw looked like. He was a rail thin, long haired, *Mötley Crüe* looking dude, complete with face make up and the S&M costume of spiked black leather.

"Now, here's what we're gonna do..." announced Chainsaw, who was clearly enjoying his role of head honcho. In his hands were two Wild West styled pearl handle revolvers which he kept waving around and using to point directions. I was hoping to hell that neither one of them had a hair trigger. Otherwise, there wouldn't be any need for this dramatic set up. He strutted around as Carrol and Lucifera secured me to the sacrificial altar with chains and padlocks that bound my wrists, waist, and ankles. Having the girl up against me wasn't bad, but Carrol up close had all the charms of a fermenting dumpster. When everything was done to his satisfaction, Chainsaw stepped up and whipped his gun across my face.

"Everyone always says you cops are tough. But me and Carrol want to see for ourselves." He cackled, pushing his face into mine. "The master doesn't care if the sacrifice is alive or dead, it just has to be fresh. So, while we wait, we're going to have us some fun! How many bullets will it take before you scream like a little girl?" My body trembled as he ran his gloved fingers across my face. "How many until you...stop?" Chainsaw's shouts morphed into shrieking laughter. When he regained composure, the leather clad bastard pistol whipped me a few more times and walked back to the porch.

I guess I'm not real tough because I was already getting close to the screaming point, but I held it in and tried one last time to talk them out of what they were doing. "Seriously guys? You won't get away with this. If you kill a cop in this state, you're done! Let me loose now and we'll go our separate ways like nothing ever happened. What do you say?"

Neither man even glanced up from setting up their toys. I looked over at the girl with pleading eyes, but she was writhing around with both hands in her pants and a faraway look in her eyes. Well at least somebody was enjoying themselves…

"It's TIME to ROCK and ROLL!" Sang Chainsaw as he and Carrol turned to face me. The huge grins on their faces made me shudder. Why the hell hadn't I just ignored this call? God damn Charlie and his chivalry! Why had he done this to me?

"Better get ready, big tough cop! I'm gonna take the first shot and then it'll be time for Carrol to blast ya with that big shotgun of his! Make sure to scream nice and loud so we can hear ya!" Their insane laughter bubbled off the back fence like a nightmare. "Ready…Aim…" Chainsaw raised his revolver and cocked the hammer back. He was carefully sighting down the barrel, when there was a sudden change of plans.

"HEY! Wait just a damn minute!" Shouted Carrol, grabbing the barrel of Chainsaw's revolver and pushing it towards the ground. Finally! Somebody was making sense! Maybe the big buffoon had a change of heart or didn't like the idea of spending the rest of his life behind bars. "I get the first shot, because I'm the one who made the fucking phone call to get this bozo out here!" Carrol raged into Chainsaw's face.

"So what? That don't mean nothin'!" Chainsaw countered unconvincingly.

"Yeah it does! Don't try ripping me off, Chainsaw, or you'll be sorry!" Carrol replied, shoving him aside. But as he lined up his shot, Chainsaw shouldered his way in front of him.

"Back off, you hairy bastard! You're not one of the

chosen!"

Waiting for two grown men to stop arguing about who would shoot me first was not my idea of a good time. Especially while I was chained to their satanic offering altar. Add in their woman, who was so heated up by her bloodlust that she was nearly burning down the fence behind her and I felt like I was trapped on the set of a really bad B-movie. *"GUNS! DEVIL WORSHIP! LUST! Will Sergeant Frank Slade Live to Tell the Tale?"* The only thing missing was Chuck Norris crashing through the fence with guns blazing and karate kicks flailing to save my sorry ass. Unfortunately, that didn't seem to be in the script for this picture. Too bad, because I would have kissed his feet right in front of God and everybody.

I was startled from my thoughts by a huge blast and whipped my head around just in time to see Chainsaw collapse with a giant hole in his chest. He gurgled and tried to drag Carrol down with him as he fell, but the huge goon just shrugged him off. After kicking Chainsaw a few times in the ribs, Carrol reloaded and stepped up to the plate. He grinned at me like a hungry alligator as he sighted down the barrel and lined up his shot. I took a deep breath and closed my eyes.

Being shot at close range with a shotgun was going to hurt like hell. That might sound weird coming from a cop who could get shot anyplace at any time. But out on the street, I had a fighting chance to dodge the shot. Plus, it's one thing to be chasing a drug dealer while shots are being fired. Your adrenalin is pumping you up and your mind is busy. Being chained to a stack of tires in someone's backyard and forced to watch an obvious madman take shots at me was a whole different ballgame. There wasn't any if in the equation anymore, just when would I be killed. By that time, I just wanted to get things over with.

A shot rang out, followed by the huge "BOOM!" of Carrol's shotgun, but no pain blossomed in my body. What the hell? A horrible wail filled the backyard and my eyes popped open. All I could see was Carrol slowly crumpling on top of Chainsaw while vocalizing his disappointment. It must be that Chainsaw retained just enough strength to pull the trigger on his already cocked pistol and wipe out the traitorous Carrol. Then the big man had made sure the other was dead by blasting his head off with the shotgun. Unbelievable! I was still standing while both of my "scientific shooters" lay still. The whole performance was capped off by the girl, who went from horny to horrified in sixty seconds. She dropped her foxy babe façade and ran screaming into the house, leaving me alone with the guys.

I watched the bodies for a while, but nobody moved. Nor did Lucifera return. Well, wasn't that just dandy as shit? There I was chained up like a dog in the yard of a Satanic worship joint, pretty much a sitting duck for whoever came along. What if the girl decided it was up to her to finish the job? She could blast me, take off in my cruiser, and be long gone by the time anybody arrived. For all I knew, there might be more freaks like Chainsaw coming out any minute to end me. I listened so hard that I was aware of when the crickets stopped chirping.

As I hung there on that twisted sacrificial altar, built by the two madmen who lay dead on their own patio, the silence was deafening. Sweat poured from my body as the air grew even hotter. Suddenly, shafts of fiery light gleamed in the grass, making it burst into flames all around me. If that wasn't enough to make me shit a brick, the ground in front of my feet split open. From the fiery pit below, deep mocking laughter boomed forth. Then two huge hands reached up from the depths and dragged the two men off the porch. As they disappeared into the flames, the laughter was punctuated by the sounds of flesh tearing and bones crunching. It didn't take a rocket scientist to realize what was going on and it wasn't anything I wanted to be privy to.

Piss ran down my leg as a pair of gleaming yellow eyes

peered at me from the depths. Then a hand started reaching upwards as the laughter began again. I wanted to scream for help, because I sure as hell needed some, but I was afraid of what would happen if I did. The Devil would not be frightened by my voice, it was the freaks in the house I was worried about. At least silence might help me avoid any more unwanted attention from them. Since no one had come to my aid with all the shooting and yelling going on, I wasn't banking on the neighbors for help. So I waited quietly on my crucifix of tires and for the first time in over twenty years, I prayed. Maybe it wouldn't help, but it sure couldn't hurt. My brain was exploding inside my head, circuits shorting out. I was losing it, totally fucking losing it! Something touched my shoe and when I looked down, a long nail slid up my pant leg…

"No! Please, God, save me!" I screamed and struggled to get away. Things looked pretty bad for the home team, but I kept shouting out every prayer I'd ever learned and begged the Lord for his mercy. How long I went on, I don't know, but an annoyed snort made me open my eyes. The Devil was looking up at me with an angry scowl on his face. He sighed and shook his huge head in disgust. The hands slid away from me and the ground began to rumble, but not before the words "Dirty" and "Next time" were spoken. Then the split in the yard rumbled shut and the fire went out. I could feel my mental health slipping away as I stared in disbelief at the same weedy patch of lawn that had been there a few minutes ago. Did I really see that? Then the porch light went out, leaving me alone in the dark as crickets sang all around.

When I saw the revolving lights flashing on the other side of the fence, I figured that I must be hallucinating because I so badly wanted them to be there. To a speeder they might be a curse, but to me they meant salvation. Then I heard the crackle of the dispatch radio and knew for sure that it wasn't a mirage. A flashlight beam explored the yard and came to rest on the pool of blood left behind by the two men who couldn't agree, then waved around the weeds. It kept missing me, so I tried to shout. But my mouth was too dry, and I was afraid that I might get shot by the flashlight owner. However, I also did NOT want to be left in that creepy joint.

"Hey! Over here!" I croaked out.

"Frank? Is that you? Asked an incredulous voice.

"Yeah, Charlie! Get me out of this!" I screamed, not caring how frightened I sounded anymore. Charlie walked closer, shining the beam of his flashlight on me, and staring wide-eyed at the chains and ceremonial altar.

"What's the deal here, Frank?" He asked, flicking the beam over at the blood. "I just got a call from a woman saying that if I wanted to see the cop I sent to 99 Rose Street alive, I better hurry. What the hell happened, kid?"

I couldn't speak. Tears were pouring out of my face, and I bawled like a baby. Charlie stared at me a minute, then called the rescue squad. They arrived a few minutes later and cut the chains off with bolt cutters. I nearly fell on my face, but two EMTs caught me and eased me onto a gurney. Out at the ambulance, I completely lost it. My mouth was babbling and screaming like a girl. I was horribly ashamed, but I couldn't stop. I guess Chainsaw got his wish after all.

Charlie kept pounding my shoulder and shouting, "You're okay, Frank! You're okay!" Which I'm sure is all he knew how to do. Thankfully, the EMTs got him to pipe down and gave me a shot of dope. Just before they shut the doors, Charlie squeezed my shoulder, looked me in the eye, and said, "I'm damn proud of you, kid! Don't worry about a thing. Before you know it, we'll be working together again!" I nodded and tried to smile, but my face didn't work right.

As the ambulance pulled away, I watched the flashing reds recede in the rear windows, feeling relief and medication wash over me until I passed out. I woke up in the hospital screaming at the top of my lungs and got transferred to a psychiatric ward. When I told the counselors the truth, nobody believed me. Well they can take their stupid mind games and shove them up their ass! None of that shit works! What I want to do is ride the edge of oblivion and never leave this secure, locked-down, ward. Charlie came around a few times but stopped when I told him the truth. I'm not *doing great!* and the only way I'm going to leave this place is in a body bag. Period! But even surrounded by security guards, cinderblock walls and locked steel doors, there are still nights when I can hear the Devil laugh. Other nights, he visits and keeps telling me that soon it'll be my turn. No one escapes.

**On September 30, 2018, an aide at our facility did a check on patient Frank Slade due to complaints that other patients smelled something burning. When the sheets were pulled down it was discovered that Slade's body had been reduced to crumbling charcoal and ash, basically burned entirely with no damage to anything else in the room. Even the sheets were intact and clean with no burn marks. Was it spontaneous combustion? Slade complained bitterly about nighttime visits from the Devil which often led to him being sedated and put into the quiet room for his own safety. Also, the rest of the patients could sleep without being frightened. Perhaps there was some truth to his statements but the representatives for the Angel of Mercy Health Center feel that at this time it is better that the case be closed. The partnership with Hendricks University is currently under review and it is unclear whether it will be continued at the time of this writing.

The Philosopher's Nightmare
C. C. Parker

I. THE EXECUTIONER

I have always wanted to kill a man. A man, specifically, who's failed to see things the way they are. Looking at myself in the bathroom mirror asking myself if I could go through with it. My eyes no longer have the crazed look of those early years, softening around the edges into a dull kind of madness. I am burnout in many ways, yet far removed from the *R. Crumb* ideal. I am a soldier of the doomed elite even in this bunker so far away from the action. Bursting with reticent paranoia and many throats slashed in the dark as I try pulling out what's left of me and committing it to the page.

I am a killer in my own way. That I have to believe . . .

Universe failing to notice—ghosts run amok while Earth sinks away like an atrophied limb into a desolate aether. Moving my alcohol-withered body through the cramped space of my room, I dig a bottle out of the closet. I hold it between my legs as I feel the seed shift, the entire Earth on its axis tipping down. I feel it in my chest making it hard to breathe.

Pulling long off a bottle and setting it aside, I look over what I'd written realizing I didn't give a fuck anymore. There are no more stories to tell unless they are in rapture of the Ghost Light that is impressed on my seared retina. Approaching without vision. Occluding sorrows of a constantly decaying center.

Meanwhile, outside, the sun is bright. Gauze of my looping thoughts settling into something more proactive. I know that I do it to myself. If I'd only learn to go for a walk instead of further destroying my one and only claim. Even though I was in with the gathering dead. The only thing they took from me was the need to participate, facilitating it with a desire to become enmeshed in a world of nocturnal gloom while waiting for the end to come.

***

Floating down the street where Oakenfell Cemetery looms to one side, half a block from my apartment, stretching in grey and green patches toward silent oblivion. Past a rusted gate flanked by a once stately hedge.

The place has gone to shit. No current burials as far as I know as most of the occupants are from the turn of the last century when Sea Town was still a sleepy village. Still, there are wild patches where fresh bodies could be inhumed in the far northern corner of the cemetery where a sparse wilderness shrouds a muddy bog. At twilight, drinking by its shore, I watch the moon through the crooked branches . . .

Thinking of a scenario, a plot, where I butcher a man and bury him there. Like now, walking down the street, I see him from the corner of my eye. A rotten stench coming from him that, weirdly, gives me an erection. Yammering on his cellphone, selling his concern to a fellow partitioner. Meanwhile, occluding truth abides, as I diffuse the barrier that lies between us.

No one is around. Nearby in a park, some children are playing. A van roars past, toward the interstate up ahead. There is only the rear of a grocery store, its hungry fellowship shielded against the coming grue.

Taking a chunk of discarded concrete from a nearby worksite, I bash him over the head many times. It isn't until his brains are oozing out his ears that I stop . . .

With no crime to my name I become fevered by the exactitude of my vision. It makes me emotional for a second. Wiping a tear as I imagine concealing my victim under a pile of concrete before coming back to get him at night with my beater car. Wrapping him in a black plastic sheet and several bungee cords, I drive around the block a couple times, parking on the quieter side of Oakenfell.

***

I don't have a car in real life. I'm not sure why I think you should know. Because I am a grievous wanderer and my streets are forked. Years of channeling and taming my demons has skewed everything I thought about myself. With each step comes a fevered emotion—love and rage—galvanizing poles, twining, electric, leading to urgent remonstrations.

This is not about how a human survives, but how the shell breaks, leaving the yoke on the floor. Ascend or become absorbed by the meat of destiny. I only wish for one example of what I mean in the real to bind the course.

Right now I don't have anything at all. No car, lady or job. I have a couple fuck buddies, Kendra and Alice, both who are getting into more serious relationships. I fill in at Cicada Video too, but it is sporadic. It is the last video store in the city, warranting a huge boon to lurkers such as myself. Otherwise, it is the physical manifestation you see. Unaware of the dying cauldron underneath, there is no extant proof of my dire rejection.

Possibly it is best to keep it inside. Continue writing horror stories and indulging in spirits over the moonlight. We all have our ways of coping or believing in the insanity of human endeavor. Romanticizing death, forgetful of the plight of life. Isn't that true horror? Why delude ourselves, when the cosmic blade rides alongside our necks . . ? I was a ghost before and I will be a ghost again—a particle of invisible sand broken up in moonlight—vaporized when the sun goes down as if none of this ever happened. But just this once I want to know what it feels like to be alive—feast, fuck, shit then die . . ! I look into their vacant eyes and am filled with rage all over again. I'm asking you, friend, what lives there?! What demon occupies those blank spaces between the surface and lost dimensions? In the guise of a disciple it walks among us with aeons on its breath and a dead tongue. It's the same smell as before, roving between worlds. A plague of understanding sealing all corpses inside.

II. THE GRAVEDIGGER

After burying the fool, I piss on his grave. I suppose it is the Thrasher in me.

Juxtaposition of youthful rage with the delinquency of my heart. For once in my life I truly didn't care what happened. Living on the edge was no longer getting drunk till six am and fucking some stranger in an alley. Times when I felt it was the most insane things will get.

We took a shit on everything, even if it never really mattered. Metal Militia kills out in the open and that's the way it's always been. But here, down in the layers of my mind, confused, even, by the layout of misgivings.

Palace of Knossos concealing the Labyrinth of the Double Axe . . .

To clarify my despair with a return to the myths; they are

a part of me, always, but I cannot confuse them with my shit or piss. Blood-stained reunions get us halfway, rituals in the dark born out of desperation. These are the demons that have come to be, surfacing nakedly from the oily pool of my consciousness.

Eventually, these will lead to other things. I've never understood the future more. No longer did I support the "no future" stance of youth. I could feel the prolonged death spasm over hundreds of years, bodies piled to grey, pitiless horizons. The cynic in me considered this to be the only future, until I pulled away from the mirror—cracked with blackened edges—to consider my one life, that I'd throw it all away to kill a single, worthless specimen. While another part of me decides it is best if we bury them all.

***

The decay is only starting to show, I think, crossing the street. I go to meet steely-eyed, truck driver, Daniel, at a nearby taco truck, wearing the same faded *Neurosis* hat he always wore. Tattoos up to his neck, charting his obsession with highway lore. Guitarist for the band *Sturgeon*, Daniel spent several months of the year on the road driving the van even though he's just truck driver, Dan to most.

"Dude, the Carnitas here are ridiculous!"

I searched my wallet and found just ten dollars, to my despair. I really need to get a bottle.

I buy one taco and eat it slow. They are only two bucks and very small, but I don't have much of an appetite. My stomach shrinks away from day like an unembalmed corpse.

"Here. Have one of mine." Daniel drops a taco on my plate, and I gobble it down. "You doin' okay, brother?"

"I get paid on Friday."

"How's life at the vid store?"

"It's a cool, easy gig."

"A video store in 20 fucking 18?!"

Daniel and I are both children of the eighties. It is the splatter decade, best years for horror and metal. Even today, we are trying to keep it alive. "Still, it's not the same," I go on. "Honestly, the horror selection is shit. Newer stuff with a decent selection of the classics, I guess. Very little foreign or underground . . ."

"I'll never forget the places back in the day." He plucks the mess from his plate with greasy fingers and crams it into his face. "Do you remember Extinction Video? That place had the sickest shit! Back in the *Cradle Death* days we used to rent there all the time. First Argento, Fulci & Herschell G. I got into. Miike's early works, too. Fuck!"

Afterwards, Daniel buys a six pack of Rainier tall-boys at Seven-Eleven that we drink in the park. He talks about his band and where it's heading. Nearing fifty, he's still touring with a working band who is recently turning heads in the doom world. "The new album comes out in October. *The Philosopher's Nightmare*. It is a series of interlocking parts, but basically one connected piece. A forty-four minute crusher!"

***

How do I wake up from this? The moment I enter the labyrinth, a new cycle starts.

Driving around town in a Chevette— faded yellow— looking for more humans to kill.

It is the same scenario as before, but this time it's for real. I go looking for men who have the smell. I keep a knife under my seat and a pistol I got from a friend of a friend in my glove box. I will only use it if my victim tries to get away. All I want to do is get them back to Oakenfell where I can perform the burial rites in private . . .

I begin digging a fresh hole when I hear crying, or possibly laughter, coming from the far side of the pond, accessible only by a weathered trail sliding into the mud. It is west of that open area, littered with beer cans, cigarette butts and syringes where, under an extended thatch of pine, my hidden graveyard swells. Pregnant with the death I gave it, inseminated by dire awakening.

I always pull my cock out at the end and ejaculate on the freshly dug grave.

This, my garden, flourishing empathically on a sea of dead. Only this time there is a visitor on my lonely isle, who wants to check on my garden. Suddenly, I can feel my life fading, becoming something else, from another life. Stepping between worlds on its way to the sanctuary of heaven. I didn't think anything in this forlorn place could abide to the logic of such incriminatory petulance.

I came here because it is a world unto itself, somehow partitioned off from the speeding juggernaut, where Lovecraft & Poe sat in my heart. There remained an ignorance of a horror beyond all this that was far more real. The blade sharper. Even as those twin giants were embroidered in horrors of their own, each against society in his own way . . . Blood is warm.

***

There's a lump in my throat as I go for the bottle. Part of me doesn't like where the story is going, as inspired as it felt. It contained a bit of the old me; twenty-five years old standing above a crowd with a pig's head mounted on his erection, spewing incantations and broken tongued litagies. I wore ash around my eyes as I personified a killer pagan at heart who fucked and worshipped nature equally. Instead, the fading idol of myself, electric nerves that have long since become the source of chronic pain. I douse them regularly, resulting in a downgradable truth.

I want to know her again. There is the meaning of this, if you need it. For those who've lost the way to her grove—who once relished the innocent violence of bacchanalian tributaries, as a full moon scintillated with the essence of youth.

I can envision when the world was new, life bursting out of every crevice even though nothing was wasted . . .

That is what the girl looks like to me under the grey arches of the tomb, one concealed away from the rest of Oakenfell. Nearly two hundred years old, black, marbled terrace overlooking the pond. The structure itself the size of a small house—densely speckled with pine needles and bird shit. Escaping to this corner for over a year, I'm impressed it lay undiscovered. For all I knew it was a junkie den, or makeshift brothel.

"How long have you been here?" I ask the girl. Ringlets of her hair like black-fire bursting to life as she enters the moonlight. A slight but heavy creature smoking a cigarette coolly in the presence of the tomb reminding me of the painful hard-on that's been with me since the night's killing. "What is this place?" Dumb, pedantic questions. Still, I didn't know it, as many times as I had loitered here.

"There's a family of settlers inside. Most of the Oakenfell dead are settlers. The tomb is walled in by pond and grove because they believed this family to be cursed."

"Why didn't they just bury them in the woods or at sea?"

"Do you understand anything about curses, mister?!" Her lips curled in a pouty snarl.

Mister! I felt old. The girl looked mid to late twenties. I could be her father! So beautiful, adorned in jewels and tattoos. If I did not know better I'd say she was a gypsy long out of her time. It is even possible she exceeded me in years. While somewhere in her gaze lurked a nauseating turn, a demeanor that spoke silently of mistrust and snake-like venom, as if aspects had decayed in her that no longer carried their traditional value.

"I think I do. It still doesn't answer my first . . ."

"Right now I have nowhere else to go!" She cried, becoming young and vulnerable, soft, nubile. "I got in a fight with my roommate's boyfriend! He was talking about taking down a gay nightclub like what happened in Florida a few years ago. Joking about it. Nazi scumbag! I pulled a knife on him and now there's a witch hunt . . . I *wasn't* joking!" Raising an arm above her head before bringing it down in a mocking series of strokes as she belted the classic Bernard Herrmann score from the shower scene in Psycho: *"Reet, reet, reet, reet . . !"*

***

I try writing it out in several ways, but the girl always comes home. I scratch out certain things and add other things in. Orders are compromised, but that is how true reality works. One minute you're a killer and the next you have a family and are surviving from week to week.

Gods dethroned before the Parthenon, when judges came down to bask on the shore.

We are subject to quick bursts of devastating change. It is the moment to moment bliss of never knowing that has become mechanical. Devices of logic, no longer able to keep shrines of normalcy at bay, toppled by an unseen web of nerve endings.

Erasing the final kill from my plot, I discard the body in a way that is common and without ritual. The writhing, bladed torment in my stomach fades as I follow the perfumed wisp of a radiant spell, devastating hallucination as I stop and stare at the wall. I will need to stop this session soon in order to masturbate. I smell her in my room as surely as she is here, the same way I feel blood on my hands when I slit a man's throat.

One thing leading to another. All objectives reflected in the labyrinth. Able to connect with such authenticity to essences without form while around every corner there is a new face. Busted mirror fastened to its bleeding wall, tumor from the future. I look into those eyes, my own, and try to make sense of the tidal wave. Incrementally, the universe shifted its weight against me. I can either live vicariously through it in order to expand the creative message, or I can shrink back into self-oblivion.

Pen thicker than my cock. Still, how the fuck should I know where any of this is going when all I want to do is dip it inside this girl I just met?

Sally, or Sal, like a more sunken rendition of an old movie starlet, a twenty-five year old ex-junkie dressed like a Hollywood gypsy, similar to Marlene Dietrich in *Touch of Evil*. Eyes of smoke gazing into mine as we pass a joint between us, the pregnant moon above the fringe of Oakenfell where we just met. Still, the persistent, nagging insistence of reason rails against the two-pronged, elemental subterfuge of my base self. I'll be a gentleman to the end, but if she opens her legs allowing me to smell the blood beating inside I'll lose my fucking mind!

Pushed from a cliff, unphased, plummeting to my death if never to see it through.

III. THE DREAMER

Somewhere between the Age of Eden and Collapse of Titus, mythologies unfolding as they rarely do, perfectly sealed in the alembic, spinning gold inside our private darknesses.

Sal, a Scorpio through and through, lunges for my junk the moment we are in the door. Even at the end that first day—love (or lust) conquers all! Coming at me like a gale instantly pushing me further out to sea. Landed on an isle, sweltering heat of tropical zones. Her cunt gushing over me with its youthful sweetness, fount of heaven for as long as it lasts. Even from that first time I am counting the days. Hours. Minutes . . .

Where am I? How much longer can we stay here?

Panting. Sweating. I go out at odd hours for a bottle and cigarettes. Living on each other's fluids for sustenance. In between we watch films, mostly horror from my personal collection. Sal is a cinephile, too, raised on the slashers of the 70s and 80s. On the second day, covered in shit, sweat and come, we watched *Dead Before Dawn* and *The Burning*. Sal laughed at the appropriate moments as she batted my shaft playfully with her tiny claws. Extracting a drop of blood from below the shimmering tip, she lifts it to her already wet lips. "Kiss me," she says, pulling me close.

That was three weeks ago. We've barely left. Cicada has been slow to my chagrin, too, and I am running out of money. I also need to go outside and breathe the air. As much as I thought I loved Sal, I could feel the experience wearing off. Never-the-less, I did not have the willpower to kick her out. Between shit rituals and blood-letting, Sal made me breakfast—when I bothered to buy eggs. There were times when I thought it'd really work. Nearly twice her age, though, I feared a heart attack. What a god damned old man way to think! Smelling her cunt for the first time made me feel nineteen again. So rock hard I could carve my name in marble, one undecipherable from the rest. Plunging below a faded stone where fresh flowers grew, over her softening bones, as pliable as clay.

***

On days I do work at the video store, all I can think about is her. On the night shift last Thursday I played three Hitchcock films in a row: *Vertigo*, *Marnie* and *Notorious* . . . If Cicada Video is a dream oasis then I am its flickering mirage. All images move through me or the ship does not leave port. Always best when constellations line up and are reflected back in the mirror-like surface of seas . . .

A customer strolling in every once in a while. Slow, even for three-dollar Thursday. The spell is hardly broken. "Due back Sunday at 7," I say, handing the movie back. Some dumb bro superhero hack job. No time for slick pedigrees when there are still starving artists! Hitch, who rose from humble beginnings, understood the economy of a shot and the power it had the potential to sustain.

Cinema, a synthesis of all the arts and, in rare instances, a reflection of true reality itself.

Living breath of artifice with a life of its own—if it can't breathe it asphyxiates . . .

Holding Sal tighter to me. Aimless night. "What do you want to watch?" I can't take it anymore. Impossible to let Sal go, her reflection shining inside me along with the ineffable garden that bonded us in primordial legend.

Wriggling out of my grasp she sits on the edge of the couch and smokes. "I don't give a fuck," she pouts. "Maybe we should go out? *Eyehategod* is in town."

In the weeks we'd spent, I'd not considered going out. I didn't know if it was because I didn't want to share her—or possibly thought she was unreal. Dead and alive as if something controlled her from the inside that was still unrevealed. It could simply be that she's a recovering drug addict having trouble letting go of all she has and all she'll lose.

Both dead in our way, which is the thing that brought us together. Mine is a slower decline—I will die with a bottle in my hand. Still, in the time Sal lived on the streets pumping cock in trade for temporary relief, she has shed years.

Nagging pain of life grinding down the nerves until there is no feeling to the touch.

Numbness erases the days. Nights become unaware.

***

Do I really want to go through with this? Share my illusions with the world? Even when a younger man railed with violent intent I held much back. We don't owe the world anything, do we? We know the score. Still, there is chaos in our blood mounting a circuitry of demons, cosmic destruction, unfiltered pain. There is a little bit of the Ghost Light in each of us born from the effluvial mass at the end of a starry stream.

I think about Sal and where she comes from. I ponder the decay of civilizations . . .

Sobbing at my desk as I've come to do, I open a window to let some fresh air inside. I feel the heaviness in my gut subside. Is it worth it? This torture? Only to codify what is meted out by hyper-aggressive worlds—sinking page after page into the repentant brine. Suicides born of lesser things; I may take that route when the moment is right. It all seems preposterous: the work we do . . .

Sal appeared to instruct me on my journey, psychopomp of the valley, where dead things go. And even though I am repulsed, I will follow her anywhere. No longer in control of my own trajectory, the labyrinth becomes a circuit board. Like the rest of the world it has become more mannered as I become more sick.

If Sal is a Hollywood gypsy, then I am its silent era somnambulist dreaming through an angular cityscape outlined in sepia tones. The more I understand her, the more surreal our surroundings become. Backdrop to a constant mental dirge.

I'm ready to go see *Eyehategod* and cancel out the ringing in my head.

Sal, unscrewing the top of a Tequila bottle, hands it to me. I swallow down a mouthful before returning both hands to the wheel. The inside of the Chevette smells slightly of rot, but neither of us seem to mind. That smell hasn't bothered me for some time, yet I hesitate to think it's her. Once the liquor hits, though, the thought fades. Reaching down to stroke my cock while jamming her hot tongue in my ear. Fading. Gone. I hold back her hair as she takes me into her mouth. Slipping into an alley where Sal climbs on top, I go to work sucking on her nipples as she grinds against me. Heating up in my balls—aborting all sanctions either mortal or heaven-wise. Digging nails into my skull, sending an electric shock down my spine the instant I release my load.

Going limp as she climbs off, a slight trickle of blood winds down my cheek—which is all I have to live for. I touch it with a frozen finger. "I hurt you . . ." Before she'd have lapped it up like a kitten. Cunt no longer purring immediately following our lovemaking. Possibly she is on the hunt again and that is the whole reason to 'go out'.

***

After the show we wander Oakenfell. It is one of the greatest feelings I know, retreating to a remote spot after being bludgeoned in a pit.

Sal looked natural among the stones, a figure of deep, preternatural beauty. Again, I am in love with her, but for all the wrong reasons. A vehicle to force my way into the deeper extremes of life. I don't know how much more my heart can take. Beyond the fringe of the page, absorbing the oiliness of truly nether zones. The entire cemetery fills up with ghosts the way the moonlight filters through her pixelating lens. I could almost see the shutters flickering open and closed over the dusky blue terrain. Dead risen from their hoary graves as they make their way toward Sal. A grey pallor I'd not seen before—like she's going home.

Sal had given me a low grade hit of acid during the show and it was kicking in. Low grade my ass! Alcohol wearing off made my hallucinations more intense. Tempted to go back to the car for the bottle, but soon it won't matter . . .

I am rock hard again watching her.

Even as the flesh melts from her bones and the dead mount her skeleton on their ragged poles. A curse runs high to the heavens where it will burn in the sun. Obviously, they are unfamiliar with the Ghost Light that pervades all living beings. It is a truly dead place and she is their lowly servant. One who brought them injustice in life now standing trial for the misgivings of unspent men. Controlling their Precambrian minds without ever having to show any faith, long before the town has a name. Priestess of the dawn who feasts naked in the wilderness, a natural concupiscence they could never understand.

Free, lustful spirits who exist in the moment . . .

Extracting my cock, I pound it furiously. Dead washes over me whether I am here or there. Dismembered spatially like plowing my vessel into a looming cliff. Out to sea for so long I am beginning to forget. I am a man who wants to be done with this, with her, everything. Suffocating on their rot as I am closer to the root of conjecture. Ending like it begins, always. Two seeds centered in a plowed trench that share a yet to be determined growth pattern. I did love Sal. I do love her. Even if she is imaginary and I am a pathetic fool. The Ghost Light in her shines brighter than most, irradiating everything in its path. Mythic obscura clouding the minds of men whether it be with sex or spirit. Fount of my pen indulging on the idea: imagination's curse throbs before action takes the place of testimony.

***

Awakening to that smell. Overpowering. I stumble into the living room where Sal is watching the movie *Pieces* with an ashtray wedged between her scabby legs. There was a time when I got off on watching her pick and eat them, but that time is long past. This idyllic scene has worn out its welcome, raw with the impunity of the Creator's urge, shifting to the whims of shadowplay among the stars.

When darkness overcomes there is no stopping it. Looking down at her rotten cunt splayed on a couch pockmarked with cigarette burns. She cackles at me like an aged crone even though she is in truth so young. "Sit down!" she says. "'I'll suck your cock after this scene."

Sores around her lips where she grins—cracked desert.

Of course she is being nice to me in this moment of betrayal. Perhaps it is residual from the night before. Labyrinth hallucinated where no one else may reach. Located on an isle of swine in a grey tropic. Olden paradise grows ashen where a residual stain grows . . .

Only this sacrifice will bring it back to life. Even though, somewhere, I am not connected to my decision in any way. Mirror shifts the disguise, showing me the flat depths of my conscience. Unified with otherworldly spaces, drifting out from under the final mask with a hateful charm.

I know I must end it in my own way. That I'll not be able to let her go. A message clear from the night before re-enacted in loving detail. To visualize her there among the dead, who followed along the banks of the Acheron where flesh constantly boiled. Gathered in the burning rain, hovering near the gate. Already it is dark outside and I can hear them whispering.

I consider calling a friend, possibly Kendra or Alice, on the off chance they'd be free for a fuck. Still, after days of feeling withered and raw I can't yet step outside the ritual circle. Down in the dungeon I make my bed where the cruelest documentations are evident. I touch the bone of violence with a pen, cutting into arteries of stone. I am a born destroyer, but this life, this sham, will not allow me to live any other way.

***

I do feel hatred in my heart, but the universe forgives me. This moment when I look at Sal and sense the eclipse come and gone. All ghosts she held inside—who supported her jerky movements and long, grey bouts of depression—oozed from her diseased meat, leaving her to the hollowed-out impressions of a pragmatist.

"You've changed," I say, as plainly as it is unreal.

"I just want to finish the movie." Sal became angry.

"Look at you?!"

"What the fuck are you talking about?!"

"You are a diseased cunt, and you make me sick!"

I did not mean for it to end this way. I am not some terrible beast, killer of innocent women. She is not innocent! And she is no woman! She has warped my head with cannibal urges and is hoping I will save her from being dead. Those first weeks when we were nibbling on each other's flesh, allowing a little more blood to escape each time. She brought me crashing down to earth in a way that is both wickedly meat-bound and sublimely preternatural.

I've given in to her every whim as she has mine, but the drug is wearing off.

At first I pull out my cock which is semi-hard. I grab her hair pulling her closer to it, but never close enough to her scabby mouth. "You're the one who's sick!" Looking up at me with writhing eyes, living nests of maggots in both sockets. It used to turn me on when she looked at me this way, but now all I can think about are the dead gathering outside. Locked into a curse that is self-designed, projection of the past onto the future. Heir to the labyrinth, descendants on a path to the furious ocean. Erecting their homes in a bath of tears—unnatural emotion.

"I can't live like this anymore!" So weak, my voice turns to smoke. Sal laughs at me while lashing her nails toward my nutsack. What kind of pedantic, weak relic was I becoming if I could 'live' on the edge of death. If I were a stronger man, I'd ask Sal to kill me instead, but that would mean an end to the story . . .

I murder Sal in many ways, but only one gets in. Every time, though, I am ripped apart the same. Fading nights. Sal's body is still on the couch where I left it. Skull bashed in with blood running from between her legs. I will not give you the full details, only how bad it makes me feel not to have her around anymore. In this world or that, a slumbering loneliness awakening at twilight. The greatest fear I've known near to the end of my life. A gaunt of contusions both sharp and vague. Many skins she wore over horizons of her longitudinal ascent.

IV. THE TROLL

I live in my filth now. Physically, for days, I haven't moved. Apartment is filled with flies as my lady-love rots in the next room. A nesting ground for writhing eggs matted under her bloated corpse, moving ever so slightly as if from a breeze.

It is an unreal life and can only be the subject of a fucked-up movie. As if those murders in forgotten chapters aren't brutal enough this is an entirely new level of unreality.

Holding her in my arms as I gaze into her rheumy sockets, I so badly need to get rid of her body even though it'll leave a pit in my stomach. Either way I'm being charged with new levels of corruptibility. Before I put the spade down—murdering years, another lifetime.

Instead, to kill one I thought I loved in exchange for the quiet it brings. Ghosts arriving through a vacuum of silence.

***

Sal is the oracle I destroyed in order to cancel out the myth. I wish I could take it back, but it was the necessary episode to connect worlds. Writing in pain, practically blind, I seek the Northern Shore. Cold waste that predicts nothing. Tracks of obscure demons or gods reduced to a frozen vista of indifference . . .

Pausing to pick up the bottle, I look over my shoulder at the rotting corpse that isn't there and decide, instead, to see what Daniel is up to. *Sturgeon* was playing that night at the Morgue and I am too jittery to stay in.

They play Nightmare in its entirety.

I keep imagining I see Sal in the crowd, blowing smoke in the air. Instead, it is Alice who glides over to me, wearing a tight, shredded *Mötley Crüe* shirt and purple battle boots, kissing the corner of my mouth. "I'm alone tonight." Whiskey on her breath—I am Risen! And just like that we are coupled for the night. Grabbing a cab after the show and heading back to her place, falling into it the moment we close the door.

Alice, letting me fuck her in the ass, reserved for special occasions. Jacked up on *Sturgeon's* set, the battle cry is on us this night. Cannibalizing each other to the bone, demands of a morbid imagination. Nibbling my way down to her rectum (as far as it goes). Farting on my tongue like I ask her to, a couple droplets of feces bubble out and I oblige her by lapping them up. "You're a dirty motherfucker!" She moans.

"You have no idea . . ."

***

Once, aged fifteen, I lived under a bridge. Summer of '85. Hot, desolate, town alive with serpents. I get caught desecrating a grave and am banished from the house. Me and my friend, Mike, were enticed by the idea of seeing the body of Bryce Pollard, a girl we'd lusted over in real life who died tragically in a skiing accident . . .

It could be anybody's life. Still, I remember the body like it was yesterday. Bryce's giant tits hanging to the sides— white as snow. Surely some myths died on that day as we stared into the gulf between her legs. Such a painful hard-on I had; beating, bloody heart born inside the cartilage—

stabbing, sickening pain, I wanted to explode inside the dead girl's cunt worse than anything.

It is a myth in my hometown to this day that Mike and I are necrophiles. My parents couldn't understand how I'd do such a thing as their normalcy—already a bane in my world—predicted cataclysmic futures.

Standing by as the rectory burns!

I did not talk to them for four months. I spent my sixteenth birthday under that bridge as high as a fucking kite. There were a couple other kids that hung around too, who stole liquor and sold it so they could buy acid and pot. We tripped that day in the searing sun as the town lurked in noonday shadow.

I contemplated murdering my parents at that time, but by the next year I was starting to write. Another potential psychopath saved by the lure of art. My friends would have gone along with it, too. They might have been my accomplices—Hal, the older kid, said he once smothered an infant in its sleep. Benny, the younger, said he had a thing for skinning cats . . .

Neither was to be my friend in the end, yet they nurtured me through hallucinatory nights as the town hissed with ancient agonies. Myth, reality, entangled in my psychosis like an electrified caduceus. Hal and Benny like crusty psychopomps. Listening to *The Doors*, *Sabbath* and *Metallica* through Hal's shitty boombox. Constantly stealing batteries to keep it going. Other kids would come down on weekends to trip and fuck. The spot was remote and the cops rarely bothered us—until Benny got caught in a Fred Meyer stealing a couple *Doors* cassettes, drawing their attention.

***

I'd not live that way again, I thought, but I know that's a lie. Draining the contents of the previous night's bottle, I step outside. Alice escaped early. The only residual sign she was here are shit stains on my bed. What the fuck?! I only remember the dirge of *Philosopher's Nightmare*. Lost in a sonic labyrinth searching for clues.

And then the dame walked in.

Mythologizing self-hood with the wink of an eye? Personally I think it's better if we die in our own shit. To visualize the forceful glow of the Ghost Light as it grows over the purple-lidded horizon ready to penetrate inferior covexes—iris shattered by lucent invaders who illumine the grotesqueness of life. What right have we to be urbane or clever? As the fire spills in over our hyperbolic ideals, revealing every nauseous fold, turning inside-out the notion that we'll go on forever . . .

There is a haze on the streets—world burns. Sun veiled behind layers of smoke as wildfires spread throughout the Cascadian barrens. At war with nature as we've always been, fading seed of propensity. Sower of regrets, blame. Even when nothingness permeates every molecule, man is unable to travel light.

I cut through the ash in a hurried stride. I want to get back and finish what I started.

Caught between stratums of doom, no fortification between the killer inside or the one that kills. Mirror has two sides in the apocryphal hour. Seared together in the blasting heat to forge a solitary seed, while all it ever harbored is trapped inside . . .

The only true escape I've ever known. All I need is a fresh bottle and a twenty bag, maybe some ham and bread for strength. I'm settling in for the final drift and, like you, I've only a faint idea of where it's heading. Outlines in a primordial fog gazing in, prepared to steal back what was stolen from them.

Ghost of my life—visions. Following since the day I was born, I bury them here.

Whether in the fog of my mind or a moonlit cemetery. In possession of a part of me that has never been more alive.

Imagination retching out the curse in an oily current. Down on my knees before the Altar of Selene. Nature's oracle pointing the way even as I am just a man on the street walking home. A familiar churning in my gut as I turn the corner toward Oakenfell.

I need to get inside before I lose my nerve and look the other way. All I want to do is sleep it off or watch a stack of horror movies—flip the illusion—go back to dreaming. Still, I dream awake, at the mercy of such alienating details. The same non-euclidean architecture as before, bubbling prismatic with angularity of change. Bordering grist-mill indifferent to the years it took to get here. Power struggle of the mind: time's irresolute contour. Around the bend another disappears to see what's there. Meanwhile, nothingness pervades its memory as consciousness is violently ripped away.

***

I no longer considered the consequences of what I must do.

Sneaking out the door for supplies, still, behind the cemetery gate I discern a row of grey faces peering through. Shackled to my mind across ongoing campaigns, each time I test the will of fate. Every crime committed is devoted to the ritual, when the labyrinth rises out of the fog revealing the intricacics of its motivations.

Tears in my eyes as I cross the street. I really fucked up this time. Somehow, a particle of the Creator's torment is showing. I will not call him God as his myths do not contain elements of manipulation. His true form, achingly tangible, no longer flickers like a cinema reel.

If I had a gun in my hand, I would splatter my brains so I could join him in his dark splendor. Only there is little time to think as I am falling fast.

Catching my breath I enter a *True Value Hardware* to

buy industrial garbage bags, lye, rubber gloves and a hacksaw. The teenaged checker looks at me crosswise as I imagine she can smell the rot under my fingernails. I'd assume my breath is rancid, too, as I've only consumed expired foods these past few days. Ogling her young, pert breasts as I try not to vomit, handing me the last of my money she takes a step back.

V. THE SAGE

I go from murderer to lover to monster. Resurrected by a Creator who is demon possessed. At the heart of the Ghost Light where the final battle is fought, I'll need to become this thing if I am to have a chance. Stepping through their numbers back toward my apartment, I am starting to see grey shapes looming out of the immaterial fabric of nascent spaces.

They part for me because they understand my intent and the deeper that understanding goes the less aggrandized they will feel. I come bearing a bundle of love to enliven their dreary state, the feeling that came before centuries of dull panic. I will cross those many thresholds and return her to the inner chamber.

First, though, I must cover my tracks, if not for the possibility of returning it as to maintain my unassuming pride. They will all know I'm secretly a monster. No impression, blank stare, unlike the Creator who is pressing down. The voice of a dismal cosmos that has violence in its heart. It is what I've understood to be the righteous path

Dismantling judgement before the throne as what lies above remains unspoken.

Everything binding us rips us apart. And we leave no trace.

I am unliving proof of its faceless debt. While Sal, my only cohort in death's domain, has been crucified again and again as only nature can attest. Unrivaled by any horror dragging its chains, or crypt marred by time, no ghosts that are strangers, or revenant apostasy. No sign or symbol to wield against ephemeral nefariousness. This cuts deeper, yet leaves no trace.

***

For a moment I think Sal is still alive. A brilliant flash coming from outside as a bus passes illuminating her corpse in brief. Turning on a light to reveal the ghastly treasure, my underworld bride. I consider fucking her one more time. Instead, I heave, rotten egg smell swirling up in the already fetid air, hamburger thick, I step through. Rolling Sal over as grey meat-sludge sluices off the side of the couch in strips. Maggots tumble off in wet piles and writhe helplessly on the floor. Flies batting against my head, drunkenly in the noxious space.

The unreality of the situation is overwhelming. "Fuck!"

Remembering it is a ritual concerning made-up deities. And I think of the line of fools that came before me: who knelt before the altar for all the wrong reasons. Even though she's not who she said she was, the initial shock of knowing Sal altered my perception and now we are on this journey together . . .

"Wake up," I say, kissing her wet, sunken cheeks. "They are expecting us."

"Who, love?" Sal's beauty shining through like a knife.

"The haunted tribe," I explain. "Those who settled on a witch's land. Those who tended sheep and worshiped at the altar of a god beyond their years . . ."

"I went to them when they were at their weakest," she recalls. Still, it's happened so many times over the centuries she's starting to forget. "I remember the trial and the burning," she says with tears in her eyes.

***

Sal's corpse falls apart in my arms as I embrace it. My grief is the greatest I've known and if I didn't have this final task I'd surely end it. No other way, the Creator persists, than back to the union of stars. We must return to the place of unification and the twining of our seeds, germinating a true, singular face.

Rising from unhallowed soil where this world waits in desperate isolation, I stand in front of the gate pleading with them to let me in.

I have what they want in tow. "Just let me in!"

Their hissing turns into shrieks. I don't fucking know if I can go through with it. And then the gate unlocks, and I'm admitted. Followed by bitter silence in a deafening vacuum partitioned by a train of jagged-tooth ramparts. Only a couple steps inside and I can feel the air change. Cold, more compressed, filtered through some invisible net, or living screen that flickers high above. Otherwise they'd be completely blind and wouldn't remember a goddamn thing. If that's all the Ghost Light is to them then why aren't they letting go?!

It is difficult to say in this Hall of Mirrors. Every facet of my character, all that has been shattered or transformed, revealing patterns that aren't cohabitational. If I'd not had Sal to put me back together, my monstrous struggle would have ended. I loved her and cursed her, knowing full well she is the one who cursed me.

***

"Please, come inside." Sal held the crypt door open wide, looking back at all the faces peering through the trees. "Fuck them!" She sneers, reaching down and liberating my cock right there, swallowing me for all to witness. Their shrieks die down as they submit to the perverse—in their hallowed grief. Gaunts, who'd rather be nature's whores than god's fanatics.

Stepping across together, Sal is whole again. Forcing me to think of weeks spent gnawing on each other's flesh until there was nothing left but nerve and bone. Content to wallow in realities that abandoned us, driven by our wailing urges. To find another who is so alone they will do anything to snare a companion. Even believe in a brooding myth: custodial monster of all who question life.

"They are the ones who wanted it this way. They are the ones who are lost."

Following Sal inside as a troop of cat's charge toward us along the crypt's innermost corridor. Names I don't recognize emblazoned onto iron cards many years rusted. It is to be the family she lived with in her final years, in that one incarnation, which somehow followed her from the wine groves of Crete to the decrepitude and lethargy of fane.

****

A slumbering sickness. Weariness compatible with new indifference. I step back from my desk, nearly slipping to the floor. Clinging to a bookshelf as all the blood rushes back into my head and toes. Transfusion of clean plasma from its shrinking form: last thing I visualize from the other's perspective—as Sal, impaled on my engorged cock, drags her claws across the naked page.

Am I alive or dead? I feel a numbness where there was warmth just a moment ago.

Moving livid hands over my animated corpse, I must disconnect from the thing before it's too late. A monster without a message. Guy gets the girl. What the fuck?! I understood the significance of crossing over, begging for lives I never had. Still a hymen of a man, unborn and lacking true courage. Accepting rot as a way of life. Going to a job that I hate. Participating in a magnate's rule, brokering demon, malefic enchanter. How could I not see it in her eyes as I am fucking her . . ?

A prisoner of the mirror? Might that have been a better way to end it? A scenario in which I'm locked out of my own creation. Utterly void of pathos, I allow the complete monster to take over. It would end in a hail of bullets, reality crashing in. Do you feel that is the logical end to such a pathetic life? Bound to machinations of civilization's past as I am forced to the ground. Bullets crashing through my skull as I am urged away from the Ghost Light . . .

What savoir? What debt? I'll not leave a trace in this life, either, as I'm exiting the scene. Only souls I've touched with the violence of my words will know the horror of being right outside your door. It has followed me my entire life, so why not you? It breathes for us when we are deep down in the dream. Sometimes I scare myself and have to walk away, looping tragedies at my door. Never of this world. Untouched by zealots or myth-makers. Untouched by reason or concourse. Blameless destructiveness of stars. Penetrated by a lover's quarrel on the edge of a death ritual. I am a necromancer in both worlds!

***

I brought her back to see myself. I carved her name in marble to not forget. Now I open the bottle and drink to her spirit, one that exists only through my imagination. After days go by, back at work, the horror of it abstracts. Connections made, the labyrinth of travails, were all set to reflect the interchangeable progress of those who are lost. It is also a paean to the fading patterns of man and his treacherous future.

The world, a graveyard, permeates the air with revenant manifestations. Densely hovering near the brink of extinction. I feel it every day. As do many of my friends, Metal Militia—doom warriors—filling the streets with their deadly tension. Who will strike against it when it comes and who will lay down? In the cannibalistic dawn when the shutters come off and the image is hard wired to the malnourished urge. Plagued by hunger, demons feeding on its sickness, a counter Eve strikes in the debilitating age . . .

"It's all in the song," explains Daniel. "It took four fucking years to write!"

"It's fucking mind blowing!" I meant it. To know the journey, no matter how grim and hopeless, is shared in number by those who are sick enough to see the difference. To feel a charge in the air that agitates more day by day pushing the urge, the art, to ruthless extremes.

Horror feeds us. Horror we bred. Maggots of trust who plague our dismay. No fear in the brine of absolution.

"Thanks man!" He shoves another taco in his mouth. Déjà vu. Rancho Bravo becoming another sign post we can count on in these final hours. Still, scenes shift with gradual reform as the breakdown becomes more evident. "Did it make sense?"

"I think so . . ." Mind drifting toward the street, aligning to the sound of traffic. Birds overhead in the blue light perched on the crackling power lines as a jet thunders through the brilliant sky, while underneath I can hear hissing as if next to my ear. Feeling cold as the sun dips behind the hills on the other side of the sea, "It's a true labyrinth," I say.

"It's awesome you see it that way! . . . I'm too old to fuck around. I'm not in this for the free drugs and pussy anymore. . ."

I thought about all the years we'd partied and how it could never be like that again.

"By the way, I've been meaning to ask you, who's the girl you were with at our show?"

"Alice?"

"Definitely not Alice," he went on. "Her tits weren't as big. Plus . . ."

"What?" All the nausea of those weeks rising against me. The smell of sizzling pork nearly thrusting me over. Stomach turning to ice as my gaze fell. A memory lingering that is not mine, evidence of a dire collaboration. With deity against man, in the circle, up against the wall, bludgeoning regret.

"You alright, brother?"

"I gotta stop drinking so goddamn much," I say, trying to hold my own. I look around for her, realizing how crazy this fucking makes me.

"Yeah, that shit'll kill you," says Daniel, not completely buying it.

"I gotta go to work, man . . . I'll catch you later."

"Cool. We should have a movie night soon. Horror season is around the corner!"

Entry

Chisto Healy

1

The man stood out on the steps staring up at the building. "Are you here for the lecture?" someone said to him.

He paid them a curious glance and saw them holding the door open for him. "Come on in. He's already talking. You're missing it."

The man smiled and nodded and then made his way up the remaining steps and through the open door.

"Thank you," he said, his smile returning. He shook the guy's hand and then headed down the hall to the lecture room. When he opened the door, he could hear the man on stage speaking and he slipped inside. Instead of taking a seat with the others, he stood in the back of the room.

"It's important to know that demons are not ghosts," the speaker said. "People constantly lump them together and that is a grave error, pun intended." The listeners laughed but it sounded nervous. The man in the back gave a genuine smile.

"I'm not going to be the one to tell you ghosts aren't real or not to believe in them, but I am going to tell you that demons are very real and whatever you believe about ghosts, the same rules do not apply. People mistakenly think that demons haunt houses, but that is entirely false. Maybe ghosts haunt houses. I don't know. I'm not a ghostologist."

This time the crowd laughed with more heart. The speaker smiled. "But seriously, demons don't haunt houses. Demons haunt people. Your house is actually your sanctuary, your safe haven. Demons can't come in on their own. It's our foolishness that constantly invites them in. We talk about them and talk to them and use Ouija boards and have séances. We allow strangers into our homes not realizing that they've already been occupied. We let them in, and once we do, they attach themselves to us.

So many people haunted or hunted by a demon try to flee, but it will never stay behind in the house, folks. Nope. Where you go, that demon will follow. It will not stop until one of two things happens. One: you die. Or, two: you let your guard down and allow the demon entry into you, just as you let it into your house."

"Can't you kill them?" someone in the front row asked.

"What about exorcism?" another person further back called out.

The man at the back of the room just watched and listened, a thin smile creasing his lips.

"No. That's fiction," the man on the stage said to them. "You cannot kill a demon. At best, you can cast it out, reject it. If you're religious—which I am not—maybe an exorcism would help with that, but I have yet to see evidence of it. Your safest bet is to never call them to you and to never ever let them in. There are precautions you can take. You can ward your house. There are symbols you can draw on the floors and ceilings or around the doors. There are signs you can see in people that have been infiltrated. You can recognize when a demon has taken residence and steer clear. All these tools are in my book and readily available to all of you. You can purchase it here today when the lecture is over."

Just then, a loud crash issued from outside and was punctuated with a shrill scream. The door to the hall opened and someone leaned in. "He's dead," they said to no one and everyone. "He just jumped off of the stairs and ran in front of a bus."

The bearer of bad news disappeared again allowing the door to fall shut, but the cameo did the trick. Everyone rose from their seats and hurried out of the room to see what had happened; everyone except the man standing in the back of the room. The lecturer sighed. "Thank you all for coming," he said mockingly to the empty room. "I'm world-renowned demonologist, Dr. Mark Ingram, and I'd just like to remind you all that knowledge is your greatest weapon against evil and I am your blacksmith. My book, *Locking Out Evil,* is only $16.95. Thank you."

The man in the back, the only other person in the room, clapped slowly. He smiled and stepped into the middle aisle facing the stage. He smiled at Dr. Ingram. "Do you take credit cards?"

Mark stepped down from the stage and packed up a black canvas bag before slinging it over his right shoulder. "Actually I do," he said as he worked to close a big box full of advanced copies of his newest book. "I have an app on my phone."

"Fantastic," the man smiled, reaching for his wallet.

Mark hurried past him to the door, carrying the big heavy box awkwardly. He braced it on his hip so he could open the door. When he had it open, he leaned against it and looked back at the man who was still smiling, arm extended, credit card in hand. "But I know who you are," Mark said. "Or rather, what you are, and I would never hand over that kind of information. You can go to the bookstore and buy it like everybody else. Maybe they won't see through you."

The man gave a quiet laugh and resumed his slow clapping as Mark let the door fall closed and hurried towards the exit and the crowd outside. He was hoping this was going to be good for him, that he would leave here with an empty box. His income wasn't what it used to be, but demons were clever. He locked them out of his house and his body, but they still found ways to hurt him.

When he got outside, his frown deepened. There were police cars and an ambulance and onlookers everywhere, discussing what they had seen or heard or what they hadn't. Mark spied what was left of the man in the street and he bowed his head. He recognized the guy. He was the door man for the lecture hall. He tried to fill the seats. He welcomed people in. Mark sighed. "Shit," he said quietly. "Sorry."

2

Mark was chopping vegetables for dinner when the doorbell rang. He kept the knife in his hand when he left the counter. He wasn't expecting company. He never married and only dated when the need for companionship reached desperation. He didn't trust that people were people, not enough to let them in that close. He got to where he was content in his isolation, and cooking was part of where that solace came from. Now he felt nervous and irritated. It felt like someone interrupted him masturbating.

He opened the door, his other hand holding the knife behind it. A woman was standing on his doorstep smiling big and clutching his last book to her chest. "I'm sorry to bother you," she said, "but can I get your autograph?"

Mark stared at her with disgust as she extended a Sharpie towards him. "I'm always going to know it's you," he said to the woman. "You will never get to me and you will never get in this house."

The woman went from being an admirer to snarling with rage. "You're a pain in my ass, doctor!" she snapped, literally spitting the final words at him.

Mark swallowed his fear and showed no emotion to the thing at his door. "I aim to be," he said. "Thank you for the good news. Now I'm going to get back to my dinner." With that, he closed the door in her face and engaged the locks. She couldn't come in, even if it was open, but it felt better to lock it.

He went back to the kitchen and his dog, Roxy, was sitting there staring at the counter and whining. Mark snickered and shook his head. Roxy cared less about the demon at the door than she did the food not being eaten. He loved dogs. They were the only companionship he allowed himself to keep. There was another benefit to them. Just like him, dogs could smell evil and tell someone's wrongness. Roxy would have barked immediately if he had not been cooking when she arrived. Everyone has their weaknesses, he supposed.

"Don't look at me like that," he said to the dog. "You can wait. We'll eat together just like always." She looked at him pleadingly, and he sighed. Giving in, he threw her a piece of cheddar which she caught in her mouth and took with her into the other room. Mark smiled and went back to chopping vegetables. He could feel the woman outside staring at him through the window, but he refused to look. He knew her gaze held the same hunger of the dog's, but she cared little for the food on the counter. She wanted his soul.

She stayed out there, staring and watching as he prepared and cooked the meal and she moved windows when he carried his plate into the dining room so she could continue watching. He went back to the kitchen to get Roxy's bowl and he felt the eyes travel with him. He sighed and forced himself not to look even though the window and the staring eyes pulled at him like a magnet. Mark made a terrible mistake. He did the one thing he constantly warned his readers not to do. He drew the thing to him.

It wasn't learning about them that had called the demon. Becoming a demonologist didn't bother these things. They wanted the world to know about them, to fear them, to feed and empower them. They have even taught college courses themselves before. It was his new book that called the thing. He was giving people information on how to protect themselves from demons, how to combat them and keep them away. For the first time, he posed a threat and that was like throwing chum in the water.

He placed Roxy's bowl on the floor by his chair and then he sat down to eat. Just a couple of bites in, he put his fork down. He couldn't take it anymore. He wanted to eat in peace. Pulling his cell phone from his pocket, he called the local police. They didn't have to know she was a demon to arrest her for harassment.

He went and got a beer from the fridge and then stood and drank it while he waited for the cops to arrive. He looked at the window for the first time as the possessed woman was being pulled away from it. Then he sat down to eat.

One of the officers came back to get his statement. Mark answered the door with caution and waited until he knew the man didn't smell wrong before he invited him in. He told them he had no idea who the woman was, but she had his book, so he assumed she was an obsessed fan. He offered the officer some food since he always made more than he could eat by himself, even with Roxy's help. The officer thanked him but politely declined.

When they left, he rubbed some tension from his face and went to get another beer. "This is our lives now, girl," he said to the dog. "I screwed up."

He knew in his heart just how true those words were. Just as he said at his lecture, this would never end. They didn't just go away. Whatever that thing was, he had to accept its presence in his life now. It was like living with only the bad parts of an intimate relationship, but the cards had been dealt and there was no going back now.

3

Mark stopped the shopping cart and pressed the button on his key-less entry to open his trunk. He held the cart with his foot and pushed the trunk open wide. When he turned back to the cart, a teenage boy was standing beside it, smiling wide. "Can I help you load those bags up sir?"

Mark sighed. "No. You may not help with anything. You will never get in my car. You're wasting your time." He was determined not to show any fear.

The boy's smile dropped from his face. "How do you always know it's me, doctor?" He leaned down and spit into the bag of groceries Mark was about to grab. "You manage to see me no matter what I'm wearing."

"I can smell you," Mark said. "Demon's smell. You stink. It's like iron, but tangy. It's like blood. You smell like blood."

The boy's smile returned. He eyed Mark with what seemed almost like respect. "That's a dirty little trick, Doc. You make people think you can teach them how to identify us but that's not something just anybody can do, is it? No. I'd say that's a God given talent."

As the boy laughed, Mark put the last bag in the trunk and slammed the door down. "Yup. I'm a bastard and no real threat to you, so let's call it bygones and go our separate ways."

The boy followed Mark around the car. Mark opened the driver's side door. He climbed in and closed it quickly, but the boy caught the door with his hand and held it ajar. "It's not that simple, Doc. There's the matter of not being able to touch you. I've heard your lectures and listened to your podcast. You know things that you can teach, symbols, wards, blah blah, etc."

Mark nodded. "That's right. I know the symbols, the scents, the powders—everything—so you'll never get to me."

The boy smiled wide, showing a missing tooth. "Oh I will, Doc. I just have to be patient and wait on my moment."

"What do you do with all of them?" Mark asked the thing wearing a boy. "Do you set them free or do you kill them?"

The boy's smile widened. "Neither, Doc. I keep them. I'm starting a collection, but don't worry. I see to it to make sure that they suffer as much as humanly possible. Pun intended."

Mark blinked, showing weakness for a moment. He didn't want to think about what that meant, about the fact that whatever they were going through was because of him. "Let go of my door," he said.

"I'm going to keep taking them," the boy-thing said. "You could stop it, Doc. Just let me in the car and we'll take a ride and talk. No one else has to suffer."

"Let go of my door," Mark repeated.

The boy let go of the door and stepped back. Mark pulled the door closed and started the car. As he did, he could see through the closed window, the boy gouging his own eye out. He knew it was a display for his benefit, so he drove away quickly without showing reaction.

When he got home though, he ran into the house and fell to his knees in front of the toilet where he vomited. Tears came from his eyes that weren't from the strain. He knew turning himself over to the thing wouldn't save anyone. It wasn't going to turn over a new leaf once it got what it wanted. He couldn't make a deal with it. Demons were notorious liars. This thing was going to use and destroy no matter what he did.

He felt eyes on him then and he looked up at the bathroom window. The woman from the other night was there again, pressed to the glass and staring at him, her red lips stretched into a smile. When the police cut her lose, the demon must have arrived to reclaim his toy. Mark was sure that the demon didn't stay inside her and sit in jail all night, or maybe he did. Maybe it decided to play while it was there. He left the inhabited woman at the window and went into the other room where he sat at his laptop and checked the news for any incidents at the local jail. There it was. Three dead in the drunk tank. Self-mutilation. Group suicide.

"Damn it," he said out loud. He had sent her there. That one really was on him. He could hear Roxy barking in the other room. She must have seen the woman at the window or maybe she smelled her. He couldn't make the mistake of calling the police again. They were just going to have to live with her company. That didn't mean he had to look at her though. He walked around, Roxy at his heels barking and growling, and closed all the blinds, shades and curtains. At each new one, she was there, staring in at him. When the job was done, he took Roxy with him and sat on the couch. Somehow he could still feel her staring at him.

4

After several days of being cooped up in the house, Mark Ingram realized he was about out of groceries. He wondered if the thing was still lingering outside. He felt nervous every time he let Roxy out to go to the bathroom. He would stand in the doorway and call her back in if he heard her bark. He wouldn't put it past that thing to hurt Roxy as a way to get at him. The truth was, a demon didn't even need that kind of motivation. Those things would hurt anyone or anything just for the hell of it, pun intended. He shook his head at himself.

He was using public speaking cues in his personal thoughts now.

He told Roxy that he was just going to the store and he would be back soon. Jokingly, he told her not to let anybody in. He grabbed his coat and his keys and went out the front door. "Shit."

While he had been safe inside the house, his car hadn't fared so well. It wasn't just disabled. They didn't flatten the tires or key the paint, remove the spark plugs or disconnect the battery. They murdered it. It was literally torn to pieces like an eviscerated animal. It was another show. It was overkill. Either the thing was venting its frustration, or he was giving himself too much credit and it was just having fun. Either way, he wasn't driving anywhere.

He nodded and then started walking. He watched every other person on the road, and realized that the thing had gotten into his head. He was paranoid. He was afraid. Even though the thing couldn't touch him, there were other ways it could get at him. Demons were anything but stupid. They were incredibly clever and resourceful. Mixed with ruthlessness, it was a hell of a cocktail. Pun not intended. He just couldn't help it anymore it seemed.

When he got to the train station, the platform was completely full of people and Mark realized all too quickly that the demon could be any one of them. The subway smelled like sweat and piss so there was no way he could pick out the thing's scent until it was too late.

He made his way through the turnstile and tried to stay away from the other people as much as possible. He avoided the edge of the platform as well. He started biting his nails as he waited for the train, his eyes dancing across everyone standing around him. When the train arrived and the doors slid open, Mark hurried past people and got on. He anxiously took a seat in the back of the car. The car filled up fast and before he knew it there was enough people packed in that it was hard to breathe. Mark glanced over at the old man sitting next to him. The man smiled. It was a knowing smile, a smile he had seen on many different faces.

The old man reached a hand over to touch his shoulder, but it seemed to hit a wall. His smile dropped and his wrinkled brow furrowed with curiosity. "I'm warded," Mark said. He rose to his feet and struggled to move through the overcrowded car. The old man rose too, head cocked to the side like a dog. Mark tugged his shirt up and showed the old man the symbol on his chest. He had it tattooed to make it permanent.

The old man righted his head and smiled. "Flesh comes off, Doc."

"Not if you can't touch it," Mark said back, weaving through the people and trying to keep his balance.

The old man laughed then. It was hoarse and dry and a single step away from a cough but there was something wicked about it. It sounded doubled, like the old man was laughing and the demon was also laughing, but the two sounds didn't quite mesh or harmonize. The lights began to flicker. "I can't touch you," he said, "but I can touch them, and they can touch you."

Then the lights went out.

Mark rushed for the door to the next car. Screams started and people began attacking each other. It was so dark, but he could hear the violence happening all around him. Some screamed in anger and some in pain. There were bangs and crashes. Someone grabbed him, but he tugged away from their grasp. A fist came from somewhere else and hit him in the face, knocking him off his feet. There were people everywhere and he couldn't move. Among the symphony of screams was the laughing of the conductor and his host.

Mark dove to his feet and started climbing over fighting people in an effort to make it to the door. If he didn't get out of here then he was actually going to die. He reached the door and hurriedly made his way through, falling into the next car. The car's occupants looked at him like he was crazy, until the screams reached them. Then they all got up and moved across the car with him.

Mark couldn't remember seeing the old man amongst the crowd on the platform. Someone had to have called to him, invited him onto the train. Maybe he was already on it. He could have known, that after his car was destroyed, Mark would have to take the train, and planned for it, jumping on the same line from a different stop. It was a trap and a calculated one, and Mark walked right into it. He just had to make it to the next stop and then he could hail a taxi. He could keep the demon out of the taxi.

The door opened with a whoosh of air and a ball of people barreled through, tearing and kicking at each other. They were already covered in blood that may or may not have been their own. The lights in the new car flickered and people started screaming. Then the train pulled to a stop toppling the combatants to the floor. Some of them still crawled at Mark, homicidal rage in their stare. He had his own eyes on the doors. It seemed to take forever but they finally slid open. He didn't hesitate and bolted.

Mark glanced back at the train as he ran and saw the car windows painted red. He ran faster. He took the steps two at a time and was screaming for a taxi before he even reached the street. A cab pulled to a stop in front of him and he tore the door open. The old man emerged from the stairwell and moved towards him. Mark jumped in the taxi. He wanted to continue the ruse and make a power play in return after what the demon did, so he said, "Get your own!" and slammed the door shut.

He gave the driver his address. He no longer cared about the groceries. He would get one of those apps on his phone where the people shop for you and deliver it. The demon had too much power when he was out in the world. At home, the power was his. He was already half a recluse. It wouldn't kill him to never leave the house again. Everything he needed could show up at his door thanks to the internet and some phone apps, even women. The demon was never going to stop, and Mark was well aware how close to death he had just come on that train. He wouldn't make that mistake again.

5

When he got home, Mark apologized to Roxy for showing up empty-handed. He didn't feel like figuring out a new app right then, so he just ordered a pizza. Roxy loved the crusts and he didn't so it would satisfy both of them.

He was paranoid when the pizza girl came to the door, but she seemed to be clean and uninhabited. He gave her a good tip so she wouldn't be afraid to come back to the crazy guy's house. Then he and Roxy sat and had dinner. The dog seemed just as anxious as he was. She seemed to know that something wasn't right. "It's okay," he told her. "It can't get us in here. It can't come in. We're safe here, girl."

He expected to see his stalker at the window, but the night was quiet. After the train fiasco, maybe the game-plan had changed. He had no idea what was coming. It could be more of the same. Maybe the demon was going to convince more susceptible people to come do the dirty work for it. Mark didn't know what he would do. Instead, he did the only thing he knew. He prepared powders, herb mixtures, that would repel evil and he spread them in doorways and on windowsills. He let Roxy out to use the bathroom and then he started drawing sigils and symbols, wards like the one tattooed on his chest.

Roxy sniffed out the dead rabbit at the end of the yard. She was delighted and rolled around to smother herself in its scent. She didn't notice the man from the lecture standing nearby under the shadow of a tree. He smiled at the happy dog not barking to alert his master of a threat. Then his neck bent at an unnatural angle and his mouth opened wide enough to break his jaw. A black mist escaped from his throat.

Roxy realized that something was wrong then, but it was too late. When she looked up, the mist was there and she breathed it in. Suddenly the man standing before the dog looked lost and confused. He began to cry, but the dog leaped on him and took him down. She went straight for the throat, ending him quickly. Then she made sure to drag the body closer to the house where her master would see it. She left the body, trotted up to the door and barked.

Mark smelled blood immediately and the hairs on the back of his neck stood up. Then he noticed that Roxy was literally covered in blood. It matted her fur. "What happened, girl?" he asked her.

Then he noticed the man in the yard. He recognized him immediately. She got one of them. Of course the dog couldn't kill the demon within but killing the host repels the demon for a time. They need to recuperate. They could move among people by choice but if they were forced out, rejected, it left them with a sort of motion sickness. Roxy might have just made them think twice about hanging out in the yard. She was a good dog. That said, he couldn't leave a mutilated body in his yard. He doubted the police would buy, "he's a demon."

He went and grabbed the dead man and hauled him to the shed. He couldn't leave him there indefinitely, but it got him out of sight for the time being. While he was doing this, Roxy was wagging her tail and creating wind that broke lines of powder. She was urinating on symbols and making the ink run and lines falter. Mark came back and looked down at his mess of a dog. "We need to get you a bath," he said. "Come on. Let's get you inside."

Roxy chuffed and trotted in. Mark followed behind her and closed the door, locking it. He felt relieved, safer, despite the fact that there was a dead body in his shed. He got a fresh towel and the dog shampoo. "Come on, girl," he said.

Roxy looked unsure and he laughed. He patted his leg and headed towards the bathroom. He started the tub and turned to make sure the dog had followed him. She pleaded with him with her eyes to allow her to remain filthy, but he apologetically told her no. He didn't want to get blood all over his own clothes, so he took his shirt off and set it on the sink. "Alright. Let's go," he said, hoisting the dog up into his arms and putting her in the tub.

Mark started to wash Roxy, but it seemed like no matter how much soap he used, he couldn't get the blood smell out of her fur. It took him too long to realize his error. Roxy lunged before he ever expected it. Her teeth gnashed and sank into the exposed symbol on his chest.

"Shit," he said, falling back onto the bathroom floor. He watched his dog's muzzle stretch unnaturally wide, the mist escape her lungs, and he knew there was no escape.

6

Mark addressed the room. "It's important to know that you cannot escape a demon. They will pursue you endlessly. They will follow you, and ultimately they will claim you. The best bet you have is to stay put and fight. When they show up at your door, don't run. Let them in. Stand your ground. All these symbols, wards, and powders people claim can hold demons at bay, are no more than gibberish. They're useless and will not do anything to save your life if you encounter a real demon. Take it from me. I'm world-renowned demonologist, Dr. Mark Ingram."

The thing wearing Mark smiled as the crowd cheered for the misinformation he fed them. Things were about to get a whole lot easier and a lot more fun. He felt excited for the future.

The Invocation
Leo J. Winters

Alaric, 8:11 PM

The night sky was alive with a spectacular lightning show that, with each thunderous bolt, cast ominous shadows behind the clouds. It appeared angels and demons battled in the heavens above to determine the outcome of little Annabelle's life. And, although the booming thunder and wind seemed to indicate so, there was not a drop of rain in sight. Still, the fury of the winds forced Alaric to grip the steering wheel of his old Plymouth more tightly than he cared to. Had it not been an urgent matter, the fierceness of the night's weather would have persuaded him to stay home.

But, that was no option tonight. The Yarvis family had beseeched him to make the journey immediately. It was his duty to care for his disciples — especially the Yarvis family, being who they were — and a strong will was necessary for what would come tonight. He had only performed a similar ritual once before, but the inflicted soul was lost that day so many years ago. That could not happen tonight.

When Alaric pulled into the driveway, he could see Randall standing on the front porch, waiting for him, slightly leaning against the strong forces of the wind. The house stood alone on the vast Texas property that had belonged to their family for generations. The nearest neighbors were almost a mile away. The house itself was the size of a mansion and had a presence that still demanded the same solemn respect that it had for all that worked its land in the generations past.

"Thank you, Reverend Drake, for coming so quickly!" Randall had to yell over the wind as he greeted Alaric.

Alaric squinted as he walked towards Randall's outstretched hand, trying to keep debris out of his eyes. "Yes, of course, Randall! Let's get inside, shall we!?"

Randall gave an agreeing nod and led him to the front door. Upon twisting the doorknob, Randall almost lost his balance as a tremendous gust flung the door inside, pulling him with it. Alaric followed through and had to help push the door closed against the blasts of the wind.

"I don't know where this damn weather came from!" Randall shouted, stating only the obvious to Alaric, who agreed out of courtesy.

"So," Alaric began, "how bad?"

"It's terrible, Reverend," Margaret answered, entering the room.

"Mrs. Yarvis," Alaric said with a nod towards her, then back to Randall, "Can I see her? I need to fully understand her condition."

"Fully understand? Didn't the school… Didn't you hear… I mean, surely you understand how bad it is."

"Yes, Randall, I understand. But, in order to fully assess what is needed, I must see her immediately. And, it was her brother that reported the incident, correct?"

"Yes. Chet is upstairs now, minding her room. She's restrained. We had to, you see."

"Yes, of course. Now, can you take me to see

Annabelle?"

"This way, Reverend," Margaret said. She turned to lead them up the stairs.

***

Annabelle, 11:47 AM

Annie removed the lunch bag from her locker in the school's second story, west hallway. Her locker number was 0776, one number shy of the one that she had wanted, but considering that next locker skipped to 0778, it was the closest she could have gotten. She deposited her science textbooks from the previous class period to lighten her backpack. She was glad that the class was finally over for the day. She loathed her Biology teacher, and the curriculum was very one-sided when it came to subjects such as evolution. She hated feeling uncomfortable with her otherwise disagreeing beliefs but hated more that she could not speak her thoughts aloud. She was not one to chance any sort of disciplinary actions.

But, now it was lunch time, and although she was not looking forward to the bologna sandwich and celery sticks in her overpriced Gucci lunch bag, she was excited about meeting Janelle in their secluded spot on the school's large terrace. There, they would pray together before opening their lunch bags to compare (and sometimes trade) food, then they would begin their secret bible study — a tradition that they had done daily for the last two years when they began high school.

Annie felt excited about their studies today. It was her turn to plan the lesson from the scripture, and she had chosen a very specific passage from the Book of Psalms. She had a smile on her face, reciting some of the passages in her head as she turned the corner where their lone table sat, where Janelle was already seated and waiting. But, she felt her smile begin to fade when she realized that she wasn't alone. With her, sat Lucinda, another girl in their grade that was always nice, but never in her circle of friends.

She forced herself to maintain the cheerful expression on her face as she attempted to hide her hesitation while approaching the table, then exclaimed, "Hey, Janelle!" and, with slightly less enthusiasm, "Hey, Lucy."

"Annie! I hope you don't mind that I invited Lucy."

"Yeah, Annie," Lucinda said with a pleasant enough smile, "I hope it's okay if I intrude. I just really wanted to join you girls today."

Annie gave Janelle a look of hesitancy, "Are you sure?"

"Yeah, Annie, of course. Lucy wants in."

Annie glanced back at Lucinda, who was still smiling — a hopeful, innocent sort of smile — then thought of Mark 16:15, *Go unto the world and preach the gospel to all creation*, and realized that of course this was for the best, and with a renewed motivation and a great big smile, she sat with the two girls and led them in a word of prayer before beginning her lesson, feeling more sure of her faith than ever.

***

Alaric, 8:36 PM

Alaric opened the door to Annabelle's room and walked in, being sure to shut it behind him. He had compelled the girl's family to wait downstairs during his initial evaluation of her. As he shut the door, he twisted the knob to prevent the latch from clicking shut. He could hear Annabelle's breathing from the bed behind him, but he needed to gather his strength before turning to face her. The room was dark, so he was unsure as to her condition or how well she was confined to her bed.

"Is someone there?" a soft girl's voice asked — Annabelle's voice.

He slowly turned to face the bed but found it difficult for

his vision to penetrate the darkness of the room. A sudden urge shot over him to flip on the light switch, and a stronger one sat in the back of his mind to leave, go back home, and let the Yarvis family deal with the problem on their own. But, he could not. This was his duty. He was the protector of his pack. He was the one that held them strong, held the entire city strong in the face of temptation to go back to the old ways. So, against his natural instincts, he stepped further into the darkness, edging closer to the bed where the girl laid, breathing shallowly. He again longed for the artificial light that modern electricity provided, but he knew what had to be done, had to be done in the dark.

The foot of the bed came into view, visible only by flashes of light that snuck through the closed curtains. The rainless storm was still raging just as strong as before. Then, a large bolt of lightning struck, forcing its flash throughout the entirety of the room for what seemed more than just a second. It was enough for Alaric to get a good view of Annabelle on the bed.

She was on top of the maroon comforter, bound with ropes, and left with no pillows to support her head. Each of her limbs was tightly tied to the bedpost that was nearest to it and a leather strap wrapped under the bed and held her forehead securely flat against the mattress. Her feet were bare, and she was still wearing the navy skirt and white button-up blouse that composed of her school uniform. But, her blouse was not in its typical pure white condition that the school demanded. Instead it was stained brown and green — no doubt from the struggle in the schoolyard — and dried blood, which was also on her knees and fingers. Her hair was in complete disarray and dried tear trails ran down both sides of her cheeks.

"Who's there?" she repeated.

"It's Reverend Drake."

"No…" she muttered and began to sob.

"Does it cause you distress that I am here?"

She continued her whimpering sob, not a bawl, not a cry, but a mere to-herself, quiet whine, followed by sniffs, and deep breaths. And, although Alaric couldn't see her face again, save the occasional small flashes of lightning from outside that only allowed him a millisecond glance at her, he knew there were tears beginning to stream down her face.

He walked slowly around the bed, checking the ropes to ensure there was no slack. The last thing he needed during the ritual was for her to get loose enough to strike at him, or even worse: get away. After he finished checking the restraints, he placed two of his fingers on her wrist to check her pulse. It seemed fine, so he proceeded to use a handkerchief to wipe the tears from her eyes.

"Why does it bring you distress, Annabelle?"

"Because I know why you're here," she responded softly.

"Oh? Why?"

"Because of what happened at the school."

"I see," Alaric stated, while he moved back toward the bedroom door. "Do you deny what your principal said? What your brother and parents have told me?"

"No."

"So, you do believe it," he asked, but not with a question as much as a statement.

"Yes."

He took a deep breath and left the room. He was going to need his bag.

***

Annabelle, 12:44 PM

Annie stood by her desk, now in her Algebra class — one of the many classes that she shared with Janelle, and the only class in which Lucinda was also in — waiting for the bell to ring so they could begin *The Pledge of Allegiance*. It was school policy that the Pledge be recited by all students twice a day. Once before first period and once before the period following lunch. If any student were ever caught not participating, then they would be forced to serve detention for an entire week.

Since detention consisted of cleaning the toilets, pulling recycling out of trash cans, or any other highly undesirable sort of work, all the students were sure to be in place, by their desk several minutes before the bell. So, there everyone was, waiting for the loud ring in silence. It was always on time, at a very precise 12:45 PM.

While waiting, Annie thought back to their lunch period. It had been a very successful bible study, and she felt very confident that Lucinda was able to take away an enlightened opinion. It was surprisingly satisfying having someone else to share her lesson plan with, especially someone that was not familiar with the Gospel. In a way, it helped Annie to feel encouraged and optimistic. If Lucinda had been interested, curious even, maybe she could reach more kids in the school. Maybe she had found her purpose.

The sound of the school bell pulled her out of her thoughts, then the music began to play with the typical rolling of the drums over the intercom system. Then, they all began to chant:

I pledge allegiance to the flag of the United States of America, and to the republic for which it stands, one nation, indivisible, with liberty and justice for all.

As she had always done since starting high school, Annie was sure to mouth the words *'under God'* in its proper place. While doing so, she glanced sideways at Janelle and saw that she also did the same. It was their secret. A silent way to rebel against the strict enforcement of the *proper* way to say the Pledge. After it was finished, everyone in the class took their seats at their desks, but as Annie was doing so, she caught Lucinda's eyes. She had been watching her.

***

Randall, 9:27 PM

Randall waited patiently with his wife, Margaret, downstairs at the dining room table. Chet sat midway up the stairs, ready to be useful should Reverend Drake call upon him. The Reverend had been upstairs in Annabelle's room for nearly 45 minutes after retrieving his large duffle bag from the car. Randall had had to help him with the doors due to the powerful winds that seemed to be increasing in strength. The sounds of their impressive blasts caused the house to creak all around and he found himself wondering if the large glass windows would hold up.

Still, despite the booming sounds of gusts against the house and the ceaseless cracking of thunder, the house seemed filled only with the sounds of his daughter's cries and the loud bellowing voice of Reverend Drake behind the bedroom's closed door. He held a firm grip of his wife's shoulder, ensuring that she knew that everything would be okay, that they would get past the malevolence that was brought into their home, into their own daughter.

But Margaret was strong. She had not shed a single tear — not one. And although he was sure that he had seen her bottom lip tremble a few times, she maintained her straight, emotionless expression that he had come to love about her. It was her strict heartless demeanor that he had been so attracted to years ago, and the pure mercilessness of her personality is what kept him loyal to her over the last twenty years of marriage.

Suddenly, the Reverend's chants stopped and the door to the bedroom swung open, causing Chet to instantly jump to attention, awaiting instructions. Only, no instructions came, but instead, Reverend Drake pulled the door closed, which only slightly muffled yelling and deceitful words that Annabelle was loudly crying out. Randall stepped to a better vantage point and could see Drake on the landing above. He was completely drenched in sweat and had fresh blood stained into his rolled-up sleeves. His hair was amess and dripped with sweat.

Randall watched, without speaking, as he caught his breath. Then, the Reverend's eyes glanced down and locked in with his own, and Drake finally said, "Don't worry, it's not her blood."

"That isn't my worry, Reverend. How is she?"

Drake simply nodded and headed downstairs to join them at the table.

"She's strong," he said when he joined them. "It's going to take more effort than I thought. It can be done, I am sure of it, but we're going to need to take more drastic steps. I'm going to need all of your help to do it."

"Tell us what to do," Margaret said with a firm, almost cold, tone.

***

Annabelle, 3:57 PM

The school day was finally over. Annie's last class, English, had ended with the final bell at 3:45. Since English was in the west wing of the second floor, she didn't have to walk too far to her locker. So, now she was already out front, waiting on Chet to take them home.

Chet was a senior this year and still had no idea where he was going to go to college next year. He wasn't even sure what he wanted to study, if anything at all. He didn't like to talk about it, and quite frankly, wasn't all that interested in sharing anything with Annie. She was sometimes saddened that she didn't have a closer relationship with her older brother, but there was nothing she could do about it. She had tried, of course, to try to find things to be interested in that he liked, which proved to be extremely difficult, but no matter how much she pretended, he wanted nothing to do with her.

Trying to talk with him about the scripture was absolutely out of the question. Yet, despite that being so, she held out hope that one day she could tell him about the wonders of the Lord and that he might be saved as well. She had to have hope in that. He was, after all, her brother, and she loved him unconditionally. It was like a rule or something, right? She was sure it was.

She double checked her watch and wondered where Chet was. He was usually anxious to get out of here, so he could either dump her off at home or storm to his room and turn up his punk music — something that she found very difficult to even pretend to like. She glanced around again and finally saw him push through the school's double doors. She began to smile at him, but then she noticed that he had a slight grin on his face, one that she did not like. Then, a cold shiver ran from the bottom of her spine, up through her shoulders, and into her head when she saw Lucinda trailing after him.

"YOU!" he yelled out as he pointed straight at Annie. "Annabelle!"

Annie felt her heart skip a beat. What had she done? She looked around and saw that everyone's eyes were on her as Chet marched his way straight for her, Lucinda wickedly smiling behind him.

She had been deceived.

Every fiber in body told her to *run*, but she was unable to move — completely frozen in place. If only time had also frozen, but it hadn't. Instead, Chet was upon her before she knew it and she could not react in time to avoid his thrusting arms that shoved her hard to the ground. Her bag went flying. She reached for it, but Chet's foot came down hard on her arm and she screamed in pain.

He bent down and grabbed her bookbag and began digging through it. Annie struggled to pull her arm back, but Chet was strong, and she couldn't pull away from him. She began to cry as she writhed in pain on the ground. Lucinda was laughing as the other students formed a loose circle around the scene, whispering to each other, trying to figure out what was going on. Then, as Moses had parted the Red

Sea, a group of students parted to allow the principal to walk through, demanding to know what was going on out here.

Finally, Chet had found what he was looking for and let Annie's bookbag fall to the ground, holding up a thick book that was wrapped in a soft cloth.

"This!" he exclaimed.

Annie looked up at her brother, eyes filled with tears, and begged, "Please, Chet... Please don't... I'm your sister. Please..."

But her pleas meant nothing to him. He shared no emotions for his little sister. No compassion. And, rather than even a moment's hesitation, he simply grinned even more maliciously at her and unfolded the cloth that had concealed the book in his hand.

Annie felt a lump begin to form in her throat — not from the consequences that she knew were coming, not from fear of what was to become of tonight, but instead from the cold realization that she truly meant nothing to her brother — her own flesh and blood. She truly had no family that would support and defend her throughout her life. Yet, rather than feeling this anguish for herself, it was for Chet that she felt woeful — for he was truly damned.

"This, Principal Garner! This is my sister's Bible!" he proclaimed as he held the book high above his head, the golden embossed 'Holy Bible' profoundly shimmering in the sunlight.

Everyone that was within ear's range gasped at the words that Chet had just broadcast. The principal stopped dead in her tracks, eyes wide and mouth partially open. "Is this true!?" she spouted.

Annie, lips quivering and shaking with anxiety, still on the ground, simply whimpered, "Yes, it is."

"And Janelle believes too!" Lucinda suddenly shouted with delight.

The crowd looked around, trying to find Janelle, but she had been lucky enough to have already been picked up by her mother. No doubt the school would call to break the news to her parents and inform them that she would be expelled until treated. Little did they know that Janelle's parents were also followers of Christ and had been the ones that exposed her to the Bible.

The principal walked up to Annie slowly, her face now displaying firmness. "Are you sure, Annie?"

In fear, she wanted to deny that it was hers, exclaim it was a joke, any of a hundred reasons that she might have that Bible, none of which that it was actually hers, but she couldn't. She couldn't deny her faith. She couldn't deny God. So, instead, despite what she knew was coming, she said, "Yes, it's mine, and Jesus is my savior."

For a moment, Annie felt firm and proud of herself while the principal closed her eyes in disappointment. Then, when her eyes opened again, her face changed, became filled with rage, and she spat down on Annie's face, lifted a foot, and stomped it right into Annie's gut, forcing all the air in her lungs to instantly expel out. The pain forced a guttural sound that she had never heard herself make before and she began to wail so loudly that she barely heard the principal order Chet to bring her inside. Then, she felt her body being drug across the grass and sidewalks toward the school, the whole time being kicked in turns by the kids that had stood around to spectate the whole thing. Each strike of one of their feet was just as painful as the last and Annie could do nothing but cry and beg for them to stop while being pulled up the steps and into the school. As she was dragged down the hallway, she overheard the principal shout to the kids outside before pulling the doors shut, "Hail Satan!" for which they shouted back.

***

Chet, 9:42 PM
They all followed Reverend Drake up the stairs toward

Annabelle's room, where the sounds of her lies and deceit were barely muffled behind the closed door. The closer they got, the more excited he felt himself become. He could recall the first time he had heard the story of the Reverend invoking a demon to possess someone. He had been ten years old and the story was preached to all the youth group at the First Satan's Church in town. The leader of the youth had been very excited that year because their church had become the largest of any religious center in the state, bigger even than the Mosque which had held the title for the last ten years after the plague of Christianity and Catholicism had been all but abolished.

Before opening the door, Reverend Drake said, "Remember, until she is consumed by one of His, you cannot think of her as your daughter, or your sister. She is sick and needs to be cured. Until she is ridden of the Holy, she is a threat to us all. Even death is better for her. Do you understand?"

"We understand," Father said, and Mother nodded with him, then all their eyes turned to Chet.

Chet smiled and said, "Hell yes."

Being all in agreement, Reverend Drake opened the door, and the words that Annabelle was quickly uttering were finally clear enough to understand.

"I have kept my feet from every evil path so that I might obey your word. I have not departed from your laws, for you yourself have taught me. How sweet are your words to my taste, sweeter than honey to my mouth! I gain understanding from your precepts; therefore, I hate every wrong path. Your word is the lamp unto my feet and a light unto my path..."

Chet drew back in disgust. Holding her Bible in his hands had been one thing, but hearing the words spoken aloud not only offended his ears but seemed to pierce into them like daggers. As they all filed into the room, he felt himself becoming nauseated by her unbroken rambling. He only felt a sense of relief when he finally entered the room and took in the surroundings which was lit by several candles that had been strategically placed around the room.

The Reverend had indeed been busy in the time he had spent with Annabelle. Each wall had affixed to it a crucifix, turned upside down to spite the Lord. The candles — five of them — had all been arranged to act as the five points of a pentagram, which had been completed with soot. On the bed, Annabelle laid, still completely constrained by the ropes he had helped to tie, but now her blouse had been completely torn open, exposing her small, bare breasts, which also acted as two points for the pentagram that had been painted on her skin by the blood of the dead dove that sat on the nightstand. Her bedding and clothes were drenched with sweat and the unholy water that Reverend Drake had doused her with.

Seeing this wonderful sight in the room, Chet felt himself become aroused and his heartbeat suddenly became very prominent in his chest. How sweet Annabelle was suffering. This must have made Lucifer very happy indeed, despite the blasphemous words that were spewing from his sister's mouth.

"Shut up!" he heatedly shouted out of impulse.

"That won't help," Reverend Drake stated coolly. "We need to all take hands, in a semicircle around her." — they all followed his direction — "Now, repeat after me, then we all chant together: Satan, Prince of Darkness, Lord of the Flies, Most Unholy, we compel you, invoke unto us a tormentor, a fallen, to possess this girl and make her unclean and sinful as you demand."

They repeated his words and began to chant along with him. Again, and again. All the while Annabelle was citing scripture, drawing quick breaths only when necessary.

"… Away from me you evildoers, that I may keep the commands of my God! Sustain me according…"

"… Most Unholy," they said in unison, "we compel you, invoke unto us a tormentor, a fallen…"

As the Yarvis family members, along with the Satanist priest, chanted louder, so too did Annabelle's scripture. Everyone was competing to become the loudest in the room.

"*... to your promise, and I will live; do not let my hopes be dashed. Uphold me...*"

"... to possess this girl and make her unclean and sinful as you demand! Satan..."

Outside lightning flashed more quickly than before. Thunder boomed louder, striking nearer the house than Chet or anyone that had ever lived there had heard before. The floors under their feet began to rumble and the window in the bedroom exploded, showering glass about the room. The curtains ripped away from their rod and were sucked outside as if a giant vacuum hose had been placed against the outside window. The powerful winds then reversed, and a gust blasted through so strongly that Chet almost lost his balance. He shot a fearful glance toward Reverend Drake who shouted for them to keep chanting. So, more loudly than ever, he continued yelling the words with his parents.

"... we compel you, invoke unto us a tormentor, a fallen, to possess this girl..."

"*... You are my refuge and my shield; I have put my hope in your word. Away from me, you evildoers, that I may keep the commands of my God!...*"

"... and make her unclean and sinful as you demand. Satan, Prince of Darkness, Lord of the Flies!..."

The entire house continued to shake as if one of the famed Californian earthquakes was commencing right below them. Then, Chet saw something he never thought he would be fortunate enough to witness.

Two of the wooden planks beside Annabelle's bed, began to split apart, unveiling a void of darkness below — a gateway to Hell itself. As the planks separated, grey fingers rose up and gripped the edges of the floor. The hands were covered in warts and decayed flesh that left a slimy film that shimmered in the constant barrage of lightning outside —

the candles now long blown out. The demon raised itself from the darkness. It had no eyes, but instead black holes where eyes used to be — black as the Hellhole that the being had emerged from.

Chet watched, with an unabashed smile on his face that ran from ear to ear, as the demon crawled up onto the bed, on all fours, until it was directly on top of Annabelle. Chet felt envy fill his heart. He wanted to be the one to carry a minion of Lucifer within his body, to experience the feeling of possession by an agent of the dark. Then, he saw the look of terror on his young sister's face. The pure expression of fright was like ecstasy to him, and a part of him — a very large part — wished he was the demon, hovering over her exposed body, about to be inside of her. The thought caused the crotch of his pants to bulge like never before, and he swore the demon faced him one last time and gave an approving smile before shoving one of its hands into Annabelle's mouth, pushing it all the way down her throat. The excitement overwhelmed Chet and he felt himself come uncontrollably in his pants as he watched the demon force its other hand into her mouth to pull it widely open. Like a snake devouring a rat, it forced Annabelle's jaws to become unhinged, and slowly slithered the rest of its body and head down her throat until it was gone. Annabelle's scripture reciting was now silenced, his father and the Reverend were still chanting, and his mother was casting a provocative smile upon him — seemingly aware of how he had soiled himself.

Annabelle now laid in silence, apparently unconscious. The lump of the entity that entered her was now dissipating as it spread evenly throughout her entire body, and the chanting of his father and the Reverend Drake ceased. As Chet began to feel that the entire ordeal was over, wanting to now excuse himself to change his undergarments, a sudden flash of lightning struck through the window and hot fire stabbed straight through his chest. He felt nothing but flames and pain go through his body. However, as he looked down, he saw that it was not lightning that had struck, but instead a blue glowing sword had impaled him like a skewer through a steak. His eyes followed the blade up toward its hilt, but the blue glowing light made it impossible for him to make out the features of the winged creature that gripped its handle.

He heard his mother cry out in agony as he understood, as if by some instant upload of knowledge, that he was going to spend the rest of eternity burning in an anguish even more painful than the burning of the sword of light that was protruding from his back. Then the sword's blade became brighter and brighter, and the heat inside him hotter and hotter, and Chet's eyes widened in unadulterated horror right before his body exploded in front of the angel that had just smitten him.

***

Alaric, 10:00 PM

Alaric stepped backwards, instinctively shielding his eyes with his hands. As he moved back against the wall, he felt Randall shove him out of the way in a mad dash for the bedroom door — running for his life, with no regard to the lives of his family members. Pieces of Chet's body landed all around him and blood splattered the entire room except the angel and the bed, which had been shielded by one of the angel's outstretched wings.

Margaret's scream of horror turned into a yell of rage and she charged toward the angel with her hands lifted high, like a crazed cat, lunging toward a ball of yarn with outstretched claws. But, as soon as she reached the angel, she was flung across the room, slamming into the wall just inches away from Alaric's head, by a simple flick of the angel's wrist. He imagined the force must have killed her but was too petrified to check.

Alaric fell to his knees on the ground, awaiting a similar fate that had just begotten Chet, for he was the priest of the house of the devil. Why would he not be executed as well? He turned his head up, in preparation for the brightly-lit blue sword to be thrust down on him, and saw the angel standing resolutely over him. He was not the size of a man, but instead stood nearly eight feet tall, the tip of his helmet nearly scraping the ceiling. His armor appeared to reflect both silver and gold simultaneously and produced a color that Alaric could not recognize. His feathered wings folded back inward from their span of more than twelve feet. It was almost as if the angel were descended from Sparta, grown wings, and traded his crimson cloak for the one that appeared before Alaric now.

Suddenly, Annabelle began coughing and wheezing from the bed, causing Alaric to slightly jump out of fright, turning his attention to her rather than the magnificent creature in front of him. He felt a moment's relief when the angel had not only turned toward her but moved to a crouching position beside the proportionately tiny bed. The angel then placed a palm on Annabelle's chest, instantly erasing the blood-drawn pentagram under the yellow light that shown from his fingertips. Then, she made a loud guttural sound and once again, her mouth opened so widely that her jaw had to have completely dislocated itself, and the demon was rapidly ejected out. It scurried and tossed about onto the floor opposite the side of the bed the angel was kneeling.

Annebelle's mouth eased back closed and she and the angel began to converse, but Alaric paid no attention to their quiet words. His focus was on the demon, which was straight in front of him, eyeless sockets aimed straight at him. For the first time in his Satanic career, he felt fear of what he had once worshiped, for the demon did not have a gratifying expression on its face, but instead one of rage and hunger. And, before Alaric could tell himself to run, the demon leapt up and straight onto him. None of his screams or kicking had any effect on the creature that was now mounted atop of him.

Then, just had he had witnessed with Annabelle, the demon shoved its grey, wart-covered, hand down Alaric's throat. The slime that composed its decaying skin, along with popping pustules along its arms, acted as a lubricant that helped the demon slide its entire lanky body through his mouth. Finally, after what seemed to be an eternity of pure torture, the demon was fully settled inside of him. He felt his body begin to convulse as random muscles began to spasm throughout his body. Warm fluid wet his pants as his body began to urinate on itself. His eyes twitched, and the right one began to roll upwards, disjoining its attention from the other's as he tried to look toward Annabelle, who was fully buttoned up in her now unstained school uniform, bruises and cuts gone, hair nearly done up.

The angel stood and walked to him, and all Alaric could do was hope that the angel would thrust his sword down and end his torment. But, he didn't. The angel reached down, took Alaric by the throat, and lifted him to eye-level. With his one working eye, Alaric looked straight at the angel's perfect face when the sound of a trumpet blast sounded from the sky outside. It caused Alaric — still in pain, body convulsing — to glance past the smiling angel and out the window. The lightning, which had been dancing across the sky all night, like strobe lights in a club, had completely ceased. Then, in a flash — not of light, but of darkness — not even the moon's reflection was visible. All that remained was pure blackness. It was something that he had never seen before. It was not simply black, nor dark in the way that we have come to know the darkest places imaginable. But instead, it was a complete absence of light that no human had ever known before, because along with the light, there too was the complete absence of hope and good.

The angel, who was only visible because of the glowing

blade of his sword, pulled Alaric's face close to his own and spoke in the most wonderful voice Alaric had ever heard, "Our Father has invoked the final judgement. You shall remain here, for a thousand years until the second resurrection." Then, the angel dropped him back to the ground, turned, and took Annabelle into his arms. He told her he was taking her Home and she wept, not as before, but with joy and a smile on her beautifully pure face. Then, the angel leapt out of the window, and with one great flap of his wings, vanished upward into the black sky. In that moment, Alaric knew this was Hell on Earth and began his punishment of eternal suffering.

Stonehedge Street Haunt
R.C. Mulhare

A failed exorcism," Jason Waite, the set designer for the Stonehedge Street Haunt Project, suggested to the planning group gathered about a table in the Kerwins' basement.

Roger Kerwin, the project head and East Manuxet's Parks and Recreation director, raised his eyebrow and sat forward in his chair. "That's interesting in a William Friedkin way, but why an exorcism specifically?"

Jason shrugged. "Why not? It's one of the ultimate fears: having your mind and body infiltrated by something from outside the realm of the natural. Like a parasite you can't treat with medicine as we understand it."

"It could work," Rebecca Taylor, the wardrobe manager, said. "There's a lot of Catholics in town."

"Why not a scary asylum?" asked Adam Kelsoe, one of their lead actors.

Rebecca side-eyed him across the table. "Considering we've got the East Manuxet State Hospital on the other side of town with its—at best—checkered past, it's a bit on the nose."

"Damn, I found some prop straitjackets at a good price," Adam said.

Kerwin leaned back. "So how do we do this?"

"Scary spray paint pentagrams on the floor or the walls. Black drapes. People dressed as cult members in black robes," Jason said. "I know where I can find a taxidermy goat's head to prop somewhere or push it through an interior window like it's lunging at someone."

"How about dressing people like devils or possessed people?" Rebecca scribbled on her pad.

"Is this really wise? We might have the moral guardians come down on us for 'glorifying Satan'." Kerwin said, making small air quotes with his index fingers.

Jason snerked, shaking his head. "If that's the case, they need to check out the photos on the Yahoo! Groups for St. Margret Clitherow Parish. They had people walk through the gates of hell, past a bunch of teens from the Catholic Youth Organization dressed as lost souls and devils to get into the all-ages Halloween Party in the Parish Hall last year."

"If your Halloween haunt doesn't ruffle a few feathers, you're doing it wrong," Adam said.

"I just had a brainstorm: how about a male possession victim?" Rebecca asked.

"Don't most cases of possession involve girls?" Adam asked innocently.

"Not always," Jason said. "The case that inspired *The Exorcist* involved a teenaged guy. William Peter Blatty just changed a lot of details to protect the guy's privacy."

"Okay, folks, do we know a guy who'd play a good victim?" Kerwin asked.

"I knew a guy at acting school who'd be perfect," Adam said.

* * *

"Would you need to tie me down?" asked Dorian Lang, a tall slim young man, the archetypal pale-skinned Goth guy with dark hair slightly below his ears, his bangs falling into his thoughtful eyes.

"If you're comfortable with that," Kerwin said.

"We wouldn't keep you tied down constantly. We're not that kind of haunt," Jason said.

"Can you give us your best Linda Blair impression?" Rebecca asked, with a wry twist.

Dorian quirked an eyebrow. "Possessed Linda Blair or cute

Linda Blair?"

"Ahh, geez, you've watched the movie more than once, I take it?" Jason asked.

Dorian chuckled, glancing away. "I might have gone through a rebellious phase when I'd pop a weird movie into the player any time I heard my mother coming to my room and I wanted to get a rise out of her. It's one of the few horror movies she didn't mind me watching."

"Is that so?" Kerwin asked.

He shrugged one shoulder. "It deals with Catholicism and Mom's a strict but not crazy Catholic."

"Oooh, a good Catholic boy, eh? This adds a wrinkle to your performance." Jason said

The haunt crew laughed. "If that's the most rebellious you got, you sound like a Good Boy, and that'll make the possessed act even creepier," Rebecca said. "Let's see it."

Dorian drew in a breath, stepping back from the table. He closed his eyes, letting his head sink back onto one shoulder. He drew in his breath in low, slow rasps, parting his lips. He curled them back, baring his teeth and curled his hands into trembling claws. He rolled his head forward, opening his eyes, showing only the whites. "Heaven's a faery tale for the weak of will."

Dorian lunged at the table, hoisting himself onto it, pushing himself into Kerwin's face, snarling. Kerwin leaned back in his chair, laughing nervously.

"Okaaayyyy, we'll need the restraints for that," Rebecca said. Jason applauded.

Kerwin looked to Rebecca and Jason as Dorian climbed down from the table. "I say he's hired."

"Seconded," Jason said, with a nervous grin.

"There's not much pay for this," Kerwin said. "We split the ticket sales: a third goes to the Youth Center, a third goes into operating costs and the last third we divide evenly among the performers."

"Fair enough. It helps a good cause, and it will look good on my CV," Dorian replied.

"I'll draw up the paperwork, but in the meantime, you've got the role," Kerwin said, offering his hand.

* * *

"Bring on the whips and chains! I dare you," Dorian rasped. "He's been a bad, bad, dirty little boy. I'm sure you'll enjoy making him screeeeeeeaaamm!"

The group of guests passing through the house startled back from the bed on which he lay, strapped down with breakaway straps. The guy in the front almost fell back onto the girl behind him. A second guy tried pushing his girlfriend toward the bed.

Dorian pulled on his bonds, sitting up. "Is that an offering to the Dark Lord who rules within?" The girl screamed, falling into her boyfriend and bowling him over. "Such a big, strong man pushed over by a weak girl." The group shuffled into the next room, hanging onto each other in a shambling conga train.

"Having fun?" Rebecca whispered in her black-veiled alcove behind the headboard.

"The reactions are priceless," Dorian whispered back.

"Glad you signed up?"

"Heck, yeah!"

"Next group's coming." Rebecca banged the wall, wailing like a banshee. Dorian shifted in his bonds, roaring before laying down quietly. A high-pitched voice wailed. He drew in a breath, growling just loud enough for them to hear.

A small boy ran through the tatty black cloth covering the hall doorway. A woman closely followed, reaching for the boy's shoulder. Before Dorian could stop the roar rising in his throat, it burst out. The boy jumped backward into the woman's arms, screaming.

"Oh, God, I'm sorry," Dorian said in his normal voice.

"Mommy, too scary!"

"It's too late for sorry!" the woman yelled.

Rebecca stepped out. "It's all right, I can help you outside. I'm sorry this happened."

"No, you aren't, you scare little kids on purpose!" the woman snarled.

Dorian looked away to hide the "what the heck?" look on his face before relaxing and looking back. "Trust me, I didn't know your son was coming." He pulled his arms from the bindings and showed his empty hands. The boy wailed, huddling against his mother as if he would bury himself in her body.

"You should be ashamed of yourself," the woman snarled. Kerwin entered and guided them toward the chicken door down the hallway, promising the woman a refund, Rebecca at their side.

A moment later, Rebecca returned. "That lady didn't read the 'No children under 12' warning on the ticket booth," one guest said.

"And on all the posters all over town?" another guest said.

"You folks want to proceed?" Rebecca asked.

"Of course! Ain't your fault some people can't be responsible with who they bring along," a guy at the back said.

"I just hope she had a situation where she couldn't get a sitter," said a girl with the guy in the back.

"If she couldn't get a sitter, maybe she should have held off till she could," the first guy said.

"Or she was short on common sense," said a woman in the middle of the pack. "You know what they say about it not being very common."

"But victims arrrrreeee," Dorian growled. "Give me the girrlll. Give her to me as a sacrifice to the darkness within."

"Soitenly," the guy at the back said, hoisting up the girl beside him and holding her toward Dorian. The girl squealed, thwapping her companion's arm as they shuffled into the next room.

"Those folks were troopers," Rebecca whispered.

"They made up for that upset."

"You okay?"

"Yeah, she sounded like an entitled customer at my day job. Nothing I can't handle."

* * *

Halloween passed. The haunt closed after a packed crowd, where they had to turn away the last dozen people at the end of the line, who'd arrived too close to closing time. They packed up the props for another haunt next year. After a cast party at Enzo's Pizzeria, with Enzo himself serving and sharing some of his grandfather's homemade wine with the cast members old enough to enjoy, they went their separate ways, with promises to come together again next October.

"Working that haunted house did you a lot of good," noted Priscilla Wazowski, the cashier for whom Dorian bagged at the town's Market Basket, the day after Halloween. "You usually look so worried that it worries me a bit. But now you've got a real twinkle in those big, dark eyes of yours."

Dorian chuckled gently as he packed a customer's cereal boxes into a brown paper bag, "I had a good experience doing it. It's why I like acting. I enjoy taking on a character and quite literally bringing them to life. Even better when it's something interactive."

"But isn't it dull, having to learn all those lines and remembering them all and saying them just right?"

"This was different. They gave me a character and a scenario. I could improvise the lines."

"Oooh, that's right. What kind of creature did you play? A ghost? A werewolf?"

"They had a demonic cult theme for the haunt, so I played a possessed person."

The customer loading her last groceries onto the belt stopped short, glaring down the lane at Dorian. "It's you. I didn't recognize you in this light. So you're the actor who scared my grandson so badly? You should be ashamed of yourself. How can you do something like that and sleep well at night?!"

Dorian looked from the customer to Priscilla and back. "I was just an actor playing a role."

"It sounds like your grandson might have been just a little too young for that haunt," Priscilla said.

"They shouldn't open places like that. Can't they have made it for all ages?" the customer snapped.

"Outside of what I felt comfortable doing, I didn't have much say in what scenes they had," Dorian said, helpless.

"Well, for what it's worth, I'm sorry your little boy got scared—" Priscilla started to say.

"You have no part of this and sorry doesn't fix it. Now my grandson needs therapy, and you should pay for it." The customer stepped into Dorian's personal space, jabbing her index finger to within an inch of his nose. He backed away, into the end of the register.

Tonya, at the next register, reached to her register light,

turning it to blink. "Cam?" Allison, her bagger, called.

Cam Barris, the front-end manager, stepped away from the point-of-sale desk where he was helping an assistant count off a drawer. "What can I do for you?" he asked.

"You should fire this monster! You need to keep an eye on what your employees do when they aren't here," the customer yelled, pointing at Dorian.

Barris looked from Dorian to the customer. "What exactly do you mean?"

"I had a part in the Stonehedge Street Haunt, and I'm afraid—" Dorian said.

"You should be afraid! I could have your job! I hope you get stuck making nasty porn movies! I hope you get possessed for real!" the customer yelled. "I hope a hundred demons tear you to pieces!"

"Ma'am, this is a family environment. I can't have you talking like that to my associates," Barris said.

"That's fine! I'm never shopping here again!" the woman snarled. To Dorian, she added, "I hope you rot in hell. Real hell!" She grabbed the bags that Dorian carefully lifted from the end of the register and held out to her. One bag slipped from her grip, falling to the floor and spilling out the boxes it contained. "Look what you made me do, you little pissant!"

Barris fetched a cardboard box, handing it to Dorian, who quickly collected the scattered items. "Ma'am, you'll need to leave once we collect these," Barris said. Without a word, the woman snatched the box and stalked out. "You all right, Dorian?"

Dorian shook his head, looking away to hide the tears in the corners of his eyes. "I'm all right."

"You go take a break and come down when you're ready."

* * *

The back door to the Langs' house banged shut. Vivien Lang looked up from her desktop computer and the spreadsheets she was combing over. "Dorian?"

Her son entered her home office, his face ashen. "Ma, you think it was wrong for me to take that role at the haunt?"

"Not at all. You enjoyed it and the haunt raised good money

for the youth center." She rose to join him in the doorway. "Something happen?"

He turned away. "Not really."

"Dorian, you call tell me what went wrong."

"Nothing went wrong, I told you."

"Did someone give you trouble at work?"

"Sort of."

"Was it something to do with an order?"

"No. They found out I'd worked the haunt and they got mad."

"One of those religious nuts?"

"I don't know, maybe. She cussed me out and wished bad shit—"

"Language."

"Sorry. She wished bad stuff would happen. Whatever."

"I'm sorry that happened."

"So am I." He walked away, heading for his room. The door banged shut, not something he did often, even when he'd had a difficult customer. "Dorian? You okay?" She went to his door, knocking on it. No reply, except for his music turning on louder than usual.

* * *

A few days after The Incident, Barris had Dorian help grocery stock the shelves, giving him a break from the front end. As Dorian stacked tomato paste cans on a shelf in aisle three, the woman who had shouted at him approached, a small pasteboard box with autumn leaves print in hand. "Young man, can I talk to you?"

"You may," Dorian replied. The three grocery clerks looked up from their work and eyed the woman.

She held the box out to him. "I wanted to apologize and to make you a peace offering. It's a large chocolate chip cookie I baked. You're allowed to have that, right? It's hard to tell with all this food allergy nonsense."

Dorian accepted the box, hiding a wince. "Yeah, I can have chocolate, at least."

"I'm sorry I went off on you. I was worrying about my

grandson and I lost my head. I hope you didn't get in trouble?"

"No, not really."

"Good, good. I won't keep you from your work. You enjoy that cookie." She scurried away.

"That the holier-than-thou lady who screamed about you being in the house haunt?" Jerry Hadlinger, one of the grocery guys asked.

"Yeah, that was her." Dorian opened the box, finding a homemade chocolate chip cookie about four inches across.

"Better break that open before you eat it and make sure she didn't bake any needles or something else nasty into it," Jerry said.

"I thought the same thing," Dorian said, bringing it with him back to the front end.

* * *

Dorian's low mood continued off and on through the following weeks. With Thanksgiving on the way, Vivien took it as a sign that work had gotten busy and bothersome. At other times, his usual gentle self returned. He came with her to Mass as usual, but he sat somewhat moodily leaning back in the pew through the ceremonies.

"Maybe you could talk to Father LaTour?" Vivien suggested after Mass on the Sunday two weeks before Thanksgiving.

"Like there's anything he can do?" Dorian muttered. He paused, blinking, looking at Vivien. "Why are you upset?"

"Dorian, are you feeling all right?"

"I feel fine now. Why?"

"You've been snappish and irritable for a while now, since you had trouble with that customer after Halloween."

"I have?"

"You haven't heard yourself talking?"

"Talking about what?"

"Just now, I suggested you could talk to Father LaTour. You snapped at me."

"I did?"

"Yes. You haven't spoken to me like that in years."

"I'm telling you I don't know what's going on." He looked

152

away, his jaw tightening.

"Are you feeling all right?"

"I don't know now." He pressed his mouth tight as he went away to his room.

A plate in the middle of the dining room table slid across the cloth-covered top to the edge and crashed to the floor.

* * *

"He's not been the same since after that haunt," Vivien told Father LaTour, one of the priests at St. Margret's later that week, when she went to confession.

"At first, I thought it could be the stress of performing, but I'm not exactly a psychologist," the priest replied.

"I didn't think it could be that. He enjoys performing and he felt honored to help. But that changed after that customer called him out."

"That could have affected him; he's always had a sensitive heart."

"He's grown stronger the past few years. He's told me that working the store has given him the tougher skin he'll need to make it in acting. But he could have taken a step backward."

It's normal for anyone, especially a young person. If this goes on longer and worsens, it's best if he talks to a counselor. I know a good one who's worked at Catholic Charities."

* * *

"I don't need a counselor, I just need you to get off my back," Dorian growled.

"Just talk to her. She can help you sort this out."

"I talk to enough people, more than I care to at the damn day job."

"In God's name, just consider it," Vivien begged.

Dorian blinked. "What… did I black out again?"

"Yes, you did. I think you need to talk to someone."

"I'd better. I don't know what's going on. I was looking for acting jobs online, and I lost time."

"What do you mean?"

"I looked at the clock and I found a half hour had gone by. I'd gone to places on the Internet I'd rather not be."

"Do I want to know where?"

He shook his head. "No. I think… you'd better take my computer for the time being. Maybe my phone, too."

"You need that for work and in case I need to catch up with you."

"I'll get a cheap phone with no bells and whistles."

* * *

Father LaTour drew in a long breath. "If it's as you say, I think this is something more than mere acting out from anxiety."

Vivien felt her stomach sink into her knees. "What do you mean?"

"I mean… this isn't something I say lightly. Your son may be possessed."

"You're kidding." Her stomach tightened inside her, but at the same time, something loosened in her chest. "How could he have gotten possessed? From working the haunt?"

He shook his head. "It takes something bigger and more serious than mere playacting for something that big to break in. I'll have to bring this to the bishop. I'd better warn you; Bishop Mallegant doesn't always take these things seriously."

"This time he'll have to. I feel like… I'm losing him to this darkness."

"I'll make sure you don't lose him."

* * *

A week before Christmas, the store crowded with customers, every register open, every one with a line.

"We need double baggers," Priscilla said.

"We need triple baggers," Allison, on the next register said without looking up.

"We need double baggers on regular days," Dorian said, packing a bag with packaged Christmas cookies.

"Oh, I don't argue that," Priscilla said.

"At least they're encouraging Christmas. Not like those stores that just have 'Happy Holidays' signs," the customer in Priscilla and Dorian's lane, a woman in her fifties with a garish red Christmas sweater emblazoned with a red nosed reindeer and snowmen, said.

"Whatever happened to Christmas being too commercial?" Allison murmured.

"It's all a racket, all a racket for a damned baby in a barn," a voice growled through Darien. "That's one abortion that should have happened."

Allison looked up, edging back. "You got a problem with that, you retarded cunt?" the same voice growled. "Don't give us that holier than thou shit. Your pulse races whenever that fat cow goth waddles through your lane, so don't pretend you're such a good widdle Catholic girl." He stepped toward Allison, getting in her face. Allison pressed back against the end of the register, staring Dorian in the face.

"Why are you talking like this?" Allison asked. "How can you know this?"

"I'm talking like this because I can, you little piglet," the voice said.

"Young man, do you kiss your mother's cheek with that mouth?" the customer in Priscilla's lane said, shaking her finger at him.

Dorian jerked toward the customer. "The same way you kiss your man's dick, and I don't mean the man who gave you that fat gold ring on your left hand."

Priscilla reached to blink her light. "Calling your master, you quim? He's not coming for a while. He's too busy to notice you and your chatter annoys him anyway. That's why he won't give you the hours you want," the voice snarled, Dorian's lips barely moving.

"We need a manager! We need one now! The bagger's gone crazy!" a customer in another lane shouted. The front-end assistant looked up from making a cash pick up on number seven. Barris looked up from rebooting the register on number twelve.

"Calling in the ape, eh?" the voice in Dorian snarled. "Who's got their hand on your chain, if you've got a hand on his?"

"Young man, stop talking like that!" the customer in Priscilla's lane snapped, swatting at him with a coupon wallet.

Dorian launched himself across the end of the register and over her shopping cart, tackling the woman and grabbing her throat.

"Mr. Barris! We need you!" Priscilla screamed. Barris rushed over, pushing the cart from the lane and grabbing Dorian's shirt collar.

With a roar, Dorian jerked free of Barris. He grabbed the much larger and huskier man by the throat, throwing him across the aisle of the front end. Barris hit the point-of-sale desk, collapsing to the floor.

"Someone call the police!" a customer in another lane screamed.

"In God's name, what's going on?" Mr. Kyriakos, the store director, demanded, approaching Barris' prone form.

Dorian staggered back against the register, blinking. "What... how... what is happening?"

"You don't know what's going on? Come upstairs to the office. This stops now," Kyriakos ordered.

"Yessir." Dorian meekly bowed his head, limping after the store director.

* * *

Two days later, on the third Sunday in December, Vivien called Dorian down several times with no results. At last, she went to his door, knocking on it. "Dorian, are you ready for Mass?"

"...no..." his voice replied on the other side, in a tiny, pained squeak.

"Are you all right in there?"

"*Go away, you rotten cunt, he's not interested in your puppet show,*" a deeper voice rasped.

She rattled the doorknob, unable to open the door. "Who's in there with you?"

"*There's no one in here but me,*" the deep voice replied.

"In God's name, what is wrong with you?" she demanded. The door popped open. She stumbled inside. Dorian's bed stood empty; the bedclothes crumpled on the floor. She straightened up, looking about her.

Someone or something whimpered above her head. Looking up, she spied Dorian, still in his pajamas, pressed against the strip of wall above the door. He peered over his shoulder, eyes wide, body trembling.

"How did you get up there?"

"Something threw me up here," he whimpered. He dropped to the floor with a thud that knotted her stomach. He lay still, eyes rolling back in his head.

She ran for the phone, dialing EMS.

Later, in Saints Joseph and John's Hospital in Manuxet, Vivien paced the waiting area of the emergency room, hugging herself. At length, one of the nursing Sisters approached, her face almost as pale as the white work veil covering her head. "Mrs. Lang? Your son is resting, but he's still recovering from the fall."

"What's wrong with him?"

"You'll have to talk to Doctor Haller, who's treating him. He's by your son's bedside if you want to speak to him."

"I need to see my son."

The sister lead her along a short hallway, past a nurses' station into the ICU. "I'd better warn you, they had to restrain him." Dorian lay on a bed close to the nurse's station, leather straps on his wrists and ankles and another around his waist, binding him to the bed frame.

"Get that wrinkled old bitch in her Jesus gown away from us!" the rasping voice in Dorian spoke, his lips parted but not moving.

"In God's name, be quiet," the nursing Sister said. Dorian twisted against the restraints before lying still.

"That's a mild version of the symptoms he's manifested," said an older man in scrubs, approaching and eyeing the IV taped into Dorian's arm. "We had to administer him enough sedatives to put a man twice his body mass into a coma before he'd relax."

"What's going on with him?" Vivien asked

"I have to ask; does he have any history of mental illness? Drug use?"

"He's never used anything, not more than once. He had some problems with depression and acting out in high school, after his father and I drifted apart. But once he went to college and especially once he got his bachelor's degree in theatre he found his footing again. He said acting helped him find an objective view on his own troubles."

"Is there any history of psychosis or dissociative identity disorder in your family?"

"No, some depression and anxiety but nothing more serious, not in his father's family as far as I know."

"I'd be inclined to admit him to the psychiatric ward, but not when he's this unstable."

"If he's suffering what I think he's afflicted with, I wouldn't advise doing that," the nursing Sister said. "Has a priest spoken to him?"

"Not him personally, but I've spoken to several priests about it."

"Have they suggested he might have something attached to him?"

"This is medieval thinking," the doctor said.

"You've seen the phenomena. Some things science can explain, but some things only faith and religion can explain," the nursing Sister said.

"Against medical advice?"

"He's my son. Let me decide," Vivien said. "I'll keep him here, but I want to bring in someone else."

"What kind of someone else?" the doctor asked.

"I'm calling in a priest."

The doctor opened his mouth to speak. Vivien held up her index finger. "It's not outside the realm of possibility. Besides, this is a Catholic hospital."

"As you wish," the doctor said.

* * *

A few days later, after Father LaTour had arranged an appointment for her, Vivien drove down to St. Anselm's Seminary in Houlton, a Gothic pile like something from a British supernatural thriller, the effect heightened by the snow covering the rooftop, the grounds, the top of the ornate iron fence along the street.

A young seminarian answered her knock on the heavy wooden front door. "I have an appointment with Father Robert Haviland?" she asked.

"Yes, he's expecting you. Come this way." The seminarian opened the door wider, stepping aside to let her enter before he shut the door and lead the way up a wide, ornate staircase, then down a hallway lined with doors, transom windows above them—the air smelling of floor wax and old books. Her guide paused before one door, knocking on it.

"*Benedicte*?" a man's voice replied within. The seminarian opened the door, letting her enter and keeping the door open.

Inside, stood two old rolltop desks, back to back in the middle of a room lined with bookcases and file cabinets. Desktop computers stood on the desks; behind the further desk sat a tall, slim young priest, typing with quick precision. Behind the closer desk sat an older priest, gray haired and with the robust build like an old Marine, who rose to greet her.

"Mrs. Lang? I'm Father Haviland." Indicating the younger priest, he added, "This is my assistant, Father Martin Crowley."

"It's a pleasure to meet you... except, I suppose, it really isn't," Vivien said. Father Crowley rose and pulled a chair from the corner for her.

Father Haviland sat down, shrugging one broad shoulder. "It will be, once we're able to help your son."

"I hope this doesn't take much of your time."

Father Haviland shook his head, with a small, reassuring smile. "This is how we serve the servants of God, by freeing them from what troubles them."

She elaborated on what Father LaTour had shared with them. "Besides everything else, he's on suspension from work. They won't have him back unless he can promise this won't happen again," she said, in conclusion.

"You say he snaps back to himself when someone invokes God's name?"

"Yes."

"That's a very bad sign," Father Haviland said.

Father Crowley asked, "Has he gotten involved in anything dangerous spiritually?"

"He went through a witchcraft phase in high school, but since he graduated and went to acting school, he's gone back to Mass with me, until now."

"That could have been the crack in his spiritual armor."

"What? It was just a phase."

"True, but at times, small things can have consequences which I'm sure he didn't intend. This curse you mentioned?"

"Yes, an angry customer cursed him."

Crowley sat up straighter in his chair. "I take it there was more than just telling him to go to hell."

"You don't think this person could have summoned a demon? But that's Old Testament talk."

"It's also New Testament talk; Christ, Himself freed people from demons. And if this woman who cursed him has dabbled in things she has barely any control over, she might well have caught the attention of something she shouldn't and it could have transferred to him somehow, by direct command, by asking someone to cast the curse, even giving him a cursed item, like food or an object."

She tensed her shoulders. "That stuff is real?"

"More real than most people realize."

"When can we start the exorcism?"

"I'll have to bring this to the archbishop's office, first, and unfortunately, Archbishop Mallegant doesn't always take these cases seriously. At the same time, we'll need his medical records from this hospital stay Father LaTour mentioned."

Her shoulders sagged. "I can get you the files as soon as I can sign off on them. But I guess this means you'll call me as soon as you can."

"I'll do what I can to convince him of the immediacy of the situation." Father Haviland tilted his head toward Father Crowley, who gave him a patient look. "And it would break this one into the ministry. He's just been appointed to the diocese, as I'm retiring in February."

"Are you sure you're ready for this?" Vivien said, realizing how entitled that sounded.

"I've assisted at several exorcisms in Rome and here in the Boston area," Father Crowley replied. With a small smile, he added, "Not all at once, but over the space of a year and a half."

"A year and a half? I didn't think it would take that long."

"It takes about nine months to cover the readings in demonology, and the next nine months, I spent assisting an exorcist in Rome. It's a challenging process."

"It sounds a bit like joining the FBI," Vivien said.

"Only the FBI doesn't deal with spiritual parasites," Father Haviland noted.

* * *

The day before New Year's Eve, Father Haviland and Father Crowley accompanied Vivien to Dorian's bedside, now in a private room, well away from the more fragile patients. Father Haviland entered, to no reaction from their client. Father Crowley followed him in, Vivien at his heels.

A growl rattled in Dorian's throat, and his body lunged against his restraints. "*Brought along some company? The old man can fuck off, but the young buck with his brand-new collar can stay. This young man would love the taste of that young man.*"

Father Crowley made the Sign of the Cross. Dorian's body collapsed on the bed. "In the Name of the Father and of the Son and of the Holy Ghost, be silent."

Dorian's eyes rolled forward. "Mom? Who are these men?"

Father Crowley opened the neck of his black wool topcoat, uncovering his Roman collar. "We're Catholic priests, here to help you at your mother's request."

"I don't know what you can do with this thing. It started talking to me and it won't shut up."

"And that's why we're here to free you from it," Father Haviland said, remaining by the door.

"You mean an exorcism?"

"We do."

Dorian laughed under his breath, before glancing away and turning serious. "I'm sorry. I've watched that movie a dozen times. I'd rather not live it."

"Neither would we," Father Crowley said. "We'll makes sure it has a good ending."

"When do we start?" Dorian asked.

"As soon as possible." Father Haviland said.

"What's today?" Dorian asked, looking to Vivien, leaning on the foot of the bed.

"The day before New Year's Eve."

"Ending the old year by casting out the darkness," Dorian said.

His eyes rolled, one eye going to either side independently, then back. *"Or starting a new one with the new way that I can show him."*

"Except it isn't what he wants or desires," Father Haviland said.

"You think you know what he wants? You're not the one inside him. We'll show him things he's barely dreamed of."

"In Jesus' name, let me speak to Dorian," Father Crowley ordered.

Dorian's body quivered and the eyes rolled forward. "Please. Get this thing out of me."

The three of them stepped out into the hallway. "Can we get him released today and do this at our house?" Vivien asked.

"It's not like what you see in the movies," Father Haviland said. "We'd perform the Rite in a church; we regularly do it, appropriately in St. Michael's, in Houlton. But first, we'll need a few days to make the necessary arrangements."

"What about the chapel here in the hospital?"

"Hospitals really aren't the best place," Father Crowley said. "For one thing, there are a lot of vulnerable patients here. For another, when the Rite progresses, there will be manifestations worse than what you've seen here. That can affect the patients here, if they hear the noises. One exorcism I assisted at, the electric lights flickered and went out, not because of a black-out, but because the demons decided to try scaring people by messing with the lights." Crowley glanced to the door. With the driest chuckle, he added, "Bad enough that the incident with the lights affected the refrigerator in the church's basement kitchen, spoiling the food in it." More serious, he added, "Imagine that happening to an X-ray or an MRI machine, or worse, a life support system."

"I guess I need to listen to the experts. I just..." Vivien rubbed her temples. "I want my little boy back as soon as humanly or heavenly possible."

"And God and His angels, working through us, will deliver him back into your hands. For now, you need to watch and be patient for a little while longer," Father Haviland said, putting a comforting hand on Vivien's shoulder.

"I suppose. I'm sorry I went off."

Father Haviland smirked. "You're doing well. I've dealt with loved ones of clients who were far less patient with the process."

* * *

The afternoon of New Year's Day, the phone rang in Vivien's home office. She nearly knocked her keyboard off the desk in her haste to answer.

"He-hello?"

"Mrs. Lang? It's Father Crowley. We've arranged to perform the exorcism tomorrow at three pm in St. Michaels in Houlton. Is that convenient?"

"I'll have to sign the release forms at the hospital and tell my boss I need another day of medical leave, but I'll be there as early as I can tomorrow."

"You don't sound well."

"No, Father, I'm not. I talked with Dorian's father last night; he's really skeptical about this, and it's gotten into my head."

He listened in silence, then said, *"Do you want to back out?"*

"No! No, I just..." She rubbed her forehead. "I just want to get through this. I just want my little boy back. Dorian wants his head back. I just feel like an idiot for wanting to back out."

"It's all right. It's normal. And actually, it's a good sign."

"How is that possible?"

"As far as we can tell, though we'll have a psychic that Father Haviland has worked with examine him, it appears there's one demon already possessing your son. Where there's one, more are likely to show up. They're going to find ways to attack, trying to divide and conquer and keep you from proceeding as planned."

"So I just have to tough it out?"

"You aren't the only one. We've had some shocks at the residence here. The computer network manager ran some routine maintenance this morning and the entire system crashed, blowing out some otherwise brand-new components."

"Could have been computers being computers, but the timing is weird."

"I won't keep you any longer. You have your son to care for."

"I won't keep you either, Father."

* * *

She went to the hospital that evening, to arrange Dorian's release. She expected resistance from the doctors and administrators. Instead, Doctor Haller agreed to an immediate release.

"I hope this exorcism works. When he's lucid, he's a good young man, but whatever has attached itself to him, I wouldn't wish on anyone," Dr. Haller said, as the nurses wheeled Dorian to the vestibule. Dorian had dark circles under his eyes, and he sat curled in the wheelchair like a scared cat. Vivien thought she saw gray hairs above his ears.

"Mom, thank God," Dorian said, rising on shaking legs. Vivien put her shoulder under his, letting him lean on her as she helped him outside to the car. She heard a growl deep inside his chest, but felt no vibration through his flesh.

She woke the next morning and on looking in the bathroom mirror, found dark circles under her own eyes, doubtlessly caused by the strange scratching in the wall that separated her room from Dorian's. She swore she'd heard whispering as well, but her mind tried to tell her that her worry could have made it real.

She tried helping the situation by sprinkling holy water inside Dorian's cereal bowl before he shuffled in and found the Rice Krispies in the cabinet. The moment he put a spoonful into his mouth, the cereal splatted out, followed by a stream of greenish stuff that should not have come from him.

"I thought it would help," she said.

"It made it worse," Dorian muttered, going for a clean bowl.

* * *

At two thirty, Father Haviland and Father Crowley arrived at St. Michael's Church, the members of their prayer team and two strong young men arrived in ones and twos by the side doors, last among them Lainie Holtz, Brett Roark and Abigail Hodgson, the last carrying a medical kit.

Lainie glanced toward the front doors, shuddering. "He's coming."

"Your Spidey sense tingling?" Brett asked.

"Don't call it that; have some respect," Abigail murmured.

Lainie smirked to Brett. "I don't mind."

A moment later, the front door opened, and Vivien entered, with Dorian at her side, literally dragging his feet. Abigail and Father Haviland approached, guiding them toward the sanctuary.

Father Crowley looked up from stabilizing the massage table where Dorian would rest—a table near it with a crucifix in a stand, a holy water sprinkler and two lit blessed candles. "I'm sorry we're late," Vivien said. "The motor kept sputtering in my car."

"Things like that happen. It could just mean the car needs a tune-up," Father Crowley said,

"I had it done last month," Vivien said.

Father Haviland helped Dorian out of his coat. "Then that means something more sinister."

"Hands off the merchandise, priest. Or are you starting to think like that fallen classmate of yours?" the voice within Dorian snarled. *"This one's ripe for the taking if you've thought of taking the ride down."*

"In God's name, be silent, demon," Father Haviland order. The voice fell silent.

Abigail and Lainie helped Dorian onto the massage table, Abigail adjusting the thin pillow under his head. The entity growled. Brett and the other robust man approached. *"Keep your hands off him, you black spade."* the voice snarled, turning Dorian's head toward Brett.

"Dorian! You don't use that kind of talk—" Vivien started saying.

Father Crowley caught her eye as he draped a purple liturgical stoll about his neck. "Vivien, it's not your son saying that."

Brett shrugged. "It's a Tuesday for me, though my grandfather would've heard that particular slur."

The prayer circle gathered in a half ring behind the head of the table. Father Haviland stepped to the foot, with Father Crowley taking a post by the head. The prayer circle started praying the Litany of the Saints, Abigail leading the responses. "In the Name of the Father, and of the Son, and of the Holy Spirit," Father Haviland prayed, sprinkling Dorian with holy water. Father Crowley took up the prayers. *"Holy Lord, almighty Father, everlasting God and Father of our Lord Jesus Christ, who once and for all consigned that fallen and apostate tyrant to the flames of hell, who sent your only-begotten Son into the world to crush that roaring lion; hasten to our call for help and snatch from ruination and from the clutches of the noonday devil this human being made in your image and likeness...."*

"Elaine, how many entities do you sense?" Father Haviland asked.

Lainie peered past Father Haviland's shoulder, her face drawing into a concerned frown. "Definitely one. Three more want to join that one, while four others await their orders to follow."

"In Jesus' name, tell us your name," Father Haviland ordered.

"Who wants to know?"

"In the name of the Father, and of the Son and of the Holy Spirit, give us your name," Father Crowley ordered, holding a wooden crucifix before Dorian's face.

"I am Azenrael, a lieutenant to Pruflas, a duke of Hell," the voice replied. Tilting the head, it looked past the priests to Vivien. *"Be fortunate you aren't this whelp's type, bitch, or I would have had this carcass plow you like a boar would a sow."*

Vivien clamped her hands over her ears. "Stop it! Stop it! Be quiet!"

The electric lights above them flickered. "Mrs. Lang, step back; you need to stay safe," Father Haviland said, without taking his eyes from Dorian. Abigail looped her rosary about her wrist and—approaching Vivien—took her by the arm, steering her toward a side-chapel. Vivien hesitated, her eye on her son. Abigail tugged on her, finally getting her to walk toward the Mary altar.

"Hrrrr, bring her back. Her grief, her fear for her whelp." Azenrael purred.

"Then it's good we cut you off from it," Father Crowley said. *"I command you, unclean spirit, whoever you are, along with all your minions now attacking this servant of God, by the mysteries of the incarnation, passion, resurrection, and ascension of our Lord Jesus Christ, by the descent of the Holy Spirit, by the coming of our Lord for judgment, that you tell me by some sign your name, and the day and hour of your departure....*"

The lights overhead flickered more violently. Dorian's body struggled, legs jerking against the man holding them. One arm slipped from Brett's grasp. The lights went out, leaving the light from the candles on the altar and the nearby tables. Crowley laid his hand on Dorian's head, per the Ritual. Dorian's hand whipped up. "*They shall lay their hands upon the sick and all will –* Uffgh, no – *be well with them..*" Crowley's voice faltered. The copper penny tang of blood rose in the air.

"Hold him down," Crowley ordered, his voice huskier.

"I *was* holding him down," Brett said.

"*Weak little boy...*" Azenrael's voice rasped.

The electric lights flickered back on. Crowley stood back from the circle. His shirt front hung open, torn diagonally. Three long gashes angled across the skin of his chest, from his left shoulder across to his right flank, blood oozing from them.

"*I bet you taste of wine, little priest,*" Azenrael purred, trying to lift Dorian's right hand. Brett pulled it back, laying it on the table.

"Get Crowley out of here, he's injured," Father Haviland ordered.

Abigail helped Crowley onto a nearby chair before she opened her medical kit, taking out a gauze pad and pressing it to the wound.

"*So worried for your pet.*" Azenrael sneered.

"In Jesus's name, be silent," Father Haviland ordered.

The voice growled, then went silent. Dorian sagged onto the table.

"Anyone have a cellphone on them?" Lainie asked.

"No," Brett said.

"Not on me," the man holding Dorian's feet added.

"There's a phone in the sacristy," Father Haviland said, heading there.

Dorian opened his eyes, shaking his head as if clearing cobwebs from it. "Ugh... God... oof... what happened?" He looked toward Father Crowley, then toward his left hand. "Oh my God, what happened? Did I do that?"

Father Crowley looked Dorian in the eye, shaking his head. "No! No... you were out."

"I'm sorry. I didn't mean—"

Crowley lifted one hand, waving off these protestations. "You don't have to apologize for something you haven't done."

"But it harmed you."

Crowley smiled, one corner of his mouth quivering, but still reassuring. "That's what they do. They parasitize and attack and try to destroy things for their own sake. They're they ultimate nihilists, trying to tear down everything by any means possible. But it wasn't you that did that."

"Why did it do this?"

"Sheer hatred of everything good and beautiful. Others say that because they cannot create, they destroy instead."

Vivien came forward. "Is it over? We heard a cry."

"No, at the risk of a Hollywood line, I'm afraid it's just starting," Father Haviland said, going to the door to open it for the EMS crew.

"Go on without me," Crowley said. "The pain is something I can offer as a sacrifice."

Dorian's eyes rolled back again. *"Weaving your own martyr's crown, eh? You used to dream as a whelp of bringing your fairytales to the natives of Bongobongo,"* Azenrael rasped. *"If your meatless bones can't feed the cannibals, you'll let us gnaw them, eh?"*

"You created the raw materials for me to put into the Blessed Virgin's hands," Crowley replied. Father Haviland returned, helping Crowley to his feet and out the side door, as the EMS crew arrived.

"Don't bring her into this! She's coming, that little wretch is coming! Get her away! Get her away from him!" Azenrael screamed something, the words undecipherable to the untrained. Dorian's body went slack under the hands of the men holding him down.

* * *

A few Sundays into January, Vivien, with Dorian at her side, went to Mass at St. Michael's. Father Haviland offered the Mass, while Father Crowley assisted, his left arm in a sling.

Afterward, Dorian approached the vestry, peering through the open door, to where Father Haviland helped Father Crowley out of a white robe worn over his black shirt and slacks.

"I'm sorry, I'd better give you some space," Dorian said.

Father Crowley pulled his head from the robe. "Not at all. Come right in. How have you been?"

"My head is my own. I stopped blacking out and no one's seen me do anything weird." He paused, and added, "I just wanted to thank you for what you did, and to apologize again for what happened to you." He eyed the sling which Father Haviland helped Father Crowley pull back on.

Father Crowley adjusted the straps with his right hand. "It's all right. I let myself become vulnerable. I didn't show it, but let fear get the better of me."

"Does it hurt?"

"Only when I try doing something with my left hand, which isn't often."

Dorian reached into his coat pocket and took out his wallet. "I still wish I could do more to make up for it. That had to cost money." He took out what bills he had, totaling about fifty dollars.

Father Crowley waved it off. "No worries, we have health insurance arranged by the diocese."

"But this has to help somehow."

"You could donate it to St. Michael's or to Catholic Charities," Father Haviland offered.

"I just wish I could do more."

"That shows you have a good heart," Father Crowley said. "I pray you find your most satisfying role in life's drama."

"Did you just make a joke?"

"A metaphor, but metaphors are close to jokes, since they both play with words and concepts, in different ways," Father Crowley said.

"Maybe I can make that metaphor a reality," Dorian said. "May I have your blessing?"

"Of course you may," Father Crowley said. Dorian knelt. Father Haviland fetched a holy water sprinkler, blessing Dorian, while Father Crowley offered the prayer.

Dorian crossed himself, glancing around. "Sorry, I was bracing for a black-out, after that thing attached itself to me. Nothing happened?"

"No. And that's a good sign: that you're free," Father Haviland said.

"I guess that means I'm free to go and find my role," Dorian said. Once they exchanged goodbyes, he went on his way.

Crowley glanced down at his chest, touching the bandage pad just visible under his shirt. "Need an aspirin?" Haviland asked.

"No, if anything, it feels all right. But… there's been times when I've felt pain for no reason, not because I lifted my arm wrong, but when I've gotten near a person who isn't exactly willing the good of one of their fellow humans. That's when I feel a twinge."

Haviland raised his eyebrows, nodding. "As if they might have an unpleasant companion that hasn't become parasitic?"

"That's one way to put it."

Haviland looked at Crowley's collar. "As if you had a spiritual Geiger counter strapped to your chest."

* * *

Twelve Years Later

Visiting Vivien for a weekend that October, with permission from his Father Abbot, and Brother Damien (ne Dorian) had gone into the East Manuxet Market Basket, a place he barely recognized, to pick up some groceries for his mother. The company had renovated the shopping plaza from the ground up, completely modernizing it and doing the same to the store. His old self would have gawked at the sushi bar near the fish counter.

"Oh, going to a costume party?" asked the bagger, a blonde girl in her mid-teens.

Brother Damien glanced down at his brown monastic robes. "No, I'm a Franciscan brother, visiting family,"

"Aw, thought you were a mad monk escaped from the house haunt," said the cashier, a college-aged lad.

A cold hand touching Damien's heart. "House haunt?"

"Yeah, it's a fundraiser at the golf course clubhouse over on Stonehedge Street," the cashier said, ringing through the cans of tomato and chicken noodle soup Vivien had asked him to buy.

"Not sure it's smart though. Isn't that place built on top of an Indian burial ground? They say the place is haunted with the ghosts of the people whose resting place got disturbed."

"I heard it's haunted because there was a house there. Back in the 1800s, the daughter of the rich family who lived there went crazy. First they were going to put her in the East Manuxet State Hospital, but the mother was ultra-religious, so they brought in a priest or something to perform an exorcism. But it went wrong, and the family got possessed for real. They trashed the house, then they all killed each other. That's why the town finally tore down the house. I heard they had a haunted house in it and some of the workers got possessed."

"Really? I remember they used to have that house haunt when I was a teenager and in college, but I hadn't heard that," Brother Damien said, innocently.

"Did you ever go through it?" the cashier asked.

"I worked it once, a long time ago. It's different, seeing the haunt from the inside."

The bagger handed the bags of groceries to Brother Damien. "Hope you had fun."

"Try it this year. My sister and her friends in the drama club are playing ghosts in it," the cashier said. "She's been bugging me to tell everyone to go,"

"He's a priest or something. He might not be allowed to go," the bagger said.

"Just because I've taken vows doesn't mean I'm not allowed some harmless fun," Brother Damien said. "I might swing by it for old times' sake."

While driving back to his mother's house, he took a detour down Stonehedge Street, passing the playground and the baseball diamond. The town had taken out one tennis court and set up a skateboard park, clearly constructed with the care and enthusiasm of the high school wood shop class. Across the way, where the old house used for the Stonehedge Street Haunt had stood, a golf driving range had taken its place, the clubhouse decked in fake cobwebs and tatty gray cloth over the doors and boards nailed across the windows, with the name "Haunted Clubhouse" across the signboards.

He contemplated getting out to read the freestanding placard displaying the times and ticket prices. A pang of memory gathered his heart. *You won't become possessed again from a house haunt,* he told himself. For a moment, the memories of that dark time crept back. *That's a door I don't need to reopen.* He turned the car around, heading back to Main Street and back to his mother's house.

Saturnine, Saturnine
Henry Myllylä

The painting strikes me with awe at the spacious, red bricked lobby of the villa. Encased in gilded, ornamental frames, a bewildered man kneels devouring a disfigured torso, his eyes frozen in ecstasy.

Cufflinks on his interviewees black suit reflect the warm spotlights aimed at the painting as he caresses his sharp, hoary beard, "Goya. *Saturn devouring his son.*"

"Stunning," I admire.

"Not original of course, but the finest reproduction I have seen. A gift from a friend."

"Quite an exquisite choice. For a gift." I cannot help myself from seeing my mother's face, if she were receiving such gift. I smile, yet haste to grave my face after realizing he doesn't get it.

"Well, it has a special meaning for the Cultus."

I press the rec-button on my recorder and pull the simplistic, black notebook out of my leatherette purse.

"The cannibalism, the reversion of generative impulse it portrays, is highly sacramental." His eyes go sharp, yet steady across it, following the frames as if invoking the presence they contain. "The painting can be read like a map if you will, as an allegory of a very specific operation."

We enter a library where a metallic chandelier illuminates a vast collection of tomes arranged upon massive, carven bookshelves. At the center, grapevine ornamented pedestals support a marble tabletop that divides apart black, leather coated armchairs.

"Please, make yourself comfortable." Aside, he opens a reservoir of green, non-labeled wine bottles. "Before we start," he pauses for a moment, tilting his head a little towards me. "You're sure about the secrecy?"

"Yes, all identities and localities have, and will be kept anonymous. I guarantee, I'm used to working with... secrets."

"That is good. Just wanted to make sure." He comes to the table and serves a glass of red wine next to my notes. "As you know," he smiles, "We like to keep skeletons in our closets."

"That is certain," I nod and give him a smile. "But why the exception?"

"The truth is that, despite all the miracles of science, my body is finally giving up. I'm afraid, I don't have much time." He gives a glass in his hand a spin, studying the viscosity of the red liquid. "Therefore, as the head of the Cultus, I have decided to take this unusual course."

I nod again, despite his failure to surprise. He's not the first unusual personality who felt the need for confession. The need for social recognition, being accredited for our labor, applies even to the most eccentric of us. And it sure made the best stories. "You mentioned the... operation. In relation to the painting. Can you enlight any of that?"

"Yes." He raises his chin, holding his stature high. "Like all true art, the painting receives its power from its honesty at a humane experience. Even so that it becomes timeless, archetypal. Something that goes beyond generations."

"I can relate to that."

"The painting is sacred in a sense of absolution. Saturn,

the outermost deity of harvest, returns the creation back to its source. His ecstasy is the secret, sacramental unity of all things."

"I see. Somewhat similar to the Christ offering salvation through his flesh and blood upon the eucharist?"

"Yes, the power of blood to restore is universal. But there is a difference. In tradition of the old ways, we seek to partake it *within* the flesh. More than the otherworldliness of the divine, we are rather concerned about the miracles of its immanence. The true sovereignty of it here, in *now*."

I could not help myself from making a notion that he reminded me of those old, perverted Hollywooders who had a good reason for orgies under the guise of satanism or neo-paganism. "If I'm correct, isn't it that Saturn is—at least somehow—often related to the Christian Devil? So... are you a Satanist?"

He smiles, clearly understanding the catch. "Satan is but a mask painted over the face of God. The devils, evil spirits, they are all shapes of the divine trying to address us its totality. We needed Satan so we would not have to look upon... to glorify the filthiness of God."

"That is a rather interesting notion."

"It sets a curious dilemma for those, who are attempting to truly look at it. As if true worship would have been destined to become a witch's sabbath. Reserved for a chosen few, somewhere amidst the dark."

His straightforwardness had made me forget my wine. I raise the glass and notice the exceptional thickness of its content. At the other end of the library a skull and a sickle have been mounted upon the wall, pairing in totemic fashion that has an archaic appeal to it. There is intriguing charisma in his simplicity and taste, I admit. It's a shame that without photographs or any relatable details, the story might feel too far out, since I really had a feeling for the content itself. I taste the wine, that is as strong as its structure. Dry roundness of grapes blend into an herbal vigor and iron staying in the aftertaste. *Definitely as eccentric as he.*

"Please, let me show you something."

We pass through an empty hall—that repeats the clapping of my heels in precise tick-tocks—and enter a tight stairway, that slopes downwards in a dim glare of occasional light bulbs. The bottom is but a black corridor, build so uneven, it feels as if it was still descending. I reach a wall, balancing against its rough surface.

He has vanished.

"Just a second," I lean myself, *God, I feel—* my eyes close for a moment.

The black behind my eyes turns to blackness of the room. I think I'm alone for a second, until I see him in the corner. His pale, naked back phantasmal against the black rough. He's no man. Rather a ravaged sheet swathed about a storm-swept tree. I hear a breath from behind me. Asphyxiated croaking. Suddenly he's closer. Every blink of my eyes makes his ghost change. Still backwards, he's not touching the ground with his feet. *A* goat laughs in crimson somewhere. Then ululating fire. Ululating fire.

II

Rain scourges the wind shield, breaking the lights of the villa into a tentacled spectacle. The surrounding fields and the road across the valley have disappeared into the night as the raging sky licks the roof in a fiery choir. The car starts roaring, headlights burning and red digits blazing inside. It's 02:06. *Eleven hours.* I almost gas into the blurred visual of what lies ahead in the headlights. *I never told anyone.* I release the pedal and let the car stop only a few yards away. I reach underneath the seat, all the way until I grasp a cold handle and pull it out. The black matte finish disguises the cold design in the dark, yet the practice allows me to release the clip even without seeing. The topmost bullet shimmers brazen against the dark. I press the clip back in and the familiar knack after a pull tells me it's ready to work its way, the bullet entering hungry to its place within the system.

Outside, the cold rain flails, drumming its thousandfold march, as I pass through the pawed front and in through the door again. I confront Saturn, devouring, waiting, his eyes lit in his golden cage.

I pass onwards into the library. He stands there, his suit straightened to its perfection, lights of the chandelier firing off from polished tips of his shoes. The skull and sickle rest mounted in their silence. I raise the gun and take a deep breath. Contemplated, I align my eyes, the barrel and his center mass for the ceremony of his undoing before the first release exalts its roar across the walls. His suit twitches. Then his expression. The numb thumb cries aloud as he falls into a half-seated position, coughs once and takes a long, strangled breath. I repeat the procedure and fire again, releasing the second bullet at the height of a controlled inhale. He falls to his back, his eyes falling apart due to trauma and his body twitching for the shock passing through his system. The death could take time even if I hit him hard. His left leg shakes a little, as if to fight back the inevitable and his throat spasms, despite the reason being already gone from his bloodshot, bewildered eyes. I step closer, kneel and listen. The errant, coarse voices calm and fade within a minute, and his blood begins to navigate its way across the gaps in-between the floor tiles, building into a scarlet mosaic throughout the room.

Downstairs, the black corridor shows its paint flaked and peeled, almost cruel in its design of disheartenment at the passage upon his mysteries. I walk through and enter the black room, all the while the rending pulsation of his violent demise still echoing about my arm and shoulder. Dripping of condensated water haunts the interior, splashing sharp and loud in its solitude, until every single rasp of my soles accompanies it acute. Every breath reverberates, going empty about the walls that stand as if alert against everything existing within their vestiges. Then the stills in-between my exhales and inhales begin to quiver. Roar like mighty waves clashing ashore. Almost fulfilled with the tongue of stones, I feel stranded upon a deathbed of existence; this paternal deep.

Then on my left, a shadow beyond black grows about the corner. A clap sounds from afar, as if from outside the chamber. Then another. This time from inside. I turn and a shape of coarse hair, crowned with a pair of horns separates itself from there, the smell of dung oozing thick in the air upon its birth. Darkness turns scarlet about its hoofs, as fiery red dawns, stripping the black bare of its silhouette. Grandeur and feverish, a choir of fires emerge and carry the darkness away with their hearse. Now my other arm begins to tremble too, and a growing fatigue unfolds from the tips of my fingers towards my center as if my bones themselves were suddenly obsessed with their frailty. The fire rises above its head and anchors in-between the horns, engaging their spirals like the sun rising about the rugged mountains at the first of dawns. Then the day breaches upon me blinding, enclosing the darkness upon itself.

On the road, my car *a*waits me, still roaring. I step in and shove the gun underneath the seat. 08:42, the wheel is heavier than ever to turn. I feel I'm being pulled straight down through the seat and my blood fed into the bowels of the earth. Despite the editor's argument, the story will be untold. Luckily I never talk too early and keep my stories to the last. For the cops it's about to be a hell of story if they ever ask.

III

The phone rings on my desk, somewhere under the newspaper clips and scattered sketches of timetables and notes. I haste to shut the door, enclosing the office from the shared space chattery of the lounge area. For a month and a half, I've faced every inquiry, every doorbell and phone call, other than those from my mom, with equal shock. Though over the past couple of weeks I've begun avoiding her too. There's just very little to say to her about me these days.

"Hello?"

"Hi, it's Dr. Bengtman. Just calling to tell you the results."

My heart releases from my throat. "Ah, great. So, what is it?"

"We found pretty much nothing abnormal. So now that everything else is closed off, my earlier conclusions remain. I know it is rare, but it occurs."

"I see, well. Thank you for calling me."

"Remember, if there is anything else I can do for you, just visit and we can talk more about the options."

"There's no need for that, at least now. Thank you."

The chair rams under my weight. *Menopause. At 32?* I shake. The flare of my gun never left my arms. But no police, still. I look outside at the children running in their circles two stories down. The sun is high on them, marching onwards to a midday zenith, still warm despite the autumnal winds. I breath deep, but stall as if hitting a bottleneck about my chest. There it remains, lying in wait. Expectant, ravenous, inching closer at every beat. The great scythe encircling its reap. Saturnine. So saturnine. It seems I ate my children before their time.

Second Glance Girls
J.B. Toner

Like a chime, the dark itself was rippling. It shimmered in the space behind my eyes, zephyred intangibly across my naked skin. It tasted dark.

"*In nomine Dei nostri,*" I whispered. "*Satanas Luciferi excelsi.*"

The floor pressed up against my knees. Pressed up against the statue and the book. What was underneath yearned upward toward the earth.

"*In nomine Dei nostri.*"

A shadow of silence. Here was no cosmos. Only a voice in the void.

"*Satanas Luciferi excelsi.*"

And Him.

"*In nomine Dei nostri, Satanas Luciferi excelsi!*"

And Her, of course. The statue began to tremble. In the deep blackness, a quiet azure luminescence grew. Her blue robe, her white wimple. Her pressed and praying hands.

"In the Name of Satan. Ruler of the Earth. King of the World!"

My secret Bible pulsing in my grip. The twin candles sparked into sourceless flame, and the shades of night sprang back. My body was there, sleek in the dimness, and there was the statue: the image of the one on whom I wove my spell.

"Mary, by your name I summon you. By the Name of Satan I command you. Mary, by your name I summon you. By the Name of Satan I command you."

The dark became four walls around the isle of candlelight. Within that tiny chamber, my will was the world. I focused my soul on her face and conjured her by the power of my Craft.

"Come to me!"

The smell of roses filled the room.

"Daughter." A strong, sweet voice. "Why have you done this?"

Smiling, I rose. A lady in blue stood before me. A radiance was in her face.

"It's lovely that you came," I said. "I suppose you'll say it was to pray for me?"

"Why else would I be here, Elise? You don't truly believe the Fallen One could sway my will and mind."

"Of course not, my lady. But as long as you're here, let's play a game."

"It's the fire of Hell you're playing with."

"Oh, I know. Now tell me: according to Scripture, who is the Lord of the World?"

Her beautiful eyes flicked up to the ceiling, as if seeking aid. "God is the lord of all."

"Is he, now. We both know better. Your own holy book says differently. Who is the Lord of the World?"

Her gaze dropped to the ground. "It is—He. The One below."

"Say it all."

"No, I . . . I . . ." Her eyes squeezed shut. "Satan is—is Lord."

"Again."

Her shoulders moved back and forth as if she were

struggling. "S—Satan is Lord."

"One more time, Mary."

"Satan is Lord," she murmured, and her body relaxed. She nodded, as if remembering, and her eyes opened. She smiled.

"Good. Now, my game. I'm going to put a spell on you. I'm going to count down from three and snap my fingers, and when I do, you'll go into a deep trance. You'll be completely and utterly under my control. You'll remain in that state until I say the words, 'Hallelujah, praise Jesus!' Do you understand?"

"Yes, Elise."

"Three. . . two. . . one."

Snap.

Her eyelids fluttered, and her face went blank.

I reached up, softly, and touched her cheek. "You're awfully pretty." Leaned close and kissed the corner of her mouth. "But not a sexy woman, not at first glance." Turned back her collar and kissed her throat. "Like me. We're second glance girls."

Around her neck was a crucifix. I took it off.

"Let's change that, Mary." I took the Pentagram I wore around my neck and looped it over hers. "Nothing's sexier than Sin." I took her face in my hands and kissed her like a lover. "You want to sin with me, don't you?"

The blankness left her, and a strange new smile arose. "*Yes.*"

Slowly, I untied the blue sash around her waist. Parted the blue folds of her robe. Pressed my palm against her thudding heart, between the virgin breasts. "We're going to spread the Lust of Satan, you and I. We're going to make converts for our new Unholy Church."

To obey me was her only desire, her only destiny. As I spoke, the words became her purpose, reshaping her whole personality. "All these wasted centuries, Mistress. Teach me Satan's Lust."

I took her hand, and a shiver went through her slender frame. "Come with me."

But as I opened the door to my bedroom, I felt another Presence in the house. I paced into the dim-lit room, leading my pet, Queen of Heaven by the hand, and saw a languid form upon the bed.

"Goddess," I whispered, and fell to my knees.

A soft red smile curved her lips. "Oh, Elise. You've done so very well."

Raised Catholic, I began practicing the Craft in secret at the age of ten. I'd seen the Dark Lady in my dreams and visions, but never before in the flesh. Yet here she was: clad in crimson silk, her hair a flood of obsidian shadow, her eyes twin purple pyres. Her body, the Platonic form of Satanic allure.

Until I released her (and Hell froze over), the need to serve me was the innermost core of Mary's being. When she saw me kneel, she instantly knelt as well. The Lady rose from my bed and glided silently across the floor. "Well, well," and her smile grew wider. "My old friend, Mary."

Mary raised her eyes. "Lilith," she murmured. "It's been a long time."

"Since Loudun. What a lovely crop of nuns that was— once so pious, now so loyal to their eternal owner." The Queen of Hell reached down to caress Mary's cheek. "I see you too have changed your loyalties."

"Yes." No hesitation. "Elise is my Mistress now."

"And I am hers," said Lilith. "Is it not so, my dear girl?"

"Yes, Goddess," I said reverently. She was beautiful—so beautiful. The scent of myrrh and pomegranate.

The violet fire in those eyes grew stronger. "Then worship me, woman of Nazareth. Eve was my replacement, and you were hers—but I am the true Left Hand of Omnipotence."

Slowly, as if some part of her was still resisting, Mary prostrated herself. "Hail Lilith," she breathed, and began to kiss those perfect feet.

Lilith turned her gaze to me. "Rise, my daughter."

I got to my feet, glowing with awe.

"A simple binding spell," she marveled. "In all this time, we never thought to try it. We've been weaving massive, complex rituals involving the fates of nations, seeking to break through the barriers with sheer force—and one doe-eyed girl walks up and tries the knob."

I found myself smiling. "Your Ladyship is too kind."

"Because you have brought me this tremendous gift, Elise, I will give you one in turn: a gift reserved for the ultimate practitioners of the Craft. I will bring you with me to present this slave to Our Lord."

Exultation. Dread.

"But first—" a new shade of sin crept into her smile "—we must prepare the offering."

Desire.

"Get up, Mary," Lilith crooned. The lady in blue rose and stood before the Lady in red. "It's time for you to learn of Lust."

Inaudibly: *Yes*.

One finger traced the line of Mary's jaw. Tipped back her chin. Two lips touched her cheek. Her eyelids. Her lips. I saw Mary's body yielding to the kiss, leaning into Lilith's, trembling with passion. I trembled too. The hands of my Goddess pulled open the blue robe and let it fall. They pressed against the pristine shoulder blades, the curve of the innocent back.

Then Lilith tossed Mary across the room like a soap bubble. She landed in the center of my bed with a gasp, and the Dark Lady laughed a sweet and terrible laugh. I found I was laughing too. No longer waiting to be invited, I leapt onto the rumpled covers and pushed Mary's knees apart. Transfigured, rapt, I kissed the pure thighs and felt her shaking fingers in my hair. Heard that special moan, the low moan deep in the throat that only comes in response to one thing. Lilith slithered past me and knelt with her own thighs straddling Mary's face. A moment later, she too began to moan.

My hand encountered the crucifix I keep in my bed for this very purpose. I traced the folds of Mary's sacred temple with the wooden face of her son, not penetrating, but stimulating. As she pleasured my Goddess, her own sounds became higher pitched, frantic whimpers of ecstasy. I heard myself chanting, "*Ave Satanas. Ave Satanas.*"

Then, somehow, we rolled over in the bed and I was on my back. Mary and Lilith were kissing my breasts, kissing my midriff—two tongues flickering in my place of bliss. I screamed His Name when I came, and then I was pleasuring Lilith in turn. The Virgin was fucking me with the crucifix, and the rapture was a beautiful damnation.

"Now," Lilith panted. "Now, Mary. Renounce your old false god. Renounce him forever."

"I do," she cried. "I renounce him!"

"And give yourself to Lord Satan for eternity!"

"I do! I give my body and soul to Lord Satan, now and forever! Hail, Satan!"

I raised my face and sang out: "Hail, Satan!"

And Lilith: "Hail, Satan!"

The room went dark.

I was floating, it seemed. The solid bed was gone; the soft skin, hot on mine, was gone. Gradually, I felt a hard surface under my feet. I was standing—I was dressed. A hard red light grew all around us.

Lilith was back in her gorgeous silken garb, the embodiment of Lust. I found myself dressed in a plain white gown, but with a black clerical collar, like the photographic negative of a priest. And between us, on her hands and knees, was the Blessed Virgin. She still wore blue, but only the garment-wisps of a concubine. Around her neck was a leather collar, and Lilith held the leash. On either side of us, I realized, were grinning Demon hordes.

Lilith began to walk, and Mary to crawl. I kept pace with them, darting my glance from side to side at the leering, foaming jaws and staring yellow eyes. We were proceeding down a long aisle, and the Demons flanked us like parishioners. I looked ahead, and then I saw.

A black stone altar. Two empty thrones. Between them, the Master Throne. And there He sat. He was horrible, and beautiful, and horrible. His eyes were—

The One True Lord, The One True God. He cannot be described, but don't worry. He is with you now as you read this. You'll see Him for yourself.

"At last." His voice was everything, everywhere. It resonated through me, backwards and forwards from that moment, filling my whole life, touching me in the womb, binding me in the hour of my death. "The daughter of the father. The mother of the son. Come to me."

She crawled to the foot of His Throne. "Hail," she whispered. "Hail to Thee, Lord Satan, God of All."

"I heard your renunciation, Nazarene. It pleased Me greatly. Now please Me again."

She rose to her knees and took His rising Godhead in her mouth. The shadow of a smile touched His impossibly divine countenance.

"Queen Lilith," He said. "Won't you join Me?"

She curtseyed with a twinkle in her eye. "As my Lord commands." She took the throne at His left hand. I knew without knowing that the other throne was meant for Mary—had been predestined for her since the Great Beginning. Some mighty turning point in the ancient détente of Hell and heaven was at hand.

Our Omnipotent Master reached down without effort and raised His new slave high in the air. For one last moment, she was the Virgin Mary—then He lowered her, and entered her, and she was His.

"Oh my God! Oh my God, Lord Satan!"

As He filled her everlasting soul with His Everlasting

Power, He turned His gaze to me. "Elise."

I knelt in absolute worship. "My Lord and my God."

"You have struck a key blow in the age-old battle. Rich rewards of power and pleasure will be yours."

"Master, I exist only for You. All that I am is Yours."

"Yes. You will awaken back in your own world. You shall be My herald and prophet. You will speak of what you've seen. Let it be known that the once-virgin Mary will bear a daughter. The Daughter of The Dark. And very soon, she will tread upon the earth."

"Yes, Master."

Like a chime, the dark itself was rippling. It shimmered in the space behind my eyes.

Back in my secret chamber, the white robe no longer on my flesh. I got to my feet and walked slowly into the bedroom. It was the same night, the same hour. To the mortal eye, nothing had changed.

But change is stirring. The universe, the heavens, all creation, will soon feel it, and know His Almighty Power. For She is coming.

Ave Satanas.

Strange Kind of Love
Glen Damien Campbell

Something next to him stirred, prodding Joseph Armstrong in the stomach. He opened his eyes, just a sliver, and through a hazy, letterboxed field of vision, saw a swastika staring him in the face. Jolted by this, Joseph rubbed the crusts of sleep from his eyes and looked again, this time with his eyes wide open.

The swastika remained.

Standing up to scrutiny, the swastika wasn't a hallucinatory vestige of a nightmare, but body art, a tattoo inked over the right scapula of the naked woman sharing his bed.

"This is not good!"

"What 'cha say?" asked the woman with her back to him as she reached over to scratch the crown of her ass crack.

"Nothing," answered Joseph, "go back to sleep."

Her head buried in a pillow, in reply, the woman muttered something. Unable to make out what she had said, and not caring too much, Joseph ignored the woman's semi-conscious mumble and continued to explore the gallery of ink on her back. The swastika had company!

Over her left scapula, opposite the swastika, held by the talons of a spread eagle, she had a tattoo of a black sun, or sun wheel, an emblem Joseph, who had been fascinated by WWII as a teenager, recognized. The Nazis had mosaicked it onto the floor of the SS

Generals' Hall of Wewelsburg Castle. At the nape of her neck there was the blood red cross of the English Defence League, and beneath that, completing her dermal catalogue of fascist iconography, the twin lightning strikes emblem of the SS was tramp-stamped to her lower-back.

"All that's missing is the Disney logo," wisecracked Joseph to himself.

Whoever this woman was, she seemed to be proud of her convictions, regardless of how abhorrent they were. Given this fact, though, the obvious question was why was she in bed with a black man?

Joseph sat up and looked around, hoping he'd be able to piece together the events of last night from the evidence at hand. How had he ended up in bed with a neo-Nazi?

He licked his lips and, along with his companion's briny vaginal fluid, tasted whiskey. The two flavors on his tongue were a tell-tale sign of Astaroth, who had a fondness for cunnilingus and Jack Daniels.

Joseph couldn't see a bottle of Jack anywhere—and from where he was sitting he could see pretty much all of his dingy, disheveled motor lodge room—so that probably meant he had gone to a bar or a pub, which was probably where he had met Eva Braun.

Joseph thought back to last night. After the call he made to Father Joyce, to confirm their appointment for today, the last thing he could remember doing was sitting up in bed, reciting the prayer the sympathetic priest had given him, the 'Prayer against every Evil'.

"Banish all the forces of evil from me, destroy them, vanish them, so that I can be healthy and do good deeds."

After that, from then until this morning, Joseph's mind was a blank.

When he had been on the bed reciting the prayer, Joseph recalled that the midsummer sun hadn't gone down yet. Where was the sun now? Joseph couldn't tell. The black-out curtains drawn across the window weren't giving anything away.

He reached over to the nightstand, picked up his phone, and lit up the screen.

"Shit!" he cursed, reading the time on the display. It was past noon. He was going to be late.

With his phone still in his hand, Joseph got up, teetered unsteadily for a moment owing to a head rush, and then lurched to the en suite bathroom, making a point to close the door firmly behind him.

First, he relieved himself. Dehydrated from alcohol, his urine ran like treacle. Next, he filled the sink with water and washed himself down. Only then, once the taint of sex had been cleaned away, did he feel ready to call Father Joyce to apologize.

"Hello, Father, this is Joseph."

"Joseph, it's good to hear from you," replied the priest in his cordial Irish drawl. "I was just in the process of making preparations for your arrival."

"Thank you, Father. Unfortunately, though, I'm calling to apologize. I'm running a bit late. *It* took possession of me again last night. I've only just now regained control."

"Oh dear, are you alright?"

"I'm fine, a bit of a hangover, but nothing I can't handle. I'm still in Leeds, though. I'm leaving now, but I'll be a couple of hours late."

"That's fine, Joseph, just as long as you get here so we can put an end to your plight."

"Thank you, Father. I'll see you soon."

"By the way, did Astaroth cause any trouble?" asked Father Joyce, speaking quickly, to get the question out before Joseph hung up.

"Nothing out of the ordinary, it seems, just his usual antics; I woke up with a woman in my bed," explained Joseph, stopping himself from adding, 'and the taste of cunt and whiskey in my mouth,' out of deference to the priest.

"A woman?" repeated Father Joyce. "Long dark hair?"

"Yeah," said Joseph.

"Is she okay?"

In his mind's eye, Joseph pictured the woman in his bed. There had been scratches and welts on her back and her buttocks were ruddy, besides these she was fine. Astaroth, a sadistic lover, hadn't gone too far on this occasion.

"She's okay," said Joseph. "Sorry, Father, I've got to go, I've still got a long drive ahead of me, so I better get moving."

"Of course," agreed the priest. "I look forward to seeing you soon, Joseph."

***

When Joseph walked out of the bathroom he found the woman with long dark hair sitting up in bed, smoking a cigarette.

"I've never fucked a nigga before," she announced as soon as she saw him. "Did I tell you that last night?"

"You may have," he said, electing to ignore the racial epithet. "I don't know." Joseph spotted his trousers lying crumpled on the floor beside the bed and went for them. "To be honest with you, I don't remember anything about last night, not even your name."

She laughed. "Well, shit, don't you know just how to make a lady feel special. The name's Becky. Does that ring any bells?"

Joseph shook his head. "No, not really, Becky. Do you remember my name?"

She smiled. "Joe."

"Yeah, that's right, so if you could call me that and not nigga from now on I'd appreciate it, Becky."

"It didn't bother you last night; actually, you seemed to get off on it."

"That was last night."

She scoffed. "What, you're not a pervert during the day?"

Joseph stepped into his trousers and pulled them up.

"Yeah, something like that," he answered, zipping up his fly.

He walked over to the window and pulled back the black-out curtains, flooding the room with eye-searing daylight. He then sat down in the tatty armchair beside the window and, from there, for the first time that morning, really looked at the face of the woman in his bed.

Her eyes were dark, her cheek bones high, her nose prominent, and her complexion pallid. Her figure was tall and athletic. She was exactly Astaroth's type.

***

The midday sun radiated down on Paul 'Jizzer' Blyth mercilessly, making the chrome plating of his Triumph 5T's fuel tank searing hot to the touch. He wiped some sweat from his brow and flicked splatters of it onto the tarmac. Beneath his black leather jacket, he had already sweated through his Burzum T-shirt, leaving the cotton clinging to his torso uncomfortably. Even though he was desperate to take off the jacket, which was absorbing the sun's rays like a photovoltaic, Jizzer kept it on; taking it off would expose the ink on his forearms. His far-right tats would attract attention and arouse suspicion, the two things most likely to get him a 'move it along' visit from the authorities and, if that were to happen, then Jizzer would have done exactly what Lee had told him not to do, he would have fucked up. With another blemish on his club record, Lee would surely not only see to it that his probate time with the club gets extended but also start hazing his ass even harder than he had been.

From off his wristwatch, Jizzer checked the time. 12:42. He had been parked outside the motor lodge for over ten hours now, watching and waiting. After the first five hours he had gotten fed up, but now he was getting worried. What if he had missed them, he wondered? No, don't even think it, he told himself, but the thought lingered.

What if Becky and the nigga had left their room while he was sleeping, while he had taken that ill-disciplined two hour shuteye between 5:00 and 7:00? Surely they wouldn't have left that early, not after a night of drinking and fucking. After a night like that, a few hours' sleep was a must. However, the more Jizzer thought about it the more likely their slipping away while he was asleep began to seem, for wouldn't that just be typical of his luck since becoming a Spears of Destiny Motorcycle Club prospect.

He was still copping shit for screwing up a beer run by picking up a DUI and also, and more seriously, for not keeping Charlie, his sponsor, out of a pub fight, a fight which had gotten Charlie a night in jail and an arraignment.

"You should have decked that guy so Charlie wouldn't have had to," was the ensuing advice given to Jizzer in the days after the incident.

In addition to those errors, just in case there was anyone left at the club who didn't think he was a dud prospect, there was also the episode with the stripper which had earned Jizzer his road name.

This incident occurred one night while he, Lee and two other club members where at a strip club sharing a lap dance. As the topless dancer grinded her bare ass up against him, for some reason, maybe because he hadn't been with a woman in a few months, or maybe because the dancer bore a striking resemblance to his slutty sister, who shared his flat and habitually came home drunk, passing out on the sofa in skimpy dresses that always left her tits hanging out, Jizzer lost control of himself and, like a pubescent boy seeing boobies in the flesh for the first time, jizzed his pants. The wet patch at the crotch of his faded blue jeans was quickly spotted by Lee, who immediately pointed it out to the rest of the guys so the laughing could begin.

In the wake of those blunders, if Becky and the nigga had indeed managed to get away because Jizzer hadn't properly followed through on an order, he would definitely be in the shit, first with Lee and then with the rest of the club, once Lee put the word around. Lee wouldn't share any of the blame, that's for sure, even though he was the one who wanted to play the fucking watch and wait game.

"Why don't we just rush 'em now and take care of that fucking coon?" Jizzer had suggested eagerly last night as he and Lee watched the couple traverse the motor lodge's car park, heading for a room.

In response, Lee smacked Jizzer upside his head, saying, "What are you, fucking stupid?" He then pointed to not one but three surveillance cameras positioned around the complex.

Lee was just coming off a suspended sentence for assault so he had good reason to want to be a little cautious. But, still, was he really just going to sit back and watch his woman slink off to a motor lodge with a nigga.

"I'm going to get a room," Lee announced suddenly, taking out his phone. "You wait here! The moment they come out call me."

"But they could be in there all night!" Jizzer protested.

"So?"

"So why don't we take shifts?"

"Why?" Lee glowered at Jizzer like a despot who had just been told by an underling to go eat his own shit. "Because I'm the patch and you're the prospect, prospect. Don't fuck up."

With that warning, he walked away, his phone pressed to his ear so he could make a call to 'pimp' Marcus to request a tart be sent over.

Ten hours later, everyone apart from Jizzer, it seemed, had gotten themselves a room and a fuck. What's more, while the others had gotten a full night's sleep in a comfortable bed, Jizzer had had to make do with two hours sleeping rough on a patch of grass behind a privet hedge. And wouldn't it just be typical of his time so far with the Spears if those two hours spent lying in the dirt were to also land him in the shit.

But then, just as Jizzer had all but totally accepted that he had fucked up again, something happened. As he stared across the motor lodge's car park, his eyes trained on room No. 23, located on the motor lodge's second floor, Jizzer saw the room's curtains open.

He smiled.

Becky and the nigga *were* still in there and now, at last, they were up and about. He took out his phone and quickly dashed off a text message to Lee:

'They'll be out soon.'

***

"What?" demanded Becky, Joseph's persistent staring at her beginning to make her feel self-conscious.

"You're very beautiful," said Joseph.

Embarrassed, the woman with the fascist tattoos blushed and looked at him in a way that seemed to say, 'Why are you saying that to me *now*, this is the morning *after*, idiot, the need for flattery has passed, don't 'cha know!' That's what her eyes said, but her lips simply said, "Thanks."

"Can I ask you something about last night?"

The woman in the bed rolled her eyes, grimaced and said, "I know what you're gonna say, and, don't worry, I don't really want you to fill me up with brown babies. That was just dirty talk! I was caught up in the moment; I'm on the pill, so relax."

Joseph laughed.

"Well, that is a relief to hear," he said, "but that's not what I was gonna ask you."

"Oh, so what were you gonna say?"

"I need your help. I want you to tell me what happened last night, because I don't remember a thing."

Becky blew a jet of smoke and stubbed her cigarette out on the wall.

"That's quite a hangover" she said; "I didn't think you were all that drunk last night."

"It's not because of a hangover," said Joseph. "I can't remember anything about last night because that wasn't me last night."

Her eyes narrowed on him. She was angry. He had insulted her.

"Well that wasn't me last night either, Joe," she said, scooting over to the edge of the bed, "do you think I make a habit of fucking niggas? I wouldn't have let your filthy monkey paws get anywhere near me if I hadn't been so mad at my fucking boyfriend."

She snatched up her panties and T-shirt from off the floor and began to clothe herself.

"Hey, calm down," said Joseph, "I didn't mean to upset you. I'm just trying to be honest with you. When I say that that wasn't me last night, I mean it, literally. It really wasn't me last night! It's nothing against you. I have a—" He paused so he could choose his words carefully. "I have a psychological disorder."

Becky stopped dressing and looked at him, her eyes challenging him to explain further.

"You ever heard of anyone having a disorder that gives them a split-personality?" asked Joseph.

Instantly, Becky nodded. "Yeah," she said, "I have. I saw a Jim Carrey movie once where he played a character that had something like that. It wasn't very funny. You have that?"

Though not pleased at having his *condition* being thought of as something out of a Jim Carrey farce, Joseph nodded.

"Yeah, I have that, and you're right. It ain't funny!"

"So last night, I had sex with one of your *other* personalities, is that what you're saying?" quizzed Becky.

"Yes."

"And you don't remember anything about it?"

"Not a thing."

She looked at him askance.

"Are you fucking with me?"

"No," said Joseph, "I'm telling you the truth."

"So, you're a schizoid?"

He shook his head. "I'm not schizophrenic."

"Are you on meds?"

Joseph pondered this question for a moment before answering, "Yeah, I am," reasoning that the prayers Father Joyce had prescribed him were a kind of medication.

"Are you dangerous?"

"No!"

As he said it, Joseph felt a twinge of compunction; this was a lie.

With curiosity having now displaced her desire to leave, Becky sat back down on the bed, leaning her back up against the headboard.

"I knew there was something off about you," she said as she lit up another cigarette.

"So, tell me," began Joseph, "what happened last night?"

Becky smiled mischievously.

"Are you sure you want to know," she teased, "because, to be honest, I've had better."

Joseph sneered.

"I'm not asking about that," he explained; "I'm not concerned about how good I am in bed."

"Yeah, I know, you made that obvious last night." She sniggered. "So what do you want to know?"

"Where did we meet?"

"*The Fox*," she said.

"*The Fox*, that's a pub?"

She nodded and blew a wreath of smoke through gathered lips. "Yep, the *Fox & Hound*, it's a pub about half a mile up the road. It's a bit grim, and the wine there sucks, but it's local, and there's not much else around here"

"And how did you and I get together?"

"You came in, saw me, and offered to buy me a drink."

"And you let me?"

She nodded.

"Why?" asked Joseph.

"Because Jizzer was watching," said Becky.

"Who's Jizzer?"

"A friend of my boyfriend, my ex-boyfriend, and as soon as you sat down next to me he went scampering out of the pub, no doubt to run and tell Lee that I was having a drink with a co—" She stopped herself before the slur was uttered, smiled at Joseph apologetically and then resumed, "with a black man."

"So you slept with me to piss off your boyfriend?"

Becky nodded. "Well that's why I let you buy me a drink. I slept with you because..." Her voice trailed off and, as if she was struggling to find the right words to finish her thought, she knitted her brow.

"Because?" prompted Joseph, intrigued; what had attracted her to Astaroth?

"I slept with you because you impressed me."

"Impressed you how?"

She shrugged her shoulders. "I don't know. I guess, you impressed me by the way you didn't seem to give a shit! You walked into a pub full of skinheads, hooligan Leeds United supporters, and bikers, the only black face in there, and strolled around like you owned the place. "

"Listen, I have to go," said Joseph, not wanting to hear any more admiration lavished on Astaroth—Becky had gotten lucky with him, most of the facets of Astaroth's character were not admirable. "I've got an appointment to keep," continued Joseph, "but can I drop you off somewhere?"

"Sure," she jumped up off the bed and stubbed out her cigarette. "Let me take a quick shower and then we can leave. Where're you heading?"

"North up the A1," said Joseph.

"Perfect."

***

Alone in his room at the motor lodge, his hooker having slunk out in the middle of the night, Lee Riley looked down at the message from Jizzer and then called the prospect.

"Where are they?" he asked.

"They're still in the room, but they've pulled the curtains back.

I think they're getting ready to leave."

"Okay, follow them, and make sure Becky doesn't see you. If they split up, stay on the nigga. If they stop anywhere, text me details. You got that?"

"Yeah, I got it. What are you gonna be doing?"

"I'm gonna call the cavalry."

***

"So, where can I take you?" asked Joseph as his road-weary Ford hatchback pulled up at the exit to the motor lodge's car park.

Beside him, in the passenger seat, perusing a tatty paperback she had found on the passenger seat, Rebecca Morton shrugged, not sure how to answer him. She didn't really need a ride anywhere. The place she had been calling home for the past six months, a small two-bedroom flat she shared with a friend who fucked herself with dildoes all day while shooting taboo camgirl films in her bedroom, was only a few minutes' walk from the motor lodge, but she didn't want to go back there, and she also didn't want to be alone, not yet. No, she didn't need a ride. She just wanted a ride—a road trip that would go on and on and on. No end in sight and no looking back.

"I can't go home," she said, "Lee will try to catch up with me there, I'm sure of it. He'd want to lay into me for last night."

Joseph took his eyes off the intersection and looked at her.

"Are you gonna be alright?" he asked.

"Yeah, I'll be alright, he'll cool down and forget about me, eventually." She opened her handbag and went hunting for a cigarette. "Where're you heading?" she asked as she rummaged through the chaotic clutter of her bag; tissues, make-up, tampons, keys, pocket knife.

"I told you, I have to meet someone," answered Joseph.

"Where?" pressed Becky, still rifling through the miscellany of her handbag.

"Newcastle."

"Well, that's convenient, I have a girlfriend in Newcastle," she lied. "I haven't seen her in a coon's age, and it'll be nice to catch up."

Though she couldn't see them, Becky could feel Joseph's eyes narrowing on her—he wasn't buying it. But before he could say anything to challenge her, the driver of the truck that had just pulled up behind them, another overnight visitor fleeing the dubious comforts of the motor lodge, sounded his horn.

"Come on," coerced Becky, "are we getting out of here, or what?"

With an exaggerated sigh, Joseph got the car moving again, turning left out of the car park to drive north.

"Fuck! I'm out of cigarettes," announced Becky, giving up on her handbag. "We need to stop off somewhere and pick some up. And aren't you hungry? I'm starved. Let's stop off at a service station, I'll let you buy me lunch."

***

She had ordered a cheeseburger with fries, and, after the waitress had set the generously proportioned plate of food down in front of Becky, the sight of it—the cheese square melting over the ground beef patty, the herb-seasoned crispy French fries—made Joseph immediately regret not ordering the same as his newly acquired travel companion. Sticking to the diet recommended to him by Father Joyce, which dictated no red meat, Joseph had ordered a smoked salmon bagel with a side of olive oil drizzled couscous. Now, though, as he compared his meal to the one on the other side of the Formica topped table, Joseph felt almost repulsed by his choice.

"You can have some of my fries, if you want," offered Becky, noticing Joseph's covetous glances at her plate.

"I'll just take a few," said Joseph as he proceeded to reach across to her plate and snatch up a handful of fries.

"Thanks," he said, depositing the salty haul onto his plate.

"You know, after a night like last night," began Becky, squeezing tomato sauce onto her fries, "you need a good meal to get your strength back. A good meal is the perfect remedy for a hangover, I reckon. Why didn't you order a burger?"

"Red meat, apparently, is not good for my condition."

"What, your multiple personalities?"

Joseph nodded.

"How does that work," grilled Becky, "is one of your other

personalities a vegetarian, or something?"

"To be honest, I don't know how it works," confessed Joseph, "I'm not even sure it does work, it's just something I've been told."

At this answer, Becky scrunched her face up into an unflattering expression that seemed to insinuate that the concept of doing something just because you've been told to do it was complete anathema to her, making Joseph feel ashamed of his compliant nature. No sooner had this expression appeared than it was gone. Becky's features quickly flattened out, returning to their usual attractive disposition. If Joseph had blinked he might have missed it, and he wished he had.

Becky took a bite from her cheeseburger and, as she chewed on a bolus of sesame seed bun and beef patty, asked, "So how many different personalities are there scampering about inside of you?"

"Besides me, there's just one other."

"Wow. That sounds uncomfortable; I get frustrated with sharing a flat, I can't imagine what it's like to share a body. Have you always been like this?"

"No."

"What happened, you have a nervous breakdown, or something?"

Inadvertently, as he struggled to come up with a suitably misinforming answer to fob off on his inquisitive lunch partner, Joseph began to stare down at the paperback on the table, next to Becky's tempting plate of food, the dog-eared copy of Father Cornelius Joyce's *Demons, Possessions & Exorcisms: The Truth.* Since finding the book on the passenger seat of his car, Becky had become entranced by the book and had already read its first two chapters. In the car, when questioned by Joseph, she defended her interest in the book by telling him that she had always had a fascination for all things occult.

Following his gaze, Becky too began to stare down at the slim, out of print volume and, as she examined its cover, which depicted a young boy with whited-out eyes and a devilish grin, she had an epiphany.

"You don't think you're possessed, do you?" she asked. Her voice was rich with incredulity.

"Does that sound ridiculous?"

Becky ate a French fry as she pondered this question.

"Yeah, it does," she admitted.

If she hadn't before, she'd definitely think he was crazy now, reasoned Joseph as he scrutinized her, looking for tell-tale signs in her body-language that might give away what was going through her mind. This was probably for the best. He didn't need her tagging along with him and really couldn't understand why she wanted to. Maybe he could creep her out enough for her to want them to go their separate ways.

"So what are you telling me, Joe," she was looking at him square in the eyes, "I fucked the Devil last night?"

"Not *the* Devil," said Joseph, deciding to drop the deceptions, the more truth he could give her, the more crazy he'd seem, "just a run-of-the-mill demon."

Sitting back, she smirked. "Well that's disappointing. I've always wanted to sleep with someone famous." She plucked a cigarette from the freshly purchased pack of Camels on the table, but, as she placed the filter between her lips, Joseph tapped the 'No Smoking' sign glued to the window.

"Fuck!" said Becky, pulling the cigarette from her mouth. Irritated, she huffed. "I guess it makes sense," she said, after staring vacantly out the window for a moment.

"What does?" enquired Joseph.

She stared at him fixedly. "You being possessed," she said. "You do seem like a very different person today compared to the person I met last night. Last night you were a bit more," there was a pause as she searched for the right word, "demoniacal." Brandishing the redundant cigarette at him, she added, "And you didn't let smoking bans stop me from lighting up." She returned the now lipstick stained cigarette back to its packet and then, so it wouldn't tempt her anymore, threw the packet into her bag. "Okay, tell me, how did it happen? How did you get possessed, did you play around with an Ouija board, or something, like the little girl in that movie, *The Exorcist*?"

"No, that's not how it happened." Joseph took a sip of Pepsi to wet his lips. "I think I let the demons in when I allowed myself to make a mistake."

"What was the mistake?" pressed Becky.

Nonchalantly, Joseph took a bite of his salmon and cream cheese bagel. It tasted good. Not as good as a greasy cheeseburger with gherkins and mustard, but good enough. He'd buy a burger for dinner, he promised himself. It'll be his way of celebrating being exorcised by Father Joyce.

"What mistake?" demanded Becky, getting peeved at being kept waiting.

Joseph put down his bagel.

"I used to be a teacher," he began.

"Oh god, that is a mistake," quipped Becky.

"You've got that right," he agreed, remembering the endless lesson plans, the brain numbing schemes of work, the tedious teacher meetings, and the pointless fire drills, "but that wasn't the big mistake," he continued. "I slept with a student."

"Oh, gross! You're a pedo?"

"No, not at all; I taught A-level history at a college, she was nineteen. I mean, that's still too young, I was thirty-four at the time, but it wasn't criminally too young. I'm not that sick!"

"Then why was it a mistake? If she was nineteen, I guess she had some idea what she was doing, and what two right-minded adults get up to together is their own business, I reckon."

Joseph looked at her surprised. "For a woman with a swastika tattooed on your back, you sound surprisingly open-minded."

She shrugged, looking slightly embarrassed. "Well, I was young when I got that tattoo, and the others, and I used to be fond of shocking people more than I was of reading *Mein Kampf.* Anyway, get to the point, why was that a mistake and how did it lead to you getting possessed?"

"Sleeping with my student—Lana was her name—was an act of questionable morality. It got me fired from my job and left me bitter, and depressed. It was after that the blackouts started. I think that act somehow opened the door that let Astaroth in."

"Astaroth?" queried Becky.

"That's the name of the demon that possesses me, or at least that's what Father Joyce thinks."

Becky looked down at the paperback on the table. "This Father Joyce," she said, pointing at the copy of *Demons, Possessions & Exorcisms: The Truth.*

Joseph nodded.

"He's who I'm going to see in Newcastle. He's going to perform an exorcism on me. Father Joyce is one of the few Catholic priests who will still perform the ceremony. He tells me that Astaroth is a lust demon. Apparently each demon has a predilection for a particular sin."

"Well, if that's true, I think you did okay; I'd take lust over gluttony any day of the week."

Joseph tittered. "Me too," he agreed.

"So what makes this priest so sure it's this demon, what's-his-name?"

"Astaroth," said Joseph.

"Yeah, Astaroth, how does he know that it's this Astaroth fella that's possessing you?"

"History tells him," said Joseph. "You see, according to Father Joyce, I'm not the first person to be possessed by Astaroth, I'm not even the third, fourth, or fifth. Let's just say he's been around a bit, and apparently the Vatican keeps detailed records on all cases of possession that their priests have encountered over the centuries. So I told Father Joyce my story, that I blackout and then usually wake up in bed with a woman with long black hair, call girls mostly. Anyway, that lit a fuse under him and he started quizzing me about what kind of sexual practices I perform with these women, bondage, sado-masochism; all that weird stuff. Turns outs, the things I do while possessed match up with acts committed in cases of possession where this demon Astaroth had been identified as the culprit."

"BDSM and call girls," cooed Becky, "this guy sounds like a one-man party. Are you sure you want to get this demon out of you? He is kind of fun."

"It's not me though."

"You sure?" she probed. "Maybe it's more you than you care to admit. This student you slept with, Lana, was that her name?"

Joseph nodded.

"What did she look like, long black hair?"

Reluctantly, after a moment, Joseph admitted, "Yeah."

"We all have a dark side, Joe," she concluded.

"What about you?"

"What about me?"

"How did you become mixed up with fascists?"

She shrugged. "I told you, I like to shock."

***

They stayed on at the eatery long after their meals had been consumed. Over coffees, Joseph went into more detail about what compelled him to abandon his ethics and allow himself to be seduced by his precocious, alluring student, Lana Hutton. He even talked a little about his family. He was the product of an interracial marriage, a mother of Caribbean descent and an Irish father. He had a brother and a sister and was the overlooked middle child.

Becky, in turn, gave Joseph a few tidbits about her life growing up on a bleak council estate, with a strung-out mother and a mostly absent father. How she had been turned on to Nazi paraphernalia by shock rock artists like Rozz Williams and Siouxsie Sioux, and by Lemmy's quote, "From the beginning of time, bad guys have always had the best uniforms." However, what started off as a way to scandalize her parents and look Nazi-chic quickly led to her mingling with people who took it all a lot more seriously than she did.

Although their conversation was such that they probably could have carried on talking until closing time, Joseph, remembering he had an appointment to keep, brought the dialogue to a close.

He paid their bill and they got back on the road.

***

"Someone's knocking at the door..." sang the Liverpudlian accented voice on the car radio.

Becky was trying to ignore the catchy rock song, an old hit from the seventies, and get through another chapter of *Demons, Possessions & Exorcisms: The Truth* when she heard Joseph exclaim, "This can't be happening!"

Expecting to see rows of gridlocked cars through the windshield in front of her, Becky looked up from her paperback. "What can't be happening?" she asked, seeing that the traffic ahead of them was running smooth.

"I'm out of gas," said Joseph.

The line was such a cliché, delivered with such hackneyed gravitas, it made Becky giggle.

"You can't expect me to believe that," she said, "we just left a service station. Why didn't you fill up? What are you after, some nookie on the hard shoulder?" She placed a hand on his left thigh and teasingly stroked her way up to the bulge of his crotch. "I suppose I can accommodate you."

"This isn't a ruse to get into your knickers, Becky." As if it was an insect crawling on him, Joseph swatted her hand away. "I'm really out of gas! And I didn't fill up back at the service station because I didn't need to. I checked. The tank was practically full. I checked. I'm sure I did. I'm sure I did." The more he spoke, the more Joseph began to sound less certain about what he was saying, until finally, with a sigh of resignation, he admitted, "Who knows, maybe I didn't."

"Do you have enough fuel to get to the next service station?"

As if the car wanted to answer for Joseph, it began to splutter.

"I don't think there's even enough to get to the next exit and get off the motorway," said Joseph. "I better pull over. We can walk back to the service station and buy a jerrycan of petrol."

Muttering an expletive under his breath, Joseph steered the car onto the hard shoulder.

The doors of the hatchback had only just slammed shut when a motorhome with a State of Texas car charm dangling from its rear view mirror pulled up behind it.

For a moment, a fear stirred in Becky, putting a tingle in her spine as she let herself think that there was something too expedient about the arrival of this roadside assistance. But any apprehensions that were brewing in her quickly dispelled when a cheery feminine face with shoulder length mousy blonde hair, topped by a raffia straw cowboy hat, poked out of the RV's driver's seat window.

"Howdy, you folk need a hand?"

She spoke with an American accent that was dripping with Southern geniality.

"Out of gas," said Joseph.

"Is that all?" said the American. "Well, you're in luck. We can get you back truckin' in no time. I've got a couple of cans of fuel in the back; can fill you up with enough to get you to the next station.”

Joseph smiled.

“That’ll be great, thank you,” he said.

“Hey, honey, my pleasure. Go round the side, my husband will give it to you.”

The driver of the motorhome was perky and cute. She had a wide, bright, unbelievably immaculate American smile. Becky particularly liked the woman’s tank top, which placed the slogan ‘I Love Big Racks,’ capped by deer antlers, across her breasts.

“Hunters,” thought Becky non-judgmentally.

Abandoning her position at the driver’s seat, the pretty American in the straw Stetson gave Becky a friendly wave before disappearing into the back of the vehicle to help her husband procure the fuel can for Joseph.

Staying with the hatchback, Becky watched as Joseph ambled up the side of the motorhome. She saw him tap on the vehicle’s door, and, when it opened, saw him exchange a few words with an unseen occupant, and then enter the motorhome.

She waited for about five minutes for him to re-emerge. After that, feeling that she was missing out on some Southern hospitality, she too approached the vehicle.

“Hey, babe.”

When the door to the motorhome opened in response to her two knocks, the last person she expected to see inside the vehicle was Lee.

Grabbing her by her hair, a familiar move, he pulled her in and threw her down onto the floor. She landed next to Joseph’s unconscious body and noted blood coming from a wound on his head.

“Let’s go!” said Lee.

The inside of the vehicle was unpleasantly crowded. Four figures where gathered around her. Three she recognized, Lee, Jizzer, and the motorhome’s duplicitous Stetson wearing driver. The fourth figure was a bearded man in a sleeveless flannel shirt. Miss America’s aforementioned husband, Becky guessed, although he was clearly considerably older than her.

“You don’t betray your race, little lady,” said the bearded man.

“Fuck you!”

Her response was answered with a smack across the face,

which, although painful, could have hurt Becky a lot more if the bearded man had really wanted it to.

"Let's get going, Ma."

"Okay, Big Daddy."

Ma, Miss America, went back to the driver's seat and got the motorhome moving. As they sped up the motorway, Becky, acclimatizing herself to her new surroundings, noticed the tube and jerrycan that Jizzer or Lee must have used to siphon the petrol from Joseph's car.

***

"Wake up, boy!"

Consciousness returning, Joseph became aware of the sensation of a steady flow of water striking his right cheek, its impact causing splashes to pepper his nose, and rivulets to run into his mouth and off his chin.

"Wake up, boy!" said the voice again.

Joseph's eyelids fluttered and then opened.

Trying to focus his eyes made his head throb painfully, but Joseph persisted and, ultimately, accomplished the unrewarding feat of seeing the man standing over him who, fly unzipped, penis pinched between thumb and forefinger, was directing a jet of urine onto Joseph's face.

Realizing the degradation he was being subjected to, Joseph tried to move out of the way of the pungent stream of amber fluid only to discover that he couldn't. His hands were tied behind his back, fixing him to the wooden pillar he had been placed up against. His movement restricted, Joseph was left with no choice but to submit to the deluge of piss for as long as his captor's bladder could sustain it.

"If you stuck with your own, this wouldn't be happening, boy." The man pointing his pecker at Joseph was middle-aged, had an unkempt salt and pepper beard, and spoke with an American accent. He was wearing blue jeans, an army dog tag, and a sleeveless flannel shirt that showed off his burly arms that were covered in tattoos. Also, he was not alone. Behind him, standing before vast rows of dry curing cannabis, and making practice swings with a splitting axe, Joseph saw the driver of the motorhome, who was now wearing a Confederate flag bikini top and Daisy Dukes.

The stream of urine turned into a trickle and then, after a quick hip wiggle, stopped.

"If we were back home, in the old U.S. of A, I'd have given you a sporting chance." The bearded American slipped his penis back into his pants and zipped up the fly. "I'd have played the Most Dangerous Game with you, set you free in the wilderness and then go and hunt you down like a buck. Can't have fun like that in this tiny country, though. You'd just have to run fifty yards before you'd come to a motorway and flag down a car. And plus, to go hunting here I'd have to dress up like one of those red-coated fags, wouldn't I? Put on a petticoat, or a frock, or whatever those nancy things are called."

To conclude that this man, who had just been gleefully pissing on him, was Becky's scorned boyfriend would have been logical, but this conclusion just didn't seem right to Joseph. The visual impression he had been left with from Becky's few words about her boyfriend, Lee, simply didn't match the figure now before him.

"Are you Lee?" asked Joseph, wanting the facile assurance of knowing that he was being victimized by the right person.

"Not me, boy," said the man looking down at him. "Lee's in the house putting his little lady back in her place. That streak of piss is leaving me and Ma to do his dirty work, but we don't mind none, do we, Ma?"

"No we don't, Big Daddy," the woman in the bikini top chimed in. "It's been a while since we had ourselves a nigga in our mitts."

"What d'ya wanna do with him, Ma?"

Ma slinked up to Big Daddy's side.

"Well, since that race traitor, Becky, likes black dick so much, why don't we cut his off and give it to her."

"That's a good idea, Ma," said Big Daddy, puckering up to plant a kiss on Ma's equally puckered lips. "You're so creative."

***

The three of them were in the living room watching television.

Notwithstanding the room's outlandish décor, which included taxidermy, a gun rack, and bales of marijuana, the deportment of its occupants could easily have been that of a happy family of couch-potatoes, Jizzer on the armchair smoking a joint, Lee and Becky looking cozy on the sofa. This reading of the scene, though, would be wrong.

Lee's right arm draped over Becky's shoulders, a seeming gesture of affection, was, in reality, a gesture calculated to remind the troublemaker that she belonged to him, and that she wasn't to stray from him again.

The TV filled the room with the sound of a car engine purring. The motor vehicle review show *Top Gear* was on. One of his favorite shows, Lee never liked to miss an episode. He was particularly fond of the politically incorrect quips made by the show's beer-bellied, curly haired host. These chauvinistic witticisms were even enough to make Lee forgive said host's disparaging remarks about motorcycles.

Currently, a fulsome review of the Porsche Carrera GT had both Lee and Jizzer captivated, allowing Becky's furtive glances towards the window, where a gap in the curtains allowed her a partial view of Big Daddy and Ma's corrugated iron shed, to go unnoticed. She knew Joseph was in there with the two Americans, what they were doing to him, though, was a mystery. With every sly glance over at the window, she kept hoping she'd see her companion emerge from the shed. So far, each glance had only returned dashed hopes.

They were going to kill him! Becky was certain of it.

If it had just been Lee and Jizzer who had caught up with them nothing more than a thrashing would have been meted out to Joseph. Lee, with a suspended sentence hanging over him, wouldn't want to be too reckless, and Jizzer, well, he was just a lost boy trying to find himself in the wrong place; he'd go along with whatever Lee directed. These two Americans, though, they were the wildcards in the pack. Becky could remember now a few occasions, nights out in the pub with other members of the Spears of Destiny, when Lee had mentioned how 'crazy' the Americans were. On these occasions, she had assumed he was talking about Americans in general and not two in particular. But Big Daddy and Ma were crazy, Becky could tell, and when they hoisted

Joseph's unconscious body from their motorhome and dragged him across the gravel to their shed like he was already dead, she got chills, feeling that she would never see him again.

Then again, why did she even care? Let them kill the confused nigga! Why not? She wasn't in love with him, or anything, was she?

For the umpteenth time since entering the living-room, Becky glanced over to the gun rack on the wall holding a Winchester rifle and again wondered, "Is it loaded?" Lee and Jizzer seemed totally oblivious to its presence, but perhaps this was because they had been guests at this remote country cottage so many times that the gun on the wall had become just another piece of brash décor, its primary function forgotten. Mounted on the wall, above the TV, the weapon was tantalizingly close.

***

"You like white women, boy?"

With the form of a field goal kicker, Big Daddy swung the tip of his right foot into Joseph's groin, causing a current of pain to surge through the former history teacher's body.

"Yee-haw, you teach him, Big Daddy!" whooped Ma, who, wielding her axe like a pom-pom, was cheerleading from the sideline, her jubilant voice an inharmonious counterpoint to Joseph's cry of agony. Then, as the initial jolt of pain lessened, the victim's cry turned to a sob.

"Please, don't!" he whimpered.

"You gonna be putting your filthy jungle paws on any more of our women?" asked Big Daddy.

Joseph shook his head.

"No."

He had never felt fear like this before. Tears were streaming down his cheeks. He was embarrassed to think about what he might look like, and ashamed that he couldn't suffer through this unjustified beating at the hands of these bigots with a show of righteous dignity, even if such an act still led to his murder, if he was to die either way, wasn't it better to die like that? An inability to defend himself, to stand by his behavior regardless of how inappropriate other people deemed it, hadn't that always been his problem though? The confrontation with the Head of Faculty, for instance, when he was challenged with sleeping with a student, hadn't he just surrendered? Yes, it was unethical. Yes, his conduct had been lecherous. Yes, with tears streaming down his cheeks like they were now, he deserved to be fired. In an encounter that lasted no more than fifteen minutes, he had lost his job and his self-respect. Now, finding himself in a situation where the stakes were greater, could he really be expected to act differently?

Though they shared the same body, Joseph was a very different person now compared to the confident black man that, only last night, had walked into a pub full of racists and walked out again with a woman on his arm.

"Let 'em in," sang a voice in Joseph's head.

As Big Daddy got ready to score another field goal, a surge of confidence suddenly ran through Joseph and with it, somehow, came the strength to break free of his binds.

***

"What do you think they're doing to him?" asked Jizzer, festoons of marijuana smoke issuing from his mouth. There was a hint of unease in the timbre of his voice. Becky supposed that the horrific scream which had moments ago emanated from the shed outside had slightly frayed the young prospect's nerves. Maybe he was feeling some sympathy for the *Untermensch*.

"He's getting taught a lesson," said Lee, eyes still fixed on the TV screen. "Blacks and whites don't mix."

"They're not gonna…" Not wanting to speak the unspeakable, Jizzer's voice trailed off. "Are they?"

Lee looked at Jizzer sharply. "Do you care?"

It took him longer to reply than it should have, but, realizing he was hesitating, showing weakness, Jizzer promptly answered, "Of course not."

"Good."

Lee turned back to the TV. *Top Gear* was coming to an end.

"Shame," said Becky, deciding that, if she was going to try to do something to help Joseph before it was too late, his screams coming from the shed needed to be taken as a call to action.

"What's a shame?" asked Lee.

"If those Americans kill the black fella," she answered, "it'll be as shame; he was good in the sack. And his cock was so big, Lee. You know, I think he's totally ruined me for you. I mean, if you put your little pecker in me now I doubt I'd even feel it."

Savagely, brutally, Lee took hold of Becky by her hair and clothes and tossed her from the sofa onto the floor.

Not foreseeing that he was playing into her hands, and that his unruly girlfriend had used his predictability against him, Lee was slow to follow-up with another assault. A mistake Becky had been counting on. As soon as she hit the floor, she scrambled to her feet and ran for the gun rack. By the time Lee realized what she was running towards it was too late, Becky had the Winchester pointing at his chest.

"What are you gonna do with that?" he asked, taking a cautious step forward.

"I'm gonna shoot you if you come any closer, that's what I'm gonna do with it, Lee."

"It's not loaded, Becky."

He said it with confidence, but Becky knew him well enough to know he was bluffing. He didn't know if the gun was loaded or not any more than she did.

"Are you sure about that, Lee?" she challenged, "because the only way I'm gonna know for sure is if I pull the trigger, and what's gonna make me do that is you taking another step forward."

He laughed; the snobbish laugh of a man who knows he has just been bested by someone of supposedly inferior ability than him.

"I hope they've lynched that nigga," he said, backing away from Becky.

She felt a compulsion to pull the trigger at those words, but managed to restrain herself, realizing that, if the gun was indeed unloaded, with it then being two against one, she would have forfeited her upper hand. Instead, keeping the rifle aimed at Lee, she began to move towards the front door.

"Just in case there's still some doubt in your mind about this, Lee," said Becky, now standing at the four-paneled door, "this is us breaking up."

Feeling good about making an exit with such empowering

final words, Becky swung open the front door and then gasped as a figure standing at the threshold startled her, a figure splattered with blood and carrying a bloody axe.

"Joseph!" said Becky, composing herself. It looked like him, but something about the demeanor of the man before her persuaded Becky that this wasn't the same person who had ordered a salmon bagel with couscous earlier in the day.

"Astaroth," said Becky, correcting herself.

The man in front of her smirked. The same smirk she had seen when he had sat down next to her in the *Fox & Hound* and offered to buy her a drink.

"Take these!" He dangled a set of keys in front of her. "Get in," he said, pointing towards the motorhome in the driveway. "I'll be there in a sec."

She took the keys and began to make her way towards the motorhome, leaving 'Joseph' to take care of her biker pals.

She hadn't even stepped off the front porch before hearing the screaming start.

***

A body stirred next to Joseph. He opened his eyes, saw a swastika tattoo and smiled, recalling the pretty face of its owner.

"You awake?" he asked.

"Mm," answered Becky, non-committedly.

"Don't get up."

He kissed the back of her left shoulder and then reached for his phone on the nightstand. The time was 12:22 PM and he had missed eight calls from Father Joyce.

Sitting up in the cramped but comfortable bed of Big Daddy and Ma's motorhome, Joseph began to type a message to the sympathetic man of the cloth. It would be rude to leave him in the dark.

Apologies, Father, for missing our appointment yesterday. I was unavoidably detained. I wish to thank you for agreeing to help me with my condition. I have, however, decided that I will not be requiring your services after all. I've realized that having some devilry in me is not the worst thing in the world.

Cerebral Activity
Nathan Blake

D octor Dillon Quarterman chased death down white sterile corridors. With each step his shoes squeaked, making him wince, only grateful that he didn't do night shifts anymore—each squeak could have woken an entire ward. He would buy some new ones tomorrow, but there was no guarantee they wouldn't squeak either. In fifteen years of walking up and down hospital floors, he hadn't worked out which shoes would squeak and why. When he broached the subject with his colleagues they had rarely even noticed the problem, let alone cared.

He entered the oncology ward, sanitizing his hands at the entrance, inhaling sharply as the alcogel burned into an unseen papercut. He found the patient's notes at the nurse's station and located the right bed from the board: C2. He walked to bay C, steeling himself for the coming conversation: it never got any easier. Walking past bay D he noticed a junior doctor telling a nurse to run some fluids into a patient, apparently with low blood pressure and obviously with shortness of breath. He paused a moment, observing the patient's swollen legs. She was fluid overloaded, the same fluid that filled her lungs and made her breathing difficult, her legs so swollen, they looked fit to burst. And this junior doctor was giving her more? She wasn't his patient; this wasn't his specialty—he should just move on. He took a few steps further then turned back to them. The nurse had moved slowly and was still hanging the bag of fluids, perhaps reluctant to follow the instructions of a confident idiot.

"If you want to give her fluids just raise her legs," Dillon said to the doctor but smiled to the puffy patient by way of introduction who smiled weakly back, "but the real question is why you want to give a fluid over-loaded patient more fluid."

"Well I, er…"

"That's what I thought. I assume you have done the obvious things if you're grasping at giving her a fluid bolus. But we might need to consider inotropic support. Go bleep the med-reg and ask the question. I'll look after your patient while you do that."

The junior doctor skulked away. The nurse, behind the patient, failed to suppress his amusement but at least didn't laugh out loud.

"Just can't get the help nowadays, eh?" said Dillon to the patient, adjusting the nasal cannula on her face to deliver oxygen up her nose rather than her cheek, then added, "Listen, I don't really know your case, I was just passing, but here's an important question that they may not have asked you: do you want to live?"

Dillon asked because he suspected no one else had—difficult questions were avoided by junior doctors. The patient obviously had a number of co-morbidities—cancer and heart failure at least, but that was enough to deal with. If she was going to survive, she needed to want to live—really want it, not just say so for the sake of social norms—fight to the last breath and all that—said by people who have no idea what it was like to drown in your own fluids. Euthanasia was now an option, and though it had been passed into law over a year ago, even some palliative care doctors were reluctant to discuss the option with their patients.

"Yes," the patient said at last, "I want to see… great grandkid born."

"How long?"

"Two months."

Without knowing her medical history Dillon had no idea how realistic it was. But he knew that if the patient wanted it, it was worth fighting for.

"OK. We'll do everything our end—but you've got to fight for it too. Every breath if need be. Cling on."

The patient nodded. Her eyes were tired, but there was steel in them. Dillon suspected she would live to see her great-grandchild.

Dillon left when the junior doctor returned. The medical registrar was on her way to assess the patient and the nurse had found a bed on the high-dependency unit just in case. He proceeded on to bay C.

***

"Mr. Ash?" Dillon asked, looking at the chart. "First name Ashley?"

"That's right," said Mr. Ash, a withered old man who lay shrouded in the folds of hospital sheets, his eyes retreating into sunken sockets. But the eyes themselves; sparkling onyx. His head was completely bald, eyebrows and even eyelashes harvested by impotent chemotherapy, his skin so thin that it seemed his skull was fit to burst out.

"Ashley Ash?" Dillon repeated.

"You find that amusing?"

"No, not at all," Dillon lied, "just wanted to make sure it wasn't a typo."

"You'd be the first," the old man snorted past his nasal

cannula, the plastic noose wrapped around his face and neck, connected to a wall tap above the bed. "You are here to tell me whether I can die."

Terminal patients were often candid, it was part of the appeal of working with them, and usually made such discussions that bit easier.

Dillon gestured to the chair beside the bed, "May I?"

"Please," said Mr. Ash, wriggling himself up his bed. Dillon was surprised he could lift any weight at all such was the feeble emaciation of his body, but soon he was sitting up.

"Well, you're eligible for euthanasia, your doctors have made that much clear to you I understand, but your request is… somewhat unusual."

"I want my death to mean something, to contribute to the great body of scientific knowledge. When I heard about your trial I was quite sure I wanted to participate."

Dillon pretended to read something in the notes but was instead remembering Dr Hansje's words: "His body says one thing, his words another…" Dillon had dismissed it as a fancy, a projection of one person onto another, but now he understood. Mr. Ash; metastatic lung and bone cancer of unknown primary origin. Required constant oxygen therapy to maintain saturations at tolerable limits, and yet was able to enunciate quite precisely in complete sentences.

IIc regarded Mr. Ash carefully. There was a twinkle in his eye that belied his death wish. Death was dull, Mr. Ash was sharp.

"So, am I eligible, as you say?" asked Mr. Ash.

Dillon retrieved the consent form from the notes. "First I just need to make sure you fully understand the nature of the trial."

"Of course. You are interested in death. So am I."

"There's a little more to it than that. Mostly it's the same as the usual euthanasia pathway already explained to you, the only difference is that it will be done in an MRI machine so that we can see what your brain is doing as it dies. You're familiar with MRI scans?"

"Of course. You don't get to my age without having every scan known to medicine. Sounds exquisite, doctor. A shame I will not be able to see the results, but as long as someone does I'll die happy."

"I'm obligated to tell you that end-of-life research has a bad reputation, associated with a decrease in quality of life in the last weeks: more needles, tests, interventions."

Mr. Ash turned to look out of the window. Several stories up, the ward looked over a graveyard. "I think it rather cruel that they give us this view, a constant reminder of our fate, as if we needed one. Decreasing my quality of life you might say. Please, just tell me where to sign."

A scar twisted on the back of the old man's head, writhing like a serpent under his withered skin as he turned back.

"What's that scar on your head?"

"Oh, this thing. From the war. They had to remove shrapnel from my skull. It had penetrated the bone, but somehow didn't penetrate the brain."

"You had surgery to remove it? It's not in your medical history."

"Of course. It was so long ago, I forget about it."

Dillon sucked in air through his teeth. He looked down to the eligibility criteria. Near the bottom: no neurosurgery. Dillon had added that himself, had overseen all the eligibility criteria. This one was included to ensure that the imaged brain structures all followed the usual pattern, undisturbed by the neurosurgeon's scalpel which could alter the location of important landmarks. But Mr. Ash had not had his brain operated upon. It was unlikely they had disturbed any structures. Still, technically it was neurosurgery, the criteria were unambiguous.

"I'm sorry, Mr. Ash, you're not eligible for the trial."

"Ah, but that is a shame. Are you sure, doctor?"

Dillon explained the intricacies of the eligibility, made his apologies and made to leave.

"Doctor," Mr. Ash said as Dillon left, "you want to know what it is like to be this close to death, no?"

Dillon took a step closer and waited for Mr. Ash's words.

"I used to enjoy walking in the hills—I found them the best of gardens. I would see a hill in the distance and strove to conquer it. No matter how steep, how tired I was, it was a joy. Then there would be some sense of an ending. But it was soon forgotten—there was always a valley on the other side. And after that, another hill. This feels the same. I can feel it my bones, like only a walker can."

***

Dillon shuffled back through the sterile corridors of the newer hospital wing before entering block H, an old wing of the hospital where pristine white walls gave way to faded brick facades. The smell of the pathology lab always stung for a few seconds, an amalgamation of chemicals and a hint of rotten meat. On high shelves, glass jars of a jaundiced liquid were filled with livers, hearts, brains, other desiccated things.

Past the lab was the palliative care research office; the only space in the hospital free at the time that the trial was set up.

Becka looked up from a computer screen, where shades of black and white formed a slice of brain, and asked, "Get us a new recruit?"

"No. Not eligible. Damn shame really. I think we would have got interesting data from him."

"Oh?" she replied, focusing on a small brain segment on screen.

"He's a different..." —Dillon cast around for the appropriate word, but he didn't know what set Mr. Ash apart other than his enthusiasm for the trial—"…demographic. How's the data from the last patient?"

"Nothing new. The same synchronization in the anterior cingulate before moving down the—"

The phone interrupted her, and she promptly answered. "Palliative research office. One second," she held the phone out. "Your daughter."

Dillon sighed, "I'll just be a moment."

"Hey you. Yeah, I know. Listen, I can't really talk about this now. I'll be back about—" he checked his watch, "—seven. We'll talk about it then, over dinner, OK?"

"How is she?" asked Becka as he hung up.

"Final exams looming, so a bit stressed. You remember how it is."

"Too well. Talking of exams, Ed passed his. We're going out on Friday—coming?"

"I can't really."

"Come on. You've got to enjoy yourself sometimes. I'll buy you your favorite drink?"

"Really, I can't. Maybe next time."

***

The office was quiet and dark. Becka had left some time ago. Though she would never admit it, she didn't want to see Luke. Their marriage had ended amicably enough, unable to withstand the death of their daughter. Friends and family had nothing but sympathy for them—even Luke's church was silent on the subject of their divorce. The only problem with their arrangement was that Luke was still the statistician for the trial, meaning Dillon often ended up as a go between for the two. Luke had popped in at some point to talk through an analysis he had done of the last MRI scan. He talked in rows and columns of numbers, always hinting at some pattern in the data, but never revealing anything tangible. It had still been light outside then. Now only the pallid yellow lights of the streetlamp bled into the room. Dillon was about to turn the light on, still determined to see if there was anything new in the data.

"Shit." Dinner with Annabelle. He simultaneously checked his watch, put on his jacket, tried to call Annabelle and made for his car. Maybe he could get home by nine.

***

She was sleeping on the couch, an old photo album lying open on the coffee table next to the Oxford Handbook of Clinical Medicine. She didn't stir when he had blustered into the living room. She must really need the sleep. He covered her with a blanket, kissed her forehead. He was pleased to see her sleep; after all her studying it was the best thing she could do for the exam tomorrow. He picked up the photo album. The red leather book of plastic pages seemed a relic from another era, before smartphones, when Sarah was still alive. It was her who insisted on still printing out family photos and putting them in a physical album. He flicked through the pages, smiling at their silly 80s hair: how had anyone thought that was a good look? But they had looked damned good at the time: certainly Sarah had.

He took the album into his bedroom and sat before a bedside shrine. A framed picture of Sarah, resplendent in her youth, surrounded by various photos: from their wedding, Annabelle's christening, a holiday in Bali. These in turn were enshrined by catholic paraphernalia; a crucifix, a picture of Mary the Mother, several candles—which he lit. None of the stuff was his—it was all Sarah's. But he had made them his own, finding their presence oddly reassuring. Sarah was still real, everything he remembered had actually happened. He had heard once that husbands and wives could forget what a lost one looked like. He couldn't imagine it.

Not that the gradual decay of synapses was beyond his ken: being a palliative care consultant meant he saw the ravishes of dementia only too often, saw loved ones wiped out from life even before they were physically gone. No, he couldn't imagine it because the horror of it caused his mind to reel. It was another death. A mental death embedded within a physical death, like the embedded corpses of Russian Matryoshka dolls. He looked through the photo album, remembering her face, kicking well-trodden memories back into life, even some happy ones. But they all took the same path in his mind, joining to the one abiding memory.

***

"Dilly, did you get the milk?"
"Ah, I forgot."
"Well?"
"Well what?"
"Are you going to go and get it?"
"I've just done a twelve-hour shift. Let me sit down for a bit."
"Don't forget. I've got to leave early tomorrow so I won't have time to get any." Sarah had to have her cereal every morning, she couldn't function like a human being without it. Hangry they called it, though Dillon called Sarah the grumpus mumpus at such times.
He had fallen asleep on the couch. When he had woken up, Sarah was gone, though it took a little searching to find out. The bedroom was empty, the car had gone. It was late. Sarah had obviously gone to get the milk. There would be hell to pay for that when she got back. The mumpus on steroids. But she never came back. Instead the police had knocked on his door.
"Mr. Quarterman? There's been an accident…"

The only thing he really remembered from that night was seeing her on the hospital trolley. So pale, even her lips were white. Her lips were never like that, it couldn't be her, maybe some doppelgänger, there were stories like that in the newspapers occasionally, mistaken identity. He kept expecting someone to come in and explain the mix-up. He would pretend to angry with them, but really he would be thankful. But it was her. The rest was a blur.

The photos around the altar swam in a sea of tears that silently fell.

"I…" he began, but faltered. He had tried to talk to her many times, but it didn't work. A photo, a gravestone, they weren't her. If there were just some way to know she was really listening, to send her a message—just a single word would be enough.

***

"Ah, Dr. Quarterman, I'm so pleased to see you," said Mr. Ash as Dillon entered the MRI room. "I wanted to ask. What changed your mind about my eligibility?"

"It wasn't relevant to you," said Dillon, leaving it at that and hoping Mr. Ash wouldn't ask any more questions.

Dillon looked around to check that no one had heard. The radiographer gave no indication she was listening, or even cared. It was a small forgery, ignoring an aspect of patient history which Dillon knew wouldn't be relevant: his brain structure wasn't altered by the simple surgery. But it was simpler if no one else knew. If the auditors caught it he would say it was an honest mistake. At worse they would tell him not to use that particular data.

Dr. Hansje entered the room, bringing in a small blue tray containing the cocktail of medicines that would end Mr. Ash's life. He looked around, nodded a greeting.

"You don't have any family with you Mr. Ash?" asked

Dillon.

"No, doctor. I've outlived the people in my life. Promise me one thing, doctor."

"What's that?"

"That you'll look me in the eye when it happens."

"It doesn't work like that. We'll be in the next room watching. The medications will be injected automatically."

"Oh, but now. Is it too much to ask for a little human contact as I die? Surely Dr. Quarterman, you can join me for my final moment?"

Dillon looked to Dr. Hansje who said, "Well, I have no problem with it. How is it with your protocol?"

Dillon wondered for a moment: there was nothing explicitly against it. It was just a bit... odd.

"Well as long as the radiographer doesn't mind."

The radiographer did mind, but didn't say as much; it was another checklist to go through, making sure there was no metal on his person, another thing that could go wrong that she could be blamed for, but still she agreed. Doctors always got their way; no point resisting the inevitable.

***

Dillon's fingers were poised on the syringe. He looked into Mr. Ash's black eyes, pupils so large they consumed his irises, wide enough to fall into. The wrinkles around his eyes creased with a smile. Dillon blinked away a feeling of falling into a deep hole, returning his mind to the clinical tasks at hand.

"See you on the other side, doctor," Mr. Ash said. His last words.

Dillon plunged the syringe, injecting coma inducing sodium thiopental into his blood stream. He held Mr. Ash's gaze, expecting to see a haze descend as the eyes lost focus. But they pierced into him until, finally, the eyelids fell: a stone shutting upon a dim tomb.

Unsure for a moment Dillon checked several reflexes. None triggered: the anesthetic had worked.

"Is everything OK?" Dr. Hansje asked through a speaker in the room.

"Just checking the dose was sufficient. All good."

The MRI table whirred into action sliding Mr. Ash into its maw, consuming his head and upper body, leaving his hands out, allowing Dillon to administer the next medication: pancuronium.

The MRI compatible cardiac monitor showed Mr. Ash's heart slow. Not quite deceased, but soon. Dillon rushed into the control room before the image acquisition started. Once in, the MRI thumped into life, repeatedly imaging Mr. Ash's dying brain.

Dr Hansje left when Mr. Ash's heart beat no more, satisfied that a peaceful death could be recorded, leaving Dillon with the radiographer.

"Did you see that?" Dillon said, glued to the monitor.

"What?"

"In the amygdala. There was some signal."

"Maybe artefact."

"Maybe," but he didn't think so. Dillon scratched at his stubble, the grey-white slices of brain on the monitor reflected in his black of his eyes.

***

"Jesus, Dillon. Did you sleep here again last night?"

Dillon roused himself from a row of chairs aligned into something resembling a bed.

"Yeah," he stifled a yawn, "lost track of time."

"How's the data then?" asked Becka.

The data! His body jerked up like a knee flexing to a hammer.

"Look at this," he said jumping to the computer.

He didn't say anything, but studied Becka's face while she took in images, flipping through the slices. He smiled as she frowned.

"Is this for real? It's so different to what we've seen before. And what is that?"

She was pointing to a BOLD signal, where cerebral blood flow was measured by the difference in oxygenated and deoxygenated blood. In the dying brain the signal had always been useless as all of it was lacking in oxygen. But by flipping through several MRI slices fast enough a pattern emerged. And not some abstraction of data, a row of numbers that Luke would say meant this or that, but an actual branching spiral you could see. Arabesque, Dillon thought, though he didn't quite dare say it.

"I sent the data to Luke—he should've had a chance to look through by now. I'll go see what he can make of it," he said instead.

***

He walked up the statisticians' office door, studied the picture there—a glorious mountain view bathed in a resplendent sun, with the words below: *In God We Trust. All Others Must Bring Data.* He knocked and entered. A few faces looked up, but only Luke's remained up, a smile breaking out from under a ginger beard.

"Did you have a look?" Dillon asked as he hopped onto an empty chair and scooched up. A picture of Hannah on a park slide beamed out beside a computer screen—taken before they tried chemotherapy and she had lost her hair and then lost her life.

"Yeah, I had a quick look. Don't get your hopes up."

"You see it though?" The statistician had a window open on his screen, the spiral now so clear to Dillon he couldn't unsee it.

"It's an Archimedean spiral. It's how the MRI machine samples the k-space."

Dillon knew that k-space was how the raw data was acquired: something to do with the frequency domain and Fourier transforms. But when he had tried to read up on it his brain had been twisted by double integrals and imaginary numbers.

"So, it's not signal?"

"It's artefact. Gotta be, gotta be. It's almost too clear to be a true signal. Look, I'll reanalyze the data using a more standard grid method. Shouldn't take too long. I'll let you know when it's done."

***

Dillon retreated back to his office and sat looking at the same data, flicking his pen on the desk around a finger like a rabid see-saw. *Tik-tik-tik-tik.* It wasn't just an artefact of the scan—sure that was common enough—but this felt different. He snorted at himself; a man of science and reason reduced to gut feelings. He took off his glasses, rubbed the bridge of his nose. He was too close to this, just let Luke look at it.

He checked his watch: 11:34. Anna would be entering the exam hall soon. He sent her a text: **Luck is for the ill-prepared. You've got this.**

He would get her something. A congratulations present. He could nip into town, do a bit of browsing on his lunch break, get Becka to cover him in case he took a little longer. He left the office, a conveyer belt of items running through his mind. He shook his head—why could he only think of kids' toys: teddy bears and make-up boxes. Some jewelry would be better, but what did she like? What about a car?

His heart fluttered at the thought. It wasn't like he was going to spend his money on anything else—so why not? A Mercedes perhaps. She deserved it. Was there a car dealership nearby?

***

His legs had taken him into a lift as wheels turned in his mind. It always took an age to get to the ground floor as it stopped at every floor, with elderly patients ambling in and out, fighting against doors that closed too quickly for them, someone else dashing to make the lift, forcing the doors back open.

"Come this way if you want to see more…" the voice was distant but familiar. Dillon looked up just as the doors closed on the seventh floor and he jumped.

It was Mr. Ash, smiling. Their eyes locked. All black. The doors closed.

Dillon squeezed past the occupants of the lift, brushing past a woman holding onto a drip stand as if her life depended on it.

"Easy," she said. Dillon mumbled an apology while pressing the button for the doors to open. For a moment nothing happened, and he imagined himself getting off at the next floor, running back up… but the doors opened, and he burst out, looking both ways.

A bald head turned a corner, disappeared. He ran after it, heads turning to follow him: a running doctor always drew attention. He turned the corner and clattered into somebody. Things fell to the floor, but his attention remained on Mr. Ash's bald head. He was now climbing onto a windowsill. His head started to turn as if to look back, but stopped. He jumped from the window instead. Dillon shouted as he ran. He reached the window, slammed his head into the pane as he tried to look out. His head recoiled but not as much as his mind. The window still vibrated from the impact. Closed? He fumbled it open, looked down at the access road below. Nothing. He looked from the other windows. All closed along the corridor. A small crowd had gathered, but none were concerned about the window, about the man who had just jumped. It was him they were looking at with a mix of suspicion and concern. A string of curses came from the corner; the woman he had collided into. A pool of milk spread over the floor. The hostess was trying to contain the spread with a dishcloth, putting the cartons back on her tray. Dillon helped, apologizing profusely, continuously looking out of the window and scanning the thinning crowd for some kind of reaction related to the jump.

He spent his lunch at the back of the cafeteria by himself, trying to re-anchor himself in the world by watching patients and hospital workers going about their business. It worked. Eventually he could spoon peas into his mouth without losing a few. No one else had seen a thing. Apparently he had imagined the whole thing.

His pager went off. He didn't recognize the number and when he dialed it he was surprised to find Luke on the end of the line—he never paged. He downed his coffee as he listened to Luke, "You're gonna want to see this."

***

"Check this out," Luke said as Dillon took a seat. "Normally we only use the magnitude portion of the signal, right?" Dillon nodded without understanding, he found it best to let Luke run off when he was in a talkative mood, it was easier than getting him to explain. "But if we include the phase…"

Dillon's chair clattered to the floor. A thin face stared out from the MRI image, embedded in the familiar folds of the brain. It was like looking at clouds and making faces from the drifting tendrils. Pareidolia: the human tendency to see faces in inanimate objects. But he couldn't shake the feeling of being watched. Two eyes there, a nose. And its mouth—was it smiling?

"Yeah, that's what I thought. There's something else too. fMRI is basically a time series, right? You know what else is time series data?"

"Just tell me, Luke," Dillon said, rubbing the bridge of his nose.

"Sound data. Before I moved into medical stats I used to use time series to analyze audio data—wouldn't have even thought of it otherwise. But it really looks like audio data."

"And?"

"The computer is still converting the data. You know there's a load of it in MRIs. But I'm sure we're going to find something. I think we've found it," Luke said, slapping Dillon on the shoulder. "I think we've really found it."

"Found what?"

"The voice of God. Maybe Saint Peter, welcoming this guy to heaven. It's gotta be, gotta be…"

He would have dismissed it but for Luke's enthusiasm. And what he had seen… Mr. Ash. Maybe he had seen a ghost: wasn't that what he was hoping for? He sat there, eyes glued on the screen as Luke clicked away, knee bouncing like a seizing alcoholic.

"Good work, Luke. Listen, I've just got to go check something, but I'll be back later."

***

Dillon had never actually been to the morgue. He knew it was in the basement but beyond that he needed to ask a porter for directions. One was kind enough, and free enough, to take him there. The basement corridors were lined with old medical equipment: broken trolleys, outdated imaging equipment, boxes full of paperwork. Patients never came down here; rarely did anyone except the porters, ferrying the dead to the coroners. They came into a basement room lined with refrigerated units for the cadavers.

He took up a ledger at a desk, found the entry he was looking for: Ashley Ash - A2. He slid open the refrigerator door and rolled out the trolley. He unzipped a body bag of flimsy white plastic and let out a long sigh. Mr. Ash. Well, at least he hadn't seen a zombie. He read the wrist band, just to solidify his grasp on reality. *Ashley Ash*. Strange—his date of birth—it was the same as Sarah's. Not just the day and month, but the very year. A clerical error; the universe playing one of its sick jokes. Dillon unzipped the bag further, found the corresponding band on the ankle. Same name, different date of birth. But one that made him ridiculously young. With a gasp, Dillon recognized it as the date that Sarah had died. The mottled skin of the leg, purple and pale, started to shift under his eyes, slowly forming words from tortured veins: *Dilly, Help Me.*

Dillon froze for a moment then jerked away and clattered into the trolley.

"You OK, man?" asked the porter, hanging around by the desk.

"Come here," Dillon frantically waved the porter closer. "Is there anything there?"

"Where?" the porter said, frowning as he looked at the body.

There was nothing. The words had vanished, leaving only varicose veins.

"Can you check the wrist bands—the date of birth?" Dillon closed his eyes.

"Thirty, four, forty-five."

"Both?"

"Yeah. You messed up the dates, man? Don't sweat it. Everybody messes up everything and it's all OK, y'know?"

He was clearly losing it. Visual hallucinations. Go home, get some rest. If he was still seeing things tomorrow he would go see a neurologist, rule out organic causes before exploring psychiatric causes. For now it could simply be stress.

"Com'n man. This place is no good for you. Getya-self a drink, eh?"

Dillon was glad the porter was there to lead him out, to guide him back up the lift to the land of the living. He went straight to his car and drove home. Slowly.

"You don't believe me do you…" a patient once said to him, during his training rotation in A&E. She had claimed that Hitler had raped her. There was no evidence of rape, of course no evidence Hitler had returned, but plenty of evidence of psychiatric distress.

"It's real. I know Hitler should be dead, but I saw him, don't you understand?"

Dillon had said he understood. It was real for her. But only now did he really understand. It was so terribly real.

He got home, took a gulp of whiskey, the burn reassuring, and headed straight for bed. He didn't dare look at Sarah's shrine.

***

"What the hell happened to you yesterday?" asked Becka as Dillon walked into the office, her face screwed up in concern.

"I was feeling quite unwell so I went straight home. Sorry, I should have let you know. You didn't get bogged down did you?"

"Are you OK?"

"I'm fine. Are you OK?"

"The auditors came 'round. Apparently Mr. Ash didn't fulfill inclusion criteria. I didn't know what to say. We broke protocol. You should have been here, you know I hate that woman. She's like a pit bull; just forget to dot an i and she's off. Can you imagine her with something like this?"

"You're more than capable of dealing with a bureaucrat. What did she say?"

"We can't use Mr. Ash's data, we'll have to take him off the trial, delete the data. Just when we were getting somewhere—Luke was really excited about it."

"It's OK, Becka. I'll give them the data. It's fine…"

The phone rang and Becka snatched it up.

"Palliative Research Office. What?" her eyes widened, nostrils flared. "No. Yes, yes of course. I…"

She hung up, her mouth opened and closed a few times, silent words on her lips.

"What is it?"

"Luke. He's dead. Jumped out of a window."

"What? I'm going there." Dillon left, too quickly to see Becka crack, to even ask her the question, afraid if he slowed for even a moment he would never again be able to move at all. Luke held the key to another world: he couldn't die.

***

Dillon knocked on Luke's office door and entered. Only one person was there, who looked up slowly, freeing one ear from headphones while maintaining the balance of a crisp packet upon his bulging stomach.

"I just heard." Dillon said.

"Heard?"

"Luke…"

"Oh yeah, right," he straightened up, put the crisps on the desk.

"Where did he…?"

"Don't know. One of the corridor windows. Still sealed off."

"Do we know any details?" But Dillon didn't need to ask.

He knew exactly which window on the seventh floor Luke had jumped from.

"Nah." The fat statistician didn't seem aware of much beyond his screen.

"Listen, I've got the auditors in and I need some data from Luke's computer… you don't mind do you?"

"Knock yourself out." His headphones went back on.

Dillon took himself to Luke's computer. The data was on an external hard drive, which he would need to return to the auditors. He woke up the computer to eject the drive. Some statistical programme was open to a stream of computer code, all of which sluiced from Dillon's uncomprehending eyes. But buried in the code was written:

If it is burned up, the builder will suffer loss but yet will be saved—even though only as one escaping through the flames.

An audio player was also open on the computer. Luke's audio data—his last act of work. Dillon clicked play.

Static. Rustle and beat, like the regular thumping of a drum muffled in a wind, or a distal heartbeat caught on ultrasound. He turned up the volume, leaning into the screen as if that might help him hear. There was a voice underneath it all, getting closer.

"Help me. Help me. Help me." Then a deafening scream. He scrambled backwards, nearly keeling over his chair.

"Are you OK?" asked the fat statistician, one headphone cocked off an ear.

Dillon stared back at the screen, the waveforms dying away. "Yeah. Yeah, just something made me jump."

"Yeah, I saw that."

He inserted his own pen drive into the computer, transferred all Mr. Ash's data across, including the audio file and ejected the hard-drive.

He didn't dare listen to it again, not here. But it was Sarah's voice he had heard. He stood up and shakily made his way out.

***

"And this is all the data?" asked the auditor, taking the external hard-drive from Dillon.

"Yes, that's everything. I don't see why we can't just add an exception to the file, there's good grounds to include the…"

"You can submit an amendment to ethics if you want. Until such a time I will hold the data."

Becka wasn't wrong, the woman was tenacious. Dillon didn't argue with her though; too dazed, too thin. He thought about punching her prim mouth, how it might help him feel a little bit better; quickly pushed it away. Besides, he still had the data on his pen drive. But he had stopped thinking about it as data. It was a message from Sarah—evidence he wasn't seeing and hearing things. Was it really her? While there was even the slightest possibility, he couldn't let go. Luke must have heard it too. What else had he heard?

When the auditor finally left, Dillon plugged in the pen drive and retrieved Luke's audio file: the poor man's final work. Suicide they said. A clear-cut case, if surprising. He didn't seem the type though. Too Christian. Only then did he think about Becka and how she might be coping. She had left early—understandable. He thought of phoning her, but the file transfer pinged ready. He was about to click play when his pager went off. He sighed, clicked play anyway: he needed to hear her voice, to know it was real. Static: fetid rain upon a casket. His pager went off again. He knew the number—a surgical ward. It would be an oncology patient with inadequate analgesia, or perhaps requesting euthanasia. The static still cackled—he was sure the voice had not been this far into the recording before. He listened a while longer. His pager went off again. This time he answered it, speaking on the phone to a nurse concerned that one of her patients was being under-treated for pain. With a glance over his shoulder he wrenched himself away from the audio, made his way to ward D7.

***

The ward smelled of shit and disinfectant. Dillon flicked through the patient's notes as a blustering nurse explained the situation. Two weeks ago, Mrs. Moore had had major abdominal surgery for pancreatic cancer. But for the last four days she had been deteriorating, drifting in and out of consciousness all day. She had contracted C-Diff, probably from antibiotic overuse, and now constantly shat herself in a sewer of infective diarrhea. The nurse explained in more detail than was necessary that even when cleaning up the patient, shit would ooze out of her in a steady stream and the nurse would have to call it quits at some point and just let the nappies do their job, shit still oozing, until a few hours later, when time allowed, another wash would be needed to get the yellow-brown lumpy liquid out of her bed sores, some of which were big enough to fit in a fist. In Mrs. Moore's lucid moments, thankfully few, she would only cry out in pain. But this the surgeons knew; this was not the problem. The nurse was concerned that the patient was still for active resuscitation: if her heart stopped, every effort would be made to restart it.

"I don't think I can do it," the nurse said. "She asked me, *why won't you let me die?* If she goes off tonight—I don't know if I could do CPR..."

"She said that? Why hasn't the surgical team discussed this with her?"

"They didn't want to make the decision until it's been discussed with the family, didn't think Mrs. Moore was competent enough by herself. They're coming over from

France, should arrive tomorrow. But if she goes off tonight…"

A familiar story. Dillon was tempted to sign off the Do Not Attempt Resuscitation order without even seeing the patient, get back to the data, back to Sarah, as quickly as possible. But that might seem too keen.

He entered side room 2 and almost gagged at the smell. It even assaulted his eyes, making them water. Breathing through his mouth, slowly adapting to the stench, he studied the sleeping patient. He understood the nurse's concern: Mrs. Moore looked ready for death. She was still receiving hydration, a drip feeding into an arm that was more bone than flesh, and Dillon saw from the drug chart, still receiving total parenteral nutrition that keep her fed via her thready veins. Dillon nearly stormed out then, a flare of anger at the surgeons who had allowed their patient to exist in this state. There would be a surgeon on call—perhaps not from Mrs. Moore's team, but close enough for a tongue lashing. This was abysmal end-of-life care. But as he swiveled, a sound held him still. He turned back round.

The patient's mouth was frozen open in a mask of pain. A muted cry crawled from her mouth: "Help… me…"

Her lips did not move, nor did her dried and cracking tongue. The voice seemed not to be emanating in her throat but from below it, as if from a subterranean world of bile and spleen. He leaned closer, his ear to her open mouth, the smell of death overwhelming even that of infected feces. The voice, "Help… me…" was Sarah's.

Compassion took flight, forgotten as the well of his own suffering bubbled over. He lifted the patient's gown, imagining the source of the voice to be within. Below her protruding ribs, her scarred stomach sank into a pit, rising again at angular hip bones. Below the pit of skin something stirred in her abdomen. For a horrified moment it seemed that a thousand cockroaches were burrowing their way to the surface, but they soon coalesced into something more coherent. A nose, eyes, a mouth; their contours stretching out from the paper-thin skin, pushing up from the stomach. The mouth opened and closed, screaming a whisper: "Help...me..."

"Sarah?"

"Dilly..."

The face continued to take form, bulging from her abdomen, but Dillon already recognized the button nose, narrow eyes. He looked about the spartan room, seeing a scalpel in amongst the contents of a basket next to a suction kit by the bed, usually reserved for emergency equipment. He didn't question its presence there, but felt its Aristotelian call to action. A knife exists to cut...

Careful, should he cut Sarah's emerging face, Dillon cut into the abdomen. The skin split with sickening ease, he could have ripped it with his fingers like soggy paper, allowing him to go deeper. He lay a hand on Sarah's head that now protruded inches. A shriek welled up and drowned everything. No, he hadn't cut Sarah. It took him a few seconds to remember that Mrs. Moore existed and recognize the scream as hers.

The nurse entered the room, confusion written upon her face as she tried to fathom the sequence of events that led to this impromptu surgery.

"Doctor, I..."

"Help me," Dillon said, and the nurse approached. "We need to get her out."

But the nurse soon ran away, returned moments later with colleagues. Dillon couldn't understand why they tried to restrain him, why they didn't try to help Sarah. At some point in the struggle, security was called and professional hands forced him to the floor with a knee in his back. He struggled against them, screaming for Sarah, until a sting in his arm sunk him into a dark well. He was aware of hands flipping him upon his back, saw a room full of bustling bodies, as he sunk further, until he saw as if at the bottom of a receding well. There was not a light at its top, but a grinning, skeletal face, jaundiced eyes with black irises. The memory was but a sinew and was lost to the same ravages that decay dreams into oblivion.

***

"You were heard saying *Sarah* several times. Your deceased wife, correct?" asked the psychiatrist sitting across from Dillon in the little white room, legs crossed at the ankles, mirroring Dillon in order to build a rapport.

"Sarah, yes. But she needs me, she's… somewhere. Trapped." He wished they didn't know; it would have been easier to lie. He knew what was real, what wasn't. But they wouldn't accept that. But since they did know, perhaps he could use them.

"You realize what you're saying? Your wife died. Do you believe she is still alive?"

"No, of course not," Dillon said, but he wasn't sure what he believed. Was she alive? Or was it worse than that. "Listen. This isn't some hocus-pocus. I'm running a trial on dying patients…"

"Ah yes," the psychiatrist flicked through some notes. "'Brain activity during the death process: an fMRI study'. Interesting. The purpose was to identify the last areas of cerebral activity during death in order to facilitate a better understanding of the process."

"That's it. If you just look at the data…"

"We were in contact with the research office. Apparently you were in possession of some illicit data?"

They didn't believe him. Post-traumatic stress disorder would be the most likely diagnosis they would explore, linked to the traumatic death of a spouse. But why the delayed onset they would ask. What was the trigger?

"But did you look at the data? There's an audio file…"

"You know I can't look at data obtained in an unethical manner…"

"It wasn't unethical!" Dillon punched the armrest. Violent outbursts would only encourage them to pursue a psychiatric explanation. "If you just listen to that audio recording you'll realize that there is something there."

"Your wife?"

Dillon said nothing. *Skin stretched taut to ripping, a mouth pleading for help.*

"You were speaking a lot with Luke Wright, the statistician, before he died?" The psychiatrist asked.

"You can't possibly think that had anything to do with me."

"Of course not. But he did commit suicide in… sudden circumstances. And now this with you. Surely you can see why we're concerned."

Dillon nodded. What had Luke heard before he died? The plea for help on the audio, unsettling as it was, wouldn't drive a person that far that quickly. What else had he heard? Or seen?

"Look, the suddenness of this episode is a little startling," said the psychiatrist. "Would you consent to a CT head to rule out any organic causes for this?"

"Yes," Dillon replied. It was the first sensible thing the psychiatrist had said. The sooner they realize there is nothing wrong with him, the sooner they will have to believe him. Then he can get back to helping Sarah.

The CT head scan was done much quicker than the MRIs Dillon had been involved with and he was back in the psychiatric room is no time. The benefit of being treated where you worked was that procedures weren't held up in the usual bureaucracy. The downside was that the people you worked with knew your business.

The psychiatrist entered the clinical room with a little entourage: a conspicuously large mental health nurse, with

Becka and Annabelle in tow, concern etched in lines upon their faces.

"How'd your exam go?" Dillon asked his daughter, all other thoughts gone for the moment.

She looked down. "It doesn't matter."

"What's wrong?" Dillon persisted. Annabelle exchanged a glance with the psychiatrist who nodded.

"I failed the practical."

Dillon stared at his daughter. Her hair was curled. It was supposed to be straight. Like Sarah's. It occurred to him that it had been curled for some time, but though his eyes had seen, it only just registered now.

"Everyone fails at least once," Becka broke the silence, giving Annabelle a little squeeze. "I had to sit my ENT exam three times

"Dr Quarterman," interrupted the psychiatrist. "We need to discuss the results of the CT scan and I'm afraid it isn't good news."

"You found something?"

"A tumor. The cerebellum. Glioneuronal, we think. We've referred you to the neurosurgeons, they should be here to see…"

"No," Dillon stood up, "I feel fine. What about Sarah? Someone's got to help her."

Tears were falling from Annabelle's eyes. "Please, dad. Let them help you."

"It's real, Anna. You mother needs us." Dillon lashed out, meaning to take Annabelle by the shoulder but the nurse took a step forward, filled the room with his bulk. Annabelle ducked into Becka's shoulder, sobbing, as they backed out of the room. Another nurse came in armed with a syringe.

"Do what you want to me, but we've got to help Sarah. Just listen to the audio. Just listen to it. Please."

He found himself wrestling with the nurse, his flailing limbs held in a vice of flesh.

"No! No!" He tried to get them off him. "Just listen to it.

Please. You'll hear…"

This time Dillon didn't feel the needle tear his flesh, just the onset of haze and shadow, until only sound was left.

"…hold him under a section 2…"

***

Click-hiss. His throat was fire and ice, the first thing that filled his returning consciousness—a hardness that bulged into his mouth, clawed down his throat and wriggled its way into his lungs. *Click-hiss.* He moved an arm to remove whatever assailed him, but his arm would not move. He realized that his breathing was not his own. Air was pushed into his lungs, which then recoiled to expel the forced breath. *Click-hiss.* Frantically he tried to move; anything, everything. But nothing obeyed. Even his eyelids were an iron curtain that could not be lifted. Memory came like a morning fog, slow and heavy. *Click-hiss.*

Neurosurgery. Dillon knew exactly what was happening: intra-operative awareness.

Suddenly he knew the sound, and dread filled him. The click of an oxylog respirator as it reset its cycle, preparing for his next mechanical breath. The hiss as it released its thrust and air passed through a valve.

"Bag him for a moment," said a voice, vaguely familiar, but it was the weight of the words that took his attention. They meant a bag valve mask—a manual form of respiration where someone literally pumps air into the lungs by squeezing a rugby ball shaped bag with their hands.

He felt pulling and tugging at the tube in his throat as they detached the oxylog. His chest fell and did not rise again. Dillon knew that his carbon dioxide levels would be rising and his oxygen levels dropping. He tried to suck in air. His body did not respond. What was taking them so long? Indistinct chatter floated past him: he knew the kind, everyday small talk of the weather and the weekend smattered with the task at hand. He strained his ears for any sign that they were going to hook him up to the bag-valve-mask, but they didn't seem to care. He tried to tell himself that the panic that was rising in his chest was just the carbon dioxide levels, known correlates of various stress hormones. His heart was hammering. The word 'tachycardic' pricked his ears.

At last he felt the endotracheal tube being tugged, followed by a gust of dry air filling his famished lungs. But before the breath could escape, another gust was forced in, and another. His chest was fit to burst, but he could do nothing to breathe out. He was entirely at the hands of whoever held the bag: perhaps a scrub nurse, maybe the anesthetist, likely an incompetent student. The breaths came irregularly: different lengths, different forces, varying gaps.

He had to let them know he was conscious, even though he knew the futility of it. He focused on opening his eyes. They were not just heavy; it was as though another will kept them shut. He railed against this will, trying to wrest back control of his own eyes and in an instance the resistance fell. His eyes snapped open and a world of light cut into his eyes. Slowly they adjusted to the overhead lights until a masked face swam into view. The eyes! Liquid black and smiling—he knew those dark eyes. As if reading his thoughts, Mr. Ash pulled down his surgical mask and flashed his teeth in a skeletal smile.

More tugging at his endotracheal tube and the oxylog machine was again given command of his breath, his chest rising and falling to mechanical rhythms.

"Shall we begin the Whipple's procedure?"

Whipple's? Dillon cast his mind back to medical school, trying to remember the nature of the procedure. Abdominal surgery, yes. For pancreatic cancer. About half the pancreas would be cut out, along with a bit of intestine and the gall bladder; maybe a bit of stomach—he couldn't quite remember. It was a major operation; at least seven hours.

Wrong surgery! Wrong surgery! Tears were running down his face: he could not close them now, even though he wanted to, could not blink or even move his eyes. At the bottom of his vision he saw the electric scalpel.

An incision was made in his abdomen, a searing heat tearing his flesh asunder. A smell like burnt pork slowly filled the room as more flesh was burnt apart. Dillon felt his subcutaneous tissues melt under the blade as it sterilized and cauterized ever deeper into his body, until the peritoneum was punctured: the gateway to his abdominal organs.

Though he could not see it directly, Dillon could all too well picture the bright yellow adipose tissues around his intestine, crisscrossed with veins and arteries and raw nerves.

Interminable time passed as the surgeon, Mr. Ash, hacked into his body, scraping connective tissues aside. Neurosurgery was painless, the brain itself containing no sensory nerves. Abdominal surgery was anything but. Surgical clamps bit around arteries and bile ducts. He watched as first his gall bladder was removed, then some intestine, half his pancreas, part of his stomach. Mr. Ash lifted each excised organ high so that Dillon could clearly see each organ as it was removed. Dillon wished he would pass out, but the visceral pain would not allow him. Eventually came the stitches, uncountable bites into his remaining organs, stitching them together into a perversion of their original state. And finally, a staple gun shot into his skin, clamping together the last vestiges of his flayed skin.

***

Click-hiss.
The pain wasn't gone, but it was distant. A rumbling of thunder that promised the sear of lightning. He tried to

breathe out, but an iron will forced air into him instead, his chest a battleground in which his will was massacred. His eyes were open, but they saw nothing but a white haze that was perhaps a ceiling.

A face came into view, floated before it came into focus briefly before swimming away. Annabelle.

She was speaking. To him. To someone else. He couldn't tell. Someone else was there, another blurred face in the white void.

Bleeps and whirrs. Machines. They were familiar. But where? Intensive care. Yes.

"There's really nothing more we can do."

Sobs. Indistinct voices.

"…the machine… let him go…"

Annabelle leaned over, clicked a switch. The hiss died. The silence of gentle sobbing. He waited for the next breath. But it would never come. The tides of his life ebbed away in the minutes it took a hypoxic brain to die. He saw Annabelle for the last time, clear but distant. Sarah! She had been there all the time. He tried to reach out to his daughter—the living memory of Sarah. But the tide was dragging him under. He became aware of the other figure. A fixed grin of teeth, eyes black, bald as a skull. Mr. Ash. One hand was on Annabelle's shoulder and he chattered in her ear. The other hand waved to Dillon as he sank below oblivion.

***

Becka packed away the last of the files into the cardboard box destined for the hospital research archives. It had taken her an age to fill in the paperwork. How did you detail the reasons for terminating the trial early: *I'm sorry but all the researchers died, I lost my ex-husband and the man I loved.* There wasn't any provision for it: none of the tick boxes were applicable. She had to tick *other* then follow the instruction: *please explain*. But she couldn't explain what she didn't understand.

She packed the CDs, copies of all the MRIs—those taken with informed consent. The data would still be analyzed, once they found a statistician willing to take it on, and the conclusions published. Eventually. But the truth would never be printed: there was none to be found.

The tears came again, rising from some well she didn't know had existed. Why hadn't she just asked him out properly? Instead she had beaten around the bush, hoping to hook him into the asking. Maybe things would have been different if she had told Dillon how she felt.

Something fell onto the floor as she placed the last CD in the box. She picked it up—a pen drive. She didn't recognize it as part of the trial, so plugged it into the computer to check.

It was another MRI scan. She was about to unplug it, put it into the box, hesitated when she realized it was Mr. Ash's. It was supposed to be deleted. Dillon must have made a copy. She sighed: she'd have to submit this to the auditors too. More paperwork. There was an audio file on the drive.

"…Just listen to it. Please. You'll hear…" Dillon's last words. She hated remembering him like that, but it was the last thing he had asked of her. She clicked play.

Crackle and hiss. She listened for a while, hoping for… what? To hear something that confirmed he wasn't mad— like that would somehow be better. She leaned closer, frowning, sure she had heard a distant voice.

"Dillon?"

The Ride Down
Gerald Dean Rice

A re you going out in *that*?" Roger asked his daughter. He'd barely looked up from his paper this morning or from the television, but now his only child was all he could look at.

"Daaaad, I can't *do* this with you now," Alyssa said. "I told you a week ago Tyler and I were going to the concert tonight. He already bought the tickets!"

"Double... Double..." he began, trying to recall the name of the band she'd told him. In truth, he couldn't get past her outfit. He knew his little girl wasn't so little anymore but the way the flimsy amount of material of her skirt squeezed her and how much her top *revealed*...

"Triple Six, Dad. Remember, I played you that one song?"

Roger remembered the song. It had kept him awake for an extra hour after he'd gone to bed that night. Roger was no fuddy-duddy—he'd been a teen once and had liked music his parents hadn't approved of. And he didn't buy into the whole satanic hysteria like his parents had in the 80s. But his daughter—his little girl—she was checking every box he had so far, as things to be alarmed by.

For starters, her clothes. Too much cleavage. He hadn't even known she'd developed that much and hoped it was from one of those miracle bras Miriam had told him about—*God let her rest*. Roger blanked his expression, calmly traveling his eyes up and down her outfit. She was definitely becoming a woman, there was no denying that. The boys back in his day would have said she was *phat*. Hell, who was he kidding? He'd been one of those boys.

No doubt the jargon had changed, but the sentiment hadn't. Boys would be crawling all over her the moment they laid eyes on her. This *boyfriend* of hers would have his hands under her skirt as soon as she was in his car if Roger allowed her out like she was dressed.

He had to stop it. But his little girl was like a hand grenade when she didn't get what she wanted. She would explode in a temper tantrum and make life miserable for everyone around her. That was only him, now that Roger Jr. was off to college and Miriam had passed—*God bless her*. But if his wife could see their daughter now, knowing she was about to leave and be with her... her...

Roger knew his name. Tyler. But the boy wouldn't even dignify her enough to call her his girlfriend. The first time she'd mentioned him to Roger he'd just been 'a guy'.

"What do you mean, 'a guy'?" he'd asked. "You mean your boyfriend?"

She'd had a few in school, her first—a puppy love thing in fifth grade, a summer-long thing with the neighbor between 8th and 9th grade—thankfully, he'd been gay, even Roger had seen that a mile off, and then the kicker for the football team in the 10th grade. All of them had had the title of boyfriend.

Not Tyler.

He was just 'a guy'.

Roger hadn't known how to take that. A guy implied someone she barely knew, or had met by coincidence. He could deal with her liking a guy. That more than likely meant she'd see him a time or two and then he'd be gone. A guy was forgettable. But Tyler hadn't been just a guy.

He was 'a guy'.

He had almost the same anonymity as a stranger. When Roger had asked her details on the young man, she hadn't known.

"How old is he?"

"What's his last name?"

"Where's he from?"

"What school does he go to?"

"Where'd you meet?"

"I don't know," his little girl had said to all his questions, save for the last one. That one she actually did have an answer to, but it had deepened the sick sinking feeling inside him at the time.

"Loco Tattoo," she'd said. It had been all he could do to not leap out of his La-Z-Boy and peel her down to her underwear and examine her for tattoos, and she'd seen the look on his face. "Relax, Daddy. I didn't get one. I was there with Sara. Her mom let her get a tattoo. Linda's actually pretty cool."

Sara's mom was *not* pretty cool. Linda Collins was an unemployed drunk living off monthly alimony checks in the house that had been passed down through her ex-husband's family for at least three generations. She was in desperate need of a friend and had made one out of her daughter. Roger kept a mental countdown of when the girl would be single and pregnant with her own rugrat, and he was certain it would be before graduation.

He'd played that relationship cool.

Roger knew that if he blew up at his daughter and forbade her from seeing Sara she would just go 'underground' with their friendship and wind up doing all kinds of things he wouldn't have approved of and wouldn't have known about until the police called. He'd encouraged as gently as possible for Alyssa to bring Sara over here to do homework, hang out, eat pizza, or do whatever girl stuff teenagers do and it hadn't taken too much longer for the friendship to self-destruct on its own.

He hadn't asked his daughter for details, simply letting her cry on his shoulder and dried her tears. He'd taken her out for ice cream and for a couple hours it had been like he'd had his little girl back again.

Roger could play it cool again.

This 'Tyler' sounded like the arrogant type who would treat a girl like garbage and dump her once he'd had his way with her. But he didn't know Alyssa like Roger did—she was a princess. The moment ol' Tyler called her babe and slapped her on the bottom or made eyes at some other girl on the street Alyssa would walk out.

And right back to dear old dad.

She was around the corner from seventeen and he'd have to start preparing himself for the idea of his daughter being away from him but dammit, not now. Not yet. She was still his. And Roger wasn't about to let some leather-jacket wearing punk take his child and *use her*.

"I remember the song," Roger finally said. "I hated it. Sorry." He shrugged.

Alyssa laughed and sat on the footstool in front of him. She placed a hand on his thigh.

"Could I have some money for the concert?" she asked.

Roger looked at her again. Something about the way she put her chin down and looked up at him. No, not puppy dog eyes, she knew he'd see that a mile off. Something about her face at this angle made her look like four-year old Alyssa. Something about that age was magical. Roger put up a fight even though he mentally was already reaching for his wallet.

"You're telling me this Tyler doesn't have the money to

treat a lady?"

"Daddyyyyyy," she said. "*He* bought the tickets. It's only fair that I pay for concessions. Get with the times!"

Roger considered himself a modern man. In principle, he agreed that a woman was equal to a man in every way that mattered. But his mother had raised him to open doors for a woman. To walk on the outside of the sidewalk, hold the umbrella, and pick up the check. It was hardwired into him and despite how many odd looks he got from women in their twenties and sometimes thirties, he couldn't help opening doors and letting them go ahead.

"Oh. Right," Roger said, attempting to roll with it. "What time does he get here? He *is* picking you up, isn't he?"

Alyssa smiled a little too wide as Roger fished his wallet out. He removed two twenties and placed them in the flat of her outstretched palm. When she left her hand hanging there he took the last twenty and reunited it with the others.

"Thanks, Daddy!" She leapt at him, wrapping her arms around his head and crushing his wallet against his chest. Roger was briefly aware of the soft flesh of her bosom against the back of his hand.

"Anytime, baby," he said once she'd let him go.

He was about to ask what time her date was going to get here when the doorbell rang.

She squealed and ran upstairs before he could tell her he'd get the door.

"I have to finish getting ready!" Alyssa said as she fled. Roger was confused, she'd looked ready to him. Well, not ready to *him*. That would have meant a bland burlap dress with a high collar that went to her ankles. He seriously doubted she was going to put anything more on and she had her face made up as well. As near as he could figure it was a stalling tactic meant to show Tyler that she hadn't been waiting on him and to make him wait on her.

Roger girded himself for what he figured was the worst possible situation. Some middle-aged man lousy with tattoos and piercings and a braided beard down to his beer gut. He was certain his daughter had better taste than that and hoped he would be somewhat relieved to see the man.

'Tyler' was an actual shock to Roger once he'd opened the door. He was a tall, slender, blue-eyed young man with a headful of thick black hair. He was white, but as bad as it *could* have been, Roger could definitely let that pass.

"Mr. Sand?" Tyler said, flashing a full, all-white smile. Roger had to admit he was handsome.

"Tyler," Roger forced his own smile, pushing open the screen door slightly, and stepping aside to invite the young man inside. He smelled nice and was dressed... well, better than Alyssa. He had on cream slacks with a black-and-white checkered button-up beneath a burgundy sports jacket. Roger shut the door and locked it, making his way back to his recliner.

"Have a seat." Roger gestured to the loveseat adjacent to him and Tyler nodded. "She's almost ready." He'd intentionally not shaken the boy's hand. He'd obliged as much he was going to.

Tyler sat, lacing his fingers in his lap, and faced Roger.

"So, sir, Alyssa tells me you're a comptroller?"

"Huh?" Roger wasn't actually expecting conversation on top of being referred to as 'sir'. "Oh, yes. Yes. At Medline Diagnostics."

Tyler smiled and nodded. "Cool. I go to one of their patient service centers whenever I need my blood drawn."

Roger froze with the remote poised in his hand. Was this boy actually engaging him in conversation?

"I... I... actually don't go to the PSC's often. I work at the Michigan headquarters in Auburn Hills.

"So you have a degree in accounting then? Where from?"

Despite himself, Roger was starting to like the boy. He was engaging and seemed really interested in what Roger had to say. He blinked several times.

"Um, OU. I actually used to be in construction, but I had

to get out when I wrecked my back. Got my degree in '06." He put the remote on the end table and shifted in Tyler's direction. "What about you? Are you in school?"

"No, sir. I graduated last year and put off college."

Figures. Now here comes the wreckage, Roger thought.

"I can go to college anytime and I figured I shouldn't waste my parents' money until I know what I want to do. So I spent about six months in Ghana with the Volunteer Service Overseas. I figured if I'm not any use to myself I may as well be of use to others.

"What, uh... what did you do in Ghana?"

Tyler laughed. "Got dysentery half the time I was there. The only reason I came back when I did was because I came down with a parasite. I just finished my treatments two weeks ago and I'm thinking of going back."

Roger realized at some point his mouth had fallen open.

"Hi, Tyler!" Alyssa slowly walked down the stairs, and the boy stood. He'd dialed back his smile and Roger watched him, watching her.

"Hey!" They embraced. When he pulled back, Tyler looked her up and down. Roger didn't like that much and then the boy surprised him again.

"A, it's going to be chilly tonight. I think you should put on a sweater."

One thing Roger's daughter had never been was a pushover. He was prepared for her to give Tyler a piece of her mind, although Roger was conflicted. He would have preferred for her to be covered up. She looked like she'd exposed even more cleavage than before. Roger was honestly surprised she was so... bountiful.

Alyssa nodded. "Okay, give me a minute," she said. "I know just the one!" She turned and dashed back upstairs. Roger was standing now too, and he approached Tyler.

"So are you from around here?"

Tyler looked at him and shrugged. "As much here as anywhere. Army brat. I was born in Germany, spent a few years in Japan, a few in North Carolina, etc. etc."

Roger nodded. Despite himself, he was starting to like this boy.

"What time does the concert start?" he asked.

"Oh, nine o'clock, sir."

Roger nodded. "Any idea when it'll be over?"

Tyler shrugged again. "Probably after one, but we'll probably leave before then. If I don't get at least five hours sleep I'll be dead on my feet at the soup kitchen tomorrow."

"Soup kitchen?" Roger asked, surprised yet again. Tyler slowly looked away from the stairs and back at him.

"Yes. That's always been one of my first stops since I was fifteen. Finding a place that feeds the underserved."

"Is this through the church you go to?"

Tyler laughed. "I actually don't belong to a church. My grandpa was a preacher, but he fell in love with my grandma and left his wife. He kind of never looked back and well, it was never important to my folks. I believe in God, but I find it's more important to actually do good things than just believe in them."

Roger opened his mouth to say *something* but then Alyssa was coming down the stairs. He found himself feeling a little disappointed their conversation was being cut short. She still had on the skirt that was entirely too high up her thigh but there wasn't a peek of cleavage to be seen, although the 'sweater' showed plenty of midriff.

"You look amazing," Tyler said. "We'd better go before we get snagged by traffic."

Roger felt a little rebuffed that the boy had completely lost interest in him and he had to remind himself who Tyler was actually here for. He watched the pair, and for just a moment thought they might make a cute couple. Roger was a hair's breadth from approving.

A hair's breadth.

Alyssa hugged and kissed him and no sooner had Roger shook the boy's hand that Tyler turned and used that same hand to pat her on the bottom, ushering Alyssa to the door.

"You two drive safe," Roger barely managed to say. He felt like he'd been kicked in the solar plexus. They stepped outside, Tyler uncomfortably close to his daughter. Roger was wavering on stepping onto the porch to watch them leave but Alyssa turned around while they were on the walkway.

"Goodnight, Dad," she said, flashing an embarrassed smile. "Go back inside. I *am* coming back!"

Tyler whispered something to Alyssa and she laughed, Roger getting the sinking sensation the boy had said something about him.

Tyler never turned to look back and it made Roger feel like their conversation had all been an act for his sake. He'd thoroughly been disarmed and now the boy was making off with his daughter. Before they rounded the corner, though, Roger saw a mark of some kind on the back of his neck. He squinted and was reasonably certain it was part of a tattoo.

Roger went back in and locked the door. He walked into the powder room and was barely able to make out Tyler's car from a sharp angle at the window. It was some sort of classic car. Black. Maybe a Chevy. He hoped it had been retrofitted with seatbelts. The engine revved to life and the car began backing out of the driveway.

He was grabbing his keys before he'd even thought about what he was about to do.

Roger figured he could let them get a head start because he knew where they were going. The Brutus Arena was in the thick of redevelopment downtown. All four major sports teams were within a square mile of one another with Ford Field and Comerica Park essentially right across the street.

Roger still hadn't consciously decided to follow them when he got in his car, a gray Volvo. He slid his key in the ignition, hit the button to open the garage door, and had his seatbelt buckled before he realized he was really going to do it.

Alyssa would be upset with him if she spotted him. It would probably take at least a dozen trips to the mall before she forgave him. But the thought of her with that tattooed boy… He'd been just so *slick*.

Roger was out of the subdivision, headed toward the intersection when he spotted them four cars ahead. The sun was already low and that would help him hide. They were in the left turn lane behind one other car when the Chevy's top began to retract.

Roger. Saw. Red.

His little girl was on the passenger side, but she was snuggled up to him, her head on his shoulder. It wasn't so much that anything inappropriate was happening, but that had always been what she'd done with him when she was younger. Roger had known she should have been buckled up, but he cherished the time he'd had with his daughter and the bench seat in his truck had made it so easy.

It was like a betrayal of the time they'd had together.

Rather than get in the left turn lane to follow them he stayed where he was, going across the intersection. The light would have turned red well before he would've been able to make the turn and he didn't want to fall too far behind. Even though they were supposed to be going to the concert at the Brute, that didn't mean Tyler wouldn't make a pitstop and try to press his luck.

There were cars coming in the opposite direction and Roger swung right then u-turned, cutting off a car going in the opposite way before getting in the right lane and turning in the direction Tyler had gone.

It was a chilly spring evening with the sun going down already, but he could still make out the pair. Traffic was light so he should've hung back but he couldn't help himself. He had to see what *Tyler*—if that even was his name—was tempting his little girl into doing.

In a few miles they were merging onto I-75 and rather than putting the top back up to protect themselves from being buffered by the wind, Tyler kept it down. Roger caught himself pulling up too close to them twice before intentionally letting a PT Cruiser between them for a good two miles.

Tyler had begun playing in her thick mane of hair, easily one of her best features considering she had hair just like her mother's. Roger had smelled it so many times since his Miriam—*God be with her*—had passed.

A light drizzle began, and Roger was certain Tyler would put the top up. Alyssa was going to get soaked. He silently promised that if she woke up tomorrow with a cold he was going to throttle Tyler. She put her hands up as if welcoming the rain, swaying her arms back and forth. She was behaving so... irresponsibly.

It made Roger uncomfortable to see his daughter this way.

He checked their speed—he'd begun pacing them a few miles back—and saw they were going seventy-six miles an hour. Alyssa pulled away from Tyler—*finally*—but she got up on her knees and hung nearly half her body out of the car.

Roger's heart leapt. This was getting out of hand. Not only was Tyler being inappropriate with his daughter, but he was putting her in danger too. His instinct was to pull alongside them, flag them down, and force her to come back home with him. But he knew his daughter. The tantrum she would throw would be epic. He couldn't even guess how long it would be before she forgave him. Besides, she sat back down after a moment when Tyler seemed to be rubbing her behind.

No! Roger thought as Tyler's hand slid underneath her skirt. She whirled on him, slapping his hand away. Roger resisted the urge to pump his fist in the air. That was the little girl he knew. But he could see the look on her face and... she was smiling.

That couldn't have been. She couldn't have enjoyed that. Roger rolled down the window. He was getting too hot. He mopped his brow with the sleeve of his shirt as Alyssa playfully slapped at Tyler's shoulder.

The boy made some sort of gesture and then Alyssa grabbed the steering wheel with one hand. Roger didn't understand what was happening as the young man seemed to be doing something with his hands below the steering wheel. Roger felt a stab of panic as they came to a curve in the freeway, but Alyssa handled it seamlessly, the car not even slowing.

Tyler's hands came back up, one pinching the steering wheel while the other wrapped around Alyssa's shoulders. No, not wrapping around her shoulders. He... put his hand to the back of her head.

"Stop it," Roger said aloud. "Don't do that." He was certain this was where things turned around. There was no way his little girl was going to do—

Gently, Tyler pushed at the thicket of her hair and Alyssa's head disappeared into his lap.

Roger thought he was going to be sick. His foot slacked from the gas pedal until he was doing forty-nine. Cars blew past him, including a truck with a trailer that nearly blew him onto the shoulder.

His little girl. He'd held her in his hands when she'd been just seconds old. He'd patched up her booboo after she'd skinned her knee when she was learning to ride her bike. He'd had to convince her he wasn't the tooth fairy when she'd found her baby teeth in his sock drawer in a plastic bag.

How could she?

"No." Roger shook his head. "It's not her. It's *him*."

He got his speed back up, the rain falling harder now, but he didn't care. He had to save his daughter while she still had a shred of virtue left. Roger didn't care if he had to drag her kicking and screaming from Tyler's car. He'd do it, consequences be damned. She could be mad at him until she left for college for all he cared. Roger knew, in the end, she would thank him for saving her from herself.

He weaved around cars, not looking at his speed as he scanned the vehicles, looking for Tyler's classic black Chevy. For a long moment of panic he thought he'd lost them. Or worse yet, they could have skidded off the freeway and could be lying in a ditch or thrown from the car.

"Please, let her be okay," Roger said, feeling the tears come to his eyes. He didn't think he could have stood it if she were taken from him too. It had been hard enough when Miriam—*God rest her*—passed, and he'd been lucky enough to have his good girl to lean on to get through it.

He spotted the Chevy ahead in the left lane and slowed so he wouldn't overtake them. He just wanted to see what they were doing first. For a moment he thought he might have had the wrong vehicle but then she rose from his lap, *wiping her mouth.*

Roger thought he would be sick. He steeled himself and got in the center lane so he could pull alongside them. But before he could speed up, the Chevy cut him off, slicing across all three lanes and onto the ramp for the Nine Mile exit. Roger was surprised, but he managed to get over in time to take the exit as well, cutting in behind a Jeep in the right lane.

Where were they going? The Brute Arena was downtown, and this was Hazel Park. They weren't even in Wayne County yet. Roger's mind was set now. Tyler was now actively lying by not going straight to the arena. Roger wasn't even going to waste words with him. He was going to floor him and drag Alyssa off if need be.

They stopped at the red light coming off the freeway. Roger was surprised he was bothering to obey a traffic light. It wouldn't be safe to do it here, he'd wait until they were on Nine Mile to stop them. The light turned green and they turned right, headed toward Ferndale. Roger had to weave around a Honda with a mismatched door to get behind them. There wasn't room enough for him to get next to them without his car being in the opposing traffic lane. Alyssa turned as if she were about to look over her shoulder and he panicked. Roger didn't want them to see him until he had them stopped, but he didn't know how to do that.

Perhaps by some act of divinity, smoke began to pour from the hood of the Chevy. They turned into the next lot and Roger was behind them a moment later. Maybe old Tyler wouldn't have a ride home in the next few minutes, but Roger was going to protect his daughter.

They were out of the Chevy by the time he pulled in behind them, parked by an abandoned building. Roger got out of his car as he saw his daughter rounding the corner of the building with the boy, giggling.

"Alyssa!" He slammed the door and jogged after them. When he'd turned the corner of the building he caught sight of what appeared to be two figures standing—well, one standing—by a dumpster. As he got closer what appeared to be a person kneeling in front of another turned out to be a trick of shadow and a stack of three cardboard boxes.

A door at the back of the building creaked as it closed, catching his eye. Roger jogged over and yanked on the handle, but it was locked.

"No, dammit, no!" He kicked the door in frustration and looked around. There were three iron-barred windows to his right. He stood in front of the one with two bars already pried up. The glass blocks of all three looked like they would collapse with a good shove. He gave the bars a yank and they didn't budge. Then he moved to the next window and the bars came out with a slight tug.

Roger was surprised by the weight and was barely able to keep from being pulled over, straining his back in the process. It felt like a flame had licked up his lower back and he stayed in that position for a count of twenty before he was confident he could move.

Roger stood and slapped at the glass blocks in the window. They didn't budge despite how flimsy they looked.

He scanned the alley for something to shatter them and his eyes settled on a chunk of concrete a little bigger than both his fists.

His back twinged in protest and instead of bending over he got down on one knee. For the briefest moment, proposing to Miriam—*God love her*—flashed through his brain and he laughed, seeing how ridiculous this whole thing looked. But thinking of his dead wife got him back on track.

He had to rescue his little princess.

Roger grunted through the pain as he stood, straightening his back. It actually didn't hurt as much as he'd been expecting, and he was able to get the chunk up to shoulder level by the time he got back to the window. Throwing it might not be enough. Roger figured he needed to get a little oomph and did a loping spin before launching it.

The glass blocks didn't hold up beneath the chunk as it smashed into the building. Roger pushed out as much of the broken glass as he could before climbing in. Still a shard scratched down his back as he pushed through and fell inside.

It was dark in here. Roger laid on the floor for a long moment, listening. There was something in the distance he couldn't make out. It sounded like human voices but neither of them sounded like his little girl's.

Roger slowly got to his feet, his hand coming down on something cold and metal. He carefully stepped around what felt like the bowl of a mixer—he'd worked in a pizza restaurant in his college years—feeling his way past several more pieces of large equipment until he came to what had to have been the dining room floor of the restaurant.

Somebody giggled.

Roger's ears prickled. That *was* his Alyssa.

"Baby?" he said without thinking.

The voices continued.

He advanced in their direction, biting his lip to keep himself quiet. Maybe he'd blown the element of surprise and maybe he hadn't. Whoever he'd heard seemed so preoccupied with what they were doing. Maybe they hadn't heard him call out.

Roger's eyes gradually adjusted to the dark. He could just make out a table ahead of him and a row of booths to his left. But he bumped into another table, barely not falling over it and crashing to the floor. The voices were coming from somewhere to his right and he turned his head to listen.

Yes, definitely over there.

He began shuffling in that direction, careful not to trip again. Roger would have to surprise them, overwhelm Tyler and then grab Alyssa and get out of here as quickly as possible. There was only one reason why they would be in here and Roger only hoped he could get his little girl out of here before that could happen.

He was less than a dozen feet away before he realized they were in a restroom. It was such a cliché. Of all the places, they were in the clichést of clichés for... for...

For sex.

The thought alone propelled him inside. Roger was bumping against walls until he'd reached the stall before he realized he was in the wrong one. Their voices echoed overhead, and he listened for a moment.

"I never saw one like that before."

"It's okay. You can touch it. It won't hurt."

"Is it always that red?"

"Your hand is so *cold*."

Roger felt along the wall, working his way backward until he was out of the restroom. He continued moving toward the voices until it sounded like he was right on top of them.

"You'll go slow, right?"

"Yeah, baby. However you want it."

He rounded the corner into the other restroom and was prepared to shout for them to stop but was surprised to see something other than the restroom. Roger subconsciously turned off the flashlight app on his cell and peered down into a slanted hole wide enough for two men to crawl through.

It was dark down there but well-lit enough for him to see several people in various stages of undress. Three men with their shirts off, wearing what looked like criss-crossed suspenders holding up black pants. There was also a slender woman, half a head taller than the men at least and one particularly scared-looking Tyler holding a black, wavy-looking knife about the length of one of his skinny forearms. The... the woman also had on no top, her bare breasts huge and swinging back and forth as she walked.

Roger shook his head as if not wanting to believe what was before his eyes. He went on watching another moment until he realized they were walking around something. A big, stone table. Something in his mind said it was an altar and something in his mind clicked.

Alyssa was on the altar.

And she was as naked as the day she was born.

His eyes lingered a moment before he snapped into action. Roger had to protect her. He bent and scuttled down the decline as quickly as he could, narrowly avoiding losing his footing and going tumbling down. He stopped at the lip of the decline, peering over to see a sort of bowl-shape before the altar where at least two dozen figures in hoods stood, watching the proceedings.

"You stop right there!" Roger shouted. As his eyes adjusted to the light he found a winding pathway to a landing between the stage and the bowl where all the hooded figures were. Everyone turned and looked at him.

Roger was unphased, though. He was too heated that his child was in such a compromised position. He had to protect her even if she wouldn't protect herself. He stepped onto the stage, brushing past the first shirtless man who was easily half a head taller than him and nothing but a wall of muscle.

Tyler was standing over her, the knife held loosely in his hands. Something about his casualty further upset Roger, the irresponsibility of the young man's grasp a danger in and of itself like it would slip from his grasp and plunge into her virginal flesh.

Roger plucked the big knife from the young man's hand, horrified at his daughter's exposed body, and ripped open his button up shirt before placing it over her. Tyler stepped away from them, cowed and unable to make eye contact. Alyssa was so tiny his shirt covered everything from her neck to mid-thigh. The tall woman glid over to him, stopping mere inches away and Roger stood, half anticipating a slap or a punch.

He was eye level with her breasts, and they were so rigid and upright for a moment he thought one of her nipples might poke him in the eye. Roger took an involuntary step backward and looked up.

She had on a ton of makeup, gold and green coating her face. At a glance he would have guessed her to be in her mid-fifties—at least ten years older than him. But the makeup, as gaudy as it was, could easily have been concealing an additional decade. Her breasts were obviously fake, but the rest of her body was taut, thin and lightly muscled like a dancer or a runner.

Her eyes were dark as night, Roger could only see a bit of white at the corners, like the irises were twice the diameter they should have been. Her thin, wrinkled mouth hung open in surprise and Roger thought he saw the tips of sharpened teeth.

He felt the briefest spring of panic, but he recognized he'd caught them all off guard. Roger had to press his advantage while he still had it. He and Alyssa were in danger here and the quicker they could get out of this hole and out of the building the better.

"Alyssa, we're going. Now." He still held the knife as he pulled her onto her feet.

"Daaaaaaaddyyyyyyyyyyy!" his daughter said, trying to shrug off his shirt. "Stop ruining my *death*!"

Roger cast a glance over his shoulder at his daughter. Her eyes were glazed, and he imagined her pupils had to have been large. She tried weakly to resist him, and he jerked her closer to him as they wound the dirt path back up to the restroom.

A hooded figure stepped in front of him and Roger held up his knife hand like he was about to punch the man (?) but in truth he had no idea what he'd been about to do and settled for tremoring the clenched fist in front of the figure's face.

Someone behind them hissed and Roger looked back to see the tall woman baring those sharpened teeth like a million letter V's that seemed to wind all the way back to her tonsils. The figure took a big step out of his path and rather than questioning it, Roger continued up the path, ducking his way back through the floor of the restroom and putting a hand over Alyssa's head to guide her through as well.

He kept waiting for them to follow. Roger's hindbrain told him to run, the logical part said to call 911, but some mysterious bridge in between told him to keep a steady, measured pace and calmly go back the way he'd come.

"Why are you here?" Alyssa asked, her voice dreamy.

"I *followed* you," he said, a swelling of righteousness in his chest.

"You followed?" She coughed a laugh and clapped her hands once in front of her face and in the near dark he saw something on her face. Maybe not *on* her face but something was off about it.

Roger thought for just a moment it had had way too many teeth that were far larger than they should have been. He blinked several times and Alyssa's face in the low light was just a face.

"Daddy, let me go."

"You're coming home."

"No. Go away!"

"Little girl, don't make me drag you out!"

She tried to pull away from him, but she was either still weak from whatever they'd given her, or he was just that pumped on adrenaline.

Alyssa slapped at his arm and screamed. "Daddy, this is my life!"

Roger was taken aback a moment, his mouth working until he found words to speak. "You are my child," he said with measured rage. "Until you are an adult you have no life!" He was done arguing.

A pair of eyes caught a hint of light behind his daughter and he pulled her behind him. Roger could only make out the silhouette of a thin man he guessed to be Tyler.

"Baby," the boy said. Roger could imagine the sly smile on his face that he'd so easily wielded to almost win Roger over. *Almost.*

Roger's fist leapt away from his hip, catching the young man right in the mouth and sending him backward. Roger didn't wait to see if he'd knocked him off his feet, turning and yanking his daughter toward the exit.

Alyssa whimpered as he roughly guided her around the tables he could see in the dark now that his eyes had adjusted. The fight had gone out of her as they crawled out the window opening and back into the alley. She kept sniffling and making crying sounds, further bolstering Roger's sense of indignation. They walked past Tyler's car, Roger resisting the urge to key its black paint job.

Roger opened the door for Alyssa and half-shoved her in. He even buckled her seatbelt for her like he'd done back when she was a child.

"I'm so sorry, Daddy," Alyssa said once he was in the car. She was turned away from him, hiding her face in shame. Roger nodded as if acknowledging to himself that he had done the right thing. He started the car and slowly backed out of the narrow lane and onto the street. In a minute they were back on the freeway, headed home.

For several long minutes he didn't know what to say. He was upset, but she was his baby girl. And he had gotten to her in time, hadn't he? Roger shivered—he didn't want to think about what she *could* have been doing. Something niggling at the back of his brain still asked the question.

What was *she doing?*

As horrifying as the idea of some boy copping a feel was, what she'd actually been up to had been even stranger. There were a million places they could have gone if they were just going to make out—Roger knew of several that were still around from back in his day and he'd definitely made good use of several.

Where they'd actually gone had just been so... out of the way. And was any of that stuff real? Had Roger not been on their tail practically the whole way he would have never found them. And he doubted a patrol car would have stumbled across them, either. The Chevy had been parked next to the abandoned restaurant and on the opposite side was an overgrown hedge that would have obscured practically the whole vehicle from westbound traffic.

Drugs. It had to have been drugs. Roger shook his head. He'd had his run with marijuana when he was a teen and had been offered cocaine a time or two. He tried telling himself this was normal. And at least all her clothes were on when he found her.

But wait a second.

Roger glanced at his daughter, still resting her head against the window. She looked like she might have been asleep. He almost lost the thread of what he was thinking before he trailed his eyes down her body. From the rise of her bosom, to the curved, flat plane of her stomach, she was no little girl anymore—but that wasn't it.

And then he noticed the smell.

It was thick and earthy, with a bit of ash. So, she

probably had been smoking. He was disappointed, but it wasn't the end of the world. He could still have his baby.

Roger licked his thumb and reached over to wipe a smudge of filth off her cheek. It didn't come off so much as it smeared.

It felt thick and tacky as he rubbed it between finger and thumb. Roger turned the light on and looked at his hand.

It was blood.

"Daddy," Alyssa said. Her voice was thick and heavy. He glanced at her and she hadn't moved save for the rise and fall of her chest as she breathed. "Am I your little girl still?"

"Yes, baby." Roger wiped his finger and thumb on his shirt subconsciously, noticing several more dark patches on her skin. "You know you are. We'll get through this, okay?"

Roger still hadn't turned off the dome light. He glanced at his daughter again, confused. The splotches that were obviously blood now trailed with the sweat pouring off her.

"You should pull over," she said. "I don't want to do this while you're driving."

"Do *what*?" The smell was suddenly dominating the inside of the car. Roger felt on the verge of being overwhelmed by it and powered down all the windows despite the cool weather.

"I don't have long. I have a curfew," his daughter said.

Roger's foot had slacked off the gas pedal and he was drifting out of his lane. A car honked at him as it blasted past and he corrected his vehicle.

"Baby, what are you talking about?"

He felt a sick feeling coursing down his spine.

"Who... who were those boys? Who was that *woman*?"

She sat up, shaking her head.

"We can do this the gentle way. You'll go to sleep."

He didn't want to ask the obvious question. He didn't want to know.

You're... you're not my baby anymore. Are you?

The car had slowed to just under thirteen miles an hour in

the center lane. Cars were honking and shaking them as they flew past. Without looking up, 'Alyssa' grabbed the steering wheel, almost dumping them into the ditch. Roger sat paralyzed, finally putting his foot on the brake and stopping them.

She put the car in Park.

Then she turned her head up at him.

"Your-your head. Your *face!*" Roger whimpered, scuttling backward in his seat. He was too panicked to open his door, fumbling uselessly at it as he stared into an open chasm in his little girl's head. From her chin to the point of her skull was simply open and he could see veins, muscle tissue, slick and shining in the headlights of passing vehicles.

Her voice came out of the gaping emptiness. She turned to him, the seatbelt tearing off her like a strip of paper. She laid an ice cold hand on his shoulder. "I love you, Daddy." She straddled him and leaned in close. Roger could see things deep within that hole that he was certain weren't inside of a normal human body and somewhere in there was the voice that was so much like his little girl's. "I don't have to rip you apart. It can be kinda... gentle. Over before you know it. You might even enjoy it."

Same Day Delivery
Ricki Whatley

Neil DeBlasik launched himself off the top step of 512 Gates Street with all the grace of a Bolshoi ballerina. With his toes pointed in his black leather walking shoes, and his slim calves scissored open at a near perfect, one-hundred-eighty-degree split, he could have been the Sugar Plum Fairy herself. His slow motion decent regained the momentum of real time the instant his lead foot met the pavement and his blue, polyester-clad frame came crashing to the sidewalk. He landed in a full sprint, cleared the front walkway in three mammoth strides before vaulting over the chain-link fence that surrounded the unassuming Cape Cod. Neil lay panting in the safety of the curb just beyond the reach of the resident guard dog. Samson, a wiry German Sheppard with an attitude problem, threw himself against the gate, snarling and wrestling with the woven metal. "Thank you for your service, Samson," Neil muttered sardonically. He saluted him with a middle finger and barred his own teeth in a silent growl. "Protect and serve, you mangy dickhead." Neil hauled himself to his feet and brushed the grass from his skinned knees and now-stained uniform. His days on the job had been far more peaceful prior to Samson moving in a little over a month ago. His presence seemed wholly unnecessary on the quaint, tree-lined street. There had not been any recent break-ins or surges in criminal activity. Neil could not fathom what possibly would have possessed the reclusive old lady at 512 to suddenly become so security conscious that she would invite Cujo's long lost brother to move in with her. The least she could do was replace the pressed tin mailbox mounted on the side of her house with a freestanding one that Neil could reach without having to brave the perilous, twenty-foot, death march through Samson's territory.

Ten years earlier, when he had first applied to become a mailman, Neil had actually liked dogs. He thought the legendary feud between mail carriers and man's best friend was a trumped-up myth, perpetuated by the cartoon and comic strip industries. Similar to how milkmen somehow won the reputation for being randy, housewife fertilizers. However, his first year toting greeting cards and bills for the United States Postal Service, had quickly changed his perspective.

It had been a bright, sunshiny day when Neil had stopped to hand deliver a cumbersome box, too large for the customer's mailbox. As he stood, grinning like a lunatic on Mrs. Bemett's front porch, her toy schnauzer slipped between her varicose veined legs and sunk its teeth into the unsuspecting flesh of Neil's ankle. At that moment, he had learned the irrefutable truth: Dogs were the *fucking worst.* He stole a regretful glance down at his right foot. Sure enough, tattooed in mauve dots of scar tissue across the top of his *lateral malleolus* was a small row of teeth, forever stamped in his pasty skin.

The deafening clamor of Samson's barking brought Neil's thoughts back to the present. *At least this asshole didn't get ahold of me*, he thought; staring into the gnashing, foam covered maw of Samson. *I probably would have lost my whole fucking foot.* He glared down at the slavering jaws still working tirelessly to rip a hole in the fence and continue his hungry pursuit. Thick ropes of canine saliva dripped through the hexagonal fence pattern making it look like some kind of oozing, stainless steel beehive.

Neil grimaced in disgust and shouldered his carrier bag emblazoned with its official eagle head logo. He sighed heavily and turned his weary feet in the direction of the next house. As he did, the door of 512 creaked open and he saw the bent shape of Mrs. Betty Ann Weaver peer out from the shadowy depths of her front room. At first, he thought she meant to check on him. Maybe offer him a band aide and verify that her rabid, man-eating quadruped was not contentedly devouring Neil's entrails in the middle of the sunny lawn. Alas, Mrs. Weaver's perceived concern was short lived. She wound her arm around the door jam and extricated her mail with a sinewy arm. She cast the papers into the house with barely a backward glance, and then turned her sunken eyes on Neil. Her gaze was devoid of any worry or kindness and she made no attempt to call off Samson. Instead, she waved her arms like a maniacal referee and yelled unintelligibly at Neil. The ancient skin on her arms swung in lazy arcs at opposition to her flailing hands. Her flesh was so pale and thin, it billowed like cotton. Neil struggled to discern where her nightgown ended, and her skin began. As he stood staring, bewildered, she seemed to grow increasingly agitated.

"Go!" She shouted from the darkness of the porch. "Get out of here while you can! NOW!" Neil could barely hear her commands over the sound of her dog, but he gathered the overall sentiment and trudged away dejectedly. Mrs. Weaver had lived at the same house for as long as Neil had been delivering mail, and she had never spared a kind word for him. She did not tip at Christmas or offer a cool drink on hot days. In fact, this angry reprimand was the most she had ever spoken to him in the last decade. Neil glanced around the street. He felt eyes on him. Certain he had an audience, he scanned the yards and sidewalk up and down Gates Street. Nothing. He shrugged to dislodge the uneasy feeling of being watched and walked on. He could still hear Mrs. Weaver and Samson howling in unison behind him as he approached the neighboring mailbox at 514 Gates Street.

514. A solitary pearl on the string of turds that comprised Gates Street. 514 was a low maintenance rental property. It was a two story, unassuming, red brick cube. Three cement steps led to a wraparound porch bedecked with white trimmed windows. The curtains were always drawn but the gauzy window sheers did little to conceal the beauty within—Lily Trumble.

Lily had only recently moved to Gates Street. Prior to delivering her mail, Neil had stuffed number 514's mailbox with letters addressed to a Mr. Donovan Ramsey. Mr. Ramsey had been pleasant, but he was a nightshift worker at the local power plant, and he hung heavy, blackout curtains that offered no inside view of his tidy little house. Lily, on the other hand, seemed to revel in performing a coy peepshow for Neil.

Since moving in, she had paraded semi-weekly in front of her living room bay windows, always in various stages of undress. Sometimes she would be clad in only a t-shirt and panties. Other times she would saunter from room to room in a satin robe left open and billowing around her voluptuous frame. On one particularly magnificent afternoon, Neil had seen her emerge from the hazy darkness of her house into the light of the front windows, fresh from a bath. He assumed that is where she had come from since she was wearing nothing but a towel…coiled in a turban around her hair. Her skin looked dewy. Almost as if it glowed from behind the translucent window shades. She walked straight ahead as if she were going to step right through the plate glass and he was treated to a full frontal view of her magnificent body.

Neil's shorts grew tight at the mere memory and he

tugged self-consciously at his fly, trying to loosen the fabric's grip on his swelling cock.

Lily just appeared to be so…ripe. A woman in her prime. Thick and luscious as a peach. The downy curves of her breasts and hips swelled to the brink of overabundance, before tapering in slow, narrowed descents around her navel and slim, feminine ankles. She was a renaissance vision. A goddess plucked from the oiled canvasses of a time when a splendid, plump ass epitomized beauty and opulence.

Neil halted in front of the white metal mailbox perched in the ground like a crane. He opened the box and the empty cavity gaped like a hungry mouth. There were only two letters that day. Something from the electric company and an offer for a preapproved line of credit. Nothing delivered to the house ever provided him with any kind of glimpse into her personal life.

Neil had a decent knowledge of the people he served; simply based on the packages he brought day in and day out. He knew Will Grandy at 309 was a secret doomsday prepper who had boxes of gas mask filters, rainwater purification tablets, or hermetically sealed, ready to eat meals delivered monthly.

Elizabeth Misner, the portly redhead at 1028, was having an affair with her air conditioner repairman. Neil delivered bi-monthly shipments from Adam & Eve. Most of the boxes were relatively light and likely contained something tame like a sized 14 French maid apron or plaid, schoolgirl miniskirt. Every now and then, Neil came across a delivery with something substantial inside that rolled heavily from side to side. He prayed it was a cylindrical bottle of warming oil and not some industrial grade, jackhammer dildo. The image of Elizabeth's middle aged, pudgy frame quaking with the reverberating frequency from a huge, animatronic member made the acid in Neil's stomach roil like a choppy sea. Without fail, every afternoon following the arrival of one of the naughty little boxes, Neil would see the Frosty

Fix-It truck parked in Elizabeth's driveway for the duration of the 12-1pm lunchbreak.

Yet, despite this intimate glimpse into the lives of the other Gates Street residents, Lily's life remained a mystery. Where had she come from? Where did she work? What did she like in a man? Did she ever go to the movies with scrawny mailmen and eat nachos covered in steaming, nuclear orange goo?

No.

The short answer, which Neil heard echo pitilessly in his mind, was *no*. A guy like Neil would never, *ever*, have a shot with a woman like Lily. He morosely set the letters inside the yawning mailbox and gently closed the lid with a dull click. He glanced up at her windows, hoping to catch even a fleeting glimpse of his lady fair.

Nothing. Her windows remained stubbornly empty. Not even a twitch of the curtains to hint at her delectable presence concealed within.

Never a break, Neil silently lamented. As if in response to his own depressed thoughts, a car sped down the street and came to an abrupt stop at the curb outside Lily's house. Neil could hear the thump of the heavy bass emitting from the glossy red sports car. He craned his head and gazed forlornly at the official, white, box truck parked down the block.

Gee, tough choice, Lily, Neil scoffed internally. *Whom would you rather date? The trendy millionaire with the eighty-thousand dollar car? Alternatively, we have the delivery boy who drives a rattling, door-less box with the steering wheel on the wrong side...*

The music inside the curbside coupe sprang open and the driver leapt to a standing position. Neil locked eyes and realized he had been standing in the middle of the sidewalk, staring at the recent arrival the entire time he had been hosting his imaginary dating show. His cheeks flushed awkwardly, and he rustled aimlessly with the mailbag, pretending to look busy. What shocked him more than the apparent economic status of the hip, young visitor was that this was obviously *not* Lily's hot boyfriend. It was a hot *girlfriend*.

She strode around the front of her cherry red car with a confidence that suggested she not only knew the way to Lily's front door, but she was welcomed and expected to return on this day, at this very moment. Her slender calves clenched atop the needle-heeled stiletto sandals she wore beneath a virtually nonexistent, black leather mini dress. Neil had seen bigger tubes of manicotti.

"You coming in too?" The skinny blonde asked with a wry grin.

"M-me?" Neil stammered. "Uh, no. No, I'm not."

"Pity," she said with a sympathetic tilt of her head. She crashed through the chain link gate and strutted up the narrow cement walk as if it were a runway. "Better luck next time," she hollered over her shoulder without turning to see if Neil was even still standing there. Of course, he was. Lily's front door swung open as the blonde mounted the top step of the front porch and she pushed her way in before slamming the door securely behind her. Next to Neil, the car's security system chirped, and the headlamps blinked playfully back at him.

Neil gazed longingly up at the house. How he wished he could waltz up to the front door, with even half of the blonde's confidence, and step into the warm center of their love nest. Alas, the lonely mailman had neither the guts, nor the disposable time. He regarded the paper-stuffed satchel weighing down his left shoulder and plodded on toward the next customer. Behind him, the curtains in Mrs. Weaver's sitting room split, and her meddlesome face briefly emerged from the darkened room. Her beady eyes squinted to mere slits as she watched Neil's retreating, blue-clad figure grow small. Samson sat vigilantly in the corner of the front yard. His snout greedily probed the air, undoubtedly inhaling the lingering scent of the leggy guest.

Good boy, she mentally praised her animal companion. *If the new girl makes it out of that house alive, you scare her enough to make sure she never comes back.* If.

Mrs. Weaver slid back into the inky blackness of her dwelling and let the curtains drop against the intrusive sunshine. Four houses down, Neil shuddered and cast another suspicious glance down the street. He could not shake the feeling of being watched. Or was it, he felt hunted?

Neil finished out his deliveries down the 500 block of Gates without incident. The afternoon was warm and calm. Almost too calm. As he crossed the street to double back along the odd side of the street and retrieve his mail truck, it occurred to him: Mrs. Weaver and the self-delivering blonde were the only people he had seen that day. No one was mowing their lawn or driving home for lunch. Samson was the only animal he had encountered, domestic or otherwise. No birds flitted from tree to tree. No lazy porch cats sunned their bellies or stalked unwary, fluffy snacks hiding in the grass. Silence hung over Gates Street as if the entire neighborhood had a giant, noise-cancelling cloche dropped over the top of it. No breeze stirred the leaves on the lush trees. If a tourist had ridden through the streets and taken a photo of the neighborhood, the picture would have appeared charming. The image was of a perfectly manicured, sweet community. Actually standing in the middle of it, Neil had a different perception. It felt forced. A two-dimensional postcard designed to look inviting to unsuspecting tourists. It reminded Neil of the carnivorous plants in the Amazon that wait with cupped petals dripping sweet, irresistible nectar. As soon as a hungry fly landed to take a sip, the flower snapped shut and instantly began dissolving the squirming body alive.

What is it with me today? Neil wondered. *I walk this street every day. No one is watching me. I am not an insect flying toward a hungry pitcher plant. It is just a quiet day. Stop being weird.*

By the time Neil had finished his personal admonishment, he was almost directly back in front of Lily's house. Her house seemed so far away and even more unattainable from across the street. As if in direct rebellion of his internal thoughts, an ear-shredding scream suddenly impaled the quiet insulating Gates Street. It wavered somewhere in between pain and pleasure, making every hair on Neil's body stand erect. The electric jolt from the shocking cries, spurred him into action. He dropped his mailbag on the sidewalk and bolted across the street towards Lily's house. As he burst through her gate, Samson once again resumed his slobbering onslaught of the fence, but Neil ran on, heedless. He did not hear the dog's frantic barking, nor the drumming of Mrs. Weaver's desiccated fists against her side window.

Neil cleared Lily's front three steps in one stride and landed panting on her shaded porch. The screaming subsided as quickly as it had started and for a moment, he wondered if he had imagined it altogether. With one hand poised to knock on the door, he stole a glance over his shoulder at the abandoned mailbag. The bright red sports car that should have been parked on the curb, obscuring his view was missing. He had not noticed it drive away, but it was indisputably absent. That could only mean… It was Lily he had heard screaming!

Neil snapped his head forward once again, intent on breaching the door and rescuing his darling but before he could rap his knuckles against the painted wood, the door opened. It made no noise as it swung on the hinges and as the doorway widened, a gust of warm, dry air blew against Neil's face. His hair ruffled and he raised a forearm to shield his eyes from the dehydrating blast. With it, the heat carried a faint, sulfuric odor. It was metallic and chemical. Neil's eyes began to sting and water, but the sensation was fleeting.

The toxic air quickly dissipated in the open air of the front yard and he blinked away the tears blurring his vision. Standing just inside the threshold of the house, in glistening, naked glory was Lily.

Her dark hair spilled in thick waves down her shoulders. Beneath the veil of glossy hair hung massive breasts that rose and fell sumptuously with each breath Lily took. She stood with her legs crossed modestly, obscuring her sex. The smooth flesh of her ample thighs flowed seamlessly downward through delicate kneecaps and finally ended at tiny, feminine feet. Her right foot was perched on top of her left and her perfect toes were stacked in two identical rows. They were so small and dainty; her feet almost looked like fleshy hooves.

Neil's respiratory rate had been elevated from his panicked sprint across the street and the vision of Lily within arm's reach did nothing to calm him. His breath rasped in desperate gasps and sweat tickled his scalp as it spilled from his pores.

"Neil," she exhaled his name with a lusty ease that suggested they had been lovers for years.

"Yes…?" Neil's response was, by contrast, uncertain at best.

"I've been waiting for you. I'm so glad you've finally come." Lily extended one narrow hand, palm up. Whether as an offer to Neil or in expectation of her own tribute, he did not know and did not care to deliberate. He slid his fingers into her tight grasp without hesitation. Her skin felt hot and faintly powdery, like freshly kilned pottery. Lily cinched his clammy hand in her spidery fingers and firmly pulled him inside. Neil complied without blinking. He moved as easily as if his body floated weightlessly on the sweltering air. He did not pause to wonder how Lily knew his name, or why Mrs. Weaver pounded her ancient fists against her window and screamed for his attention.

Once inside, Neil's eyes took a few seconds to adjust to

the gloom. Not a single ceiling light or lamp shone in the entire bottom floor. His vision was limited to the thin film of light that saturated the gauzy window treatments. The small foyer was empty except for a four-foot tall podium carved from a single piece of thick, black wood. Atop, a large leather-bound book lay open to about halfway through the sheaves of thick, antique paper. Neil stepped closer and realized it was some kind of ledger. Names, dates and times ran down the page in fine, handwritten columns. They progressed chronologically and the last entry read, "MALLORY KEEN," followed by the date. According to the book, Mallory had entered the house less than 40 minutes before Neil.

That must be the leather girlfriend's name, he thought absently.

Before Neil could wonder why Lily would keep such fastidious records of her visitors, she petted his cheek with her long fingers, and he forgot about the book entirely.

"This way, my darling." Lily led him stiffly into the next room, situated at the heart of the house. The center of the room was bare, hardwood. No furniture or décor of any kind filled the space. What monopolized the majority of the room were piles, upon piles, of clothing and personal effects. Male and female clothes of all sizes and styles reached nearly to the ceiling, and further obscured what little light spilled in through the side windows. Amongst the garments, Neil could detect the glint of eyeglasses, car keys and patent leather shoes. A distant memory of his high school lessons covering the Holocaust briefly invaded his mind, and he shuddered in spite of the oppressive heat. Lily's living room looked like some kind of disorganized Auschwitz and he nervously scanned the corners of the room for the piles of shaved hair and gold teeth.

Lily gently turned his chin with her surprisingly strong hand and his gaze once again focused on her. She was all he could see. His beautiful, curvaceous goddess.

"Kneel, my darling," she commanded with a sensuous pucker of her lips. "Do not mind the clutter."

"I don't," Neil replied hypnotically. And he truly did not. His mind was devoid of any worry or concern regarding… anything. Lily's unexplained nonchalance; her strange guest book at the front door; the discarded hoard of clothing. None of it mattered, and he placidly knelt on the floor at his beloved's feet.

"Good," she cooed with an indulgent grin. Her eyes flashed with hunger, and Neil grinned back foolishly. He was elated that Lily would be equally enamored with him. It gave him immeasurable pleasure to please her.

"Strip," she commanded firmly. Neil scrambled to undo his belt and work his shorts and boxers down over his sticky skin. In his haste, he forgot to address his shoes first and awkwardly wrestled the leg of his trousers, black knee sock and right sneaker off in one motion. He repeated the ungainly battle on the left side and without thinking, cast the damp wad of clothing onto one of the towering mounds lining the room. The floorboards were warm against the front of his bent legs. His erection bobbed eagerly from under his shirt, and Neil fought to loosen his top buttons.

"Good," Lily said again and sucked her bottom lip. She gently pushed Neil's shoulders until he lost his balance and fell in a clumsy seated position with his legs sprawled out in front of him. He stopped fiddling with his shirt and planted his hands on the ground behind him as bracing. Lily stepped between his legs and Neil strained forward to inhale her scent. Between her legs smelled like Sulphur. It was the same acrid smell that had greeted him at the door; forebodingly toxic. The kind of smell that certain fruit emitted to fend off predators. Neil sucked it in with lecherous enthusiasm. His tongue flickered like a hungry snake to steal a taste of her. Lily squatted and brought herself eye to eye. She entwined her sharp fingers in his hair and jerked his head backwards exposing his throat and pulsing carotid. She pushed her own tongue out of her mouth and slapped it against the side of Neil's neck, lapping up his sweat.

She groaned with pleasure and spoke in a breathy whisper against his ear, "Such pleasure these bodies provide. What delicious succor."

"Yes," Neil readily agreed.

"The Master will be so pleased with you, my little darling. You're doing so well."

"Yes," he repeated thoughtlessly.

Lily rose slightly on her knees and brushed her silken nipples against Neil's open mouth. His lips closed tightly around the pink flesh and he sucked wantonly. He reached his hands around Lily's back and dug his fingers into her soft flesh, pressing her body against him, nearly smothering himself in her creamy breasts.

"Drink, my darling. Drink from me as scores of your offspring shall feed."

Thick streams of milk poured down his chin and threatened to drown Neil as he suckled with abandon. He struggled to balance the need to breathe, with the urge to swallow, but refused to part himself from Lily's embrace. She chuckled hollowly and straddled Neil's seated frame. He whimpered helplessly as her slick pussy devoured his cock and Lily began to ride him mercilessly.

Around the tangled lovers, the room began to glow with an unearthly, orange light. Fiery red embers glittered between the floorboards and the whole room seemed to heave and expand with heat. Smoke rose in thin, gray geysers through sporadic gaps in the floor, but Neil continued his desperate rutting, oblivious.

Lily tossed her head back, her hair dangling nearly to the ground behind her. She laughed in deep, guttural tones that defied her womanly form. Her eyes were wide and crazed as she rocked her hips rhythmically and without pause against Neil's trembling pelvis. Her ample size engulfed his quivering body, and he was lost almost entirely between her gargantuan breasts and thighs.

"Spill your seed, mortal!" Lily's voice was no longer her own and it rumbled like a demonic thunder inside the shuddering house. Around them, the floorboards began to buckle and splinter, letting more of the hellish, orange light shoot into the room in jagged spotlights.

"Become father to LEGION!"

Neil could not contain himself any longer. He gritted his teeth and moaned as his lust exploded between Lily's spread legs. He was finally able to pry his face from the unrelenting tide of her overflowing breasts and he cried out in infinite pleasure. His shrieks were so overwrought with bliss, a passerby on the street outside might even have mistaken the sounds for screams of pain.

"YEEEEEEESSSS!" Lily shrieked in a chorus of inhuman octaves. She dug her fingernails into the sweaty flesh of Neil's throat. The well-manicured fingertips had become grotesque, gnarled claws. She easily pierced the skin with her talons and ripped his neck nearly in half. His partially decapitated head lolled back and flopped lifelessly against Neil's back, revealing the gaping tunnels of his trachea and esophagus. It happened so fast, his vocal chords did not have time to realize they were dead, and the disembodied mouth continued to scream in a horrifying, ragged gurgle. Blood streamed down his chest and soaked the front of his embroidered uniform, obliterating his sewn nametag.

Lily stood but made no attempt to back away from the twitching corpse. The floor around her fell away entirely, revealing the fiery, seething depths of Hell. Lily stood in midair as if her feet remained firmly planted on solid ground. Her chest and rounded belly glistened with a macabre mixture of lactation and arterial spray. She smiled broadly, revealing uneven, jagged fangs. Neil's fingers still unconsciously reached for her as his unfortunate body tumbled back into the swirling vortex and disappeared into the unholy realm of the Dark Master. The heat singed his hair and made the still-spirting blood from his artery bubble and steam. He blackened as he fell until he appeared to Lily as nothing more than a tiny, charred morsel disappearing in the blazing throat of an enormous predator.

Once satisfied Neil had been disposed of, the floorboards rose back into place and the room was again whole, just as suddenly as it had disintegrated. The house groaned uncomfortably as the wood and nails settled back into place. It was much harder for inanimate objects in the mortal plain to undergo otherworldly transformations. Lily's human form had remained largely unchanged for centuries, but this humble brick tenement would likely have to be abandoned after only a few more weeks. The mortar would start to crumble between the weight of the bricks, and cracks would begin to tunnel through the plaster like ant colonies. Human construction was too brittle for extended shape shifting. After Lily was finished with it, the house would never go entirely back to normal.

The next tenants would feel it too. There would be doors that did not close all the way. They would close certain cabinets each night, only to find them flung open in the morning. The contents of the cupboard strewn around the room. If they were foolish enough to bring any Christian iconography into the home, well... the Master rarely encountered a crucifix he could resist inverting. Once a portal had been opened on Earth, it never truly closed. It was unlikely any of the future tenants at 514 Gates Street would live in the house much longer than Lily did.

Lily sighed and coolly ran a finger up the inside of one thigh. She sucked the salty cum from her finger and smiled happily. The Master would indeed be very, *very* pleased. She sauntered to the foyer of her small, human dwelling, leaving a trail of bloody footprints behind her. She approached the podium where the Devil's book lay open and unassuming. Lily swiped her index finger through the bloody mess on her stomach and smeared a line beneath the last entry on the page. The red smudge instantly transformed into lilting calligraphy that spelled out, "NEIL DEBLASIK," followed by the current date and time. One more added to the Master's book. It had been a very productive day.

Outside, Gates Street shimmered with late afternoon sunshine. No cars drove up or down the street, but that in itself was not overly strange. It was not yet quitting time for the working masses after all. Lily peeked through her translucent front curtain and looked impassively at the sad mail bag tossed like so much garbage on the empty sidewalk. She imagined that it was tucked safely inside Neil's mail truck, and it was. Just as when she had imagined Mallory's red sports car was parked safely inside her garage, it had been. She debated imagining the mail truck safely back at the post office but decided against it. No one would come looking for the rogue mail carrier. They would assume he had grown weary of his pathetic life and simply wandered off the job. They were a notoriously unpredictable bunch. The mortals had even coined a phrase for it: "going postal."

Lily turned and sashayed up the stairs to the barren second floor of her temporary post. She wanted a blistering hot bath to help relax her and prepare for the next job. Overall, it was a very easy assignment. Her work on Gates Street was steady and unopposed. This was the best century she had worked in yet. The superstitions and nosy practices of the old days were largely gone by the wayside. Nowadays, people were so quick to see the Devil in vaccinations, or same sex marriages, but they never thought to check the house next door.

Meanwhile, at 512, Mrs. Weaver opened her front door to survey the street. She did not see any trace of the red car, nor its svelte driver. She did not see Neil making his deliveries, but she thought she saw the distant outline of his mail truck farther down the street.

Another one gone, she thought woefully and patted her leg to summon Samson inside. She could not put her finger on the manner of evil that had moved in next door to her. Nor did she have enough evidence to call the authorities and report the recent string of people who had gone missing on her street. At any rate, she felt safer with her door locked and a badass dog prowling her front yard. Samson obediently climbed the stairs and sat at his master's feet, waiting for her to invite him in. "Come on, boy," she muttered softly and closed the door securely behind the both of them. Tomorrow was a new day. The post office would likely already have a replacement for Neil and send him around with her letters at roughly the same time. Whenever he came, she would be ready. Ready to warn him, and hopefully she and Samson could scare him away from that evil, red house next door.

The Girl Scouts from Hell
Carlton Herzog

The Devil's Advocate

Fiends come in all shapes and sizes, but I had never seen one packaged in a blood smeared Girl Scout uniform. This pint-sized killing machine, stocky with brown eyes and dimples, sported an iconic beret atop thick blonde curls fashioned into ringlets. The bloody merit badges on her sash ran the gamut from "Special Agent" to "Programming Robots." Prophetic sigils as I would soon discover.

I expected some glimmer of emotion, some flicker of remorse, but got none. Instead, her unblinking reptilian eyes dissected me with intense predatory concentration, searching for my tells and weaknesses. And I suspect that if an opportunity had presented itself, she would have tried to kill me.

I said, "Considering your situation, I'm surprised you don't seem the least bit bothered by any of this. Is it that you can't appreciate the gravity of the situation?"

Maintaining her nerveless poise, she said icily, "Just

because I don't care, doesn't mean I don't understand."

If she had been a Gary Gilmore or a Ted Bundy, her glacial rationality would not have surprised me. But she was a fourteen-year old girl splattered in her victims' blood and cuffed to a chair.

Before I could ask her anything else, she said:

"You want to know why I did it. And after I offer up some psychologically plausible explanation or whatever other bullshit I fancy, you will turn to the *Diagnostic and Statistical Manual of Mental Disorders,* flip to the listings of antisocial personalities and see where I fit.

Mind you that manual has its limits. It doesn't mention the so-called 'warrior gene' a monoamine oxidase polymorphism associated with 'psychopathic behavior. Nor would it direct you back along Darwinian vapor trails to prehistoric Europe where the Neanderthals—prognathous jawed, ridge browed—were making the psychopathic rounds. Whatever else they might have been, they were natural hackers and slashers, and so, shining examples of the proposition that lethal aggression comes naturally to us all.

But even if you had the complete scientific picture, you would still not have the truth. Frankly, to borrow a line from Jack Nicholson, 'you can't handle the truth.' Not from me, and not from the private investigator who offered you incontrovertible proof that your wife is a serial cheater."

I was flabbergasted. "How do you know that?"

Without skipping a beat, she said, "I'm the devil; I know everything."

I said, "The devil? Lucifer?"

She said, "Okay, not *The* Devil. I'm the demon, Astarte."

I said, "Forgive my skepticism, but the idea that a demon put a saddle, bridle and bit on a Girl Scout and then went for a ride sounds ridiculous. If you're a demon, then do something outside the laws of physics to convince me. Why sit here bandying words with a lowly child psychologist when you can remove all doubt with a snap of your fingers?

Turn yourself into a wolf or something equally dramatic."

Astarte said, "I may know what the wolves say to one another when they talk among themselves, but I have no desire to scratch myself or sniff another canine's genitals. Besides our greatest trick is convincing men we don't exist. So, shapeshifting, like floating beds, spinning heads and projectile vomiting are all counterproductive absent a compelling reason for such legerdemain. My job is to peddle Hell's influence while maintaining a low profile."

I asked, "I thought Hell's go to guy was the Anti-Christ."

Astarte said, "You watch too many movies. From the beginning men have been drawn to us, the way moths are drawn to a flame. So, our play book focuses on bottom up, grass roots malignity rather than top down. Like most revolutions, it's all very egalitarian."

I asked, "And the Christ?"

Astarte howled with laughter:

"Let me set you straight about Jesus. First, Mary Magdalene, his publicist, wrote all his ponderous dialogue. I met her—she had a camel's face and reeked of farts and hay. I wouldn't fuck her with *your* dick. Second, Jesus didn't die on the cross. He fell off it. The Romans did a shitty job nailing him to the crossbeam. When the first strong wind blew, he popped off and landed on his head. Everybody thought he was dead, but he was just out cold. He woke up in that cave a few days later. Didn't remember a thing. He slipped out the back and headed North where he lived out his days as a wandering foot washer."

I said, "That's some story. If it's alright with you, I'd like to talk to Mary."

Astarte said, "You can't, she's resting in the sunken place. Possession takes a drastic toll on the host. Even if she were awake, she would not have my deep understanding of the events that took place, nor the ability to eloquently explain them. So, you're stuck with me for now."

I asked, "How did you get Mary, your host, to buy into

your bullshit?"

Astarte said:

That's a good question and I'm glad you asked it. I appeared to her mind's eye as an imaginary friend named Glinda, the Good Witch. It was a tour de force performance with me as a beautiful young woman. I had long rich red hair and blue eyes. I wore a pure white dress. I was attended by no less than fifty nymphs.

I fed her the line that I was a sorceress supreme and master of the air. I went over my resume with her. I told her that in Oz, I protected the rabbits of Bunny-Burry and the paper dolls of Miss CuttenClip. I also told her that I had freed and befriended the flying monkeys.

I asked, "And that's all it took?"

Astarte said:

Heavens to Betsy no! I bribed her with promises of better grades, superior athletic ability, and increased popularity. Consider that when I found her, she was clumsy, homely, slow-witted and thick. I made her smarter and stronger. Then I went to work on her peer group.

They proved to be exceptionally stubborn. So, elimination rather than persuasion became my preferred course of action. I began with Danny Racer, Mary's lead tormentor and the most popular boy in school. For all his athletic and academic success, he was an insecure little shit with low self-esteem. Like all bullies, God included, he felt that belittling Mary somehow made him better.

But turnabout is fair play. I had Mary follow Danny home. I made her invisible. As we neared his home, I had her pick-up a good sized sharp-edged rock. Igneous of course, since they tend be harder. I told her to fling it at him. She protested. I told her not to worry.

'Relax nobody can see you. I will make sure it hits him'

She protested some more, then hurled the missile. It was child's play for me to manipulate its flight path and ramp up its acceleration. It didn't just hit him. It split open the back of his skull and penetrated a good three inches. To quote Hamlet, 'it was a hit, a very palpable hit.' He dropped like a bag of dirt. Frankly, I'm surprised he survived, but survive he did. To this day, he remains in Our Lady of Perpetual Sorrow's coma ward. I had Mary bring him flowers. Good publicity made all the better by crocodile tears and some get well cards.

His army of skanks and thugs, however, remained. Sooner or later, a new Alpha asshole would emerge, and Mary's torture would begin anew. I knew we couldn't keep throwing rocks, so we threw mud instead.

Like I said before, we demons know all your dirty little secrets. I knew where various criminals had stashed guns and drugs. I pointed the way and Mary retrieved them. Then once more under a cloak of invisibility, I had her plant them in the lockers of her enemies. A few phone calls, and locker searches later, and all her antagonists had been expelled.

Fratricide

Once her principal tormentors were out of the picture, Mary became pure putty in my hands, open to any suggestion or idea, regardless of how malicious or perverse. I take great pride in her. After all, I had taken a lily-white, Rebecca of Sunny Brook farm type and turned her into a monster. And like I always say, the best dark angels are made, not born.

The real test came when I decided Mary's twin brother Timmy had to be eliminated. Born with cerebral palsy, a stutter, and a slow wit, Timmy got the bulk of the parental attention. He always needed Mary's help with anything that required a measure of physical dexterity—from climbing stairs to changing his clothes, and on certain occasions, going to the bathroom. Since he had no friends, Mary was his inevitable and reluctant playmate.

Although Mary's parents saw nothing amiss with that

relationship, Mary herself felt overburdened. Despite her newfound popularity, her friends remained unsympathetic, shunning her because she could go nowhere without dragging her brother along. They saw Timmy as a nuisance; Mary saw him as something between an unwanted appendage and a tumor.

I told Mary to take things in stride: 'Surely, things will get better as Timmy gets older. Eventually, he'll want to be more self-sufficient, so just hang in there, kiddo.'

But I knew things would get worse before they got better. I just needed to wait for the right moment.

As I expected, he became excessively, and some would say obsessively dependent on his older sister. He never gave her a moment's peace. Each day saw one indignity after another piled on Mary under the rubric of sisterly obligation. The more helpless Timmy became, the more his parents stepped aside and placed the responsibility for his well-being and happiness on Mary. Her resentment grew exponentially. She came to hate Timmy.

I stopped giving Mary pep talks. Instead, I filled Mary's mind with lethal scenarios that included everything from pushing Timmy in front of a car to poisoning his lime Gatorade with anti-freeze.

I interrupted Astarte's narrative by calling her out. "You have the soul of a scorpion. First, you murder her classmates, then you convince her to murder her own flesh and blood."

Astarte said:

"You didn't experience Mary's torment that way I did. She had zero social life. It was all school, sports and Church. All her free time was dedicated to babysitting that whiney, spastic little shit. He parents would pat her on the back then step out leaving her holding the diaper. They had the money to pay a caregiver, but chose to turn their own daughter into a slave instead. She was better off without him and I let her know it.

As the weeks passed, Mary's anger at her brother reached a tipping point. When the bus arrived in front of her house, she was, as always, out there to walk him up the steps. Once in the house, he followed her into her bedroom and sat on her bed. That's when she noticed the smell. He had gone in his pants and then unceremoniously seated himself on her clean comforter. She stuck tissues in her nose and marched him to the bathroom where she cleaned and wiped him.

Plugged up nose notwithstanding, Mary gagged at the smell. I said, 'I can't take his stink anymore. You need to put him down now. This nonsense has gone on long enough.'

Without hesitation, Mary agreed: 'You're right; I can't live like this. He's got to go.'

So, on a sunny Saturday, Mary made it a point to take her brother up to the third floor and out onto the balcony that overlooked the concrete driveway. She brought a camera. She told him that they could take pictures of the hawks nesting in the backyard.

Once she had helped him up the stairs and onto the balcony, she urged him to move to the railing. No sooner had he done so, than she hooked his braces from behind, and in one swift fluid motion, pitched him over the side. He landed headfirst. Mary looked over the railing. A smile crept over her face as she watched the blood and brains ooze onto the concrete from her brother's motionless body.

Given Timmy's extreme spasticity, there was never any suspicion of foul play. Mary gave an Oscar worthy performance as the grieving sister. Life went on after that.

At that point, I interjected and asked Astarte, "Aren't you the least bit worried that God himself will intervene."

Astarte said: "Fifty million people died in World War II and God was nowhere to be seen. So, no I 'm not worried in the least."

I asked, "Why haven't you killed her parents?"

Astarte said: "They still have their uses."

I said, "There's something you're not telling me.

Astarte said: "What gave it away? My bloody saddle-shoes?"

I said, "Possessing someone too young to drive or vote or have any consequential influence seems pointless."

Astarte said:

You got me. So, here's the deal: we demons take a perverse delight in tormenting the damned. Whether it be immersing them in boiling blood, fusing them to dead trees, or tearing them apart again, and again, most of the Fallen relish their opportunities for otherworldly sadism. It takes the sting out of eternal incarceration and helps pass the time.

But even among demons, familiarity breeds contempt especially after eons of the same old same old. One can only rend so much flesh before one gets jaded and yearns for something more. Many demons resent their position as divine torturers, for in their eyes, they are grinding souls to appease their mortal enemy, the Almighty.

To alleviate the boredom, we more high-minded demons have routinely debated what type of possession produces the greater evil: turning an otherwise pure soul dark or steering a pre tainted one into greater acts of depravity.

To that end, I told Mary that Lucifer was looking for someone with whom he could share power. The Queen of Hell, so to speak. 'And I have been preparing you to compete for that honor.'

Mary didn't seem very eager, so I sauced the goose. Gave her the old 'better to rule in hell than serve in heaven' speech. I told her heaven sucks. It's as boring as Sunday school but for all eternity. You spend all your time floating on a cloud, strumming a harp and singing Hosannas to the biggest ass hole the universe has ever seen. In hell, there's always something to see and do, such as orgies, dismemberments, and incinerations just to name a few of the non-stop attractions.

Mary said, "I can't see myself married to a guy with

horns and a tail. How does that even work anatomically. Does Lucifer have a dingus?"

I said, "My, underneath all that quiet reserve and goodness, you are one cheeky sausage. You forget the devil has the power to assume a pleasing shape. He can make his dingus in any size or shape that suits your fancy and he can ramp up the duration and intensity of your orgasms with a wink and a nod. But let's not put the whore before the cart. Before you can sit on Hell's magnificent throne of golden skulls, and bounce on Satan's big red dick, you must occupy a seat of power here. At the very least, we want you to be Senator, but we're shooting for the Presidency. I'm getting tingly just thinking about it."

Mary asked me, "What do I have to do?"

I said,

Kill your opponent. She is a black-haired, angel faced devil-eyed little bitch named Nicky Swango. She hails from a family of arrant scumbags: Father a stumble bum drunk; mother a trollop and meth head; sister a whore and crackhead; brother a thug. Her rider is none other than Azazel, my brother. He is the patron devil of lost causes. And Swango is as lost as they come.

At the tender age of 15, she had already succeeded in blackmailing two of her teachers for making inappropriate advances toward her. That guaranteed her two A's and a steady supply of cash to support her crack habit.

Eventually, the two teachers compared notes and came clean. They lost their jobs. The state sent Nicky to the Trenton Home for Wayward Girls. That living situation offered her the fantastic possibility of recruiting an army of like-minded fiends to do her bidding.

In no time at all, her gang of distaff hoodlums had set fire to schools, shoplifted as a gang, and robbed the elderly. But it wasn't until they made war on Girl Scout Troupe 88 that we felt that it was time that the two of you should meet in battle.

You see they didn't just go in for the traditional catfight—clawing and pulling hair. No, they went at it with the gusto of hardened thugs. They broke jaws, blackened eyes, and fractured limbs. They stole Troupe 88s uniforms and made the girls scurry home naked as jaybirds. Even now Swango's soldiers are masquerading as Troupe 88 Girl Scouts selling the cupcakes the real Troupe 88 intended to sell.

I told her 'Your mission is to collect the real Troupe 88 and whip them into shape. Make the phrase 'a dimple on the chin, a devil within' to mean something again. I want you to burn Swango and her army of skanks to the ground.'

Mary said, 'And if I refuse?'

I didn't mince words. 'I will put a bug so far up your scrawny ass you won't know whether to shit or wind your watch. That's a crass way of saying you will experience hell on earth until the day you die, and once you are departed, I will personally see to it that you are extradited to Hell, where you will spend Eternity being trampled by Centaurs. So, take your pick, Cupcake. Pick up the gauntlet laid at your feet or slide down the infernal sink into misery unending.'

She thought about it for a moment, then said, 'Where is the bitch now?'

The Cupcake Wars

Although Mary had no compunctions about going head to head with Swango's crew, the girls of Troupe 88 were deathly afraid of them.

Mindful that something more was needed, I had Mary claim she was a white witch.

Mary asked me, 'I thought you were all about the low profile.'

I said, 'Convincing a group of naïve girls that you're a white witch is not the same as convincing them the devil exists and you need an exorcism. A witch could be anything from a mutant with telekinetic powers to a garden variety mystic, so the powers of hell would not necessarily be implicated.'

Once Mary gave her consent to play the role of a white witch, I had her go from house to house gathering her recruits in short order, injuries notwithstanding. Mary levitated herself, read minds, moved objects with a thought, and even threw a lightning bolt or two. In the process, the girls went from cowering adolescents to bloody thirsty para-demons eager for revenge against their erstwhile oppressors.

The first order of business was to bake a new batch of cupcakes. I used my powers to spin up the process while making the cupcakes bigger and tastier than the ones stolen by Swango and her mob. I also made them highly addictive to enhance the repeat business.

When Swango got wind of the cupcake competition, she had her girls conduct surveillance of Mary's girls. I read her mind. She wanted to do more than put them out of business. She wanted the secret recipe.

Azazel didn't do much to help her. Girl Scouts and the cupcake business were not his purview. When Swango asked him for advice, he would just say, 'I don't know anything about baking beyond what goes on in hell with the ones I roast. Frankly, I don't get along with little girls. You give me the creeps, what with your pigtails and berets. You remind of Hitler Youth.'

Swango said, 'Do you mean to tell me that after all this possession business and all the promises you made, your dumbass can't come up with a single idea? Man, you are as useful as tits on a bull. Maybe you should change your name to Jesus. He's another big talker who always fails to deliver.'

Azazel was taken aback by her sass. 'I want to hit you,

but I can't because you're a minor. And I'm also inside you. But if you really need a suggestion, then go beat those girls up again, only this time make it stick. And if you want the secret cup cake recipe, beat it out of them. Coercion isn't rocket science.'

Swango, having been given a heads up on the competition's infernal endgame, said, 'if the Devil is anything like your lame ass, then my marriage will surely be one made in hell. Then again, I'll probably be running the show in no time at all.'

Swango gathered her teeny-bopper battalion and went looking for Troupe 88. They looked high and low. When they found them, they were marching down Fulton street in lockstep like a bunch of continental soldiers about to fight in the Revolution.

Swango didn't waste any time. She led the charge of screaming banshees straight at Troupe 88. I did not expect such ferocity. Nor did Mary. Her jaw dropped as her fledgling band of pint-sized assassin scattered to the four winds in fright. They ran down alleys and into backyards; they hid under cars. Some waved down passing vehicles for a ride to safety. A few fainted. Others played dead.

Swango and her not so merry band of angry adolescent girls surrounded Mary. Mary knuckled up to fight Swango. But she was hit from behind and fell face first onto the sidewalk. As she lay there spitting out teeth, Swango stood over her.

She trumpeted, 'Did you honestly think your weenie brigade of whiners could go toe to toe with my girls? Thanks to Azazel, I'll be the new Queen of Hell and you'll be shoveling hot ash for all eternity.'

Then Azazel spoke directly to me through Swango: 'This just goes to show that you can't let a woman do a man's job. You picked weak recruits. Sad. And even worse, you didn't train them to stand their ground. I told Lucifer you were not up to the challenge. You should have stuck to sticking pitchforks into adulterers. Possession is not for you.'

Then we went all sibling rivalry on one another. I said, 'Don't get too cocky, pinhead. I've still got a few tricks up my sleeve. Or haven't you heard that old expression 'hell hath no fury like a woman scorned?'

Azazel said, 'I've heard the saying. I've got one for you: the most talented demons are the ones that can make people worse than they already are. You are nothing more than a tiny stumbling block I will crush underfoot. Be smart and delight in my unparalleled wickedness.'

Amused I said, 'Well since we are trading platitudes, have you heard the old Bible saying that 'Pride goeth before a fall'?

Azazel laughed at that. He said, 'Seriously you're quoting that Book of Lies to me? I would have expected that even a demon as dull as you would have more sense than to put stock in that bit of pulp fiction. The next thing coming out of your mouth will be a quote from a comic book. Sad. But I guess when you're stuck on the bottom, there isn't much in the way of theological ammunition. Face it: you're the ant and I'm the boot.'

I laughed in his face. 'I don't need biblical quotes to take you down. This game was rigged from the start. Wife or no wife, I will always be Lucifer's paramour, while you, my mouthy mephitic moronic brother, will be nothing more than hell's bagman.'

At that moment, I changed Mary from adolescent girl into one of Hell's airborne soldiers: a fire breathing, bat-winged dragon with enormous fangs and talons.

Azazel protested: 'No fair. The rule against encouraging belief prohibits such transformations. Disqualification.'

I said: 'Intent is everything. This metamorphosis is purely defensive and directed solely at you, another demon that would do me harm. I am free to tear you a new one right here and now.'

Taking his cue from me, Azazel transformed Swango

from petite girl into an enormous three-headed wolf.

I tried to incinerate the wolf with hell fire breath. The Wolf, nimble even for its gargantuan proportions, leaped out of the way as my fiery breath turned the street macadam into a molten, bubbling tar.

Not to be outdone, the Wolf took its mighty paw and batted an SUV at me. Flapping my wings and flying just out of harm's way, I let loose another infernal blast of fire. This time I singed the Wolf's shoulder. It let out a murderous cry and bounded down the road in agony and stopped.

Now, I—a dragon—and Azazel a wolf, stared at each other from a distance. Both of us were imbued with full demonic power and wasted no time in escalating our private little war. On the one hand, I turned all of Mary's cringing querulous minions into ferocious bat-winged, fire-breathing dragons with razor sharp talons and teeth and on the other, Azazel transformed Swango's platoon into enormous wolves with deadly venom dripping from their fangs.

Then time froze. Our two hellish factions were unable to move. I suddenly popped out of Mary and Azazel popped out of Swango. A glowing disk of eldritch fire grew larger and larger between us. A moment later, Lucifer himself stepped through the portal. He had not come as an incarnadine horned devil. Rather, he manifested as blond, athletic well-tanned young man dressed in Hilfiger.

He eyed the combatants. Then he smiled and said, 'Sorry, but I have decided I don't want to share power after all. The whole child bride idea was bad from the start. So, I'm releasing you from the game and sending you back to live out your earthly lives. In the theater, this is called a *deux ex machina'*

With that Swango and her army and Mary and hers returned to human form. But instead of going their separate ways, they glared at one another spitting mad and eager to throwdown.

Azazel said, 'See sister. That's what I love about humans

most. They're overriding desire to kill one another, a desire that is surely baked in at birth.'

I said, 'Yes, they are some tribal bitches. Let's stick around and see what happens next. This will be the catfight to end all catfights.'

Lucifer said, 'If they try to kill one another, then something good will come out of this possession business after all. My money's on Swango.'

I said, 'I'll take that bet. Now let's find some good seats to watch them throwdown.'

So, Mary and Swango went at it. At first, it was standard cat fight fare: hairpulling, kicking, slapping, biting. Then they each started looking in the debris for something lethal to match their bad intentions.

They both found tire-irons and began to duel. I must admit they were natural fencers. But as they got winded, Mary the nimbler of the two took control. She parried, she thrusted, and eventually cracked Swango across the jaw. As Swango reeled from the blow, she spat blood and teeth on Mary. Before Swango could gather herself, Mary struck her in the temple. At that moment the fight was over. Swango collapsed into a moaning heap. Mary however wasn't finished. She jumped on top of her and opened up Swango's skull with blow after blow until Swango's head was nothing more than a pile of blood, brains and crushed bone, and Mary was drenched in bloody splatter.

The police showed up moments later. I jumped back into Mary's body as they took her into custody. I had gotten her into this hot mess, and I wanted to get her out. So here sits Mary, bloodied and handcuffed, but victorious with me inside holding the reins. Giddyup bitch.

I said, "That's some story. From a clinical perspective, it will prove very valuable to me. This is the kind of case that can make a career."

Astarte said: "If the video camera had recorded it, then yes, you would be a celebrity. But I can't have you spreading my narrative, so I took the liberty of erasing the footage."

I didn't believe it. But when I played back the recorder, there was just static. Until that point, I was skeptical as to the narrative that had come from Astarte. But the dead video and the knowledge about my wife's numerous affairs made me wonder if I were in the presence of some malignity from hell.

So, I asked, "If Mary is in custody, then how can you use her to advance your agenda?"

Astarte said: "Not a problem. I saw to it that there were no witnesses to the battle. That's called a glamour. Hence, the police merely assumed that she was the perpetrator. But there is no physical evidence suggesting she is. As for the blood, I used a genetic sleight of hand to change it from Swango's to Mary's own, the same as that coming from those cuts on her knobby knees and elbows."

Mary will claim that they were both attacked by person's unknown, and Mary narrowly escaped with her life. The lone survivor angle will play well in press releases about her heroic efforts to defend her troupe and Swango's.

I asked, "And me?"

Astarte said: "If you play along, then I'll consider you a friend of hell and reward you accordingly. I can see you with a string of offices and a headquarters on Park Avenue. Not a bad day's pay for repeating my talking points, wouldn't you say?"

I said, "I am the moth and you are the light. What would you have me do next?"

Astarte said: "Just follow my lead, and all will be well."

And that's just what I did.

Sinister Hand
Len M. Ruth

Banging in the hallway woke Jordie. He dressed in jeans and a t-shirt and opened his door to go to the bathroom. In the hall, a man knelt on the old pine plank floor and yanked on a wire sticking out of the wall.

"Hi," Jordie said, his voice still hoarse with sleep.

"Hi kid," the workman grunted.

Jordie combed his short brown hair, but couldn't get the cowlick out of the back. He brushed his buck teeth and washed his face, wishing the water would take the freckles with it down the drain.

When he finished and stepped out of the bathroom, there was a loud crack from the wall and a section near the floor gave way. Something large and obscured in plaster dust dangled from the wire in the workman's hand.

"Holy shit!" The workman dropped the wire and stared at it.

As the dust cleared, Jordie saw that the workman hadn't

been pulling on a wire at all, but instead, the tail of a giant dead rat. Jordie pictured it crawling around in the walls of his room, and shivered.

"Good thing your parents had the exterminator come before we started. Imagine if that thing was alive? I'd hate to pull that guy out of the wall with those teeth gnawing at me. He's a big one, huh kid?" The workman smiled at him, one tooth edged in front of the other like crossed fingers.

"Uh, yeah." Jordie went down the stairs and did his best to sneak through the dining room unnoticed. His mother had the sewing machine on the table.

"You can't go to school in that raggedy old T-shirt, Jordan. You're in fifth grade now, you need to look nice. Here, try this on." She snipped the thread from a red and white checked shirt and pulled it from the sewing machine.

Jordie sagged, trudged over to her, and put the shirt on. He buttoned down the front and the cuffs. "The collar is too wide, it almost runs off my shoulders."

"Well, we can't afford new shirts or new patterns. You look so handsome. I don't know what you're complaining about."

"No one at my school wears shirts like this, mom. I'm going to get beat up again."

"For wearing a nice shirt? I don't think so."

Jordie nodded.

"You tell those other kids to go dry up. You'll be fine."

While it was a new shirt, it was an old argument, one Jordie knew he couldn't win. "Okay."

He took the brown paper sack from the kitchen counter and peeked in: peanut butter and jelly, again. The bushes in the front yard were an excellent place to take off the shirt and stuff it in his book bag before putting on his orange safety patrol sash with its meaningless tin badge. Even as the plan was forming in his head, his mother called from the dining room.

"Don't you have safety patrol this morning?"

"Yeah."

"Put on your sash then."

Jordie did. Now he was locked into the shirt.

"I love you. Have a great day, Jordie."

"Yeah, right," he muttered slamming the screen door hard.

On the corner, he prayed that Nick DiFruzzio, a sixth grader, had already crossed the street. He walked each knot of kids across the intersection. When it was just about time to go, Nick came down the sidewalk. Close enough; he turned to pick up his school bag where it rested against the stop sign.

"Hey, Jordie," Nick called, "you're supposed to help me cross."

Jordie slung his backpack over his shoulder and turned away.

"Hey, douchebag! Do you want me to tell Mr. Robinson that you left early? Huh?"

Shit. Jordie didn't want to go see Mr. Robinson again. He had enough trouble at school. Shoulders slumped, he stepped onto the street to let the older boy cross. Nick bent down and rub his hands in the dirt by the curb. As Nick passed him, he wiped his hands on Jordie's shirt.

"Nice shirt, douchebag. See you after school, I'm going to kick your ass."

Jordie tried not to worry, but he couldn't help it. He worried he was going to get his ass kicked, he worried he'd get in trouble with Mrs. O'Connell again, and he worried about the shirt.

At math time he kept his head down, hoping Mrs. O'Connell wouldn't notice the calculator on his desk. As she passed out the worksheets, Jordie put his hand over it. The *swick* of Mrs. O'Connell's massive thighs rubbing together in her polyester pants drew closer, then stopped next to his desk. She stood in the isle next to him, her avocado pants struggling to contain her girth.

"All right, Jordie, what are you hiding?" she bellowed in a voice that cracked and gurgled.

He moved his hand.

"A calculator, for math time?"

"I have a note."

"Oh, I know all about your note. Your mother told the principal. Apparently," she rested a plump hand on a fat hip, "you're special."

She hated him. Jordie knew it.

"Why don't you take your special self, your calculator, and your precious note, and go sit at the table at the back of the room so that you are the only one cheating."

"I'm not cheating."

"Using a calculator at math time is cheating, no matter what your little note says."

"It's not cheating. It's a learning disability." Jordie bit his tongue to keep from crying. He felt the eyes of the whole class on him. Muffled laughter burned in his ears.

Mrs. O'Connell leaned down. He smelled the stink of her breath and traced the jagged red lines on her nose with his gaze. The giant mole on her chin looked as if someone stuck a black pencil eraser on her face and planted black hairs around it. "You're a lazy boy, that's all. You'll never amount to anything. Take your things and go to the special ed room. I don't want you in here encouraging the good children to cheat."

Jordie met her gaze for a moment, chanting fuck you, fuck you, fuck you, in his head even as he wondered if she was right. Maybe he was just lazy. Probably he would never amount to anything. No one in his family did. When Mrs. O'Connell moved on, Jordie gathered his things and walked out of class, head down, not meeting the eyes of the kids he knew were staring at him.

The special ed room was a dim cinder block cave. Mrs. Henderson kept the fluorescent lights off, she said they hurt her eyes. The blinds were open, but the sun never saw the inside of that little room.

"Jordie," she said in a flat voice, "having trouble with Mrs. O'Connell again?"

Jordie nodded.

"What would you like to work on?" She made Jordie think of fish he caught on the rare occasions his father took him. Partly because of the dry skin on her arms, cracked and scaly. Partly because her voice was as cold as brackish water in springtime. "How about a story prompt? You always like those."

Jordie nodded.

She withdrew a sheet of lined paper from her desk. "You're quiet today."

Jordie nodded. If he opened his mouth, he might cry.

"Here's a nice one about a snowman. That should be fun to write about."

Only if the snowman tells Mrs. O'Connell to go fuck herself. Of course, he'd never write that story. He'd learned not to express himself in his stories. He'd written one about beating up Nick DiFruzzio once. That landed him in meetings with the principal and his mother. Then more sessions with Mrs. Natalie, the school counselor, and her ridiculous 'talking pillow.' "Okay."

"You work on that; I'm going to step out for a few minutes."

"You're going to smoke cigarettes and sneak a grownup drink, is what you're going to do," he thought, but what he said was: "Okay."

He sat in the darkest of three little cubicles. The paper had part of a sentence at the top. It said: Sparky the snowman was happy because… Jordie looked at it for a minute. He could read it just fine, but sometimes when he tried to write, the letters all jumbled up in his head and came out wrong on the paper. He crossed out 'snow' and wrote 'spase,' then crossed out 'happy.' He was going to write 'angry' but couldn't get the letters the right way, so he wrote 'mad' in spidery letters. He finished the sentence so that it read: "Sparky the spase man was mad becuz he lost his spaseship." Better.

The door opened behind him, and a stranger came through. He had black hair and a bushy black beard that covered most of his face, and he smelt like ashes.

"You must be Jordie," he said.

"Yes."

"Mrs. Henderson went home sick. I'm your substitute, Father Ollie."

"Are you a priest?" Jordie had the impression that the man was smiling at him, but he couldn't really see the man's mouth through all that hair.

"Something like that. Are you okay? You seem sad."

"I'm fine," Jordie lied.

"I don't think so, Jordie. I can see that you're having a hard time."

How could this man know that after just looking at him for a second? Jordie just wanted to be left alone to write his story.

"It's okay, I won't tell, promise." Father Ollie held up his hand in a scout's salute.

Jordie said nothing.

Father Ollie put a hand on Jordie's shoulder. The hand was very hot. Jordie flinched away. He didn't like being touched, not even by his mother, and especially not anyone who's name started with 'father.' It made him think of Father Finnegan.

Father Ollie removed his hand. "I'm sorry, I didn't mean to upset you. I heard you are having trouble with Mrs. O'Connell."

Jordie froze, doing his best to melt into the floor.

"It's okay. Can I tell you a secret?"

Jordie nodded.

"I think Mrs. O'Connell is a bitch."

Jordie couldn't believe it! He'd never heard a teacher talk

like that before, especially about another teacher! He snorted, holding in a laugh.

Father Ollie laughed. "It's okay to laugh, Jordie. I said it, not you. You can't get in trouble for laughing."

Jordie knew that wasn't true, but he laughed just the same.

"Now, let's see what you are working on." He looked over at the paper on Jordie's desk. "You don't like writing about snowmen?"

"They're boring."

"Yes, they are."

"Spacemen are okay though. Like Star Wars."

"Would you like to try something different?"

"Like what?"

"Well, if you're having a hard time sometimes it helps to write about it."

Jordie shrugged.

Are you afraid you'll get in trouble?"

Jordie nodded.

Father Ollie seemed to smile.

"Tell you what, Jordie, I've got some special paper. If you write down what's bothering you on this paper I won't even look at it." He pulled a tan envelope from his jacket. It was big enough to put papers in without folding them. He took a sheet of paper from the envelope. Then he took a gold lighter, the kind with the flip top, clicked it open with a flick of his wrist, and lit the paper on fire. There was a *whoomp,* and the paper vanished.

"Wow, that's cool!"

"It's called flash paper. You write your troubles down, then I'll burn the page. I promise you'll feel a lot better, just like magic. I won't even look if you don't want me to."

"Okay, but how do I write the story to make me feel better?"

"Well, what's your biggest problem today?" He took another sheet of paper from the envelope.

"Well, Nick DiFruzzio said he was going to beat me up after school."

"I see. Maybe you could write a story about something bad happening to him so that he can't beat you up. I bet that would make you feel better."

"Like what?"

"Use your imagination. I hear you have a good one."

"I'll try."

"You'll do fine. And, Jordie, it would be best if you didn't talk about this. It isn't exactly in the teacher's handbook."

"Okay." Jordie didn't know what the teacher's handbook was and he didn't care. He was already thinking up terrible things that could happen to Nick DiFruzzio.

"Good boy. Say, are you left-handed?"

Jordie dropped the pencil, afraid Father Ollie was one of the teachers that insisted he switch hands.

"It's all right. Do you know what Latin is?"

"It's the language they speak at church sometimes."

"That's right. It's an ancient language, a *dead* language."

Jordie shivered.

"And the Latin word for 'left' is sinestra, or sinister. Do you know what sinister means?"

"Something bad?"

"That's right. Smart boy. Why don't you take your sinister hand and write a sinister story about Nick DiFruzzio."

Jordie liked that Father Ollie seemed almost excited about his being left handed. Even though they'd just met, Father Ollie was already the nicest teacher Jordie ever had.

Once he got into the flow of writing, he really enjoyed it, more than ever before. The letters didn't jumble up in his head. The sentences seemed to come right out of him from somewhere else. When he finished, he did feel better. It made him feel strong and in control. He liked having the power to decide what horrible thing happened to Nick, even if it was on paper.

"Done," he said putting his pencil down.

"Do you want me to read it?"

"No."

"All right then." Father Ollie lit the paper with his gold lighter. There was a *whoomp* as before, and the paper was gone.

Jordie thought he saw the flame reflected in Father Ollie's eyes even after the fire was gone.

"Do you feel better?"

Jordie nodded.

"See, what did I tell you?"

Though he felt better, Jordie still worried about Nick DiFruzzio beating him up after school. He thought about pretending to be sick and going home before safety patrol. If he did, then there'd be a visit to the school nurse, calls to his mom while she was at work, and all kinds of other problems.

He worried a little more with each group of children he helped cross the busy intersection. Nick was among the last to cross.

"Look at that douchey orange sash over that faggoty shirt," Nick said, shoving Jordie aside as he crossed.

Jordie shoved him back.

Sound exploded, metal on metal. A blur. A cloud of thick black smoke. The smell of burning rubber. Nick DiFruzzio… gone. In his place, tire marks on the pavement. A smear of blood led under the dump truck screeching to a stop. Jordie thought of when his mother grated the special cheese on his spaghetti. Only, Nick didn't look like the cheese, he looked like the spaghetti.

His ears rang. He coughed on the smoke from the truck's tires.

The truck driver climbed under the truck yelling something. People got out of their cars. Jordie turned in a circle.

A woman grabbed him by the shoulders and sat him in

the grass by the side of the road. "Don't look."

Jordie didn't.

Sirens, ambulances, police, and people filled the intersection.

The woman sat with him until the police came and talked to him. Then after a while, his mother came for him.

No one talked about it at dinner. No one talked about anything. That night Jordie lay in bed and stared at the ceiling wondering why the exact thing he'd written in his story for Father Ollie happened, just like he wrote it. He wondered if it was his fault somehow if that flash paper was something more. He worried that he'd go to jail, and he listened for the rats.

The next day Jordie's mother kept him home from school. That was fine with Jordie. He sat on his bed staring at his hands. Was he a murderer? There was no such thing as magic, he knew that. Stories didn't come true just because you wrote them down, he knew that too, but in his heart, he knew that Nick was dead in his story. And dead in real life.

The day after that, most of the kids and teachers were wearing black. No one spoke to him. No one even looked at him. He used his calculator at math time, and Mrs. O'Connell pretended not to see. She pretended he wasn't even there. No one spoke at dinner that night. Jordie didn't sleep much. Every time he closed his eyes he saw blood on the pavement and heard rats in the walls.

The next day Father Ollie was in the special education room again. Jordie stopped in the hallway.

"Jordie, hello, what is it?"

Jordie stood frozen.

"You can't just stand in the hallway all day. Come in, come in. If something is bothering you let's talk."

Jordie took a few hesitant steps into the room.

"Sit down, Jordie, tell me what's on your mind?"

"I'll get in trouble."

"No, I promise."

Jordie hesitated.

"C'mon, it's going to be okay."

"The story I wrote...on that special paper…"

"Yes?" Father Ollie leaned in closer resting his hands on the desk.

Jordie smelled ashes again. "I wrote about Nick getting hit by a truck," he sobbed.

"Oh, Jordie," Father Ollie reached out to touch Jordie's hand.

Jordie recoiled.

"Sorry, I forgot you don't like to be touched." Father Ollie drew back. "Don't worry, Jordie, what happened to Nick was an accident. The story was just a coincidence. Do you know what that means?"

"Yes."

"Good. Jordie, you can't make things happen to people just by writing them down. The world would be a terrifying place if any boy could do that." He gazed at Jordie. "You don't seem convinced. Jordie, sometimes things just happen. Sometimes bad things happen to good people, and when that happens, it's sad. But sometimes bad things happen to bad people, and I don't think that's so sad. Do you?"

"Well…"

"Are you sad that Nick died, or are you sad because you think you had something to do with it?"

"The second thing."

"Jordie, do you believe in magic?"

"Not really."

"No. Jordie, I'm just a man. A regular man. And that paper is just flash paper. You can buy it at any magic shop. All you are doing is letting your feelings out, putting them on paper. Nick was mean to you wasn't he?"

"Yes."

"Did he beat you up?"

"Yes."

"More than once?"

"Yes."

"What were you going to do about it? Just take it, forever?"

"I don't want to talk about this."

"Do you want to talk to the school counselor?"

Jordie thought of Miss Natalie and her stupid talking pillow. "No."

"Then tell me, what you were going to do about Nick?"

"I started carrying a pocket knife."

"A knife!"

Jordie thought Father Ollie was going to yell at him, but he just smiled.

"What were you going to do with it? Stab Nick?"

"I don't know."

"Well, I don't think you would. You're a good boy. Still, we can't have you walking around school with a knife. Besides, you don't need it anymore, do you?"

"I guess not."

"Why don't you just give it to me to hold on to so that you don't get in any trouble?"

Jordie felt the weight of the knife against his thigh, but he didn't move.

"You don't want to get in trouble, do you? Your mother would have to come down here for more meetings. You'd have to see the counselor, all that stuff. You don't want that, do you, Jordie?"

Jordie squirmed in his seat.

"Come on, Jordie, do the right thing."

Jordie gave him the knife.

"There." Father Ollie rose from his chair and withdrew the envelope with the flash paper from his coat, then held out a piece to Jordie.

As Jordie took it, Father Ollie's fingers brushed Jordie's in a slow, smooth way. Jordie jerked back.

"Yes, the boy who doesn't like to be touched. Why is that Jordie?"

"I don't want to talk about that."

"No? You'll feel better."

"No."

"All right. Why don't you write about it."

"What if the same thing happens?"

"Oh, is it because of a person?"

Jordie was silent.

"Well, we've talked about this. What happened to Nick is a coincidence. That can't happen again." Father Ollie leaned in close to Jordie, so close that Jordie could smell ashes on his breath. "Even if it did, would you feel bad about it? Really?"

"No. "

"Good boy. Then go use that sinister hand."

Jordie wrote the story. His pencil slashing and stabbing at the paper. His letters didn't jumble up in his head at all. Every letter of every word was perfect. He was almost sad no one would see it, but no one could. No one must ever see this story, ever. His pencil pushed through the anger, through the hatred, and through the paper in some places.

"Done." He dropped the pencil on the desk.

As before, Father Ollie smiled, closed-lipped, and set his lighter to it. And as before, Jordie thought he caught a hint of flames lingering in Father Ollie's eyes even after the paper was gone.

When he got back to Mrs. O'Connell's class, she was meaner than ever.

"Well, I hope you had a relaxing time while the rest of the class was learning. Do you think you'd like to learn anything today? Or would you like to go back to the special ed room and take a nap?"

Jordie sat down, face burning, and did his best, which wasn't very good, with the spelling words.

Guilt about the story he wrote, and about Nick DiFruzzio, ate away at him all day. At home, he broke down crying. When his mother was able to coax out of him that he felt guilty about Nick she had the same answer she always did—a visit to Father Finnegan.

Jordie resisted, stopping just short of absolute refusal. He hated church even more than was normal for a boy his age, but he wouldn't disobey his mother. What he really hated, more than church, were visits to Father Finnegan.

When he came out of Father Finnegan's office, he held up a finger to his mother and ran for the bathroom. There, he threw up in the toilet, then washed his face and hands. He wadded up some paper towels, wet them, washed himself front and back, pulled up his pants, and re-washed his hands. The nausea hadn't gone away, but he felt like he could face his mother and pretend nothing was wrong, at least, nothing new.

He didn't sleep at all that night. Thoughts of blood on pavement, rats in walls, and whether or not today's story would come true kept him awake.

At school the next day, Jordie couldn't keep his mind on his work. The story he'd written haunted his thoughts. Though he knew it was silly, he kept wondering if it came true like it did with Nick DiFruzzio. He saw the blood on the pavement. He smelled the smoke from the truck's tires. He heard angry voices. One of them was Mrs. O'Connell. She stood over him.

"You are the laziest boy I've ever had in my classroom." She looked over his unfinished spelling worksheet. "You are the only fifth grader I've ever seen who still can't tell the difference between a 'b' and a 'd.'" She reached down and grabbed his paper. "I can't believe I have to waste my time on a brat who doesn't care to learn. Or maybe you can't, that's what your precious note says, isn't it? That you have a learning disability? So are you lazy or stupid?"

"I care." Jordie took a breath, trying not to cry in front of the class. "You just won't give me a—"

"Chance? I've given you chance after chance. Don't try to blame me for your laziness. You're going to stay inside for recess, and while the rest of the class is outside playing, you're going to finish your spelling worksheet. Then on the back, you will write 'I will finish my spelling on time' one hundred times."

Jordie couldn't hold in the sob. It came out like a bark, and tears were close behind it.

"Crying might get you sympathy at home, but not in my classroom. Everyone else, line up at the door." Mrs. O'Connell leaned down. "You are lazy and stupid, and you'll never amount to anything," she said so that the other kids could hear.

The class lined up and filed out.

"You'd better be done when I get back, sitting with your hands folded on your desk." She closed the door behind her.

Spelling was hard. Jordie struggled through the rest of the worksheet, then began to write on the back. He kept looking over at where Mrs. O'Connell's lunch bag sat on her desk. He imagined her grabbing a giant sandwich from it, white mayonnaise dripping from her fat, wrinkled chin as it worked up and down, devouring, smacking, gobbling. Then he imagined her choking, her hands at her throat, her face purple, eyes red and bulging. She dropped to the floor in his mind, writhing, clawing at her neck, and then lay still.

When the vision was over, he looked down at his sentences. He dropped the pencil and began to get up, then, sat back down and wrote 'FUCK YOU' in large letters across the blank part of the paper.

He banged open the door of the special ed room.

"What—" Father Ollie half-rose from the desk.

"Is there any of that paper left?"

"I set a piece out on the desk in the corner cubicle. I've been waiting for you."

Jordie looked at him, wondering how he knew.

"It's best to get started while the fire of inspiration is hot," Father Ollie smiled through closed lips.

Jordie's pencil flew across the paper. He'd never seen the

story and the words so clearly in his mind. Each sentence was letter perfect. Hatred, rage, and revenge flowed through his sinister hand onto the page. When he was done he handed the paper to Father Ollie.

"May I read this last one?"

The last one, Jordie thought. "Go ahead." He folded his arms across his chest.

Father Ollie read the paper then looked at Jordie. "Delightful! The dripping mayonnaise and the big mole going up and down, wonderful imagery! It's almost a shame no one will ever read it. Are you sure you want me to burn this one?"

"That's how it works right? For coincidences to happen?"

"Yessss," Father Ollie hissed, "that's how it works." He lit the paper, and it disappeared with a *whoomp*.

Jordie sat down, his anger spent, eyes heavy.

"Are you tired?"

"Yes. Couldn't sleep."

"Well, you'd better get some rest. Did you know if you go long enough without sleep you hallucinate? See things, people that aren't there? You can't make good decisions either. Why, without sleep, you could see and do almost anything. Best to get some rest. Why don't you put your head down on the desk and take a nap? I'll make sure Mrs. O'Connell doesn't bother you."

"Okay."

"Oh, before I forget," Father Ollie took a crumpled white cloth from his pocket. "Here is your knife back. I wrapped it in a handkerchief, so you're not tempted to take it out till later. Wouldn't want you to get in trouble." Father Ollie smiled, this time showing his teeth. One of them edged over another, like crossed fingers.

Jordie couldn't help thinking he'd seen that smile before, but his eyes were already closing as he laid his head on his desk.

Someone grabbed his shoulder. Jordie raised his head in

confusion. Mr. Robinson stood by him. Jordie rubbed his eyes and looked around. Outside the window, he could see only darkness. How long had he been asleep?

"We've been looking for you, Jordie," the principal said.

A man in a suit stepped into the room, two others stayed in the hall. He looked mean. "Where have you been today?" He asked.

"Um, here."

"Here in this room? All day?"

"No, at school."

"Were you in Mrs. O'Connell's class today?"

"Yes."

"By yourself?"

"Well no, it was a regular class day."

"She didn't leave you alone in the room while the rest of the class went to recess?"

"I don't know." Jordie struggled to keep himself from trembling. He gripped the thighs of his jeans, suddenly sure that his story had already come true.

"Yes, you do, Jordie. She left you inside by yourself at recess. Didn't she?"

"I guess so."

"Is this your paper?" The man held up his spelling paper. The 'fuck you' side faced him.

"No."

"Really? It has your name on it." The man put the paper down and pulled a plastic bag from his pocket. "What about this?" The bag had his knife in it. There was blood all over it.

"That's not mine."

"We found it in your room."

"Why were you in my room?"

"Because you were the last person to see Father Finnegan alive. He was found this morning with his cock cut off and shoved up his own ass."

"Really, detective! I don't think—" the principal began.

"You shut up, Principal Pencil Dick, or I'll find a way to make you an accessory." The mean man turned back to Jordie. "Are you sure this isn't your knife? I think it is. I think that's Father Finnegan's blood on it, but don't worry, we have ways of finding out for sure."

"It's not mine. Father Ollie gave me mine back this afternoon. It's in my pocket."

"Who's Father Ollie?"

"Mrs. Henderson's substitute."

The detective looked at Principal Robinson.

"I don't know what he's talking about. There is no substitute," the principal said.

"Yes, there is! He's been giving me writing prompts all week!"

"No, Mrs. Henderson says you've been coming in here and sleeping on your desk all week. You told her it's because you weren't sleeping well at home on account of the rats."

"Is that right?" the detective asked.

Jordie looked down at his hands. He thought of what Father Ollie said about seeing things.

"You said this Father Ollie gave you your knife back," the detective said. "Why did you have a knife at school?"

Jordie's stomach knotted.

"Okay. Why did he take it away then?"

"Because I'm not supposed to have it at school."

"Do you still have it?"

Jordie felt the weight of it on his thigh. "Yes."

"Show me."

Jordie stood, pulled the hankie with the knife in it from his pocket, and held it out to the detective.

"I'd better not touch it, just in case. Put it on the desk. Why is it all wrapped up?"

"Father Ollie said it was so I wouldn't take it out and get in trouble."

"I see. Unwrap it."

Jordie did, and let out a sob. It wasn't his knife at all. It was a long thin box like the kind his mother kept her pills in.

"That's not a knife, Jordie. What's in there?"

"I don't know."

"Open it."

"It's not mine! Father Ollie gave it to me!"

"It was in your pocket. Open it."

Jordie opened the box, heart pounding against the prison bars of his ribs.

"Looks like rat poison. The same rat poison we found in Mrs. O'Connell's sandwich a little while ago. The same rat poison that's all over your house. And I'll bet we'll find some in Mrs. O'Connell's stomach at the autopsy. Do you know what an autopsy is, Jordie?"

"No."

"It's like a doctor's visit for dead people to find out why they died."

"Mrs. O'Connell is dead?" Jordie felt like he was falling down a well.

"Does that make you happy, Jordie?"

Jordie looked down. "No."

"Well, if what I hear is true, you should be happy. She was very mean to you. So mean that you wrote 'fuck you' on your paper and put rat poison in her sandwich."

"No."

"What about Father Finnegan? Did you know he was dead?"

"I...no...you just said he was."

"That's right, someone cut his dick off with a knife just like that one." The detective pointed to the bloody knife in the bag. "He was mean to you, too, wasn't he? Did he do terrible things to you? Huh? Maybe things with his cock?"

"Really!" the principal shouted, "this is not the right venue detective, uh—"

"DiFruzzio. Detective Nick DiFruzzio. This little murderous bastard pushed my son in front of a truck, then killed two other people. Now you shut the fuck up."

"He pushed me!" Jordie shouted. "He pushed me! He pushed me!"

The principal stepped between them. "I'm sorry about Nick Jr. but are you really supposed to be on this case?"

Nick's father grabbed the principal and shoved him aside.

"Can I get a little help here!" the principal called into the hallway.

"You were going to do my Nick with that knife, weren't you, you little murderous bastard, but the truck did it for you. Then you had a taste for it." Spit flew from Detective DiFruzzio's mouth as he spat the words at Jordie. "Couldn't let the knife go to waste, so you thought you'd have a little revenge, on Father Finnegan, give him a taste of his own medicine, huh? Shoved his pecker up him like he shoved it up you! Then that old bitch O'Connell pushed you—"

"Detective!" The principal yelled, getting between Jordie and Nick's father.

Jordie was looking for a chance to run, but two men in white were walking into the room blocking his way out.

"All right, Jordie," one said in a sing-song voice, "we're going to take you to a special hospital where we can sort this all out—"

"No! I didn't do it! I didn't do any of it! It must be Father Ollie!"

The other man in white smiled at him with a crooked tooth like a crossed finger, just like Father Ollie.

"No! No! It was him!" Jordie pointed at the man with the crooked tooth. "It was him! It was himmmmm!"

Jordie heard someone say: "Sedate him." He put his fists up.

Crooked tooth took a case from his pocket and pulled a needle from it. Someone grabbed his arms. He felt the sting of the needle. He saw crooked tooth man smile wide. Fire flashed in the man's eyes.

"Father Ollie's eyes!" Jordie felt the world slowing down.

"He has Father Ollie's eyes!" He began to feel tired, heavy. "Father Ol...eyes. Father Ol eyes…" The words jumbled up in his mind. "Father O lies… Father of Lies… Father of Lies…"

Charity Begins at Home
Vivian Kasley

On a quiet picture-perfect street live the picture-perfect family, the Noblemans. A two-story Victorian home sits on a sprawling lawn and snow blankets the ground like waves of marshmallow fluff. The front of the house is decorated for the holiday season with large festive wreaths, warm colored lights, and a single star adorns the front door. The door opens, and out pops Mr. Nobleman to retrieve his morning paper with a steaming cup of French roast. He tilts his head full of dark hair toward the sky and shields his blue eyes from the glare of the sun, then grins with his gleaming white teeth and breathes in the crisp air.

"You know tomorrow is Christmas Eve?" Mr. Nobleman said as he set the paper down on the table and winked at his daughter.

Mrs. Nobleman was preparing pie crusts and her platinum blonde hair bounced as she turned around. "Of course, dear. I have everything in order."

"How lucky am I? I have a beautiful wife, beautiful children and a beautiful home. Which reminds me—Bree, honey? Did you invite anyone to dinner this year?"

"Yes, father. A struggling artist outside of the coffee shop

I go to. He was holding a sign asking for money and food. He said he had no family or anywhere to go tomorrow, so, I invited him. I gave him some money, the address, and told him to come around six."

"Oh, sweetheart, that's great!" Mr. Nobleman beamed proudly at his daughter.

"Jim, dear, I'm making a turkey, sausage stuffing, apple pie, pumpkin pie, mashed potatoes, corn, sweet potato casserole, and salad. Is there anything else you think I should make?"

"Goodness, no—you always make too much and I'm always filled up before I even reach the pies!"

"Oh, Jim, it's ok to be gluttonous this time of year!"

Bree smiled at her parents. She was excited about Christmas, too. She was hoping for something special this year. At only seventeen, Bree had almost everything she'd ever wanted.

"Good morning, mother, father...oh, and Bree. It's a glorious morning, indeed. No school. Snow on the ground. And it's Christmas Eve, Eve." Brannon poured himself some juice.

"Bran, have you invited anyone to dinner tomorrow?" Mr. Nobleman stared at his son.

"Not yet, father. There're so many needy people out there, though. I'm sure I'll find someone today." Brannon smiled over his glass and sipped his juice.

Mrs. Nobleman frowned at her son, then said, "Well, honey, today's the last day before...well, before you know what. Remember, we're very fortunate, and also, it's good for your soul, sweetie. Last year you didn't invite anyone and I don't want you to feel left out again. Your father and I have both invited someone this year. Why, I met a lovely woman who was sitting outside of the laundromat who I almost mistook for a pile of clothes! Poor thing, she was bundled in so many layers of clothing. And your father, he spotted a man asleep against a tree. He said the man was so tipsy he could barely stand, the poor soul."

"Well, he could stand, he just stumbled a bit is all. A hot meal would do him good, I think. He actually asked me if he could bring anything, can you believe that? I said, just yourself!" Mr. Nobleman chuckled, then mumbled, "I'll be surprised if he shows actually."

"Oh, honey, he was trying to be nice and I'm sure he'll show, they almost always do. People shouldn't be alone on Christmas. No one ever truly wants to be alone." Mrs. Nobleman turned back to her pie crusts.

"I'm going to the mall. Bree, you wanna come with? Jayden might be there." Brannon playfully punched his sister's arm and wiggled his eyebrows.

Bree scowled, then punched him back. "No, I have too much to do, and mother needs my help."

"Ok, whatever. I'll tell *Jayden* you said hi."

"Bran, I'm gonna need help with the firewood. We don't want a cold house. Think of our guests? Nobody likes cold food, am I right?" Mr. Nobleman asked.

"You are absolutely right, father."

Without turning around, Mrs. Nobleman said, "Brannon, before you go, please try and remember that we have so much to be thankful for. We've been granted so many wonderful things. Remember in order to receive, you must give back. I know as a teenager you're enjoying yourself, but just remember how you got where you are, will you?"

"Mother, don't worry, I get it."

"Bran, your mother's right. Don't be selfish. It can all be taken away. We have what we have for a reason. Every year we must give back." Mr. Nobleman hit the table with his fist to drive home his point.

"I said I get it, jeesh, could you give me a little credit? It's winter break, that's all. I promise I won't be out too long."

"Of course, go get em', son."

Brannon grabbed his black peacoat and headed out the

door to his Mercedes. He smirked at his reflection in the side mirror, then sped out of the driveway.

"Boys! They're all like that, right? Girls, girls, girls—it's all they think about!" Bree rolled her eyes.

"Bree, don't you like a certain boy? Jayden, is it?" Mr. Nobleman tilted his head.

"Father!"

"You've been fluttering around here for days like a hummingbird." Mr. Nobleman flapped his arms.

"I have not! Anyway, I'm not sure he even notices me."

Mrs. Nobleman said, "I'm sure he'll notice you, sweetie. How could he not?"

"Your mother's right dear, he'll notice sooner or later. Well, alright, my beautiful ladies. I'm going to get started on the wood." Mr. Nobleman kissed his wife and headed outside.

Mrs. Nobleman put a pie in the oven, then her and Bree went to hang four black stockings from the fireplace. The top of their tree almost touched the ceiling and was littered with a multitude of decorations. Bree frowned and touched one of the dangling ornaments.

"What is it, sweetie?" Mrs. Nobleman's eyebrows knitted together.

"Nothing…it's just that…I was just thinking of something. Remember that older man a couple years ago, the one with the eye patch? He was a Vietnam War veteran and he spoke about so many things and shared all those stories before dinner…he was so nice, that's all."

"Oh, yes, I do recall. Your father invited him. He was very nice, sweetie. You know we do what we can and we do a lot more than other people do. Just try to keep in mind how happy their faces are when they're seated around the table enjoying a hot meal."

"I know, it's just that...I hope what we do eases their suffering, even if just a little."

Mrs. Nobleman took her daughter by the hand, then

turned her toward the large mirror that hung above the fireplace. Bree was the spitting image of her mother. They could have passed for sisters. She smoothed her daughter's hair and said, "Just look at yourself. You're stunning, Bree…do you know that I wished for you? I couldn't be happier. A higher power truly exists and he's always watching and counting on us. Be grateful and praise him every day. I know I do."

Mrs. Nobleman wiped a tear away from her daughter's cheek and turned her attention back toward the stockings. Bree watched her mother in the mirror and felt her heart swell. *Mother is right, we are lucky.*

Mr. Nobleman enjoyed the crunch of his foot falls in the snow as he went to the shed to get the axes. They needed sharpened. He counted the piles of wood that sat out by the shed that Brannon and he would chop together. It was a ritual and the Nobleman's believed in their rituals.

Brannon pulled into the driveway, hopped out of his car, and jogged over to his father. "I did it! I've invited someone!"

"That's great, son. You did the right thing." Mr. Nobleman handed his son an ax.

Together they chopped firewood in silence as the snow began to fall around them. By late afternoon, they had already stacked all of the wood. Mr. Nobleman reminded his son to bring his ax inside and place it in the coat closet.

"Of course, father. Man, I can smell mother's pies baking from out here!" Brannon stomped the snow from his boots, then went inside.

"Mother, guess what? I've invited someone to dinner!"

"Wonderful, honey! I'm so glad!"

Bree stood at the table rubbing down a turkey. She looked up at her brother. "Let me guess? It's a girl, right?"

Brannon grinned. "Why, how'd you know? She was hanging outside the mall and we got to chatting. She said she was staying at a motel."

"Is she a prostitute?" Bree pursed her lips.

Mrs. Nobleman shot her daughter a look of disapproval. "Bree, it doesn't matter. We don't discriminate."

Mr. Nobleman walked into the kitchen and sniffed the air. "Jill, you're cooking something special this year. Did Brannon tell you the good news?"

"Yes, he did. I'm so happy too, I hate setting the table with an uneven amount of plates. It's such a bother."

Mr. Nobleman kissed his wife, then swirled her around to dance with him. Bree threw a sprig of thyme at her brother and he threw it back, then he picked up a wooden spoon and began to croon holiday songs into it. Everyone laughed and joined in. Later, as they sat by the fireplace, the Nobleman's relaxed and drank hot cocoa with candy cane sticks. The fire crackled and popped as it warmed them and they all went to bed feeling merry and bright.

On Christmas Eve morning, the family sat in their breakfast nook and stared down at their individual pieces of gold lined paper. Brannon folded his over first.

Mr. Nobleman looked up at his son. "Made your wish already, Bran?"

"Yup."

"Good." Mr. Nobleman nodded, then folded over his paper next, then nodded at his wife and daughter when they folded theirs. "Ok, I believe we're all finished. Shall we?"

The Nobleman's all went to the fireplace and put their folded papers into their individual stockings. Then they bowed their heads and prayed silently until Mr. Nobleman clapped his hands together and said, "It is done. Let us all get ready for tonight!"

The day went by quickly and by six o' clock in the evening the first guest was due to arrive. Mrs. Nobleman asked her husband to check the turkey in the oven when the doorbell rang.

"I'll get it," Bree yelled and ran to the door. She opened it and looked over a pretty girl in an old grey sweater, ripped jeans, and worn black boots. She smiled and Bree smiled back. The girl pushed her brown hair behind her ear and put her hand out for Bree to shake.

"Hello, I'm Sage. Brannon invited me to dinner here and I—"

"Of course, come in out of the snow! I'm Bree, Brannon's little sister. It's so nice to meet you."

Sage walked in and her eyes were wide with wonder as she took in the lavishly decorated home. She began to spill her guts. "This's weird. I've never had a holiday dinner with complete strangers. It's just that, well, I have no home to go back to right now. I just came here not too long ago, and when your brother asked if I wanted to—"

Bree put her hand on her Sage's shoulder. "Please, just come and get warm."

Brannon walked in and smiled at Sage. He held a mug of warm cider out to her. "You came! Would you like some hot cider?"

"Um, sure." Sage took the mug, then said, "Your home is gorgeous! Thank you again for inviting me."

"You're very welcome," Bree and Brannon said.

"This drink is actually delicious. I've never had hot cider before, at least not that I know of."

"We're so happy to have you here, we really are." Brannon gently took Sage by the hand and led her to the couch, then he excused himself.

"He's so sweet. You're lucky to have a brother like that," Sage said and sat down.

"Yeah, he's pretty cool, I guess." Bree sat down next to her.

"So, where're you from? How old are you? I mean, you don't have to tell me, I'm just curious—alright and I'm nosy." Bree blushed

"No, it's fine. Where to start, let's see, I'm nineteen and my pop threw me out. I have Facebook friends all over, so I crashed with them a night here and there, but suddenly found myself shit out of luck when one supposed friend bailed. I don't expect people to keep taking me in or anything, I was very lucky they did at all. Don't worry, I'm not going to ask to stay here or anything."

"I'm not worried." Bree smiled.

Brannon came back and the doorbell sounded again. Bree stood up to get the door and Brannon looked over at Sage. He moved a poker in the fire and tried to make small chat. A tall well-dressed young man strolled into the living room with Bree.

"Brannon, Sage. This's Toby."

Toby stuck out his hand to Brannon, and then Sage who stood to greet him. His nails were manicured and his blonde hair perfectly coiffed. "It was so nice to be invited to a holiday dinner! And at a stranger's house? This's so cool! I love it!"

"I'm going to get Toby some cider." Bree skipped out of the room.

Sage laughed nervously. "This's kind of weird isn't it?"

"What is?" Brannon asked.

"This whole thing. Any other random runaways coming to dinner?" Sage snorted.

"Oh, I'm not a runaway honey. I'm just down on my luck. Struggling artist and all. My insane Christian family wants nothing to do with my homosexual lifestyle. Christians and all their fucked-up rules! I don't believe in any of it…sorry, no offense."

"None Taken." Brannon laughed.

Sage shook her head. "That's it? You're gay? You're homeless, because you're gay?"

"I don't like to call it homeless, more like, sophisticated nomad," Toby said.

"We're homeless." Sage rolled her eyes.

"Perhaps we should change the subject? So, Toby, you're an artist?" Brannon asked.

"Yes! Painting, drawing, and that sort of stuff. I used to

work as an artist at this one place where I would paint people's bodies for parties and other events. Sometimes, I even used my—well, never mind. Anyways, I got fired for sleeping with someone's husband. I sold a lot of my paintings once upon a time, but I spent most of the money I had on blow and meth. I don't mess with meth anymore though, that stuff's nasty with a capitol N." Toby snapped his fingers in a zig zag motion.

"Ahh, well, we all make mistakes. I know I have," Brannon said.

"Same! I'm just so psyched, honey. I haven't had an actual holiday dinner in years. I've always spent it shacked up with some random in-the-closet douche canoe." Bree came back and handed Toby a mug. He sipped, then put his hand up and said, "If there's a heaven, this is it, queens!"

Sage sat back on the couch and watched the fire. She jumped when she heard the doorbell again.

"I'll get it," Bree chirped.

"I wonder who it is this time?" Sage sighed.

"You came here on your own, little miss miss. No one forced you. You could go if you're gonna keep being so negative," Toby snapped

"I'm sorry. I just…I'm not used to this type of thing. I mean, a nice family doing nice things. It's just so different then what I know. I just hate feeling like someone's charity case. It's embarrassing."

"Only if you let it be. Just relax and enjoy," Brannon said.

Bree brought in a middle-aged woman in a long musty looking coat. She had short dark oily hair and tanned leathery skin. "Everyone, this is Sheryl. She's mother's guest."

"Hi, Sheryl," everyone said.

Mrs. Nobleman came out with a tray of hors d'oeuvres and a mug of cider. She placed the hors d'oeuvres on the coffee table and handed the mug to Sheryl. "So happy you came, Sheryl."

The woman took out a silver flask and poured some brown liquid into her mug. "It's nice to be here, thanks. Smells like a real holiday!"

"Why, it is a real holiday," Mrs. Nobleman said.

"Oh, yeah, I suppose it is, ain't it? It was so cold out there I almost froze my tits off!" Sheryl cackled.

"Yes…well, we're waiting on just one more. My husband, Jim, is carving the turkey. He's excited to meet everyone. Please, sit down, have a snack, and get comfortable before supper. There's plenty of cider if you want more. I'm so happy you've all come. If you will excuse me," Mrs. Nobleman said and dipped her head.

"Your mother is very beautiful," Sage said and reached for an appetizer.

"I'm a homo and even I admit that," Toby said.

Brannon chuckled. "I'm sure she'd be flattered."

"She sure has on a fancy dress. I haven't worn a dress like that in ages! My ex-husband used to buy me fancy dresses. Then he went and screwed my sister and here I am—in a stranger's house for Christmas Eve wearing dirty clothes! Mighty nice house, too. Finest I've ever been in. Jesus, that tree is ginormous!" Sheryl tipped her flask to her mug.

"These appetizers are delicious. What are they?" Sage asked.

"Oh, my mother makes them every year. One is a spinach and goat cheese tartlet and the other is a crostini with thyme roasted tomato and an olive tapenade," Bree said.

Toby took a bite and said, "Holy Shit! These are fabulous! She's an artist in the kitchen."

"I'll make sure she knows that," Brannon said. Him and his sister stood side by side and smiled at their guests who looked uncomfortably back at them.

"Where the hell did that music come from?" Sheryl asked with her mouth full of crostini.

"Oh, mother probably hit the button on the wall from the kitchen. We have a pretty cool sound system," Bree said.

"I feel like I won the lottery," Sage whispered.

Toby started to sing, "Oh, the weather outside is frightful and the fire is so delightful and since we all have no freaking place to go, Let it snow! Let it snow! Let it snow!"

They stopped singing when the doorbell rang, and Bree excused herself. The others waited to see who else the Nobleman's had invited to dinner. Bree came back with an old man who reeked of beer and sweat. He had on dirty khaki pants and a pit stained dress shirt. The man gave a toothless grin and a bow. "Pleased to meet'cha. Name's Albert."

"Hi, Albert," they all said.

"So, what's your story, Al? I see you got the same invitation we all got." Toby gestured to the piece of paper in the man's trembling hand.

"My story? I don't know. I can't quite remember what my story is anymore." He looked around bewildered.

"We're very happy to have you for dinner, Albert," Brannon said as he led the old man to the couch.

"Well, it seems we have everyone here now. Dinner should be real soon," Bree said, then looked away from them.

Mr. Nobleman came into the room with a mug. He handed it to Albert, then smiled warmly at him. "Here ya go, good sir. Warm yourself up."

Albert took a sip of his cider. He closed his eyes and smiled.

Mr. Nobleman turned to face everyone. "My name is Jim Nobleman. My family and I are so happy to have you all for our holiday dinner. Let us give thanks, and praise the almighty. Now, if you could excuse all of us. I need my kids help getting the table ready. We'll come and get you in a few minutes. The bathroom is down the hall, second door on the right, if anyone needs it."

Toby, Sage, Sheryl, and Albert sat on the cream-colored leather couches. Albert took a crostini and sucked it like a baby sucking on a cookie. Toby hummed along with the music and Sheryl nursed her spiked cider with one eye cocked open.

Sage asked, "Does anyone else think it's weird that these people invited total strangers into their home for the holiday?"

Toby shrugged. "I'm not looking a gift horse in the mouth, miss miss. Sometimes people really are just good people. I learned that over the years. I've gotten all kinds of stuff from strangers. Maybe they do invite people every year, so what? I'd been dead long ago if everyone that invited me in off the street had a motive."

Sheryl popped her other eye open and slurred, "I think they're a bit whacky. They just left us all alone in this big room full of fancy stuff. Complete strangers; strangers who ain't got money and nothing to lose. What if one of us was a thief? What if one of us was a murderer? Any one of us could be planning something. I should've just took the money they gave me for that Uber and bought some more rum."

"Speak for yourself, girlfriend. I'm not planning shit," Toby scoffed.

Sage nodded. "No, I get what she's saying. They don't even seem worried at all. Are they that kind or just that naïve?"

Albert stopped sucking on his crostini and said, "Or maybe they're the murderers. Who knows? Mm, this little cracker thing is so tasty."

The others looked at him then reached for more appetizers.

"Seriously though, this isn't weird to anyone else? What about the fact that they seem too perfect," Sage whispered.

Toby waved his hand at Sage and said, "No, it's not that

weird. Stop looking for something, you're digging. We're all fine. Gawd, miss miss, chill out. You've watched too many movies! We just have such fucked up families that we can't imagine anyone being the way they are."

An odd feeling swam in the pit of Sage's stomach as she stared at the four black stockings hung above the fireplace. She looked away from them, and instead scanned the family portraits that hung on the walls. *How'd they get so lucky*, she wondered.

Toby glanced at the picture of Brannon in his football uniform and licked his lips. He marveled at how perfectly everything was decorated, then stared back at Brannon's picture.

Sheryl sat and looked around at what she might be able to take and fit in her coat. *The bathroom is where you find some of the good stuff,* she thought. "Whelp, I need to go to the little girl's room really quick," she said, then got up and stumbled to the bathroom.

Albert noticed nothing other than how warm he was. He thought of how good it was to be eating food that wasn't out of the dumpster. *You could only eat so many Twinkies or moldy gas station hot dogs. It's nice to sit with regular people, on a nice couch.* He wasn't exactly sure how long it had been since he last had that, but he didn't care. He grabbed the last crostini and sat back against the soft buttery leather.

Sheryl had just come from the bathroom, when Mrs. Nobleman came to gather them from the living room and lead them to the dining room. A platter of carved turkey sat in the middle of the table with all the trimmings piping hot around it. Each guest's name dangled from a glittery gold pine cone.

"Such a neat idea," Toby said and fingered the tag on his.

"Thank you, Toby," Mrs. Nobleman replied.

Once everyone was seated, Mr. Nobleman nodded and looked around. He told everyone to join hands so he could lead them in a prayer. Everyone did as they were told and closed their eyes—all except Sage, who only pretended. Mr. Nobleman's voice seemed to echo around the room as he spoke. "For all the years on earth we've roamed, it's on this night where charity begins at home. We invoke you, Almighty, to accept the gifts each year we offer up to thee, so that we all may live on this Earth so bountifully. Before we let this yearly feast begin, we open our hearts and our souls and fully let you in. Hail! Hail! Hail the Almighty!"

A chill ran over Sage's body and she shivered. She'd never heard such a strange prayer before, but what did she know, she wasn't raised religious. She looked to see if anyone else thought it was odd, but they were already holding their plates out for food.

"Ok, let's dig in…and don't forget to try everything. My wife makes the best food!" Mr. Nobleman said as he placed turkey on their plates.

Bree, Brannon, and Mrs. Nobleman helped scoop out the mashed potatoes and other sides onto their guest's plates. Sage took some of everything. She felt guilty for being so suspicious and ate a forkful of turkey. It was delicious. Soon, they were all so busy eating, they didn't seem to notice that the Nobleman's all had empty plates.

"I hope everyone is enjoying their meal," Mrs. Nobleman said.

Albert spoke with his mouth full of mashed potato. "Finest meal I ever had."

"Pure Art," Toby added.

"This sweet potato shit is great," Sheryl slurred.

"It's so good, Mrs. Nobleman. Reminds me of my own mother's cooking. She used to cook like this on the holidays," Sage lied.

Brannon excused himself from the table. Mr. Nobleman watched his son leave the room. Mrs. Nobleman looked over at her husband and then at her daughter, who began nervously chewing on her thumbnail.

Sage stopped eating and put her fork down. Her stomach had begun to cramp and her head throbbed. She picked up her glass of water and took a sip. The cider had made her mouth feel funny and she had a very uneasy feeling.

Toby was still filling his face when he suddenly stopped. He coughed then grabbed his glass of water. The music that played in the background sounded far away and his vision seemed off. He looked around the table. Everything was blurry, his mind fuzzy.

"Are you alright, Toby?" Bree asked.

'Yeah, I'm fine. It's just…I don't know." Toby drank more water. He felt stoned.

Sheryl wiped her mouth with her napkin. She felt drunker than usual. Her mouth had a funny taste in it, like bitter almonds. She closed one eye and looked around, then burped.

Mrs. Nobleman reached out and touched Sheryl's shoulder."Sheryl? You ok?"

"Yup, just took many sips of the good stuff…always been a slave to it. Gotta give it up."

"Yes. We all have our vices. Let me know if you need anything, sweetie," Mrs. Nobleman said.

Albert was helping himself to seconds and Mr. Nobleman watched him intently. Sage sat back in her chair. She definitely did not feel good and she wondered if it was something she ate. *Where's Brannon? He left the table a while ago.* She looked at Bree, then at Mrs. Nobleman, and then at their empty plates.

"Excuse me, I need to go to the restroom." Sage stood up.

"Of course," Mrs. Nobleman said.

Sage made her way to the bathroom. Maybe she would see Brannon on her way. She felt faint and had to steady herself with a hand on the wall. Brannon was by the front door. *What's he doing*? The closet door was opened and he was bent down. Sage called out to him, "Brannon?"

"Yes?"

"You all good?"

"Yeah, I was just getting something."

Sage watched for a few more seconds, then continued to the bathroom. Before she entered, she peeked around the corner and saw Brannon holding something in his hands, but she couldn't make it out. She closed the bathroom door and locked it, then slid down to the floor with her hand over her mouth. Saliva filled her mouth, so she crawled to the toilet and opened the lid. She hung her head over and vomited, then wiped her mouth with toilet paper. Something definitely wasn't right. Sage squinted around the bathroom and noticed there was no windows, then she vomited again.

Mr. Nobleman watched as Albert ate a third helping of turkey and mashed potatoes. He looked at his wife, chuckled, and said, "Albert sure is hungry. He seems to love your turkey, honey."

"Good. Let him enjoy it. We'd never eat all that food."

Mrs. Nobleman looked over at Sheryl, who was sitting back in her chair with her napkin over her mouth. Sheryl did not feel well at all. *I shouldn't have drunk so much*, she thought. She felt like she had to be sick, so she closed her eyes and waited for the feeling to pass.

Toby stopped eating. He began to get nervous. *Sheryl doesn't look so good. Sage didn't either before she left the table*. And now he was feeling sick. *What are the odds? Although, that Albert guy's still eating and he seems fine*. Sage put all those bad thoughts in his head earlier. He drank more water and smiled at Bree and she smiled back halfheartedly. Toby's head started to throb as he tried to push away the feeling of panic that had overcome him.

Sage vomited one more time before flushing the toilet and crawling to the sink. She pulled herself up and looked in the mirror. Sweat saturated her sweater. Whatever she'd drunk or ate had made her sick, she was sure of it. Something told her that she had to get out of there, and fast. She had a feeling that if she didn't, she wouldn't be leaving at all.

Albert had finally stopped eating. He smiled at everyone around the table, then his smile faded and his mouth hung open in puzzlement. His body trembled briefly before he slumped over in his chair. Toby yelped, causing Sheryl to jump and knock over her drink.

"Calm down, no need to panic," Mr. Nobleman said a she stood up.

"No need to panic? Seriously? That man looks like he just died in his chair," Toby shouted.

"I assure you he did not die. Look, he's still breathing."

Toby looked over at Albert. Drool hung from his mouth, but his chest rose slowly up and down. He then looked over at Sheryl, who looked as if she might pass out next. Sweat ran down her temples. Toby slid his chair away from the table and tried to get up, but a hand firmly pushed him back down. He looked up and saw Brannon with an ax in his hand.

"Going somewhere?" Brannon asked.

"Uh, yeah, I um… have to go to the bathroom if you don't mind," Toby muttered.

Brannon sucked his teeth and shook his head. "No can do pretty boy."

Mrs. Nobleman offered her hand to Bree and they got up out of their chairs. When Sheryl finally passed out, her head hit the table with a hard crack, and Toby cried out, "What the fuck did you do? What the fuck's going on?"

"What do you mean? We didn't do anything, sweetie." Mrs. Nobleman smiled at Toby.

"Both of them are passed out in their chairs! What the fuck did you do? Where's Sage?"

Brannon groaned. "Oh, crap."

"I 'll take care of it." Bree came from around the table and left the room.

"Take care of what? Sage! Sa—" Mr. Nobleman shoved a napkin into Toby's mouth.

Toby struggled, but he was no match for Mr. Nobleman. A sharp pain pierced his chest and he knew he was about to pass out. He fell with a soft thud onto the plush rug beneath him and looked up into the faces of Brannon and Mr. Nobleman. Toby turned his head and saw blood pooling beside him and wondered, *whose blood is that*? He put his hand to his chest. It was wet. He looked back up and before he could even scream, he saw Brannon raise the ax up over his head, then bring it down. Blood shot up like a geyser and rained back down onto his face.

"Oh, dear, I hate to see them hurt while they're still awake," Mrs. Nobleman said. But she beamed with pride as she watched her son raise the ax and bring it down again and again and again.

"Good work, son. Nicely done," Mr. Nobleman said.

Mrs. Nobleman sat back down at the table as her husband and son swiftly took apart the guest's limb from limb. Each body part was cleanly cut and stacked in tidy piles. Her eyes shone when their blood sprayed across her husband's face and soaked his festive green sweater. She tucked a cloth napkin into her dress and took a deep breath in. When a drop of blood landed on her lips, her tongue darted forth like serpent and she savored the briny taste.

Sage heard commotion coming from the dining room. She thought she heard someone scream, and though she wasn't sure, she also thought she heard someone shout her name. She turned on the bathroom sink, left the light on, then quietly opened the door and locked it behind her, hoping they'd think she was still in there. As quickly as she could, Sage made her way to the front door, but then she saw Bree coming from the dining room. She dashed into the living room, grabbed the poker by the fireplace, and crouched behind the couch.

Sage waited until she heard Bree knocking on the bathroom door before she made a run for it. She opened the front door and slipped out, but didn't close it all the way, fearing someone would hear. She felt terrible about leaving the others behind, even though she didn't actually know what was going on. All Sage knew was that she felt safer outside. She made her way around the side of the house and stopped. Her breath rose in plumes around her and she gripped the poker as she stood on her tip-toes and peered inside one of the windows.

At first, she couldn't see much. Brannon and Mr. Nobleman were standing and they were both covered in something. *Is that blood?* Then she saw Brannon raise an ax. Soon, Mr. Nobleman also rose an ax. Sage saw the red spray shoot up and splatter across their faces as both men swung their axes and she covered her mouth to stifle a scream. Her knees buckled beneath her, and she had to force herself to get up and run.

"Hello? Sage?" Bree knocked loudly. She could hear the sink. "Sage? Are you ok? We're getting ready to do dessert. Would you like apple pie or pumpkin?" Bree put her ear up to the bathroom door. She wiggled the door knob. She supposed Sage fainted, so she started to run down the hall to alert her family, but then she noticed the front door was ajar. Bree looked out and saw footprints leading to the side of the house, so she hurried back to the dining room.

"Father," Bree cried.

"Yes, sweetheart." He was slick with blood.

"Father, I think she got away—the girl! The bathroom door is shut, but she didn't answer…I came back to tell you and the front door was open!"

"Calm down. Are you sure the door wasn't open when you went to check on her?"

"I don't think so. I looked outside and saw footprints in the snow leading to the side of the house." Bree had tears running down her cheeks. "I'm so sorry! I didn't see her!"

"It's alright. Daddy's got you under his wing. Mother and you need to get everything ready while your brother and I take care of this little matter."

Mrs. Nobleman came around the table to meet her daughter. Her heels slid in the gore, but she composed herself and grabbed Bree's hand. "We're going to be fine. Daddy will take care of that girl. Don't worry. It will all be ok. Do you think Daddy would let anything happen to us? And do you think our Almighty would let anything happen to us? C'mon, let's organize everything so that when Brannon and Daddy come back, we can sit down as a family and enjoy. Here, take the parts you like and put them on your plate."

Sage shivered behind a tall pine across from the house. She wasn't sure what she saw or what was happening. When she spotted Mr. Nobleman and Brannon step out of the house, she moved deeper through the woods, careful not to make too much noise. The poker was like an icicle in her ungloved hand and it hurt to hold. Without the light of the Nobleman's house, she couldn't see well and struggled to pick a direction to go in. She stopped behind another tree and could hear them shouting to one another.

"Bran? She's not on this side!"

"Or this side, father!"

"The woods! She probably went to the woods," Mr. Nobleman shouted. They ran towards the woods and when Mr. Nobleman spotted the girl's footprints in the snow, he grinned from ear to ear. *Nothing wrong with hunting for your food,* he thought.

Sage heard them running towards the woods. She ignored the branches that slapped her face as she ran. After several minutes of running, she panted and doubled over. Her body and legs were weak. She would not be able to outrun them for much longer. She could scream, but she didn't know if anyone would hear her other than them. There was one other house on the street. It looked like no one was there, but she had to try. She ran back the other way, toward the street.

"Father, she might've gone deeper in."

"No, she didn't. She'd get lost in there, it's too dark.

She's probably headed toward the Dyer's house. I'd bet that, son. Let's just meet her there, shall we?"

There were no cars parked in the driveway at the house. *They might have a landline*, Sage hoped. She ran across the street and went to the back of the house. She banged on the back door and cried out. No one answered. She raised the poker to break the window, but someone grabbed her from behind.

"Oh no, ya don't. You can't go breaking the Dyer's windows. They wouldn't be too happy if they came back from Florida and saw that." Mr. Nobleman turned Sage around to face him.

"Please…don't hurt me," Sage pleaded.

"Come on, now. It's going to be ok. What're you running and carrying on for?"

"I got sick. And then I saw…I saw blood everywhere and…" She gasped for air.

Brannon sighed and twirled his ax like a baton. "Father, let's just get her back to the house already. I'm starved."

"Good idea, son."

"No, I don't wanna go back! I wanna go home," Sage cried.

"You wanna go…home, was it? But you have no home to go to, do you?" Mr. Nobleman pat Sage's back and held her to him. He let her cry into his blood-stained sweater. "There, there. That's what I thought. Oh, you poor sweet little lamb. Just come back to our house where you won't have to suffer any longer."

"I just wanna go home," Sage whined.

"I'm sorry, honey, I truly am, but it's going to be ok. You don't have to run anymore."

Sage crumpled into Mr. Nobleman's arms and let herself be led away. Brannon walked behind them whistling a cheerful tune. They took her back inside the house, where the warmth of the fire made her feel exhausted. The food smells mingled with the tang of death made her dry heave. It smelled like a holiday slaughter house. She collapsed onto the living room floor and looked up at the tree. The lights twinkled like hundreds of stars and she stared until it hurt her eyes.

Mrs. Nobleman came out and looked down at Sage. Bree followed, and stood behind her mother, chewing her thumbnail. Mrs. Nobleman walked over to her husband and touched the ax in his hands. "It's time, Jim. You know what has to be done," she said.

"I know, dear," he whispered, "I know."

Brannon stared blankly and bit the inside of his cheek. He was hungry. *Get it over with already.* He tapped his foot in tune with the music and raised his eyebrows at his father.

Sage could hear them talking, but she didn't care. She thought about her own family then and remembered the last Christmas she'd spent with them. Both her parents had gotten wasted and slapped each other around the kitchen. Her bloody nosed mother had shouted and cried while chain smoking over the holiday ham. In their grassless junk piled yard, her brother had smoked meth with his friends, and when they tried to grab her, her brother stood by and watched. *No wonder I'm so fucked up, fuck it.* Sage drowned out the voices of the Nobleman's and listened to the instrumental of, Have Yourself a Merry Little Christmas. She closed her eyes and smiled. *Fuck it all.*

Bree felt mixed emotions. She looked at her family and all their beautiful things. She thought of the decadent meal they would have and how all that they'd wished for would be waiting for them when they awoke the nest morning. A calmness came over her and she walked over to her father and grabbed the ax from his hand.

"Let me, father," Bree said.

Bree stood over Sage. She took a breath, then lifted the ax and brought it down on Sage's neck in one clean swipe. Brannon watched his sister in awe and marveled at her precision. He walked over and put his arm around her. Then they dragged the girl to the dining room, separated her into pieces, and dined at the table as a family.

The Nobleman's awoke to a beautiful white Christmas and came downstairs to gather in the living room. Mrs. Nobleman looked in the mirror. Her face was ten years younger and her hair was as bouncy and shiny as ever. Mr. Nobleman kissed his beautiful wife and told her that his boss called to say that when he came back to work, he would be made partner and make double his regular salary. Bree was squealing about how Jayden had just texted and told her how much he'd been thinking about her and wanted to go on a date to the movies. Brannon smiled at his sister and looked out the window at his new black Porsche 911. The family joined hands and shouted in unison, "Happy Holidays and Ave Santanas!"

W.F.F.
Carson Demmans

It was the summer of 1985 and it was hotter than Hell. I was later to find out that was not literally true, but at the time it was a perfectly logical choice of words, and that's how I think of the day I first met a dear friend of mine I hope to never see again.

I was stuck in Saskatoon, Saskatchewan, desperately trying to keep my career as a freelance journalist alive by chasing what was a hot topic in the press, mainly the Satanic abuse of children. For once, there seemed to be a credible case of it that would actually go to trial. There was no physical evidence, but there were a dozen kids telling exactly the same story, and the psychiatrist said they had not been coached. There were even some slightly believable suspects: neighborhood teens who had been ritualistically killing animals and leaving Satanic symbols behind. I have no idea if these guys were true Satanists or not, but they had tried to act the part, and the world was waiting to see how much was an act and how much was true.

In a case like this where the victims and the accused are all minors, you can't get anywhere near anyone who might actually know anything. The best you can do is find a friend of a friend, who is more likely a friend of an acquaintance of a neighbor who used to live nearby but moved years ago but always thought those kids were weird.

Some days I wish I had a respectable writing job, like the letters editor at *Hustler*.

It was an incredibly hot day, and my vision was occasionally going pure white as sweat dripped into my eyes. I was skulking around the back alleys where everyone involved had lived at the time in question, looking for anyone who might want to talk to the type of guy who skulks in back alleys. It was then that I saw him for the first time. He was obviously doing the same thing I was, but he was doing it with style. His large brimmed hat shaded his face, although it was obviously to conceal his identity and not to shade his face. I say that because there wasn't a drop of sweat on him, which was a miracle considering that he was wearing gloves and a full-length trench coat with the collar pulled up.

"Find any leads, pal?" I asked in a pleasant tone. He jumped visibly, as I had snuck up behind him. He looked me over thoroughly, and then laughed.

"I'm not a cop," I explained. He laughed again.

"I know that, Lionel Hart," he said without a trace of smugness in his voice. "Police forces don't hire writers for *SCREW Magazine*."

Maybe that should have surprised me or shocked me, but my ego interpreted as meaning he was familiar with my work and had seen my byline once or twice. There were a couple of other guys skulking around who were in the same business as me and who knew me, so I just figured he was another one of them.

"A freelancer has to get published where he can, pal," I replied. "But I assume you're chasing the same story I am?"

He thought for a second before he answered, and then smiled broadly.

"I suppose I am," he said. "But I'm not a writer. I'm just trying to get to the bottom of this."

I nodded. I met a lot of private eyes in my business, usually waiting in line to go through the same bags of garbage I was sifting through. There was something different about him though. He had a certain air about him that was different from anyone in my business, me included. He looked like he didn't belong in that alley, whereas most people would say that I wasn't classy enough to be there.

Nobility. That was the word. He looked noble, in the sense of aristocratic.

"Look," I can tell you're no threat to me or my story," I said. "Let me offer you a deal."

He was taken aback by that. At first, I thought he was offended, but his broad smile returned again.

"Friend, I'm usually the one who says that!" he said happily. "I'll listen to whatever you have to say."

"Let's team up," I said. "You're not a writer, and whatever you are I don't care as long as it's not a writer. Let's go somewhere, compare notes, and share everything. The only rule is we don't horn in on the territory of the other."

"You're right," he agreed. "I'm not a writer. And I know you can't intrude on my business here, even if you did know what it was. You have a deal. Lead on."

As we walked together, I noticed he had an unusual gait. That must be the reason for the long coat, I decided. He had some injury or deformity to his legs that he was hiding. In any event, he had no trouble keeping up. I led the way to the lounge of a small restaurant that had become my unofficial headquarters for this story. We took a seat in the back and ordered, but he kept his hat on indoors and drank his beer with his gloves on.

"So, are you looking for someone or is someone looking for you?" I finally asked.

"Why do you ask?" he said coldly.

"The get up," I replied. "Nobody who saw you today could tell what you looked like under that disguise, and you're going out of your way to not leave fingerprints."

He looked puzzled and then realized I was talking about his gloves and shook his head.

"You are wrong but not as wrong as some people might think, Lionel," he replied. "I have enemies. One very powerful enemy in particular, wouldn't like me horning in on his territory, as you put it. I need to solve this quick and get out of here even quicker. So the answer is both. I am looking for someone, but someone is always looking for me."

"Then who are you looking for? They've already made arrests."

He shook his head slowly as he said, "I'm looking for the real person who victimized these kids. I have no problem with the kids they arrested being punished, but they are technically innocent of what they are being accused of. They have an alibi."

"Not that they've told anyone," I countered.

"They can't," he said with a chuckle. "Their alibi is that they were busy committing other crimes at the times they were supposedly torturing these children in Satanic rituals, and some of what they were actually doing is worse than what they are accused of."

"So, the bad guys get punished," I said. "That's a good thing, right?"

"But at least one bad guy goes free," he said grimly. "Don't get me wrong. I have spent longer than you can imagine punishing the guilty. Somebody did something to these kids, but it wasn't what they are saying happened, or who they said did it. Deep down, you know that, right?"

I didn't answer the question, which in a way was the answer he was suspecting.

"I report the facts," I said gloomily. "If someone says something, as long as I accurately report what was said, that is a fact. Whether or not the truth is said doesn't change the fact that it was said."

"But?" he asked.

"But I am pretty sure if kids were witnesses to gang rapes, mutilations and animal sacrifices, not to mention what they said was done to them personally, there would be some kind of evidence. Injuries to the kids, a crime scene, something. Instead, we have a bunch of kids repeating the same story, and that's it."

"I wish I could find these kids," he said with a sigh. "Even if I could just have them tell me their story once, directly to me, it would tell a lot. That's what I was snooping around for in that alley—some clue as to where they are being hidden."

"Oh, I can tell you where they are," I said. "But it won't do you any good."

"Oh?" He arched his eyebrow slightly.

"Sure," I said, "I was telling the truth when I said I was putting all of my cards on the table. A cop bragged to me about where the kids are being hidden, but only because he was so proud of how tight the security was. They're under lock and key in a hotel downtown. Police on every floor, every entrance, and inside and outside every room the kids are in. Each one is in a different room so they can't talk to each other about the case."

"Get me there," he said confidently. "I'll get us in."

I am known to the police, which is inevitable in my profession. It can be a good thing and a bad thing. It is good when they look the other way when I do something illegal because it's just Lionel digging for some story for some trash bin liner. It is a bad thing when they can recognize me a hundred feet away and I'm trying to get well beyond their checkpoint. That's what happened at the hotel. The cop on the front door recognized me long before my friend and I actually reached him. But then, when we reached the cop, he just waved us through. I stopped and stared in disbelief.

"Keep moving," he whispered to me. "Don't look back and move as fast as you can without running. I look really strange when I run."

I didn't ask any questions as we breezed by police officer after police officer to the fourth floor, where I had been told that the children were being housed. My friend stopped at the first guarded door we found, walked by the guard and faced the guard inside the room directly. After staring into the cop's eyes for a few seconds, he pointed at the door and the cop left without saying a word. The child on the bed, a girl of about six, stared at us blankly. She had apparently grown used to strange adults coming and leaving her room to the point where she paid no notice of it, a disastrous skill for a victim of sexual assault to learn.

My friend, as that is how I thought of him, and still do, knelt before her as she sat on the bed. He told her to tell him what happened. Out of habit, I turned on my tape recorder. If I take notes after I have been drinking, half of them are about how much I hate the son of a bitch I am interviewing.

I have to admit that the kid was scary to listen to. She gave graphic detail on what was done to her and her friends and what they had seen. She said how it felt, what it smelled like, and when it happened.

During the whole time she was talking, my friend stared intently into her eyes. At the end, he was disappointed.

"She believes everything she just said," he said with a frown. "It's not possible, but she believes it. She could pass any lie detector test ever invented, but it's not true."

"Maybe her friends convinced her," I suggested. "Young kids can be like that. Do you think you can get us in to see the others as easy as we got into this room?"

If anything, the other kids were even easier. With a mere wave of his had, my friend had doors opened for us and we walked in like invited guests. The kids all told the same story, but the more I heard it, the more suspicious I became.

"They all believe every word of what they say," he said sadly. "How can that be?"

"I have an idea," I said. "Come with me. First, we're

going to borrow every tape recorder we can find even if we have to ask every person I know in this town. Then we are going to my hotel room for a special presentation."

There was something about being invited into my room that my companion felt was inherently funny, and he made an off-hand comment that it had been centuries since that happened. I ignored it because I was intent on finishing my project. I had recorded each child on a separate cassette and had borrowed enough tape recorders that I could play them all at once. It took a couple of attempts before I had the beginnings of all of the tapes synchronized, but once I accomplished that, I played all of them at once.

The effect was startling.

The timing, speech inflexion and tone of each child was exactly the same, and they all said exactly the same thing, word for word. It was like listening to a recitation at a school play if the children of the Addams Family and the Munsters all went there.

"These aren't kids," I said. "These are little robots with tape recorders inside them! But that's impossible!"

"No," my friend said. "But it's only ever been tried once in a little town in Connecticut, and the cost was prohibitive. Someone taught these kids to say this, but how is it so perfect? Even the best choirmasters in the world can't teach kids to be in such perfect unison."

I looked at him in surprise as he gave a low chuckle.

"Sorry," he said. "Church choirs have always been a guilty pleasure of mine. Besides, even if they were taught, they wouldn't all believe it to be true, and trust me, that is exactly what they believe. I know."

"Then it wasn't teaching," I said. "Somebody made them believe, and I can only think of one person who would be able to pull that off."

The office of Gregory Temple was easy to find. As the psychiatrist who had gone to the police once all of the children had made disclosures to him of the abuse they had suffered, he had become as famous as the story itself. The names of the victims and accused had to be kept officially secret due to their age, although it had been easy enough to figure out; Temple though, had been in the spotlight and the newspapers were full of the story of how one child had been brought to him by his parents and then he relentlessly tracked down everyone else who had been victimized. The kids had all told the good doctor first, before their parents, friends or stuffed animals (confirmed by the webcams the trusting parents had implanted in those animals; strange how parents so concerned about their children's well being routinely let them watch 8 hours of television per day unsupervised).

As usual, little things like security guards, alarm systems and locked doors proved no delay for us as I let my new friend lead the way. Why didn't I question how he did it? I have no idea. The people who are your friends are your friends; there is no logic to it, and you trust them.

We found Dr. Temple still in his office, working, but it wasn't his practice that he was working on. It was a book detailing his role in the case. If he had ever been given a chance to finish it, I am sure it would have been an international best seller. He was never given that chance.

He recognized me instantly from my previous attempts to interview him.

"Get out!" he said bluntly. "I told you before—no interviews."

"I don't have to interview, you son of a bitch!" I snarled. "I already know how you did it. You've been bragging how you hypnotized these kids and helped them recover bad memories that you had blocked out. They didn't recover anything! Instead, you left something behind, namely a lovely little fairy tale that you had tape recorded and played for them. You basically implanted little tape players inside their brains."

"Cost effectively too," my friend said begrudgingly.

"Much cheaper than actual tape recorders."

The doctor said nothing. Very smoothly, he pulled out a semi-automatic pistol from his desk and began firing at me, but just as smoothly my friend stepped in front of me and remained there until the doctor had emptied his gun. I could hear the bullets thud as they hit my protector, but his body didn't even flinch as they hit his chest again and again. Once the doctor's gun was empty, my friend turned to me and said he would take it from there.

He walked confidently to the doctor, taking one of his gloves off as he did. His gloves had been padded to hide their true appearance, which were talon claws. He put the bare claw on the doctor's bald head and the smell of burning flesh filled the room. When he removed his claw from the doctor, a second-degree burn in the shape of the claw was left behind.

"Your guess was right," my friend said. "Exactly like you said. I have to leave now, and quickly. My little mind reading trick just now was too much of a display of my power to not catch His attention, and in case you're wondering, that's His with a capital *H*."

He took off his other glove to reveal another claw, and also removed his coat and hat. He had short horns which had been covered by the hat, and the lower half of his body was animal, much like the Greek satyr.

"People hate me enough now without getting blamed for stuff I haven't done. I'm taking this guy straight to my home, and I suggest you run. Enough lightning to power this city for a month will probably hit this building in a few seconds"

"I'm a lousy runner," I said. "Take me with you."

"If you come with me, you can never come back," he said. "You were right. We are friends, and friends look out for each other. If you keep going down the road you are, you're going to end up a permanent resident in my realm, and I wouldn't wish that on any mortal other than the truly evil. I'll give you a short cut. Run."

The room was engulfed in flames which did not burn me, but which burned a hole in reality itself. My friend pulled the doctor through the hole, which sealed itself. The flames burnt a hole through the walls of the office building to safety. As I ran through it, the sky lit up with lightning, and there was little left of the building. The doctor was presumed dead, and the Satanic abuse trial never started without his so-called expertise.

Since then, I have tried to walk the straight and narrow but often fail. Then, I get a note in the mail or on my phone or the spaghetti I am eating suddenly creates a mini-billboard, splattering me with sauce. The messages are simple, and when I follow them, I know I am doing the right thing.

Lots of people say they have guardian angels, but who else can say that they have a guardian fallen angel?

Addicted to The Night
Alexander Marais

If you were ever to call me pretty, I'd laugh at you. I'd fucking laugh at you. That is, until my more diplomatic instincts would kick in and have me making you wish in a variety of ways you were dead. I don't appreciate boys, men, girls, and women who lie. Never have. Never will.

If I were to tell this story in chronological order, you wouldn't get the half of it. I mean, you'd *obviously* get the technical flow of the unsightly events that would befall me after my sixteenth birthday. But you wouldn't get it the way I now understand it. Which, as far as I am concerned, is the only way to *really* get it because I'm me and you're you.

As I said before, it all started after I hit the sweet age of sixteen. The age where, allegedly, you gain empathy as a teenager for the first time. I guess I got a C minus in *that* class. Probably a bit more of a B, by now. Yet as I look back at everything that has occurred, well, really *fallen* would be the better word, I'm shocked while simultaneously a little cocky about the fact I haven't entirely lost the small amount of regard for others that I just began to possess myself. And just began to possess when shit splattered, and I mean *splattered*, against the fan.

I always was bound to snap. You'll learn a little later why in these pages. The home environment I was from, privileged as it may be, proved to be the most surprising — if luxurious — of prisons. The old saying is true. Money can't buy you happiness. And the folks who raised me, *happening* to be my parents, were pretty unhappy people. Yet I hesitate, pondering whether or not the word *snap* really describes what happened to me. Prior to this whirring cyclone of shit, I didn't have a history of mental health issues. Of course, I was told constantly that I did. But I didn't. I *really* didn't. Never saw any files. Never was able to be told explicitly what indicated the nature of my "ailment." I was just continually brainwashed via the black magic of constant, negative reinforcement. Which, as I got older and started to ask more questions, needless to say got worse, and worse, and worse.

I'll formally begin my story's narrative with waking up.

Dirty. Scared. Alone.

I had become a rather feral creature in my own eyes, rising only in the early hours of night after a long day's sleep inside my dumpster. When you reside and hide in such a place long enough, the usually nose-pinching aromas become like old friends. Covering myself with seemingly infinite bits of waste and shredded paper didn't even trigger an afterthought. I could only imagine the bewilderment of those who lived their whole lives this way seeing the life I used to lead. Needless to say, though, it appeared to be all over for now. *Or so I thought.*

Several years of living on the streets taught me one thing. *Embrace your unpreparedness.* Don't expect to make it through the night. Just go through the motions of someone trying to survive, and well…do your best *to* survive. I was surprised at how seemingly easy such a thing appeared to be, but learned the hard way time and time again you didn't disappear into the night without earning it first. Sleeping in dubious concealment during daylight hours seemed the safest of all unsafe options. The freaks and the truly heinous — much like myself — were creatures of the night. Somewhat paradoxically, I had decided it would be best to be awake when they were. To be prepared for such encounters, rather than avoid them. To be ready to run when danger truly was present, lavishing the few and filthy splendors of safety when able.

The abandoned warehouse I called home was never a place safe to inhabit. During the day, due to its close proximity to an artist colony some yards off, there was minor supervision of comings and goings courtesy of the armed guards before the chain-link fence. Night, however, was when residents of the former military units were told to deadbolt their doors. Management could only do so much, or would. Needless to say, such hours proved to be go-time for the crawlers, bottom feeders, cutthroats, and those who enjoy burning both people and things.

The fact my dumpster was never touched, day or night, I considered to be a great blessing of impossibly metaphysical proportion. My residency amongst the colonists proved undisturbed for quite some time. To say I was content would be a statement of seventy-five percent accuracy. I had forgotten what happiness was years ago, and coupled with external reinforcements it showed no signs of soon returning. But oddly enough, I found solitude and purpose in my life being homeless. It was more real to me than anything I had ever experienced. Until I met Dom.

He was working outside his pale white apartment, his hands covered in thick, wet clay. There was nothing particularly extraordinary about him, not that my allegedly troubled mind was attuned to such distraction. Silhouetted against the red, evening sun, his life was the epitome of what I had always imagined for myself. A life free of convention, yet conventional to those who shared it. The life of an artist, a poet, a creative person. A life beyond the Siddhartha effects of my societally acceptable, yet undeniably bizarre rearing.

He saw me before I saw him. Like I said, my mind was not fixated on things such as romance. *Obviously.* Sauntering cautiously out of my unstable haven, the hairs on the back of my neck prickled almost instantaneously as I grew parallel to the colony. *Someone has seen me.* My first instinct was to run, quickly made secondary by my turning to judge the witness. He simply stared back at me in response, never once moving his hands from the rotating device sweating sheets of gray.

"Hello."

My head snapped at the sound of the greeting. I had grown accustomed not only to my own silence, but simultaneously the stillness of others. When the words managed to reflux into my throat, I was shocked to hear how much my voice had changed. "You gonna bust me?" It was deep and gravelly, my tone somewhat threatening.

Dom frowned, for the first time moving one of his hands away from the spinning machine. "No," he said finally, eyes peeled for what he must have deemed potential threats. "Should I?"

"No." The word escaped my lips with an even greater fire, fear momentarily overcoming my hardened exterior. Then I remembered. *The guards have gone home. This belongs entirely to me.*

"Very well then," he said, instinctively glancing in the direction of the chain-link fence. "I will not bust you."

"How long have you been around here?" I interjected, still terse.

Dom raised an eyebrow. "Here?"

"Yes, asshole. *Here.*"

"About eighteen months."

Now it was my turn to raise *both* my eyebrows. "Eighteen months? Huh. You like it so far?"

"It has its advantages." His eyes were focusing back on the clay formations, and for the first time I began to feel a flicker of mortification. *He's no longer looking at me.* "You can stop staring now. Unless you want to come up here and help."

My eyes bulged. *Was this man insane?* "Help you?" the words barely escaped my mouth, complete with hardboiled egg formation.

Dom merely shrugged in response, leaving me in maddening silence again to contemplate my next move.

"I'll help you."

When he didn't respond, I began to turn around and walk

away. I couldn't help noting in that moment the girl I used to be. Several years ago, I would have been bold enough to challenge this by walking straight towards the apartment and smashing his device. Things now, however, had changed me along with them.

"Hey!"

I kept walking, yet slowed my pace. After several more steps, something within me broke through the ice — forcing me to turn around.

He stood, continuing to be framed against the magnificent sunset, arms outstretched. "What happened to helping me out?" His tone was the perfect mixture of baffled and inquisitive, complete with a cloying if not unworldly sincerity.

Helping him, as it turned out, lasted about two months. During this period, I finally began to recoil at the filth and shit that once coated my tongue. What he saw in me, at that particular moment in time, is anyone's guess. My hair was long, ragged, and unkempt. My teeth were yellow. And I was said to have had glowing eyes in the darkness — a small but significant adaptation to my usual routine. I ultimately never asked him, and he never proceeded to tell me. I started living with him as the ultimate opportunist, in complete awe at his actions while wondering what the hell his shtick was. On a certain instinctual level, such thoughts were deemed irrelevant. Sliding back into a life with a few creature comforts was like a slow but steady addiction. It became transcendently surreal to rediscover what "good" food was, the feeling of water hitting my skin, and soft fabric touching the back of my head. Yet it always remained disconcerting to feel clean, cool clothes touching my naked figure. Such revelations made the truly new things, like Dom's lips pressing into my own, that much more revolutionary. My parents had always said such things would be out of my paygrade. *How wrong they were...*

It was our own, private world — his apartment being its facilitator. Surrounded by tall, exotic, and sometimes frightening shapes Dom crafted with clay. Like me, he was the ultimate outsider in his youth. He just found a way to make money with it. To be something *because* of it. I always envied that about him. But more than that, I envied his open heart. Granted, I had now seen enough to make me never smile again. Yet the pain of rejection, in any context, is what can make wrists bleed. But not Dom's. His wide-eyed stares and bright smiles contained no inkling of sardonicism.

He was the yin to my yang. Someone who chose to believe in the good of the world, overlooking any indicator of *bad to the bone.* That was the only time we would fight, our little universe threatened with breaking apart. He would accuse me of affecting his art courtesy of my cynicism, my retorts equating him to a bastard with no spine. Making up often consisted of some of the best sex I've ever had in my life. His innocence seemed to become undone every time. A darker side of the man would emerge — shining and feral. He would pin me to the bedclothes, digging so deep inside it felt like I'd burst. Needless to say, the mortality vibe to such carnal moments made the occasional shatterings that much sweeter.

Such pleasantries were never things I could find myself getting used to or taking for granted. Something else connected to what drove me wild about him. He never was able to comprehend that, despite knowing my story better than anyone. It was too easy for him to suffer vexations courtesy of my night terrors; to slam glasses onto floors when I'd be in one of my many moods. He simply didn't have the patience for a girl used to life on the streets still incapable of a steady step in modest means. Something, I would come to understand, that lay the foundation for what ultimately caused us to suffer our worst fight — for the hundredth and final time.

He came home late that night.

The thought beat and beat relentlessly against my thick skull as I surveyed the icy waters.

He would have come home earlier if I hadn't fought with him.

Why I chose to blame myself in this instance is anyone's guess. Perhaps it was easier than the truth. It felt better to blame myself, rather than both of us or him. Such self-loathing seemed to delay the impact of realizing my new life was gone. Almost as quickly as it had begun.

Dom had been followed. Dom had been followed, and it was all my fault.

You should never be outside past the unspoken curfew after the guards return home.

It's all my fault.

The devils always come to dance the moment authority disappears. That night was no exception…

It is all my fault.

My hand instinctively moved between my legs. I winced twice, first upon the impact my fingers made with the damaged tissue. Then again when retrieving them I saw they were covered in blood. A broken cry erupted from the furthest depths of my throat — the most painful thing about it being its failure to communicate the entirety of the anguish within.

Taking one last look at this wretched world, I cursed it quietly under my breath. *Hopefully the next place is better.*

And with that, ignoring the painful throbbing, I closed my eyes — waiting for the sea's harsh embrace. It came, but not in the sense that I hoped.

It is all my fault, it is all my fault, it is all my fault.

I continued to let the words dance through my head as I made slow, heaving motions onto the sandbank. The water stunk of pollution, the smell embedded deep within my sinuses and making every breath arduous. Shore was just a foot or so away. I couldn't help letting out another, agonized wail. Even Death wouldn't stay.

At long last, I felt the entirety of my belly make contact with the lukewarm surface. Closing my eyes again, I proceeded to breathe in as much reek as I could.

Maybe this could stimulate his return.

Yet all it did was jerk me further into the present, courtesy of a familiar nausea. "Oh God," my words subsequently escaped. "Is this my burden? Is this my curse? To continue to carry a most unpleasant weight of the world upon my shoulders?"

If there was a God, and he was merciful, this would have been his time to answer. To reassure me this was just part of the journey. That all this was a test of my strength, in an effort to maximize the redeeming qualities of my character. I laugh at such thoughts now. As if he really were merciful…

Perhaps the ensuing silence is what finally drove the final shaft of pain into my heart, blackening it forever. Accompanied by the stink and filth that I knew so well. The familiarity was the most potent aspect. It formed the grail from which a new kind of feeling emerged — one terrifying in its implications, but so very enthralling in its promises.

Walking around the endless megalopolis only cemented this new sensation. Much like a tentacled parasite, it spread across my body until I could almost swear I felt as if I were growing bigger. Badder. Smarter. Yet there was still an undeniable air of melancholia. It wasn't as if the gratification and adrenaline freed me from the origins of its existence. It was as if I had become synonymous with my pain, this newfound persona a child of that marriage. While I no longer felt disenfranchised enough to wander complete with psychologically induced limp, every confident step now taken *depended* upon my awareness. *Awareness of the damage. Awareness of the disillusionment.* Awareness of my own, innate drive to self-destruct. Not that it was entirely of my own making…

"Remember, sweetheart. You are ill. *You are ill*. Now repeat after me, *I am ill*. I am *ill*." Those words became the mantra of my household role. Routinely coupled with dubious feedings of multiple medication. My birth trauma planted the seed of the seemingly endless paranoia. Plus, I made no eye contact. I preferred being in a world of my own. Worst, I didn't care to please — such traits deemed especially damaging for a girl. The oddities performed on me, unpleasant as they were, all were done in the name of "love." Or so they called it. The means was to an end titled *not losing me*, and from there the list went on and on. I may or may not have had measles, dyspraxia, and motor dysfunction. Needless to say, it was hard to tell where the condition ended and the side effects began. I never feel well as a general rule.

Call it a blessing or sheer dumb luck that I was a block away from the soup kitchen. Every single sad sack flocked to their charity, often trekking from miles away. Getting an actual meal from the place equated to winning the lottery. So naturally, in spite of my short-lived comforts, I gladly wolfed down everything they gave me. The entire time locking eyes with the server, staring back at me blankly. *Had it really been so long?* Molly was just a grade above me when we both attended high school. Was my appearance alien enough to her that she truly did not recognize me? I still wonder.

Following her home proved easier than I thought. She had the awareness of a child looking through a keyhole. For that reason alone, her very presence after the initial shock irritated me. It must have been very stimulating for her to do a bit of volunteer work. Seeing "the real thing" for twenty-four hours made her an expert in her mind, I am sure. Yet not enough to understand leaving one's door open, regardless of seconds, is an easy way to the hereafter. She was lucky in that the interloper was only me. A "damaged" young female after twenty bucks in her precious, sequin-coated wallet.

Buses wouldn't run for the next couple of hours, so I squatted in her closet for a small eternity. It was a relief there appeared to be no man in her life. The seemingly endless piles of ladies' underwear and bright pink bras confirmed it. When sounds dissipated and the apartment grew dark, I finally mustered the courage to half-slither my way from the smelly quarters. Rifling around in the darkness was easy. I had grown used to it in my street formative years. Making my way through the small kitchen towards the door, my finger pricked a corner of newspaper. I proceeded to grab at it, instinctively. *Something to remind me of the other world is always welcome.* Outside, the air was cool and crisp. The kind that could quietly creep up on you and leave the unlucky dead by morning. I paid it no heed as I continued walking towards the nearest station. The stink of dried diesel left itself in my wake. Pity the fumes weren't enough to cause anything more than a headache.

Sitting down amidst the dim fluorescent light, a particular article caught my eye. Not the writing, so much. The ten to twelve-point font was little more to me than dots. It was the photograph, framed beneath text too large to see. I blinked several times, part of me tempted to stick a cuticle in my left-dominant eye. The photograph matched Dom's face. In every way. The cliché in films at this point depicts the heroine crumpling up the newspaper and falling to the ground. But I had fallen many times over the years, and even in the face of this had no plans to do so again. Catching a breath, I squinted in the hopes of turning the small print to information.

Dominic Larson. Twenty-five years old. Believed to be the victim of a homicide involving the Pelphry Gang.

I could interpret little passages. Such a trait is the closest I'd get to howling in despair. Being reminded of a tragedy I wanted to forget seemed like the universe's ultimate *fuck you.*

He is survived by his mother, Angela Larson of Point Pleasant, New York, and his father, Arthur Prescillio of Mill Valley.

Edit my comment on clichés. Forget the bullshit I just

wrote. The name *Arthur Prescillio* did not hit me slowly. It drove a freight train into my chest. *Running over my heart.* The paper fell out of my hands, splashing messily in a puddle by my feet. *What did this all mean?* Arthur Prescillio was the name of *my* father. *In* Mill Valley. Here, in the northern part of the state of California.

What did this all mean? A painfully naked sob escaped my lips when the answer cruelly flashed itself, in hideous glory. My small-time love, albeit necessary affection, was my half-brother. The infamous, unspoken child of my father's "other" family. What didn't hurt me was the incest. It was the realization of the profound irony. *Dominic wasn't good enough for my father's form of child-rearing. I was.* In a way, looking at it now, you could say he was blessed. Blessed because in spite of a life of luxury, I was a prisoner in a golden cage. While he rose, I had fallen. The small nexus that was our romance proved the ultimate cruel joke. For us both, *equally.* Only I was further cursed by living to see the results.

After I boarded the transit, I decided not to ride the bus toward the Oregon border. The same demeanor overtaking me after I jumped had other plans. I was returning to Mill Valley. There was a score I could not bear leaving unsettled. My knuckles were white balls entrapped within walls of skin. My jaw was so tight, I was surprised my teeth didn't crack. Over the grief had spread the plasma of a wrath I couldn't have contemplated — even in the presence of already such revelatory moments. As the doors slowly closed and the vehicle began to chug along the dimly lit streets, the ethereal nature of my predicament began to film. *He didn't choose him. He chose me.* The words angrily played out, over and over, beating evenly on either side of my head. My father had chosen me. Chosen me as a superior target to break. The only thing worse than the epiphany was my own self-doubt that followed. Perhaps everything I now felt was the ultimate marker of *why. I am weak. I am vulnerable. They have won.* I blinked hot tears back around my eyeballs. There was no denying it, least of all to myself. *Congratulations, father. If nothing else, this is how you have succeeded with me.* The fire that had engulfed my heart would not break. The damage caused could no longer be undone, if it ever could have to begin with. They had won. And through winning, they had created a monster. A creature of the ultimate malice, as you will no doubt understand the further you delve into my story.

"Excuse me, miss?"

I slowly turned with a brazen stare. Needless to say, I was unhappy to be yanked away from my critical and depressing thoughts.

The voice belonged to a figure next to me, reaching out with a gnarled hand. His face was completely obscured within the depths of an olive-colored hood. No matter how hard you squinted, there was no telling just who…or *what*…was in there.

"Yes?" My voice was calm, but my fists were cocked. Not that it would have been a fair fight. *Yet nevertheless…*

"Are you hurt?" The words were maddening because of the bizarre calmness with which they were spoken.

"No." My tone now communicated impatience. You told it like it was. That, or played the game. The latter was not an option for me right now.

"I didn't mean *physically.*"

I slowly turned to face him again, finding the hood cocked at a funny angle — almost levelling with my right tit. "What's the matter with you? You want to fuck me?"

The hood moved up and down slightly as a hollow laugh emerged from its depths. "Not particularly. You're not my type."

"Then fuck off." I was not in the mood for games. Yet, in spite of the harsh words, I found myself literally unable to look away.

"Be careful with what you do. Don't regret what you wish for. And remember above all else, *tread carefully in the darkness*."

My eyes didn't widen, despite wanting to. Frozen, my mouth moved without my consent. "What do you mean by that?"

The figure laughed again, silhouetted slightly against the growing blue light outside. "Exactly *what* I meant."

"No," I found myself able to blink, regaining some control. "What do you mean *tread carefully in the darkness*? What does *that* mean?"

The figure simply stared back in silence. "You should be fully back in control in several seconds," the voice – almost a separate entity due to the visual disembodiment — finally spoke.

I blinked again. "What?"

The figure folded its arms across its chest as it reached its punchline. "Then you will understand all that there is to comprehend."

Despite my best efforts, my eyes were beginning to close – sleep covering me with its bitter sheen. The only thing I can remember was the figure flickering slightly. Yes, *flickering*. And I know it wasn't because of my trembling eyelashes.

When I awoke some hours later, he had vanished. I was being roughly shaken by the driver — a pig-faced man displaying apparent disgust. "Time to get out, time to get out," he was saying.

"Where are we?" I yawned in reply, rubbing my eyes with my fists.

"Mill Valley," the man replied curtly. "Now scram before I call the fucking cops on your bum ass."

"Mill Valley?" I sat up slowly, looking around me. "I thought this bus was headed to Humboldt County." Despite the reassurance of not having slept through getting home, I was struck by the odd disconnect — *plus* the hooded figure — all in one night.

"Don't know where you heard that," the driver spat. "But I'm not fucking around. I'm going to count to three, and by three you better make me feel sorry. Get!"

Finding my way home was an odd experience. One would think after so many years I'd forgotten the way. Yet my feet knew exactly where to go, my conscious mind in tow. The pavement was terribly hot in the autumn sun. The soles of my feet felt like burnt leather every step of the way. Yet I had been through enough pain that I had developed an elaborate system of clouding. Shutting in everything sensory and otherwise until I reached the present goal. But in that moment, such a habit fluctuated in its effectiveness. I grit my teeth as the feeling refused to go away, instead merging with the overall tapestry of misery. *This will only make it harder...*

Before I knew it, though, I was home.

Looking around me, I had forgotten just how beautiful everything was. *The spacious two-story house, atop a large hill, overlooking the great mountains ahead.* A soft breeze rippled through the trees, touching the back of my hair. Cocking my head as my eyes closed, I couldn't help feeling for just one second like the young, wide-eyed girl I used to be. It was as if by being here, I could finally mourn what I had lost. *Even if just for a moment...*

It wasn't long before the stink of diesel signaled the return of my newfound character. Eyes opening, I proceeded to lock such reek inside the furthest confines of my heart. Taking several steps forward, I knew exactly where I would seek refuge until the new night fell. The garden my mother and I had planted felt like an old friend. It was bleak-looking and rotten in places, just like me. Waiting there proved to be so much of a comfort. There was nothing too beautiful to remind me of what I had been missing.

When the right time finally came, my lips were chapped and sore while my head felt it would burst. It was an all too familiar feeling, intense in its being suddenly alien. Despite consuming so little for many years, being home spoiled not only my mentality but also my senses. It was as if physically I had undergone a transformation. What normally I could take I found myself oddly averse to. It was hard to cloud this particular pain, or to make it another motivator for what I was about to do. But looking upwards, my newfound demeanor burned fire in my throat. They needed to pay for what they had done to me. And they would.

Climbing onto the roof no longer scared me. Back in my days of privilege, I had suffered bouts of severe vertigo. I couldn't even ride in elevators. *At least that's changed.* I scuttled without hesitation towards the far left of the house. From there, I could safely jump onto the upstairs deck. If they were anything like how they used to be, my mother and father would have left the sliding glass door open. They preferred that to AC. On such a hot night, the faux worldliness of this made me stifle a hooting laugh. *Fucking ridiculous, as always.* Sure enough, the door was open. Walking towards it proved easy. It was as if I had never left. Yet I froze the moment my front permeated the space within its frame. Terror welled up in the back of my throat, like a flapping second tongue. In the darkness, the grandiose nature of our living room was bizarrely intimidating. Perhaps it was the large, pointed chairs – resembling monstrous entities writhing before me. Or maybe it was the large painting of my grandfather – eyes staring directly into my soul. It took a lot of willpower, boosted by my revelatory ferocity, to finally put one foot in front of the other – returning to a world I had known intimately for so many years. Looking back on it now, I wonder if I was feeling the superior mortal fear of a guilty executioner. Someone needing to be intimidated by anything they could conjure that was greater than themselves. Needless to say, it would have made perfect sense to whatever sliver was left of my former self...

There was only one other time I approached their bedroom in this fashion. It was twelve years ago — and like today, I planned to kill them. Of course, I was a lot more naïve then. I thought I could strangle them both with my bare hands, bless me! Almost turning the knob, I regret irrationally in retrospect chickening out. It would have been the perfect scene for making the ultimate point. Not that they would have understood, of course.

Heavy moaning had emanated from within, creating an uneven paradox. *Brutally dying while in the highest state of life. Maybe even while creating it.* Yet such sentimentalities mean little to me now. The memories of such a feeling only hardens the grail of my *un*feeling cruelty. I suppose my need to note this adheres to an overall sense of protectiveness. I spent the first three quarters of my existence living a hideously cauterized life. A life that ironically subjected me to the very things my parents claimed to protect me from. *Manipulation. Sexuality. Death.* Needless to say, there were many reasons for my finally turning into what they proclaimed I always was. For my *needing to be* such a person. But such details are stories for another time.

"What are you doing?"

For a second, I thought the voice in present time was my own. Thinking out loud was one of my many weaknesses. The crack beneath my parents' bedroom door emitted no visible light. It was late enough so both of them must have been asleep. Then I jerked into the moment when I remembered my voice wasn't that high anymore. Turning slowly, I found myself further floored at the sight now lying before me. She was a beautiful little girl, about eleven to twelve years old. Dressed in pajamas reflecting the precociousness of Generation Z. Eyes shining in the darkness — *just like mine*. There was no mistaking it. I was looking at my new, little sister.

Neither one of us moved for several more seconds. It was as if we were both judging — then subsequently regretting — our roles in this scenario. Hers being confronting me at all. Mine being the cold pragmatism surrounding what I was now compelled to do. It was just a question of who would act first. Her, or me. The girl did not disappoint. Turning on her heel, she ran with surprising speed down the stairs. My eyes gleamed. *I knew the way.* There was only one place she could be headed. Racing after her down to the house's first story, my eyes locked on the closing door of what used to be my bedroom. *No*, the fire burned. *My bedroom. It's mine. It's rightfully mine.* The outrage accompanying this epiphany increased my already fearsome stride. My left foot jammed itself between door and frame, the ensuing pain prompting me to use my right to kick it hard. There was a shriek from the other side, indicating the back of it probably hit her in the face. As the door swung violently open, my assumption proved correct. The girl had been knocked into a sitting position, eyes wide with fright, blood escaping her nose. She wasn't one to play victim too long, however. I couldn't help smiling as she grabbed at a fluffy toy — admiring her grit. *It reminded me so much of myself.* The stuffed animal proceeded to harmlessly bounce off my left breast. I cocked my head slightly. "Never hit a woman there, young lady." Even I was struck by the loss of innocence in my thick, ragged tone. A feral cry escaped the child before me. Seeing she was out of options, my little sister wasn't going down without a fight. She came at me, utilizing everything she had. The teeth were the only effective parts — two especially sharp incisors sobering my initial amusement. With a roar of my own, I proceeded to grab ahold of the young girl's throat, slamming her onto the gray-colored carpet beneath us. "You think you know how to fight?" The demeanor was all I had now.

"Fuck you," my sister wept. Even displaying such naked

and childish vulnerability, her magnetism never faltered.

"Do you know who I am?" I said, something in me bridling slightly at the sight of fresh tears.

"No," the girl said, closing her eyes slightly.

"I'm your sister." The words escaped my throat right as the revelation caused it to close. Whatever shred of humanity that was left was being used up courtesy of this encounter. "I'm your fucking sister, that's who."

"I don't have a sister." The girl's voice was weak. Clearly all the stress inflicted upon her was taking its toll. She looked like she could barely stay awake.

"Is that what they told you?" The demeanor reared its head again, the tears slowly running out of gas.

"My sister…" the young girl struggled, "is dead." Her eyes opened right after she said this, as if such a statement reinvigorated her own fire.

"So that's what they told you," I assessed, slowly moving my hands away from her neck.

"Why are you here?"

The question was simple enough. The diabolical answer caused my tongue to waltz and my blood to sing in my veins. Yet looking into her face, the response became so complicated to word. However would I do it justice? The young girl stared at me, armed with an expression best described as vehement curiosity. "I…I don't know," I finally said. This reinvigorated my own tears. Yet it remained unclear to me whether their existence depended upon her or myself. Several seconds of this newfound grieving passed. Then my sister proceeded to break it.

"Get off of me."

If the words weren't so demanding, weren't

so…*entitled*…I might have complied. But as a response to her tone, my face hardened while hers subsequently crumpled. The fire in her eyes was beginning to dim. Childish hopelessness and childish submission were beginning to make their entrances.

"*Please*," the young girl begged. Stripped of her mane, her plea came wrapped in excessively sweet sincerity. Yet to no avail. Whatever chance she had to reason with me, she had wasted.

My hands began to close themselves around her throat, naturally her breathing beginning to quicken at this.

"Please, don't." More tears. More slightly stifled cries. Now more *stifled* cries. "Please don't. *Please don't.*"

Yet looking into her petrified face was cherry on top of the visceral sundae. In it I saw something even worse than Dom's scenario. This was someone who was kept. Someone who was spoiled. Someone who, in *this house*, wasn't groomed for a life of shattered stability and lost hope. As her life began to escape, the words the hooded figure spoke to me suddenly flashed to mind.

"Be careful with what you do. Don't regret what you wish for. And remember above all else, *tread carefully in the darkness.*"

My hands went limp, the process suddenly interrupted. Beneath me, the young girl struggled for breath — her cheeks slightly blue. Her eyes were completely stripped of their power. Wild and terrified, they stared at me with the circumference of saucers. I simply proceeded to stare back, coldly. When my mouth formed the words, I realized her life was the last roll of the dice I had had. The last chance to *trust* and to *spare*.

"I'm not here for you," I heard myself say. "I'm here for them."

Tread carefully in the darkness.

To Be Human
Mark Towse

So that's it.

She's gone.

I draw the covers up to her neck, but she will not feel the cold anymore. Dirty yellow light from the streetlight sneaks through the side of the curtain, giving her eyes a hint of life, making it look as though she is sleeping with them open.

The room still smells the same, just the slight essence of perfume.

Eighteen years together and two children with this woman, and it's as if she never existed. Music intrudes from across the street, and I can hear the constant hum of traffic from the main road. Moving the curtain slightly aside, I see the neighbour's cat outside their front door. It meows to try and get their attention.

It's all too normal.

My wife is dead; she has passed. Where was her God? The one she worshipped every Sunday for as long as I can remember. There was nothing spiritual about what happened. She stopped breathing and never started again.

I feel nothing.

You see, I'm not human. Flesh and bone, yes—but that is where the similarities end. I want to cry; I do. I want to mourn, to feel something, but I simply cannot.

Fifteen years of marriage, and I have nothing for her, not a single tear.

It wasn't always like this.

Everything changed after his visit—the man with the pale skin and dark eyes. He stepped out from the shadows of the bedroom one night and made his way towards my bedside. As he reached out to touch my shoulder, he told me that I had been chosen, that he was relieving me from the burden of emotion. Before I could even process what he was saying, he stepped back into the darkness, leaving me with the words, "When the timing is right, you will be reborn."

I've been waiting ever since.

That was over ten years ago now. Suzie wasn't even born, and George was four. To think about all those moments that should have carried such emotional resonance. But I'm incapable of feeling anything—anger, guilt, sadness—it's simply not in my programming. To try and explain—it's like being imprisoned from life. I can smell it, taste, and hear it, but cannot feel it. It has driven me out of my mind with only the promise of reawakening to keep me going.

I've done many bad things since then, gradually getting more violent and horrific in my pursuit to feel. Things that would have made the old me sick to the stomach.

I lost control a long time ago.

The kids could sense something yesterday at dinner. Perhaps my hopelessness. George kept nervously glancing up from his meal. Suzie, of course, mimicked him each time. Amy was the one that was good with them. I struggle with human interaction of any kind, for obvious reasons. She organised all our social activities—the parties, nights out with her tedious friends or work colleagues. I would smile and laugh in the right places, but it was exhausting.

I know there are others like me. The man with the pale skin and black eyes told me that. He said we are just anaesthetised, that one day we will wake up and feel again. He visits me now and again, and each time I ask him when I will be able to feel again, he nonchalantly replies that it isn't the right time.

My pursuit of such awakenment is a secret I have lived with for far too long. It's not easy pretending to be human, and I have grown weary of it. I have lost hope.

As I sit on the edge of the bed, the sheets shrink back, exposing her neck. The red marks that circle her skin are visible, even under the subdued lighting.

There are no pangs of guilt or regret. I have spent nearly two decades of my life with this person and—nothing! I am wrong. Incomplete. Unfinished. I thought it might help me feel something, but even when her pleading eyes looked directly into mine, and as she desperately flailed at my hands around her neck, I felt nothing.

I'd already done the children at that point. I felt nothing then either.

It's over now, though.

I could say that I am sorry but wouldn't mean it.

How could I do this? Because I wanted to feel again. I have tried everything else. You don't know what it's like to feel disconnected—unplugged. Over the years, I've lost the ability to care about anything. I am just numb, inhuman. So, spare me your anger and disgust because I simply do not care. I don't have the ability to.

Do I make myself clear?

It was my last effort to feel something, to attain some level of humanity. Oh, the irony.

I lie down on the bed next to Amy and stare at the ceiling. He appears then, at the end of the bed, the black-eyed man. He walks over and touches me on the shoulder, and suddenly, my mind is overloaded with imagery. My entire life flashes before me, and all at once, I feel everything.

I'm witnessing the birth of Suzie all over again—and it's terrifying but beautiful—unlike the previous soporific experience. I witness the arguments, the kid's school plays and sports days, Amy's recitals, Mother's funeral—the highs and the lows that should have been—and all these emotions surge through me simultaneously like a thousand bolts of electricity. My heart is racing, adrenaline pumping—and the man with the face as pale as the moon leans towards my ear and whispers, "Wakey, wakey, rise and shine."

Amy's face flashes in front of me, and I can see the yearning behind those emerald eyes. I am filled with love for her, so much that it hurts. My children's faces are next, and I'm hit by an overwhelming feeling of regret and shame. And grief. There is tightness in my chest and a lump at the back of my throat. I think I'm going to be sick. Warm tears begin to run down my cheeks.

The room starts spinning then as the visions keep flooding through. But this time, Amy's eyes are straining, raw, bulging and her face is almost blue. Another vision—my hands are wrapped around Suzie's neck; she is looking at me terrified and confused. I witness the entire episode and helplessly watch as the last of her life slowly seeps from her eyes. And poor George—he put up such a fight through those teary eyes. My boy.

What have I done?

I feel, for the first time in years, I feel— nothing but pain and sorrow.

I am awake. And it feels like hell. My eyes are raw with tears, and there is an intense pain building across my chest. I remember some of these reactions, but this goes way beyond—a pain beyond the physical—a different plain of turmoil and grief.

Pushing myself from the bed, I hang the loop of the belt over the corner of the heavy oak wardrobe. The dimness of the room emphasizes my sallow face in the mirrored doors—oh, how I hate it.

I feel everything. And it's too late.

I should have done this long ago, and I guess if I had an element of empathy or compassion, I wouldn't have been able to live with myself and the things I've done. But I always hoped I would be reborn—not like this, though.

I wrap the belt around my neck and pull it as tightly as possible. The pain is immediate and frightening. Panic ensues, and it takes everything I have to not reach for it. I am already light-headed and gasping for air, and my chest feels like it might explode. The man with the black eyes steps out of the shadows and edges towards me. He stands two feet away, frowns, and then slots his thumb under his chin as though studying a piece of art. My legs begin to kick against the door as the pressure around my neck becomes unbearable.

I see the sheets of the bed wrinkle as my wife turns over.

There is a blackness filling my vision as he begins to laugh. The room is getting smaller and—

***

From the end of the bed, I stare at her as she begins to wake. There is no apparent redness around her neck.

The morning sun seems desperate to fill the room—a brand new day.

I can hear the children playing downstairs. No, now they are fighting. In the corner of the room, my body hangs limply from the wardrobe door. She will see it soon. Please don't scream, Amy. I don't want the kids running up here.

The bad things I thought I'd done were just creations— manufactured dreams and fantasies of an unhinged mind and attempts to placate the hunger for sensation.

He stole my ability to feel, only giving it back when I had lost all hope.

There are higher beings out there, observing and watching over us. I met some of them when I crossed over. But they're not all good.

Some of us are merely pawns in a game played for their pleasure.

OTHER HELLBOUND BOOKS

The Toilet Zone: Number Two
"Restroom reading at its most terrifying!"

Imagine, if you will, you're traveling through the unknown, hellbound, with no roadmap or stars to guide you. The light fades as you descend into a shadow realm where supernatural terrors make their lair and evil lurks at every turn. Here, dead things don't always stay dead, for this is a world where things that shouldn't be… *are*, and things that should be are not.

In this world, it takes between 2,500 and 4,000 reading words to pay a visit to the smallest, but terrifyingly necessary, room, and stories are written precisely to chill the bones as you wait for nature to make its call.

You open up the book, and one of the 32 tales skulking within its hellish pages chooses you…

It's too late to turn back now.
You are about to set foot into another dimension, so best watch out for that signpost up ahead...
You've just crossed over into... The Toilet Zone

Blood and Blasphemy

If you enjoy your horror dipped in buckets of blood and sprinkled with generous amounts of blasphemy, then you've come to the right place!

Blood and Blasphemy is a collection of over thirty of the most sacrilegious horror stories ever written.

Within these irreverent pages, you will encounter a priest that keeps his deformed spawn chained in a root cellar, a convent where a poisonous species of salamander is worshiped, a demonic altar boy, possessed religious relics that kill, blood-drinking clergymen, a Son of God who feeds on sin, an unsuspecting couple who run afoul of religious lunatics in a small town, the divine (and deadly) turd of Christ, and other terrifying tales guaranteed to make church ladies faint and nuns clutch their rosaries.

Schlock! Horror!

An anthology of short stories based upon/inspired by and in loving homage to all of those great gorefest movies and books of the 1980's (not necessarily base in that era, although some do ride that wave of nostalgia!), the golden age when horror well and truly came kicking, screaming and spraying blood, gore & body parts out from the shadows...

This exemplary 80's themed/inspired tales of terror has been adjudicated and compiled by one Mr Bret McCormick, himself a writer, producer and director of many a schlock classic, including *Bio-Tech Warrior*, *Time Tracers*, *The Abomination*, *Ozone: The Attack of the Redneck Mutants* and the inimitable *Repligator*.

Featuring stories from: Todd Sullivan, Timothy C Hobbs, Mark Thomas, Andrew Post, James B. Pepe, Thomas Vaughn, Edward Karpp, Jaap Boekestein, Lisa Alfano, L. C. Holt, John Adam Gosham, Brandon Cracraft, M. Earl Smith, Sarah Cannavo, James Gardner, Bret McCormick, and James H. Longmore.

Graveyard Girls

Female authors + Horror = something spectacularly terrifying!

A delicious collection of horrific tales and darkest poetry from the cream of the crop, all lovingly compiled by the incomparable Gerri R Gray! Nestling between the covers of this formidable tome are twenty-five of the very best lady authors writing on the horror scene today!

These tales of terror are guaranteed to chill your very soul and awaken you in the dead of the night with fear-sweat clinging to your every pore and your heart pounding hard and heavy in your labored breast...

Featuring superlative horror from: Xtina Marie, M. W. Brown, Rebecca Kolodziej, Anya Lee, Barbara Jacobson, Gerri R. Gray, Christina Bergling, Julia Benally, Olga Werby, Kelly Glover, Lee Franklin, Linda M. Crate, Vanessa Hawkins, P. Alanna Roethle, J Snow, Evelyn Eve, Serena Daniels, S. E. Davis, Sam Hill, J. C. Raye, Donna J. W. Munro, R. J. Murray, C. Bailey-Bacchus, Varonica Chaney, Marian Finch (Lady Marian).

**A HellBound Books LLC
Publication**

http://www.hellboundbookspublishing.com

Printed in the United States of America